Enchanting Secrets
R. L. Wells

Copyright 2012 by Rusty L. Wells

Cover Art by Jenny Miller
Edited by Steven Lyons

Author's Dedication

I would first like to thank my editor Steven Lyons, you rock (of course you know that) and Jenny Miller for the amazing cover. To my husband the hero in my love story, you are and always will be the most precious treasure I hold, you are my heart. To my family and friends I want to thank you for all your love and support.

Now to the most important the readers, this is the first book of many. I hope you enjoy it as much as I enjoyed writing it. My characters are like old friends that I hold near a dear to my heart.

Happy Reading....... R.L. Wells

Enchanting Secrets

By: R.L. Wells

PROLOGUE

In the deepest part of the castle, where all was dark and musty, there was one lone candle burning, casting shadows about. The one remaining servant looked around and saw nothing at first, but out of the corner of his eye he detected movement. "Master I have all the ingredients that you asked for," he said.

"Don't just stand there. Bring it all here to me." The servant placed everything on the table and stepped back. He had watched his master, Drake, gradually progress from a strong, carefree man to a cold, bitter shell. All of his master's strength had gradually been consumed by one thing - revenge. He was growing older by the day and bitterer, pouring every last ounce of energy into the only thing that he craved.

At one time everyone had lived together peacefully. Their world had thrived and everyone was happy. His master at one time was a fair and wise man, and he was respected by all. Drake had many friends, but his most loyal and most loved friend was Lucian. They were both masters of their world but then the whispers had started about a woman whose beauty was equaled only by her great powers. It was said that everyone, from the young to the old, fell in love with her. She was known as Rianna the Enchantress. Drake and Lucian had met her at the same time and both men had fallen hopelessly in love with her. This had eventually led to battles where thousands died. Sides had naturally formed - good against evil.

In the end Lucian married Rianna and his old friend Drake never forgave either of them. He told all who would listen that Lucian had cheated him but only they knew the truth. No one spoke of it and his master had grown bitterer. Looking at Drake now, the servant trembled as Drake put the ingredients to use.

"Brome, how long have you been with me?" he asked with his back to his servant.

"Master I have been with you always." Drake didn't respond but kept on working at his foul potion and muttering to himself, his sanity rapidly slipping away.

He gave his servant a cold stare with eyes that were black and empty. "You have always been loyal. My time here is almost up but before I go I have one last request of you."

Brome looked at his master closely. He had aged almost overnight. His hair was pure white where not long ago it had been as black as the night. His shoulders were no longer held high and his walk had grown slower. Famous for his brilliant robes of deep rich colors, now he wore a plain brown one that had seen better days. In a matter of only a year he had wasted to an old bitter individual with only one final goal. His revenge was so consuming that it was draining the life out of him but he didn't seem to care. "Yes master, I will do anything you request of me."

With an evil twist of his lips his master smiled. He almost looked like the old Drake but a closer look revealed eyes as cold as ice, and his smile was truly cruel.

"Tell everyone what you have seen and heard this night. I want everyone to know!" All Brome could do was nod then his master went back to work. He started a fire with the kindling that Brome had brought from the Black Forest where evil dwelled. He waited for the flames to rise high then set the black pot over it. Drake added all the ingredients in a strict order accompanied by some ancient verse that Brome could hear clearly but could not understand.

Everything started to bubble and a heavy fog draped the room and floated out of the chimney. Drake threw his hands in the air... "I, Drake of Darkness bestow a gift, a gift that cannot be returned on this, the anniversary of the marriage of Lucian and Rianna the Enchantress and for all of their offspring. Never again shall there be another!"

With those final words his master released the most cruel and evil of laughs and fell to his knees with his head stretched forward.

Brome ran to him and laid him down. "Master, are you all right?" Putting his hand up to silence him he spoke. "Leave me, do as I ask," his voice was gruff and only a whisper. Shaking his head

Brome turned to leave. At the door he looked back one last time and there on the floor lay his master, eyes closed, breathing stilled but with a cold evil smile on his face. He had given his life for the thing that he had wished most on two people he hated… Revenge.

1

The day was warm and humid; a light breeze blew through the trees and stirred the flowers on the ground. Leaves danced in the breeze as the flowers swayed back and forth to the age-old song of summer. It was mid-June, the trees were full, and the flowers were a bloom. The colors and smells were as close to heaven as you could get.

Alana looked up and shielded her eyes from the sun. This little piece of heaven was where she loved to spend her days. The breeze stirred the hair that had come loose from her ponytail. A hint of a shiver ran through her body. It was cooling down some and soon it would be dark.

Alana sighed and put her book down. She felt she had no real purpose in life. She was almost twenty-one and at a time when most people her age were certain about their goals, Alana still didn't know what she wanted to do. She was the sort of person who wanted to make a difference. She just hadn't figured out how. Good thing she had a very understanding mother.
Her mom was cool. She had always told Alana to enjoy life and had stood by her every step of the way. Her friends nagged her a lot and told her she was weird, but sometimes she actually *felt* weird - like she didn't belong - as if she was different in some way. When she was younger she had asked her mother if she was weird or strange. Her mother had just smiled and told her she wasn't weird or strange - she was special. Alana hadn't understood that when she was ten and she still didn't understand it now at twenty. Of course her mom would think she was special - she was a mother after all. She was supposed to say things like that to make you feel better. Smiling, she thought back to that long ago day and yes, she had made her feel better at the time. Laughing to herself she picked up her book. She needed to get ready, even though she really didn't want to go. She had been seeing Todd for over a month now and he was starting to pressure her into making a commitment that she was not ready to make. She didn't know if she would ever be ready to make it - with Todd anyway.
As she walked slowly to the house she thought about the night

before when Todd had told her she needed to decide something soon. He told her she wasn't getting any younger and that he was on his last year in college and already had a job offer. Of course it was with his father's firm. He would soon be graduating top in his class. All he ever wanted was to be a Lawyer like his father and his father before him. He came from old money and he was used to getting everything he wanted. A month ago he had decided he wanted Alana. At the time she loved the attention he gave her and the fuss made by all of her friends on campus. They all talked about how charming he was, and how handsome he was - which they were right about - but they overlooked how self-centered he was, and how arrogant he was, or how everything had to go his way. He was spoiled rotten. Like today, his family was throwing some kind of a big do at their estate and he wanted her to be there. He *expected* her to be there! She never felt comfortable going to his family's home. The few times she'd been there she felt they were looking down on her. When she mentioned this to him, he just laughed and told her to relax, that they loved her. But she still felt like she didn't belong. She wasn't considered rich by any means, but she wasn't poor either. Her mother owned her own business and had done so for as long as Alana could remember. She was very proud of her mother.

Ever since Alana's father had passed away when she was very young, her mom had always been there for her in every way. She had never wanted for anything, and she adored the flower shop. She liked helping out when she could. Of course her mom had struggled when she first opened the shop, but for many years now it had been a blooming success. She has full time employees and can take time off now when she wants. Customers come from miles just to order flowers from her mom. People always exclaimed how beautiful her mom's flowers are.

Alana remembered what she had told one lady when she was younger. "Mom always puts all her love into every arrangement she makes so the person who receives them will know just how special they are." The older woman had smiled sweetly to her. She wondered what had happen to her. She remembered she used to come in all the time, and then she just stopped. She remembered how she would always bring her cookies or candy. She was going to ask her mom what ever happened to her. She was a sweet lady, but for now she must get inside and prepare herself for another night with Todd and his whole family.

Eudora moved her fingers gently through the water of her fountain and the image that had been there vanished. "Well Brigham what do you think of her?"

Brigham moved away from the fountain slowly turning his back on Eudora. Absently reaching for his beard he gently stroked it. Eudora knew not to disturb him. He was deep in thought so she stood there quietly. "She is lovely, yes, but she has a troubled soul," he sighed and turned to Eudora. "After all these many years she does seem to remember you."

Eudora smiled, "Yes she does, as I have remembered her. We have kept our end of the arrangement and have stayed out of her life. But I too felt something was troubling her. Do you think she knows that she is different?"

Again Brigham was silent as he walked to the table and sat down. All Eudora could do was follow and take the seat opposite him. "I could sense that she feels she is different from all others, but I do not think she knows just how different she is, or how important she really is to her world and to ours. She is unaware of any particular purpose in her life, but she has so many. More than *we* even know. We need to call a meeting with the council and decide what it is that needs to be done - and it needs to be soon. If the wrong people ever find out who she really is, our world and hers would be in grave danger. When I looked upon her today I could see a slight shimmer of color all around her, and as the days go by it will only grow stronger; I am afraid for her. If one of the others senses her presence just as I can, they will know who she is, and if she is not ready, all will be lost."

Eudora agreed. Brigham shook his head slightly and turned on his heel and headed in the opposite direction. Eudora knew what she had to do; no words were needed.

Alana had just finished getting ready when the doorbell rang. Looking at her watch she groaned. Was he ever late for anything? Todd had always prided himself for being on time for everything, so she took a big breath, planted a smile on her face and went to the door. "On time as always."

Laughing softly he kissed her cheek, "Of course. Would you expect any less of me?"

9

All Alana could do was smile. She just hoped and prayed she could get through the night. Her nerves were already on edge and she didn't know why.

"My mother and father can't wait to see you again," he said. Alana could hardly believe that. Every time she was around them she felt strange.

"I'm looking forward to this evening too," she answered politely knowing it was a huge lie. He helped her into the car and neither of them spoke again until they pulled into the driveway.

"Here we are. Now show me that beautiful smile of yours." All she could do was hope the smile she gave him didn't reveal how much she disliked this whole night. "That's my girl. Your mother and father picked the perfect name for you, because when you smile like that it lights up your whole face and you look beautiful as always."

Before she could say anything he was out the door and helping her out of the car. As they approached the house Alana got the same feeling she always did whenever she went there. She couldn't put her finger on it, but it was a feeling of uneasiness and discomfort. 'Probably just my nerves,' she thought. 'The sooner we go in the sooner this night will be over.'

The butler opened the door and smiled from Todd to Alana. "Sir. Everyone is around the back waiting for you." Todd nodded his head and smiled then winked at her.

Taking her hand he led her to the back of the house and out through the french doors where they could hear music and laughter. Alana took a deep breath to prepare herself. She just hoped no one would notice that her smile was fake. As she followed Todd outside she looked around. There were more people than she had expected to be there. She spotted the headmaster from school and a couple of their professors and some other people she recognized but didn't know their names.

It looked like the party was already a big success. Todd's parents didn't do anything by halves. Tables had been set up along one side. There was live music - if you could call it music. Alana thought it sounded like something you would hear in an elevator – not her taste at all. It was loud enough to enjoy, but still soft enough so that people didn't have to yell to talk to one another.

There were candles and flowers everywhere and by the look of them they probably came from her mother's shop. She had to admit the scene was beautiful; the soft music; the scent of the flowers and the soft glow of candles. If she was with anyone else and at another time this would be enchanting and romantic.

"Alana did you hear what I said?" Alana turned to look at a frowning Todd.

"No, I'm sorry Todd. I was amazed at how beautiful everything is. What a perfect night," she smiled. Well she thought most of that was true.

Todd's face changed from a frown to a smile. "I know. It *is* beautiful isn't it? My mother has outdone herself again. What I asked was, did you want something to drink?" Before Alana had a chance to answer she heard someone calling Todd's name. When she turned to look she almost groaned aloud. Bearing down on them was his mother, so she planted another forceful smile on her face.

"There you are! I told your father that you two would be here soon." She reached out and kissed Todd's cheek and turned to Alana. Taking her by the arm she directed her toward more people. Todd asked again if she would like something to drink. She turned slightly and nodded. If she kept smiling like this she knew her face was going to crack.

"Yes dear, please get her a glass of champagne. Tonight is a night to celebrate. I will take her over and introduce her to everyone." With that said they were in the middle of the crowded yard and Alana was meeting this person and that one, hardly remembering which name went with which face. She hated this.

"Could you excuse me dear I need to talk to the cook about dinner tonight. I'm sure Todd will be back soon."

"Yes of course. I'm sure you're right. He'll find me soon," then his mother was almost floating across the yard and entering the house by a side door. Alana decided to find a secluded spot so she could catch her breath. She spotted a bench not far from where she stood. It wasn't really secluded, but it was close enough she could at least sit for a minute and catch her breath before Todd or someone else spotted her. She needed to find a way to end it. Things with Todd weren't working out. He wanted too much too soon and she wasn't ready for any of it. She was almost twenty-one and still hadn't been with a man. Most of her friends had been in and out of relationships and been with this one and that one but she didn't see any point in giving her virginity to a man who didn't love her or to someone she didn't love. She wanted it all - the fairytale romance - the ones you only read about, but it seems there are no Prince Charming's left in this world. Todd sure didn't fit the bill. She never understood why he pursued her in the first place. He had been charming and persistent. There were plenty of girls to choose from and most had money and were prettier than her. Her friends always said she was so lucky to have caught Todd's attention. Well right now, at that moment, she didn't feel lucky at all. She was so wrapped up in her thoughts she never heard Todd approaching until he sat down next to her with a glass in each hand.

"Alana I have been looking all over for you. Why are you sitting here away from everyone?"

Now what should she say? "I'm sorry I just needed some air and to get off my feet, these shoes are new and I haven't had time to break them in yet." She smiled her biggest smile. Todd smiled back and handed her the glass of Champagne.

"No problem. I was hoping I could get you alone tonight."

Alana didn't like that look in his eyes. There was something calculating and cold about it and it made her shiver slightly. "Are you cold?"

Alana shook her head. "Maybe just a little. It has gotten cooler tonight."

Todd leaned forward and put his arm around her. "Better?"

Alana smiled and nodded. There was that feeling again. She didn't know what it was but it was something like dread. Maybe she was just uneasy anyway and it was probably nothing, but still she couldn't shake it.

"Now back to what I was trying to say before. I think it's time we stepped our relationship up. You will be twenty-one soon and I'm twenty-five. I will be out of school soon and will be joining my father's firm." As Todd talked Alana's head started to spin. She was only listening to half of what he was saying, a hard knot forming in the pit of her stomach. She shook herself so she could listen to what he was saying - to focus. "…so I think we should get married. You know how I feel about you and I think I know how you feel about me. I have already talked it over with my parents and they think it's a wonderful idea. If you say yes, we can get married right away. I don't want a long engagement. My mother said she could have it all arranged with your mother's help of course in no time. What do you think?"

Alana couldn't believe what she was hearing. She always thought that when someone proposed to her it would be different. She didn't know what to say - they'd never shared their feelings - they had barely even kissed. And she didn't know what she felt for him. She knew it wasn't love though and it bothered her that he had already discussed it with his parents. It should have been with her first.

"I can tell by the look on your face you weren't expecting this tonight. I know it's all so sudden to you."

'More than sudden,' she thought and no, she wasn't expecting it – ever. She was trying to figure out a way to break things off without hurting him - she sure didn't want to *marry* him. If she had a guardian angel like everyone said, she wished he would show up now and do something – anything!

"Todd you're right - I don't know what to say and no, I wasn't expecting this at all. I don't know - it's so soon, I…" Before she could get any more out he had placed one finger over her lips. "Just think about it tonight. I'm sure once the surprise wears off you'll see this is a good match." With that said he bent down and kissed her hard on the lips. Her stomach rolled. If he thought that kiss would work he was wrong. If anything, it made it easier. Lifting her glass she drained it in one drink. She needed to wipe away all memory of that kiss; she needed to get away. She felt trapped. She wished the night was over. The dinner bell rang, and Todd reached for her hand and pulled her from the bench to the table were everyone was already starting to take their seats. Dinner went by in a blur. She didn't even know what they had served - hadn't even tasted it. She was lucky to even get half the meal down past the lump in her throat; people were talking all around her, but she didn't care. The sooner she could get out of there the better. She didn't want to celebrate. She didn't want to dance. She just wanted to go home. Then the strangest thing happened. The wind picked up, the candles started flickering wildly and one after another flickered out. Alana looked around.

The wind was getting stronger and she heard someone gasp and someone else say they should all go inside. Her head started pounding. Todd reached over and grabbed her hand. "I think my father is right. We should all go inside." All Alana could do was nod her head as they started inside.

Alana stopped and Todd turned to look at her, "Are you all right?" "No Todd, I have a headache. Do you think you could take me home?" She could tell by the look on his face that he wasn't pleased, but he nodded his head as they entered the house. He went up to his father and explained that Alana wasn't feeling well. His father shook his head and said he understood and would explain it to his mother and they were on their way home to Alana's.

They never said a word in the car. As he pulled into her drive it started to rain. "Are you sure you're going to be all right?" Alana smiled. "Yes I just have a slight headache. I think I will just go to bed - it's been a long day." Todd picked up her hand and kissed her palm.

"You just remember what we were talking about and I will come by tomorrow and check on you." When he reached for the handle Alana held her hand out to stop him.

"Todd you stay in the car. There is no reason for us both getting wet". He just looked at her and he smiled and nodded. He leaned forward, placed both hands on the side of her face and kissed her forehead.

"You go on get inside and go to bed and I will call you in the morning." Alana smiled and left the car. As she ran inside she felt like she was running for her life. That feeling she had earlier was still there. The lights were on in the house so her mother was home. When she opened the door she turned to wave but Todd was already out the driveway. She shrugged her shoulders – he never even waited for her to get in the house. "Oh well," she thought "at least I am home," and she actually did feel better.

"Mom I'm home. Where are you?" She heard some noise in the kitchen. "I'm in here honey."

Smiling she went to get a towel to dry her hair and then she headed for the kitchen. Her mom was fixing some tea. She looked up and smiled. "So how did your night go?"

Alana plopped down on one of the chairs and sighed as she pulled her wet shoes off. "It went OK I guess. It was beautiful of course.

Your flowers were the highlight, they were all so beautiful. Todd asked me to marry him." She sighed again and closed her eyes and waited to hear what her mother had to say. She could hear her mom fixing the cups and making the tea. She sat one cup in front of Alana and took the chair opposite her. Alana couldn't stand the silence any more so she opened her eyes. Her mom was looking at her with a gentle motherly smile on her face.

"Well I can tell by the tone of your voice that congratulations are not in order."

"I never had time to answer him, he told me to think about it and he would get my answer tomorrow." Alana covered her head with her hands.

"What is it you want to do honey? Do you want to marry Todd?"

"That's it Mom. No I don't want to marry him. I just don't know how to tell him. I was going to break it off tonight until he dropped this bombshell on me. I tried to tell him but he hushed me up and told me to think about it. Before I could say another word the dinner bell rang and then the storm blew up and I asked him to bring me home. I thought I would feel something special if I was ever proposed to, but Mom I felt no joy! I felt trapped and panicked and very uncomfortable. I had a very uneasy feeling. He told me why we should get married. He even told me he had already talked it over with his parents, Mom. Can you believe that? He didn't ask me first - he had to ask his parents. He never mentioned anything about feelings or caring or romantic thoughts. It was just a plan to him. Like planning a holiday or buying a car. What should I do Mom? Please help me."

Alana watched her mother take a sip of her tea then set the cup down. "Honey I can't tell you what to do, you have to follow your own heart. Listen to it. This one is up to you - this is something you must decide. I can't tell you and the only advice I can give you is, if you have doubts and your whole heart isn't in it then maybe this is something you shouldn't do. Honey you are the only one who can choose your destiny. I can only be there for you when you do. Whatever you decide." With that said, her mother reached out and grabbed her hand.

"Somewhere out there your soul mate is waiting and when you find him you will know. Now I think we should both get some sleep, although I doubt that you will have much luck with that."

Her mother took both cups over to the sink and rinsed them out. As she was about to leave the kitchen she turned and smiled at her daughter, "are you coming?"

Alana sighed "In a minute Mom and… Mom, tell me how will I know?"

Her mother stood there for a minute as if she was thinking about something long ago. She had a soft smile on her lips, as she turned on her heel and on her way out of the room Alana heard her mother's soft laugh.

"Trust me honey you will know."

Alana laid her head on the table. After a few seconds she sat up, ran her fingers through her hair and headed upstairs to her room. After undressing and getting into bed Alana lay there awake, her thoughts troubled. Tomorrow she had to tell Todd that she just wasn't ready; he would have to understand.

Sebastian entered the room. Eudora was gazing at the water so Sebastian cleared his throat. He had received a message earlier that Eudora wanted to see him. He didn't know why. As far as he knew he hadn't done anything wrong. Eudora never turned around. She motioned for him to come forward. Sebastian approached her and spared a look into the Water. He caught sight of spun gold or what looked like spun gold. As he looked closer an image formed slowly before his eyes. He shook his head and closed his eyes. He was seeing things surely. When he opened his eyes again there she was. The gold he had seen was her hair spread out on her pillow. His fingers itched to touch it to see if it was as silky as it looked. He noticed her tiny nose and the way her eyelashes touched her cheeks. They were long and full where they rested. His eyes moved lower to her lips where a sigh had escaped. He could feel her sadness and for some reason he couldn't look away. She opened her eyes and Sebastian forgot to breathe. She was breathtaking! Her eyes were the color of a misty morning when the skies are a bluish-gray and from what he could see in them there was a storm brewing. Her eyes were troubled. He felt a sudden urge to protect her. He was so busy with his thoughts and the woman in the Water that he forgot about Eudora. Right now she was staring at him closely with a knowing look. She recognized the look on Sebastian's face for what it was. Pure enchantment. She trailed her fingers into the Water and as it rippled the image vanished.

Still looking at him she prompted "Beautiful isn't she?"

Sebastian was still looking at where her image had been so he didn't notice how close Eudora was studying him. Without looking up he answered her question; "Yes she is very beautiful." He stood there still watching the water waiting for he didn't know what. For her to come back maybe? She *was* beautiful. He wondered who she was and why Eudora was watching her and why she had summoned him to her. "So Eudora, what is it you want of me? Why did you summon me?"

Eudora laughed with a snort and walked over to the table. He could do nothing else but follow her. When she sat down she motioned for him to have a seat. "Sebastian dear, you have always been one to get right down to business." All Sebastian did was shrug his large shoulders. Eudora had known him for many years. She liked his arrogance and his cockiness, but Sebastian had a soft side too. Not many people saw that. She knew he would do anything she asked. She was very fond of Sebastian and she knew he felt the same. "Sebastian by any chance did you see the girl in the Water?" she looked at him with amusement in her eyes. She already knew the answer.

He looked at her. "What about her?"

She could tell he was interested even though he tried to hide it. She wondered how to approach the subject and took the only choice; the truth, or most of it. "I will get right to the point then," she watched as Sebastian sat up a little straighter in his chair. "Well anyway her name is Alana Vaughn and she is about to turn of age. She knows nothing about her real background - well her father's background anyway. She is already starting to discover some of her powers and she does not understand them. The Council and I think there are dark forces out there and they have been waiting to capture her powers. They have taken different forms, but as of yet we do not know who they are and what harm they want to do to the Realm and to Alana."

Eudora paused. She had been watching Sebastian closely and the mention of anyone harming Alana brought fire to his eyes and his nostrils flared; she knew he would protect her no matter the cost. "So tell me Eudora. Why are you telling me all of this?"

She could see the challenge in his eyes. "She needs to be protected at all costs. You see she is special. Her aura has already started to glow. Soon, whoever the dark ones are, will know where she is. If *we* can see it, they will be able to see it too. You have to remember the dark ones used to be members of our Realm. We don't know who they are and they have themselves well hidden." Eudora sighed, "Sebastian, she is the daughter of Edmund Von Drayton." Silence followed her statement. She knew Sebastian needed to understand just who she was.

He stood up. "Are you trying to tell me she's the one?"

At Eudora's nod he ran his fingers through his hair. "Does my father know?" Again Eudora nodded her head.

"Why was I never told about her - why was something so important kept from me?" He never looked at her.

She could hear the questions in his voice. She knew he wasn't really asking *her*, but she answered anyway; "It seems there was always something that came up. Back then it was a tragic time. There were some who wanted more power, and there were some who wanted peace, so the war went on for several years. You were still young and it didn't seem so important, but we were wrong to assume it was for the best. You had a right to know."

Sebastian sat back down in his chair and running his hand over the back of his neck he thought about it. He didn't remember much about that time because he was so young at the time. He knew they were at war, but he was too young to go off with everyone else so he had never seen how bad it was. He really couldn't blame anyone. They had suffered so much, but still they should have told him before now.

He sat straight up in his chair. "I understand, but still I should have been told before now. What if the dark forces already know who she is? We don't have much time. Tell me the rest and I will leave. And don't worry Eudora, I will make sure nothing happens to her. You have my word!" Eudora reached across the table and grabbed his hand. "I know." She told him everything from beginning to end. She even showed him pictures in the Water of Alana as a child to the lovely woman she was today. After ending her story she waved her hand through the Water and the last image disappeared. Sebastian stood up and Eudora watched as he left the room, a small smile beginning. "Yes" she thought, "everything will work out and their Realm will be stronger than ever."

2

Alana looked down at her watch and noticed it was only 9:00 in the morning and already her day was not turning out to be the best. She had overslept, she snapped the strap on her shoe and she was having one of the worst hair days imaginable. She crossed the street and noticed from the window of the coffee shop that everyone was there already. Alana hurried inside, "Sorry I'm late. I have had one of those days where nothing has gone right!"
Trisha laughed, "Girl I hate when that happens and don't worry about it we haven't been here long." She looked closer, "What happened to your hair?" Alana blew it from her eyes. When she couldn't get it to do anything she had plopped it all up on her head and stuck one of those hair needles in it. Why do they call them that when they're really only chopsticks made to look fancy? But now from her rushing, some hair had come loose and was falling in her face. She knew before the day was over she'd have to put it back up.
"Don't say a word, any of you. I have had a bad morning. I overslept, that's why I'm late, then the new shoes I bought the other day - you know the ones with the cute little straps - well one's missing a strap now."
"Oh Alana not the little black ones?" this said by Jessica who studies boys and clothes - nothing was more important, "I loved those. I was going to borrow them this weekend." Alana made a face and all of them laughed.

"Maybe your day will get better," chirped in Katie. She was the quiet one of the bunch, it was amazing to her how they'd all remained friends through the years. They were all so different. Trisha was the outgoing one who never met a stranger, Katie was the quiet shy one - brains *and* beauty and then there was Jessica. What more could she say? Homecoming queen, head cheerleader, every man's dream and most women's fantasy, and last but not least Alana. She considered herself to be friendly, a little shy, a little outgoing, and full of hopes and dreams maybe even a romantic at heart.

"I hope you're right; you know the old saying, 'after the worst it only gets better?' I hope that's true. I don't know how much more I can take. Does my hair really look that bad?" They looked at each other each shaking their heads "yes" and they all laughed again.

The waiter arrived with their cappuccino. "We went ahead and ordered. We figured you were running late," said Trisha as she took a sip of her coffee.

Alana took a sip and sighed, "Thanks. I needed that. So what's up for today?" As they all sat back and discussed their day, Sebastian sat on the other side of the café and watched and listened. To him she looked good - actually better than that. He didn't understand the bad hair day thing. There was nothing wrong with it from where he was sitting. The sun was coming in through the window and encircled their table. He'd noticed how she had blown the hair from her eyes twice already. She had it pulled back away from her face, but some of the locks didn't want to be bound together and had pulled free of whatever it was she had sticking out of the side of her hair. Whatever they were, her hair was staying in place pulled away from her face. He liked it down flowing free like the first time he'd seen her. Alana had a weird feeling like someone was watching her. She looked around once but didn't see anything out of the ordinary. People were sitting at tables with friends and some were sitting reading a book or newspaper. Everything looked normal, but nothing felt that way. Shaking her head, she tried to get rid of the feeling. "So Alana, how did the party at his folks go? Were there any cute, rich single guys there? Come on tell all. We want to know!" begged Jessica. Alana laughed. Leave it to Jessica to ask about the men. "Yes, small talk is over we've all been dying to know," said Trisha. She noticed that Katie shook her head. They all leaned in closer. "The party was beautiful," she replied and looked around the group. She could tell they all wanted more, so she took a sip of her cappuccino to make them wait a little longer. Sure enough, leave it to Jessica to pout, "Come on Alana we want more than that! We want details from beginning to end. You're not leaving here until you tell us all and we are satisfied, right girls?" They all nodded their heads enthusiastically.

"All right, all right. I will give you details," Alana said and held up her hands. She bit her lip. How much to tell them and how much should she leave out? Nothing but the truth, like her mom always

said, "The truth you will always know, a lie is just that a lie, that you know is not the truth, and if *you* don't believe no one else will." Anyway her friends knew her too well. They would know she was keeping something from them and so taking a deep breath and planting another smile on her face she prepared for battle. "Like I said the party was beautiful, dinner was excellent, Todd asked me to marry him, and yes, Jessica to answer your question from before, there were several single, rich men there."
Jessica smiled than she looked puzzled, "Katie, Trisha, please tell me I didn't just hear her right. Did she just say Todd asked her to get married?" "Yes you heard right. She did say that Todd asked her to marry him." Trisha looked closely at Alana. Out of all her friends Trisha knew her the best. As they sat and stared at each other Jessica looked from one to the other. "What I would like to know is, did you say yes or no? By the way you're looking, it could be yes or it could be no. So which would it be, congrats, or you're better off without him, so to speak anyway?" Then she shrugged her shoulders. "What! Why is everyone looking at me like that?" "Congrats or you're better off without him. Real smooth Jess. If I ever decide to get married, you will be the last person I tell." "Come on Trisha you know what we all think." Someone kicked Jess under the table and under her breath she said "ouch", and clamped her mouth shut, but Alana heard and looked from one to the other. They all had a guilty look on their faces. "I didn't realize that none of my friends liked my boyfriend. Why didn't anyone tell me?"

Katie who now had a sincere look on her face answered "Alana, it's not like that at all. It's not that we don't like Todd, its well, we just don't think you like him as much as he wants. He's trying to pressure you into something we know you're not ready to do with him. Anyway, I think I'm right or you would have told him yes last night."

Alana who was very stubborn sat up straighter in her chair and lifted her chin "What makes you think I didn't say yes, and that I am not here to tell everyone the good news?" She narrowed her eyes and looked them all over. She almost smiled. None of them liked to be put on the spot. She watched as every one of them looked at each other. When Trisha and Jessica nodded at Katie she knew which one was to be the voice for all of them. She was the most level headed one of the group.

Alana watched as Katie cleared her throat and moved a little closer to Alana. "You know we're all your friends. If it was 'congratulations' you wanted you would have been so happy to tell us that you would have blurted it out earlier and you would at least have a ring on your left finger and since you *didn't* blurt it out and I see *no* ring than either you told him 'no' or he wouldn't let you tell him no. He wanted you to think about it first. I'm right. I can tell by the look on your face." Alana sighed. "Actually, it started raining so we had to go inside. My head started hurting and I asked him to take me home, so I haven't said *anything* yet." When she looked around she could tell that she hadn't convinced them so she threw up her hands, "All right, you guys win, you're right as always Katie." She looked up and saw Katie smile. "I never got a chance to say anything. He told me all the reasons we should get married. He had even talked it over with his parents, but I don't know. I was planning on breaking up with him last night and then he goes and does something like this! What am I going to do? I don't want to hurt his feelings, but I can't marry him. I thought about it all night. I don't love him and I know he doesn't love me or at least I don't feel it. When I finally do get married I want it to be for love, and I know I haven't found that in Todd. I don't even know if I really like him. My mom says it will happen and when it does I will know, and you know what?" she paused long enough to look around and catch her breath. "She's right. I don't really know how right now, but I do know for certain Todd is not the one and I know when I do find Mr. Right as everyone says or Prince Charming I'll know. I, myself, want *the* Prince Charming," she laughed. Every one still looked uncomfortable. "Come on everyone. My heart isn't broken. I know I'm making the right choice!" Jessica smiled she was never one for serious talk. "We stand behind you one hundred percent - you know that." said Katie as she looked at the other two girls.
"Girl you know we're with you all the way," added Trisha.
"I know that, but can you believe he asked his parents if it was a good match before even asking me? I couldn't believe it". Alana

sat back and sighed. "So have you decided what you're going to tell him?" asked Trisha. Alana sighed again and shrugged her shoulders.

"I think you need to decide quickly. Guess who just walked in?" said Jessica looking toward the door, then she waved. "Shit, he's spotted us," she said in between her teeth as she smiled in his direction. Alana sat frozen in her chair. She didn't know why, but she felt such a sudden rush of fear grip her that she couldn't move. She could barely breathe! What was wrong with her letting something like this bother her? She knew he would be upset or at least his ego would be bruised but he would get over it and if she had to take a guess it would be sooner than later. So she sat up straight in her chair, shook the last of the fear and doubt away, took a deep breath and pasted a smile on her face. Turning, she watched as he approached. The fear and doubt tried to resurface and she almost panicked but then she looked past him to the lone man in a corner booth. He was watching her. The fear she was trying so hard to swallow seemed to disappear. She suddenly had a rush of emotions: comfort, peace, warmth and love. It was as if he knew how she was feeling and knew what was going on inside her mind. He was her protector telling her that he was there to slay the big bad dragon. Eye contact was broken and Todd was standing right in front of her, blocking her view. She tried to look around him, but couldn't without being rude. Was she the only one who had felt that? It seemed like eternity, as if frozen in time. Looking around at everyone she knew it had only been seconds.
Todd took the seat next to her and placed his arm on her chair. "Hi" Alana managed to say as she looked over his shoulder. The corner booth was empty. Had she imagined the whole thing? She still felt warm and yes protected. Turning around she faced her friends and Todd. Maybe she was going crazy she didn't know. "So what are you ladies up to today?" asked Todd as a waiter came by and took his order.

3

Sebastian had to leave. She had felt him. She looked right at him. He had been watching all of them and had felt her fear and it was strong. An uneasiness had come over him. He had noticed one of her friend's wave and look toward the door. He saw the man standing there, but something wasn't right. Something just didn't feel right. He had channeled all of his thoughts to her which had given her a blanket of comfort and warmth. She clung to it and their eyes had locked. That was when he was able to see into her soul. She was lonely and confused and not too sure about herself. He wanted to protect her and shield her from the world. Instead, he never took his eyes from hers and sent her his thoughts: "I will be here always to protect you." Than he blinked and the contact was broken.

Looking in the window now, he felt her feelings again. She was calm, if not a little edgy and right now she thought she was a little crazy or her imagination was working overtime. He knew who the man was by Eudora's special waters and he also knew he was no real threat. Alana had no real feelings for him, but still there was something. He just didn't know what it was yet. He needed to keep his eye on him. Sebastian then turned to Alana and in a silent voice he whispered, "All will be revealed to you soon and you will finally have some understanding in your life." As he stood there and watched he didn't think anyone had heard his pledge, but several had.

4

It was late when Todd arrived at his parent's home. As he entered the study he saw his father standing by the fireplace and his mother sitting in a chair close by. "You're late! Where have you been, I called you several hours ago?" his mother was usually calm and in control, but he could tell by the look on her face she was worried about something. Walking over to the bar he poured a drink. "Relax Mother. I had some business to attend to." He took a long drink and watched as his father turned and looked first at his mother and then at him.

"We hope the business you are referring to has to do with the girl. Has she accepted your proposal yet?"
Todd sighed and ran a hand through his hair. First he looked at his mother then his father. "She has not accepted yet, I didn't have much time today to talk with her, but if that is what's bothering you then don't worry, she will say yes, I'm sure of it."
His mother leaned forward in her chair. There was an almost desperate look in her eyes. "Son, you don't understand. You have to be more than sure." She looked at her husband. Todd could see the concern in his father's eyes.
"Is there more to this than either one of you are telling? By the looks on both your faces I'm guessing there is." He watched his mother lower her head. She looked straight at his father and if not for the muscle that twitched on the side of his father's face you would think he was discussing the weather. But Todd knew better. There was a storm brewing and by the looks of it a huge one.
His father responded. "The Guardians have sent a watcher of sorts." This made Todd stand up a little straighter.
"Are you telling me they have broken the spell and know who we are?"

His mother also straightened her spine, but her voice betrayed her fear in a small whisper that sounded almost like defeat. "No. Not yet anyway, but they could find out anytime. Our Magic is the same as theirs. We use it differently but it is still the same magic. I have sensed things in the last few days. I wasn't really worried until I heard his voice. He proclaimed he would protect her." His mother nearly spat the words out.

"What are you talking about Mother? Who is he and whom does he proclaim to protect?" Todd glanced at his father for some help. He knew his mother was too caught up with her own anger and rage. She would be no help. His father on the other hand was always in control.

"Your mother doesn't know who this man is. All she knows is that he is here to protect the girl. She has been trying all morning to find out who he is but it seems whoever it is their power is great. We can't see who they are, at least not yet." His father moved back to the fireplace and stood looking into the flames. Todd didn't know what to think of this. As far as he knew, Alana hadn't mentioned meeting anyone new. Maybe it was nothing at all; maybe his parents were getting all worked up over nothing. But looking at them now, he knew there was something wrong or his parents wouldn't have said anything. They usually kept everything from him. They always said the least he knew the better off he would be, but now he wished he knew everything. Maybe he could help in some way.

"Mother, Father. I think it is time that you told me the whole story from the beginning and please leave nothing out." The room had grown so quiet he didn't think either one was going to talk but eventually his mother spoke up. "He has a right to know."
His father came forward and for some reason he looked much older. Taking the seat next to his wife he motioned for his son to take a seat too.
"Please sit down, and I will tell you everything." Todd sat down across from his parents. Finally he was going to learn everything. He waited patiently. The clock in the hallway struck the hour as his father began.

"It started over two hundred years ago. At one time we all lived together and we all got along rather well considering." Todd was on the edge of his seat. His father looked tired and older. His mother placed her hand on her husband's, if for no other reason than to support him. The fire crackled and popped at his side. The air seemed to have grown thicker somehow. Todd loosened his tie.

"The old world was different to this one and the two most powerful
wizards were the best of friends. Drake and Lucian were fair, but
hard when they had to be. They were the Masters of our Realm.
They both held the highest respect from all but then they both fell
in love. Rianna the Enchantress was lovely. It was said that all men
young or old fell in love with her in some form or fashion and by
all accounts she was as beautiful on the inside as on the out. She
was pure of heart and everyone knew that whoever was lucky
enough to win her heart would gain so much more. She held her
powers in her heart and once given to the man who holds it, their
powers would be bound together and so much greater. So of course
for years every man tried to win her heart except for at least two;
Drake and Lucian. Their lands bordered each other. They both had
great responsibilities and had no time for such things. Neither one
had ever seen her, but by some chance they all eventually did meet.
Some say it was a higher magic, and of course they both fell in
love with her. They both had to have her, but only one could. At
least that is what they both thought. They never understood her
feelings. The choice was hers. I'm a little foggy on some points;
actually not many know what really happened. There was feuding,
men died, and sides were formed; Drake went one way and Lucian
the other. In the end Lucian married Rianna; Drake said Lucian
cheated him. No one ever talked about it. Everyone was afraid, and
as the months passed Drake grew more enraged. He felt betrayed.
Some say he cast a spell of revenge, others say he died a broken
old man; no one really knows for sure. But they say for his friend's
deceit he gave a gift that could not be returned. Never again shall
there be another. Some didn't understand what that meant. Others
knew and as the years passed not another girl was ever born into
the family - only sons."

Todd didn't fully understand either, but he waited patiently as his
father took a drink. His father looked him straight in the face;
"From what I know, girls were always gifted with a pure heart and
a pure heart can conquer all. But as the years passed it became
nothing more than a story but they say that if ever it should happen
and a girl was born, her heart would be the purest and whoever was
lucky enough to gain her heart would hold the world." His father
took another healthy drink.

"Father I don't fully understand. What does that have to do with

us? That must have been decades ago." Todd was still trying to put
it all together when his father answered.

"Yes it was a very long time ago, but what happened all those
years ago will affect our future. You see, as the story goes, if ever
a girl is born she will be the purest of heart. Such a girl has been
born and according to the stories of the past, she is everything
Rianna was and more. There must have been a spell cast. We never
knew about her until now. That is why there's not a moment to
waste. From what we know her mother has raised her with no help
from anyone. We know her father was a descendent of Lucian and
Rianna. Somehow the spell was either broken or weakened over
the years. We don't really know how it happened, but she has
conquered the impossible, which makes her the purest of heart. Her
powers are starting to show; her aura glows. We *practice* our
Magic - she *is* magic".

Todd went to the bar to top off his glass. He knew he was going to
need it. "If you know all this then you should know who it is and
still I'm wondering what you want from me. Dare I ask?"
His father looked a little guilty, but his mother looked him straight
in the face. "Gain her heart and you will rule both worlds."
Todd was surprised he didn't know what to say to them. He took
another drink, loosened his tie even more and ran his fingers
roughly through his hair. He didn't understand; why would they be
asking him about Alana and then telling him this story and then
asking him to gain some other woman's heart. Suddenly it hit him.
He could hardly breathe. Sweat beaded on his forehead. Was it hot
in here to anyone else? He looked at both his parents. They were
looking back at him all in control. He felt like a bomb just went off
and he was the only one who felt it.
"I'm starting to see. How long have you known? A year, maybe a
month, and you're just now telling me that the woman I have been
seeing is a descendent of these people Lucian and Rianna and is
all-powerful? If so why hasn't she used these powers or why can't
I feel her powers?"
Todd threw these questions at both his parents wanting answers.
His father started to answer but his mother laid her hand across his
arm.
"To answer your first question; we haven't known that long. We

knew it was possible, and yes she is a descendent, and like your father said earlier, there must have been a spell placed on her so we couldn't feel her powers. And for your last question, she might not know yet that she *has* powers. The other night at the party we felt them, as the wind blew and howled and the rain pounded down." Todd sat straighter in the chair. "You mean to tell me she caused all that?'

His mother just nodded. "So now you know why it's so important that you get her to say yes and soon, for once you're married no one can stop you. Not even the one they sent to watch over her. He must have a higher power, or someone with higher powers is helping him. I have tried to feel him, but I can't. Your father has even tried to bring him to us with no luck. We have tried everything and it seems every spell is blocked. So it's very important to get the marriage over with soon. You must gain her heart before she finds out anything. Once she has given her heart it can never be taken away and it must be you she gives it to." With that said his mother stood and so did his father. Todd knew the conversation was at an end; of course it was, there was nothing left to say. As he watched them leave he noticed his father stop once and almost turn, but instead he continued out the door.

5

Alana was just finishing the dishes when the phone rang. Grabbing a towel she wiped her hands and made a mad dash for the phone. "Hello," she said trying to catch her breath. She heard a familiar laugh. "Hi sweetie sounds like you ran all the way to the phone, and it took you long enough too," there was that laugh again. "Hi Mom, I thought you would be home by now." She heard a sigh in the phone. "Me too, but some last minute arrangements came up and almost everyone has left for the day so Becky and I are going to stay and finish them. They're needed in the morning for a wedding. Speaking of that, have you decided anything yet?" Alana wasn't prepared for that question and didn't really know what to say. Everyone would think she was weird or something. She could just hear it now. People would look at her and wonder what her problem was. In their eyes he's perfect, but they need to see him through her eyes to understand.

"I don't love him and besides he scares me a little and something just doesn't feel right." "Honey there is no rush. Take your time. Remember this is forever. Make sure it's what you want with him. Sorry honey, Becky needs me. I'll be home later. No need to cook a meal, I'll grab something on the way home. Anyway it's Friday night - go out and have fun." Alana knew her mother wouldn't push the issue anymore and took a deep breath.

"Thanks Mom for everything. I don't know - I might just do that. I haven't been out in a while. If I'm not here don't wait up, talk to you later." She hung up the phone and went into the living room, sat on the couch and looked around the room. Her mother was right, it's Friday night and here she was sitting on the couch doing nothing. Maybe she should call her friends. They always went out on the weekends and if she wasn't here she wouldn't have to talk to Todd or even see him. For some reason that thought had no appeal; he had showed up that afternoon at the café. It was really weird. They had been just talking about him too. Her friends had surprised her. She thought they all liked Todd. Maybe if she sat down and explained everything to them they might understand. If anyone could it was her friends. She didn't like having to cut their gab session short. They had stayed long enough so it wouldn't be rude. She was surprised that Todd never said a word about last

night, not even after they left. He didn't stay long either. He said
he had something to do and didn't know if he would see her
tonight or not. He said he would call. So she could call up her
friends since she wouldn't be breaking a date with Todd by telling
him she was going with them. Maybe going out and having some
fun was the best thing for her. She phoned Trish. She was the most
outgoing and she knew *she* would be doing something tonight.
After dialing her number she waited - one, two, three and on the
fourth ring she heard Trisha's voice. "Hello." She could tell by the
tone in Trish's voice that she was doing something and didn't like
being interrupted. "So by the way you said hello I can guess I got
you in the middle of something huh?"
Trish laughed. "You could tell all that by the word Hello?"
Alana laughed. "Of course, now what were you doing?" this time
they both laughed. "I was finishing my last minute housework then
I was planning to get ready. What are you and Todd doing
tonight?" Alana sighed softly. "He said he had an appointment or
something to go to and didn't know when he would be through, so
I thought if you guys didn't mind I would go out with you." Alana
could tell Trish was beaming.
"You know you can go with us anytime. It's going to be a blast.
Wait till the others find out you're coming with us. They're going
to freak!" she laughed. Alana thought about that for a minute.
Would they really freak? Has it been that long since the four of
them had a night out on the town? She *had* been neglecting her
friendships.
"You really think everyone will freak Trish?"
"Well, yeah they might. You have to remember it's been a while
since you have been out with all of us. The café don't count - that's
during the day. Anyway it will be fun - we miss you, you know
that right?"
Alana was rapt. "Yeah I know. I miss you guys too. So where are
we going tonight?"
Trish laughed "Get ready. Put on one of those sexy little numbers,
I know you have and I will come and pick you up. We'll meet the
other two, and as for where we're going, well let's just say you'll
enjoy yourself. And be ready at 8:00 sharp." She heard Trish
giggle.

"Wait. Where we going?" again she heard a soft giggle.

"Wait and see," said Trish. Her giggle was now a full-blown laugh. Alana heard a click. "Wait!" she called but all she got was a dial tone. She hated when Trish left her no choice. Now she had to guess where they would be going. Sexy little number indeed. She should get back at Trish and maybe wear the ugliest thing she could find. That would serve her right. Just the look on Trish's face would be priceless. It was a little after six and if she wanted to look her best she needed to start getting ready. She'll save her ugly costume for another time. Tonight she wanted to look her best. She didn't know why, she just knew she needed to. She shrugged her shoulders and decided she would have a good time. As she went upstairs she again wondered where they were going and what she should wear. Opening her closet door she thumbed through her clothes. Something sexy huh? If only she *had* something that sexy. Biting her lower lip she stood in front of her closet looking through her clothes, hoping something would appear out of thin air. "As if something would!" she thought with a giggle. She decided to go look in her mom's closet. Maybe she could find something in there. Her mom was always going to some charity dinner or another. She knew she had a couple of cute little black dresses and since they were about the same size she might find something. Entering her mom's room, she went straight to the closet. Opening the door she looked through several outfits and made a face. Then she spotted one of her little black dresses and held it up.

It was cute, but she didn't want to be cute tonight. Something in the back of the closet sparkled and caught Alana's eye. Shoving some clothes out of the way she reached for the dress. It was a pale gray with small spaghetti straps that crisscrossed in back and dipped down and curved to show off most of her back. Smiling she went to the door and looked in the full length mirror. Holding the dress close she twisted this way and that, the beads moved with her and the whole dress sparkled. Now *that* was sexy. Now if she could get lucky and find some shoes to match, maybe even a little beaded purse... Then she giggled at her reflection. It had been a while since she had partied with her friends. She missed it.

She placed the dress on the bed to go and search for shoes. It would be magic if they could be found so readily.

6

Lily was still smiling when she entered the back room of her shop. "Do you think she'll go out with her friends tonight?" asked Becky who was one of Lily's best friends. They had known each other for years; they met when Lily first started the flower shop. Becky was her first employee and they had been friends ever since.

Laughing, Lily picked up the last foam form, "I don't know Becky, but I do hope so. She needs to explore life and have some fun." Becky nodded agreement as she placed more greenery into the foam form before adding flowers. They were almost done and if it wasn't for Becky, Lily knew she would have been there all night. "Becky, again I want to thank you for staying with me and helping. If you hadn't I would have been here all night working."

Becky lifted her head from her work, "You know I don't mind. Feels like old times though when you and I would scramble to get everything ready the night before. I remember a lot of times we took shifts during the night and made a trip to the back office where that horrible couch used to be." She laughed and Lily laughed with her. "I think we both slept more on that old couch than we did in our own beds!"

Becky was finishing up on the last arrangement, placing the final bow off to the side. "There. I do believe that was the last one. Give me that one and I will take them both and put them in the cooler." Lily handed the arrangement to Becky. "After you put them into the cooler go on home - I'll clean up. It's been a long day." Becky nodded and with both hands full headed to the back room. Lily grabbed the garbage can and placed it at the end of the table. Looking around she found the dustpan and brushed everything into the bin. From the greenery to the stems that had been cut and the discarded soft petals here and there. All went into the large garbage can. She was finishing the last of the mess when Becky came back into the room - her purse hanging over her arm.

"I locked the back door and turned all the lights off except the one next to your office. Are you sure you don't want me to stay?" Lily smiled and watched as Becky looked around. She knew if she asked, Becky would stay as long as she was needed. She was a treasure and Lily let her know it too. Grabbing her shoulders Lily turned Becky toward the door. "You go - and thanks again Becky. I'll see you tomorrow." Becky smiled and waved. Lily watched as she disappeared around the corner to the parking lot. Looking around, she admired her little corner. Her shop was on a well-populated street. There was an ice cream parlor across the way, and at the end of her street was a deli that made the best sandwiches she'd ever had, and on the opposite side there was a small bookstore with a coffee bar inside. Sometimes she would go there, have a cup of coffee, relax and remember she had met Edmund in front of a coffee bar. They had bumped into each other literally. It was love at first sight, at least for her. He was a ray of sunshine - all bright and golden. Too handsome for his own good, with a smile that took your breath away. Alana had that same smile. She stepped back into the shop and the tiny bell over the door rang softly. The lights were starting to come on outside - it would be dark soon. Glancing at her watch, it was just past eight. If she wanted to get home before nine she needed to finish getting everything ready for tomorrow. With a critical eye she looked around. The shop was just as she had always wanted it. The place had a whimsical look, with wood nymphs peeking out from around the wicker baskets that held flowers. There were colors blended here and there with greenery sitting in pots and hanging from the walls. Colorful butterflies and fairies danced around. There were also coolers that held the most exotic flowers and the roses were on the back wall in the cooler. Their colors were stunning and varied. During the day they would be fanned out in different pots and baskets where everything was in reach of the customers so that they could see and smell the different types of flowers. Even with most of them put back in the cooler their smell still lingered in the shop. Gnomes kept their watch with mischievous smiles. Lily was very proud of her little business. It might not be much, but everything was hers and people came from miles just to purchase flowers from her. Humming happily Lily started toward the back. "You should be proud. You have done a wonderful job." Startled, Lily turned around and there stood a little old woman with a smile on her face. Lily saw that the door was still closed. So why didn't she hear the bell? She must have been really daydreaming not to have heard anyone enter. Planting a smile on her face she stepped forward. "Welcome to My Enchanted Garden. I'm sorry we're closed, but we will be opened again in the morning if you would like to come back then."

The older woman just smiled and walked to the back where the work table was located. With her back turned, Lily couldn't see her face. How strange. There was something familiar about her.

"I'm sorry ma'am is there something I can help you with?" Still the woman stood there. Lily hoped she wasn't lost or didn't know who she was. She didn't know what to do.

"I'm not lost and I know who I am, and I also know who you are. Maybe this will help." With a flick of her wrist the old woman suddenly became a beautiful young lady. Lily couldn't believe her eyes. Where there was gray hair before now it was black, long and flowing almost to her waist. It curled a little at the end. The little pale blue dress was replaced with a long robe rich in color. The pale eyes behind the glasses now looked more vivid, cerulean blue with nothing to block them. She had a mischievous smile with a knowing look. Lily couldn't believe what she was seeing. Something had to have happened for her to be here.

"I know it's a shock to see me dear. If it wasn't important I wouldn't be here." She waved her hand again and two chairs appeared at the end of Lily's work table and the lock in the door slid closed with a barely audible clunk. Eudora motioned for Lily to have a seat. She could tell this was still a shock to Lily. "Would you like something to drink dear?" Lily just shook her head. If Eudora was here then something *must* be wrong. She hadn't seen her in almost nineteen years and now she didn't even look a day older.

"You're looking good Eudora - why have you come?"

Eudora could see Lily was trying to stay calm and in control, but Eudora could feel her worry and confusion. With a smile Eudora spoke lightly, "I don't want to worry you, but Alana will be twenty-one soon. Now we have kept our promise and have stayed out of her life. You wanted her to have a normal childhood and she has had just that. But now is the time for her to know who she really is." Lily stood. "I thought we had some time - to break it to her. Now you're telling me it's time for her to know right now! Why?" Eudora had to commend her; she was doing exactly what a loving mother would do. Again Eudora motioned for Lily to have a seat. When Lily sat down again Eudora continued. "You know of the story about Lucian and Rianna?" Eudora paused as Lily nodded slowly. "You must know just how important your daughter is. Your husband Edmund was a descendant of Lucian and Rianna. There was a curse, some would say, placed on them and their descendants. Because of the curse Rianna was the last female of the line - until Alana." Lily just sat there and shook her head. "I think I remember Edmund telling me the story and how important it would be if a daughter was ever born. I don't see why that should have anything to do with us." Lily laid her head in the palm of her hands. "Please tell me Alana is not this daughter!" When she looked up she had her answer. Eudora sat patiently while Lily worked everything out in her mind. Lily muttered and shook her head, then she stood. Eudora knew she now understood the importance of her daughter's heritage. Her eyes were clear, her stance was soldier like.

"So tell me what we need to do. Is my daughter in danger? Are there people out there looking for her?" As Lily stopped to take a breath Eudora held up her hands.

"I will tell you everything you need to know on our way to your house, and don't worry. Alana is being protected. She has a watcher looking out for her." Lily still looked dazed, but in control. She turned off lights and grabbed her purse. Eudora was standing where she had left her and the room sparkled and shone. Eudora shrugged her shoulders and headed toward the door as she spoke "I hope you don't mind that I cleaned up a bit." With that, she was unlocking the door and stepping out. All Lily could do was shake her head even more and follow. This was going to take a lot to get used to. Did Alana have the same powers? Or did she have more? Was that why she was so important? This was too much - and all on an empty stomach. When she turned the corner Eudora was standing by her car watching her closely.

"I had forgotten all the *modern* conveniences that you humans use," she laughed as she got into the car. "It has been quite some time since I have been in a car - it's really refreshing."
Lily got behind the wheel and started the engine. She turned to Eudora but wasn't expecting the look of fascination on Eudora's

face. "I wouldn't think anything surprised you." She said as she backed out and headed towards home.

"My dear, I have always been, shall we say, mystified by the human race. What is the term I'm looking for? Yes - modern technology. Over the centuries the human race *has* evolved." Eudora sat back silently. Lily knew nothing else would be said until they reached their destination.

7

Alana was glad she had decided to go out with her friends. She was having a wonderful time. Something she hadn't had in a while. She felt almost free. The girls were surprised at first when they saw her, but they got over that quickly. The place Trisha had picked out was one of the top spots around. Looking over at Trisha, Alana smiled "Thank you for not asking any questions and for taking me out and showing me such a good time. I haven't had this much fun in forever!" she waved her hand in the air slightly off center and laughed. Trisha laughed too and shook her head. "Girls - I think we have created a monster!" They all laughed.

"I don't know about that," said Jessica "but that really cute guy has been checking you out now for a while." She looked straight at Alana who laughed and looked at all of them.

"Me?" Alana looked around the place and spotted him again standing off to the side by himself. Her heart rate picked up. She turned back so quickly she knocked over the rest of her drink. "Oh my God, I've seen him before. You know when we were all at the café? Well he was sitting at a table close to the door and I saw him watching me," Alana said as she looked over her shoulder. He was no longer standing there watching. For some reason she was drawn to him. He made her feel safe somehow. Still looking at the empty space where he had been, she heard Trisha talking.

"Alana are you listening to me?" Alana nodded her head, well she was now anyway. "I asked do you know him." Again Alana shook her head. All three girls looked at each other and then at Alana.

"Maybe it's just a coincidence that you're both in the same place at the same time – twice in one day," said Kate, the sensible one.

"Or maybe it's just fate - you know - your destiny to meet!" added Jessica as she sighed into her drink.

Alana didn't really want to believe what either one of them said. The first was just too creepy, and the second was just plain stupid. She didn't believe in fate or destiny. She sighed. "I don't know what it is, I just know I'm ready to go home and crawl into my bed and sleep for a week." The other three voiced their agreement and decided to call it a night.

8

Lily poured them both a cup of tea and sat down at the table next to Eudora. "Now that some of the shock has worn off can you please tell me again what the hell is going on?"
Eudora had to give this woman credit. She just found out that her daughter is not just any witch. No, her powers were passed down through the generations and they were very powerful. Just how powerful no one knew. "Alana will need some training in the arts of magic, spells, everything relating to our craft. I will be her teacher of spells and help her with the many questions I know she will have. Also she will be trained in the art of war and I have the perfect teacher for that job. He is loyal and very brave, and he will also protect her with his life if necessary." Eudora watched as Lily stuck her hand up in the air.

"Wait a minute. What do you mean the art of war? Why in the world will she have to know anything about that?"
Eudora watched Lily closely and wondered should she tell her the truth. She decided only the truth would suffice. "Lily there will be a battle. Good against evil. It is inevitable. That is why we need to start her training as soon as possible. Right now she is still under a protection spell that will last until her twenty-first birthday. After that she will be on her own. Well not actually on her own. Others will be around to make sure she is protected, but they can only do so much. That is why we need to make her understand everything I have told you. The dark ones might already know who she is, but there is nothing they can do right now even if they tried. Soon we will know who they are, but for now we need to concentrate on Alana and her training. Now have I answered all your questions"
Eudora watched Lily take all of what she said in. "I can't believe this is happening. Someone is out there ready to destroy my daughter and all you can think about is her training. Well I'm sorry but I won't let this happen. Why are you shaking your head no?"
Eudora sighed then spoke again in a soft voice. "I'm sorry Lily but there is nothing you can do to stop it." Eudora turned her head listening. "Your daughter should be here in just a moment. I'm sorry Lily, but I will be speaking to her tonight." They both heard the jingle of keys as the door opened.

"Mom are you up? I'm home." The door closed and the lock was put in place.

Lily resigned herself to the whole idea and looked straight at Eudora as she called to her baby. "Honey I'm in the kitchen. Could you come in here?" Eudora knew at that moment that Lily would not stand in her way whether she wanted to or not. Her daughter was her main concern and she wanted her to be safe and protected from whatever evil was out there and Eudora knew she would be. If her radar was correct Sebastian was watching out for her. She could sense him even now in the house. "Let the battle begin," she thought. She knew it was to be one of legends.

9

Alana could hear the hesitation in her mother's voice. Maybe she was just tired - she did work late. Alana locked the door and headed for the kitchen. As she stepped through the doorway to the kitchen she hung her keys on the wall.

"Mom I hope you have some tea made. I could use some." She looked at her mother. She looked tense and wouldn't look her daughter in the eye.

"I'll have a new pot made in just a moment," she answered as she jumped up and fluttered about in the kitchen. She had been so intent on her mom she hadn't noticed the other lady in the room. There at the table sat a woman who was looking at her as if Alana should know her. Moving from the table to the kitchen, she cornered her mother.

"Who is that woman sitting at our kitchen table? I have never seen her before." Alana crossed her arms and waited for her mother to answer, but instead the woman at the table waved to her.

"I'm sorry to butt in dear, but you *have* seen me before. I'll admit it has been many years and you were a little girl then. My name is Eudora." She got up and headed toward Alana with her arms outstretched. When she reached Alana she pulled her into a tight hug. "You are so beautiful Alana, and you look a lot like your father. You have his eyes. "Alana could barely breathe, much less understand what this woman was talking about. She said she knew her and that she looked like her father. For some reason, Alana had an uneasy feeling about all this. She looked into the lady's eyes. "How do you know my father?" Of all the things she could have said that is all she could come up with. She was still trying to fathom what was going on. She looked again at her mother. She could see such sadness there, then back at the lady who was still holding her shoulders. She was looking at Alana like she had known her forever and the strange thing about it all? Alana had a feeling that she *had* known her forever.

Eudora could tell by looking at Alana that she was confused and uncomfortable. "I can sense your uneasiness and your confusion Alana, so I will get right to the point. Your father was a very important man, but Alana, you are a very powerful woman. Please, my dear have a seat and I will tell you everything." With that said, Eudora pulled out a chair for Alana and waited for Lily to put the tea on the table. She started to pour and told Alana the whole story leaving nothing out.

10

Sebastian watched everything that was going on. His senses picked up on every emotion floating around in the room. The mother felt guilty and sad and maybe a little regretful for not knowing what was to come. And not knowing what would happen to her daughter and knowing there was nothing she could do about it. But he could also sense her courage against the unknown, her strength to protect - that made him smile. Something he would never let anyone else see. He liked to keep to all the mysteries about him. He was known as the Dark Dragon and that's how he wanted it to remain. The daughter was more confused. Then the shock had registered along with a feeling of unease. She sat in her chair and listened to every word that Eudora spoke. Whether or not she comprehended it all was another question, but she never interrupted and she looked Eudora straight in the eye. When Eudora was finished a silence fell thickly throughout the room. You could hear the clock above the stove ticking. The sound was magnified when any other time it wouldn't even be noticed.

Eudora looked up into his face. He could see the concern and worry she was trying to hide. Sebastian nodded to let her know he understood and turned back to the one woman who had the power to control both their worlds. He could sense her trying to put everything in order and to absorb it all.
Sebastian concentrated on her thoughts and closed his eyes. Images of her father came into focus along with Alana when she was very young. He was sitting in a chair watching his daughter as she played on the floor. "Tell me another story Daddy please."
Her father laughed "Anything for you Princess. Long ago in a place far away a curse was made. A curse against two people who were very much in love. It was made by an evil man who wanted revenge on the couple. Through the years they lived as happily as they could, but through the generations they knew the curse had worked. None were ever blessed with a daughter, but now their princess has come and there is still hope for all!" With that he kissed her on the top of her head.
"Oh Daddy I like that story bestest of all!" She stood up and hugged her father. He laughed and hugged her back.

"And when the time comes what will you do poppet?" he hugged her small body to him and with tears in his eyes he listened to his daughter.

"You said I will be the princess Daddy, don't you remember?" she laughed and slid off his lap.

On her way out of the door her father spoke; "Of course I remember Poppet."

As she left the room he bowed his head.

11

Eudora knew it would take Alana some time to take it all in. When she looked up again Sebastian was still with them. Good thing no one but her could see him standing in the corner with that fearsome look on his face. He tries to play the demon but Eudora knew better. Sebastian had a heart of gold, but he was a dangerous opponent in battle. With the nod from him Eudora knew that he would not interfere or show himself. He would only help when it was needed of him. She looked back down at Alana, still sitting there with a blank look on her face staring off into space. She was just about to speak when she heard Alana's voice barely above a whisper. Eudora had to lean forward to hear.

"My father used to tell me a story when I was so young I really didn't remember much of it until now. I used to ask him who the princess was and he would always tell me that it was me. I was the one who would protect both worlds - that I could walk in both and that one day someone would come and ask for my help to destroy all the evil in the world. I thought it was just a story - something my father made up for me, just for me.
I never thought it was real - that this could be happening." She looked up. "How can any of this be real?" she asked, looking at her mother for the first time. She wanted her reassurance that this wasn't happening, but with one look into her mother's eyes she knew the truth. "You knew all this time and never told me? How could you do this to me?" she whispered. Alana got up from the table and ran out of the room and straight up the stairs to her room and slammed the door.

Sebastian never hesitated - in the blink of an eye he was gone. Eudora took Lily by the hand. "I know this seems cruel to you, and it very well might be, but she had to find out and it had to be now so she can prepare," she patted her hand. Lily looked up at her with tears in her eyes. "She will never forgive me," the tears streamed down her face. Eudora could feel her loss. If only she could make everything go away, but it's not that simple. "She is the one the prophecy spoke about. She will be the one with enough powers to stop the Dark Ones." Rising from the chair Eudora placed her hand on Lily's shoulder. "I will go and talk to her right now. I think she needs to understand that she *is* the princess from her father's stories and that that is a *good* thing."

Eudora knocked on Alana's bedroom door. No answer. She tried the door handle - it was locked. "Oh bother," she whispered and with a wave of her hand the door opened. Alana was lying on the bed and when the door opened she saw that woman standing there with a hesitant look.

"How did you get in here? I know I locked the door," she almost snarled it at her.

"Pish, posh" Eudora said as she shook her head and waved her arm. "You did lock the door my dear and I went ahead and unlocked it. I knew you needed someone to talk to so I took the liberty in coming up here."

Alana's head was spinning. This woman talked without taking a breath and what she did say never made any sense to her and now she's telling me she opened my locked bedroom door from the outside. Yeah right. "So if you don't mind me asking what did you do? Ask the door to please open up."

Alana almost smiled when Eudora answered, "Why yes, I did. You're a fast learner!" Eudora clapped her hands together.

"What a minute you're trying to tell me you ask my bedroom door to open up and it just did? Well if that really happened, how did you do it?" Alana crossed her arms over her chest; 'now let her talk her way out of this' she thought.

"I did it with one of my powers, and I do have many - just as you do." She folded her hands in her lap and waited for her words to register and she knew by the look on Alana's face it was sinking in fast. When it did, Alana jumped up off the bed and nearly screamed; "I'm a witch?"

When Eudora just nodded her head 'yes' Alana started pacing and mumbling to herself. "I can't believe this is happening. A witch and with some kind of powers too. She'll tell me next that I'm expected to kidnap children lost in the forest and bake them in a big oven." She turned around and looked at Eudora again. "Please explain everything to me." She sat back down and tried to compose herself, waiting for Eudora to tell her everything again. Eudora could tell Alana was trying hard to understand - that's why she had looked at Sebastian and waved him away so she could explain what Alana would have to do.

Eudora took a deep breath, "I know this is a lot to take in, maybe we should have told you sooner," she admitted "but what is done is done. There is no going back, so your training will start tomorrow. I will be your first teacher, you will learn all your spells and incantations and any other magical rituals you will need to know. We will go through the old spells and the new ones. You will learn how to use your mind as I did on the door and all sorts of wondrous things. Now you rest tonight. I will be back in the morning when your training will begin. I have a lot to teach you." With that Eudora got up from the bed and started for the door. "Wait!" said Alana. Eudora turned with a smile on her face waiting for her to speak. "How do I know this is all real and I won't wake up tomorrow to discover it was all a dream?"
Eudora thought for a minute. What could she do to relieve her mind to let her relax enough to get a good night's sleep. An idea came to her and so she walked back over to the bed and with a wave of her hand a globe appeared. She could tell this had surprised Alana, but soon this would be just as natural for her as it was for Eudora. Alana started to speak but Eudora shook her head. "Just relax and watch the flowers float to the ground from the trees. Watch as the stream flows slowly and puddles into a pool of water, listen to the birds sing and the breeze blow. As the flowers swirl and dance around all is happy in this place, all is calm and peaceful. *Close your eyes, and set yourself free. Remember my words, remember my plea. Close your eyes and only see me. Remember these words I say to thee, remember my voice when I speak, close your eyes and listen to me, close your eyes I beckon thee, sleep my sweet and have many dreams.*" Eudora watched as Alana closed her eyes and gradually fell into a deep sleep. She placed the globe on the night stand. "Watch over her," she whispered before grabbing the blanket from the end of the bed and covering her up and leaving her to her dreams. Outside Alana's room she silently summoned Sebastian. He was standing in front of her before she even opened her eyes or her mind cleared. "Watch her tonight Sebastian, make sure she has a relaxed peaceful sleep. It will probably be the last night she will have one."

Sebastian nodded. "Do *you* think she is up to the challenge that faces her?" Eudora watched Sebastian's face - he never gave anything away. When she tried to reach him she always got no emotion at all.

"She has the courage to go forward, but only time will tell if she has the strength of mind to accomplish it." With that said Sebastian was gone. Eudora knew courage was sometimes all you had, maybe with Alana that would be enough to give her the strength to reach a victory. Like Sebastian said, time would tell.

Sebastian appeared right in front of Alana's bed. She looked so peaceful lying there. He still couldn't believe this girl on the verge of womanhood would be their salvation. He didn't understand how someone so small could wield that much power, but it was written in the prophecy. Alana tossed a little back and forth. Sebastian laid a hand on her forehead to comfort her. Eudora would start her training tomorrow and when Alana mastered that he would take over and show her the ways of battle and how to win. He would be by her side through it all. His life was hers now - he would protect her with everything inside of him. She will succeed - he will settle for no less.

Eudora found Lily still sitting at the table with a cold cup of tea in front of her. "How about if I freshen up that tea a bit for you?" and without an answer steam rose from the cup.

"How is she?" Lily asked as she took a sip of her tea. She is resting peacefully.

I will start her training tomorrow, but I think it is time for me to leave and let you get some rest yourself. Now you finish that tea and I will put the kitchen back in order." With a quick sweep of her hands everything was put back in its place and she watched as Lily sat there and finished her tea. Eudora was glad to see that she had finished every last drop. She had added a little extra to help Lily sleep.

"You're right it has been a long day, and I do feel tired." Lily got up and went for the stairs. When all was quiet Eudora said a silent prayer. One of many prayers to come.

12

When Alana rolled over in her bed she opened her eyes. She hadn't slept like that in a long time. She felt well rested and relaxed. She stretched her muscles and came back to reality. Sitting up in bed she wiped the sleep from her eyes and thought about last night. She had been out with her friends the previous night and when she arrived home she had got the shock of her life. Or did she? Running her hands over her face and then through her hair she thought back to all that had happened, or rather what she had perhaps dreamed last night. Was any of it real? She turned to the clock on her night stand and froze. There next to her clock sat a globe. When she reached for it she shivered, but when she picked it up and held it in her hands it was warm and the warmth of it flowed over her like the sunshine would feel on a warm day. She suddenly felt alive. Alana looked down into the globe. It was still as beautiful as it had been the night before. The trees were still blowing lightly and the flowers still danced and the stream flowed on. She could almost here the bubble of the water as it emptied into a pool at the base of the stream. Looking around she knew it hadn't been a dream. Last night *did* happen.

Jumping out of bed, Alana grabbed her clothes and threw them on. She brushed her hair and pulled a rubber band through it. Looking in the mirror she noted she hadn't done half bad; she had on jeans and a sweatshirt. Grabbing her shoes she headed down the stairs and came to a halt. When she stepped through the kitchen door there, sitting at the table drinking tea sat Eudora. With a smile and a wave she said "Come Alana - we have much to learn today," and motioned to one of the chairs. Alana walked over and sat down. "Now then, sit down and have a nice breakfast and a cup of tea and then we'll get started". Before Alana could say a word, a hot breakfast and a cup of tea appeared in front of her. She could smell the bacon and eggs and see the steam rising from the plate. With large eyes Alana turned and looked at Eudora. "How did you do that?" Eudora waved her hand toward the food that sat in front of her. "I asked for it, and see, there it is. And hot too. What, is it not to your liking? Maybe something lighter would do." Before she could wave her hand again Alana held up her own.

"Wait this is fine, but I really don't like tea with my breakfast. Coffee would have been better." Before she got the last word out a nice steaming cup of coffee now sat where the tea had been just moments ago. When Alana looked at Eudora she just shrugged her shoulders and smiled. Alana sat there in silence for a while. Eventually she picked up her coffee and took a sip. It was delicious. When she set it back down she decided to try breakfast. It was good too! With a smile she dug in. Eudora just sat there watching. When she was halfway through the meal she set her fork down and looked at Eudora.

"Will I be able to do this - you know - ask for something and it just appears?"

Eudora answered somewhat cryptically "That dress you wore last night? My dear have you not figured it out yet? No I see you haven't. Dresses and breakfasts and pots of tea are just everyday conveniences. But as well as those things, you can *always* have your heart's desire, but only if you believe you can. I mean with your heart and soul. Without that desire, it will never be. And I am here to teach you how to use your powers, or at least what powers I know of. You will learn the old ways and the new, we will leave nothing out. Now finish your breakfast so we can get started."

Alana picked her coffee back up and thought about what Eudora said. Alana could do everything that Eudora could do and maybe even more. And that dress and shoes last night. Wow! The possibilities. Was this the reason she had felt different lately? This made her shiver wondering what evil was out there waiting for her. Would she be ready when the time came? She didn't know the answer to that question but she did know one thing; she would do whatever it took to save all those people. She had so many depending on her and most of them didn't even know it, but *she* did and that's what terrified her. Could she do it? Eudora watched as the battle continued. Alana's emotions were out there for all to see. She knew what was at stake. She knew everyone was depending on her and that was a lot for anyone to carry, much less a mere girl. Eudora knew how this weighed on Alana. If there was some other way they would have tried it. This is the only way. Feeling all of Alana's emotions Eudora stood and held her hand out to Alana.

"We should get started. We have much to learn in a short amount of time." Alana looked around then placed her hand in Eudora's. Warmth surrounded her everywhere. Closing her eyes she let the warmth pour through her bones and just as quickly Eudora was talking to her.

"You may open your eyes now," she laughed softly. Alana opened her eyes and knew she wasn't in her kitchen anymore. Where her table used to be there was now a fountain, the water was crystal clear and perfectly still as if it was frozen in time. Alana looked at the rest of the room. There was a fireplace where a fire was burning and casting shadows about the room. Two chairs were positioned on either side of the fireplace. There were bookshelves at the back of the room with every inch of them crammed with books. Turning further, there was a table that held all kinds of bottles and a shelf against the wall stacked with others things that Alana couldn't identify. Some of the things she had never seen before. Turning again she faced Eudora who seemed to always be smiling.

"Where are we and how did we get here?" Eudora lead Alana to one of the chairs by the fireplace and she sat in the other one. "My dear, welcome to my Library. This is my special room. Only a few have ever seen the inside. It is protected by a spell so no one can enter without me." Alana couldn't believe she was there much less in this woman's private room. Looking again to the fountain Alana was drawn to it. She really couldn't say why, but something about it made her eyes wander toward it more than once. Eudora picked up on this and waved her hand toward the fountain and laid her other one on Alana's back.

"Would you like to look inside the fountain?" Alana never said a word she just followed Eudora up to the ledge of the fountain. "Now my dear. What would you like to see? Name anything and then look into the fountain and you will see it there." Alana looked from Eudora to the fountain which was still very still. "Let me see my mother." She leaned back as she heard Eudora chuckled. Eudora softly moved her hands in the water. It shimmered and started to settle and there in front of her was Alana's mother in the flower shop doing an arrangement. She looked tired and sad. Alana knew that there was a lot weighing her mother's shoulders down because she could feel it. She wasn't even mad at her mom anymore. She understood. Even if there was something her mother wanted to do to help, she knew it was hopeless. Alana knew that this was something she had to do on her own. Of course there would be people like Eudora who would be there for the training and teaching her everything they could. But in the end she would be the one standing alone against whatever evil was out there. This made the hairs crawl on the back of her neck and a shiver to run down her spine. Gritting her teeth she prayed for the strength to get through this. Alana looked towards Eudora who had been watching and knew when she had accepted her fate. She could see the determination in the grim lines of her face. Yes she knew she would have to do this alone. She also knew there would be help along the way. "I think it's time to begin." With that Eudora called for her spell book. "The first thing we have to do is conjure you your own spell book so you can write down what you learn. This book will only come to you no matter who calls for it. This book is sacred. You must always protect it so I will show you how. We're going to use a summoning spell. Now if you want something you have to ask for it and no, you can't just say 'I would like my spell book' - it doesn't work that way. You have to call for it. I will help you. Now we need paper and a pencil," and just like that they appeared in Eudora's hand. "Now look at my book. We will use it as an example until you catch on, but every spell that is placed in your book can only be from your own mind and written by your own hand. These are spells I have come up with over the years. Now let's see. We will find a small one to start with." Alana watched as Eudora thumbed through her book. She mumbled as she searched - sounded like 'oh bother'! Eudora then laid the spell book down and opened it and with her hands held over the book she concentrated. The pages started to turn until it fell open to a particular page. "There's what I was looking for!" She leaned the book toward Alana so she could see what the spell said.

"You have to be kidding! It has to rhyme? You can't be serious!" Alana shook her head. "I've always been hopeless with rhymes." She picked up the notebook and pencil and looked down at both.

Eudora watched as Alana struggled with what she had to do; later on she would be able to perform spells in her sleep. Right now though it was still too new and probably sounded silly on top of it all, but she was trying.

Eventually she handed the notebook to Eudora and looked her straight in the eyes. Eudora looked at what she had written. Alana sat there and watched Eudora read over her spell. She felt silly and it sounded stupid, but hey it was her first spell and it only took her a few minutes to do. Looking at the clock she was surprised. Actually it had taken more than a few minutes - almost an hour! It just didn't feel that long. Looking back at Eudora she watched as she laid the notebook in her lap. "Sorry. I didn't realize it took so long." Eudora just shrugged her shoulders. "Some spells take longer than others," she looked back at Alana and smiled. "I think it is time to call for your spell book. Close your eyes and clear your mind." Alana did as she was told. "Now concentrate on your spell. Say the words in your mind. Think of nothing else but your spell book. See it. Feel it in your hands." Eudora became silent as Alana thought of nothing else but her spell book. She said the words over and over in her head and laid her hands upright in her lap. In her heart she called for it. She could see it in her mind and she reached for it. She could actually feel it, heavy in her hands. It had a musty smell to it and the leather was cool to the touch. That's when Alana realized she actually *was* holding it. Opening her eyes she saw it there in her outstretched hands. Hugging it to her she looked at Eudora and smiled.

"I can't believe I just did that. One minute I was thinking about it and the next I could feel it and smell it. That was amazing!"
The look on Alana's face was priceless. It was a combination of shock, disbelief and wonder. Eudora couldn't help it. She had to laugh.
"Well done my dear. That book belongs to you now. You need to copy your first spell into your book so you will always remember it and you also need to write a few more so your book is protected. You can use these same spells on many different things. Now I think we should both get busy. You write some spells while I gather together the herbs we will be going over today. You will

53

also write those all down in your book."

 Eudora heard Alana snort and smiled. Before the day was over, Alana's hands would be tired along with her mind.

13

Alana couldn't take anymore - she needed a break. Her brain needed a break - she was bone tired. "Eudora is this necessary?" Eudora turned and just stared. She shook her head and took Alana by the arm. "Let me show you why it's necessary." She placed her hand in the water and images started to appear. What Alana saw made her heart hitch in her throat. All the destruction! Nothing was left of the peaceful place that Alana gazed at and admired every day in her globe. All that remained was rubble. No more flowers, trees uprooted and bare, the waterfall no longer flowed and the little pool was muddy and stagnant. The magic of the place was gone and desolation had taken its place.

Alana wiped her eyes and looked away. "I don't want to see anymore." Eudora waved her hand and the waters cleared and became still again.

"I was hoping you wouldn't have to see all that, but now you know why it's necessary to know everything - old and new. My time with you is almost up so I have to work harder and so do you! To learn! You were born to be what you are so the task has been easy."

Alana snorted "What do you mean 'your time with me is almost up?' I thought you would be with me till the end. I guess I thought... You... I don't know - I'm not ready to face anyone yet. I don't feel ready!" She leaned against the counter. Eudora knew Alana was starting to panic so with a gentle smile she calmed her. "Of course I will be with you. Just call my name and I will be there. I am only your teacher for the spells and incantations and teaching which herbs are for what. You will have a new teacher for the next part of your journey. He will teach you how to be prepared for a battle and a magic war. What I have taught you also prepares you for that because you can take your spells into battle."

Alana stood there listening to Eudora. Soon she would have a new teacher and he was going to teach her how to battle magic with magic. This was something she wasn't expecting. She thought Eudora would always be with her but now she will have another teacher to worry about. "What is this new teacher of mine like? And what is his name?" Alana asked as she stood up straight and looked defiantly at Eudora.

"His name is Sebastian Drakon and he is the top warrior in the Realm. You will find none with more skill. He will teach you well." Alana thought this over for a minute and let his name become familiar in her mind. "Has he ever lost a battle?"

"No" she replied as she watched Alana take all of this in. "Now my next question is how many battles has he been in?" Eudora almost laughed. She knew Alana wanted to make sure he knew what he was doing if he was to be her teacher. "He has fought in many battles. Sometimes just hearing his battle name put fear in people and some would just surrender or flee." Eudora shrugged her shoulders as if this wasn't any kind of news, but to Alana it was. "Just what is his battle name to set fear in people?" Alana quizzed further as she pretended to shiver. Eudora couldn't wait until they met face to face. Sparks would fly. Good thing she would be there to watch. "His battle name is 'Dark Dragon'," Eudora spoke softly. Alana almost shivered for real when she heard those words. Perhaps he was different when he was not in battle. "My new teacher - is he smart? Does he know anything else besides how to win a battle?" this time Eudora did chuckle. She couldn't help it - it slipped out before she could stop it.

"My dear, do not let the word 'warrior' fool you. Yes, he *is* a warrior through and through, but Sebastian is also very intelligent. He graduated with top honors and that, my dear, is not easily done. He works hard and he is well respected and loved by all in our Realm. Whatever fear his name has brought to our enemy, it has also brought security to our people and joy to know that their warrior had returned victorious every time he went out to battle." Eudora had to catch what she said. She almost said their 'prince' and it was too soon for Alana to know that her teacher was actually the son of their king and next in line for the throne. That would spoil everything. Alana would mind her manners and not show her true self and Sebastian liked to be known only as Sebastian. Maybe if she spoke to him he would keep quiet. Eudora knew that it aggravated him when they came to Eudora's secret place because Sebastian was not allowed to enter. But she had her reasons. If Alana knew that Sebastian listened in when they spoke of their lives and all her secrets, then she couldn't respect him and Eudora didn't want that to happen. Their time might be just about over but Alana had thrived. Not once did she miss a beat. She might think spells are silly, but she had a book half full with them and every one of them came from Alana, in her own hand and from her own heart and mind. She knew everyone by heart - she would be ready soon. They have come a long way in a week, which might not sound like a lot, but in her world time was measured differently; of course they got off to a rocky start. That boy who Sebastian told her about would come by and call – very distracting. Then one day he just stopped. Eudora meant to find out what had happened to him but she never asked and Alana never spoke of the matter. Of course her friends came by occasionally. Eudora was introduced as Alana's aunt on her father's side. But now things were going smoothly. Alana's spells were very good for one so young. "When do I meet him?" Alana had taken everything Eudora said to heart. If he was respected and loved by his people and loathed and feared by his enemy then he must be doing something right. "I will arrange for you to meet tomorrow." Alana wanted to know more but her friends would be there soon so they needed to clean up and leave. Eudora took pity on Alana and with a wave of her hand the tables were cleared and the books were put back in their right place. "I still don't think I will ever get over the fact that I can do that too." Alana chuckled, took Eudora's hand and closed her eyes. When she opened them again they were in her living room. Eudora told Alana she would also be able to go from one place to another just like that, but that would take a little more time to master. Only the most skilled of them could travel that way. Alana just shrugged her shoulders as the doorbell rang. With a smile she dashed for the door. Eudora just shook her head and went upstairs. She needed to talk with Sebastian. She knew he was there and he would follow so she entered Alana's room and closed the door.

Alana was so happy to see all of her friends - she had missed them so much. Of course she *had* seen them, but it had been a while since all of them could get together.
And it was nice; they all piled in and headed for the kitchen where the food and drinks were waiting. Of course when Alana had left to answer the doorbell nothing had been prepared and now the counter was covered with different kinds of snack foods. There were chips and salsa for Trish. Jessica liked wheat thins for some reason. She thought because they were wheat and they were thin

there were no calories involved. Katie, she was like Alana - good old fruit and cheese was the thing. After everyone tucked in Jessica was the first to talk; "Alana we were all wondering if you're ok. I mean… you know?" she shrugged her shoulders and looked at the others. They were all nodding their heads and looking at Alana. "I'm fine, really." She looked at all her friends with a smile. "I wasn't ready to make a commitment. Todd and I were just not marriage material. We were doomed to failure and I want something special when I marry. I want to know that it's right. You know what I mean don't you?"

Trish spoke up. "Yeah, you want the 'happy ever after'. I guess I can't blame you. That's what I'm looking for too and I don't think I could settle for anything less either." They all nodded in agreement. Even though they were all different in style and personality, they at least all wanted the same thing - love. 'Who didn't' thought Alana. Out there in the world was the one person that was meant for her and she was going to find him. Looking around she almost laughed. The room was so silent.
"Come on guys cheer up" she laughed and all of them joined her. "Well at least we can have some fun while we wait for Mr. Right. You know sometimes Mr. Wrong can feel so right" added Jessica who never had trouble finding a boyfriend. They all laughed again - it was good to be normal for a while. If only her friends knew. They would all freak out except for maybe Katie. She was the one who always had her nose in a book. She might believe her.
Katie looking at Alana with concern added "I can't believe Todd meekly understood and went on his merry way. Tell us how he took it really." Alana cringed. "Well let's just say he wasn't too happy about it." Alana almost shivered thinking back to the day she told Todd it was over. You would think no one had ever told him 'no' before. She'd had a very scary moment. Todd was furious. She could see it in his movement and the narrowing of his eyes, then as if by magic his face cleared and his eyes returned to normal. He smiled and asked if they could still be friends. What could Alana do but agree? Still something about him made her nervous.

Trish was waving her hand in front of Alana's face. "Earth to

Alana. Did you even hear anything I just said?" Sheepishly Alana shook her head no. She heard Trish sigh. "I said forget him. I always thought he was a little creepy anyway." When Alana just stared Trish shrugged her shoulders. "I mean in a handsome sort of way, I don't know what it was about him. Maybe it was because he seemed too perfect."

Everyone agreed with Trish, even Alana. There was definitely something about Todd that just didn't add up. He could unnerve you with a stare. Even thinking about him made Alana's skin tingle. Hopefully she wouldn't run into him in the near future. "Let's talk about something else you guys." Alana didn't even want to think about him. Shaking those thoughts away she concentrated on what everyone was talking about. Soon all you could hear from the kitchen was low voices and lots of laughter.

14

Eudora was waiting when Sebastian entered the room. She had no doubt that he would come even if he preferred to be elsewhere. She wanted to also give Alana some private time with her friends without Sebastian watching on and hearing everything.
"Sebastian it is time." She knew he understood by the way his shoulders became straighter, his eyes more focused and his nostrils flared as if he could smell the battle to come. Yes it would come - the question was when.
"I will meet her tomorrow - have her ready. And Eudora, I will not go lightly on her. She needs to be at her best." He then smiled his most wicked smile and walked to the door. When he turned the knob he looked back and winked. "They don't call me the Dark Dragon for nothing," then he disappeared. Eudora sighed as she walked over to her fountain. After chanting a few words Eudora was back in her own Realm and Brigham was there to greet her. "All is well. My training with Alana is complete. Now it's all up to Sebastian."

Brigham turned to the table and sat down stroking his beard in thought. He looked up. "Will she succeed I wonder?" Eudora knew he wasn't asking her a question but she answered him anyway. "She has the courage to win and the strength not to quit. She's intelligent and clever with her spells. She has learned more from me in this one week than most of the elders even know. I taught her the old ways and the new. Not once did she hesitate. She's all that magic is. I trust that she will succeed when the time comes. She will make the right choices. We have to believe in her - she is our only hope, so yes I think she will succeed. I have faith in her ability." Eudora took a deep breath and waited for Brigham to speak.
"Such loyalty. I hope she knows the faith you have placed in her and I hope and pray that you are right. All we can do now is guide her along the way. It is out of our hands. Come, we will take refreshments before we speak to the rest." Brigham stood and walked away knowing that Eudora would follow. He was right - now it was all up to Alana and what Sebastian would teach her for her final lesson.

15

It had been a week since Alana told him she didn't want to see him anymore and in that week Todd tried to calm down. But every time her name was mentioned something deep down inside of him wanted to burst out but he held it in check. The bitch would get her due. He would make sure of it. He walked over and poured another drink when a deep voice came out of nowhere. "Your mother and I have been looking for you."

Todd looked toward the door. It was open. Shaking his head he took a seat. He hadn't even heard the door open much less his mother and father entering.

Sulkily Todd spoke. "What can I do for you both?" Todd knew what they wanted. He could see it in their faces. They had questions - lots of them. They both entered, his mother taking her usual seat by the fireplace and his father stood behind her chair. Todd knew they were united in whatever they had to say. "All right go ahead and say it. I'm the one who screwed up. Go on - tell me how disappointed you are in me. It's nothing I haven't already told myself so go on - I'm listening." There was total silence. All that could be heard was the ticking of the clock in the hall.

His father cleared his throat but before he could say anything his mother spoke. "We are not disappointed in you son. We just wish things could have gone better. Perhaps there is still hope. You did say she still wanted to be friends. We are going to use that to our advantage. You will call her and take her out somewhere to dinner or something then while you are there you will slip a sleeping potion into her drink. But you must remember it will not last long. Let your father and I talk it over with the others and we will come up with a plan on how to keep her here without her being able to use her powers against us. But I must warn you now, when we call upon you son you must be ready and prepared!" she looked pointedly down at the drink that was in his hand.

"I think what your mother is trying to say is clean up and take a shower. Put that drink down and start preparing for the time when we will call you. You need to be ready for anything." With that said his parents left the room. Todd sat there in silence listening to the tick of the clock and the beat of his heart. Looking at the drink in his hand, Todd stood and set it on the table. There would be time to celebrate once the bitch was dead. That put a smile on Todd's face. He would get his revenge. She had only been a witch for a short time – he had been one his whole life. She would never defeat him. He didn't care what the prophecy said about her powers being great. She was just a girl who didn't even know *how* to wield her powers much less control them. It had taken him years to perfect his craft and he had indeed perfected it. She didn't stand a chance against him and he would make her pay. All he had to do was be patient. Todd started for the door. All this talk about revenge and getting even with her actually made him excited. As he rounded the corner of the door he pulled his phone out of his front pocket, dialed a number and waited. When he heard a soft voice on the other end he smiled.

"You busy tonight?" She laughed and purred into the phone, Todd grew even harder. Tonight he would release some of the tension built up inside of him. Tonight he will take what Star was offering. There were benefits to knowing a shape shifter. They could morph into whatever you wanted them to be and tonight she will play his enemy and for now that would have to be enough.

16

Alana woke with a start. Sitting up in bed she looked around.
There was nothing there. She'd had another troubled dream.
Something big was going to happen - she just didn't know what it
was right now. Could it be the battle, before her training was
complete? Eudora had told her that she had one more task to
complete and then she would be ready. As if she would ever be
ready to fight whatever evil was thrown her way. With a yawn
Alana got out of bed and headed for the shower. Once she had
taken her shower she would be able to concentrate on the day
ahead. She didn't know exactly what she was in for but she would
be ready for it. She had to be.

Eudora was already in the kitchen when Alana came
downstairs. Eudora took her hand and lead her over to the table
where a steaming hot breakfast was laid out on the table. "Please
sit. After you have had a good healthy breakfast we will talk about
your next lesson and meet your new teacher."
Alana shrugged her shoulders and decided that eating was an
excellent idea. She had certainly developed a hearty appetite
during these training times. After demolishing most of her plate of
eggs and bacon and two cups of coffee Alana felt like her old self.
Looking up, she noticed Eudora wasn't eating. She seemed
nervous. Her hands were in her lap and Alana could see how white
they were becoming from holding them together for so long.
"You're not eating?" it was more of a point then a question and
Eudora knew it.
"I'm not really hungry this morning my dear, but you seem to be
managing. You will need your strength to get through the rest of
the week," she smiled and looked toward the door.
Alana looked too but saw nothing and turning back to Eudora felt
that something wasn't right. She could feel it, or maybe it was just
the lack of sleep getting to her. With a determined effort she
finished eating her breakfast in silence. Once she was done she sat
back in her chair with another cup of coffee. After she took a sip
and set the cup back down on the table she spoke.
"So when will I be meeting my new teacher?" She looked at
Eudora but Eudora was looking towards the door again. She
nodded absently. Alana glanced back at the door, but still there

was no one there. Suddenly Eudora was looking more relieved. "Why my dear your new teacher has been with us since you came downstairs," she said looking towards the door again. This time when Alana looked an image appeared right in front of her. Alana thought she was seeing things so she closed her eyes, took a deep breath and as she let it out she opened her eyes again. The image she had seen was of a man and now he was clearly there to see. Alana let out a squeak. He was the most beautiful man she had ever seen. Taking a few shallow breaths, Alana tried to calm her racing heart. On closer inspection he looked vaguely familiar, but she couldn't place him. He was very tall. She had to bend her neck to look up at him. He was dressed simply enough, all in black from his head to his feet. His hair was too long - it almost reached his shoulders and those shoulders looked like they could carry her or anyone else without him breaking a sweat. He looked remarkably fit with an athletic body - and what a body it was. With a narrow waist and legs that looked like small trees. Her eyes travelled back up to his face and she saw that he was watching her. She swallowed. Her mouth was so dry she didn't think she could say a word much less put two words together, and those eyes that were watching her appeared to be so dark. His eyebrows had a slight arch to them and his eyelashes would be the envy of any woman. His lips were beautiful too - full in the right places. Even though he was frowning at her, overall he was a very beautiful man, but very dangerous. She could sense the power in him.

"Come forward Sebastian and meet your new student - and have something to eat." Eudora indicated to the empty seat across from her own. Sebastian walked across the room, took his seat and waited. The room was silent for several minutes - something that made Alana nervous - and she didn't like to feel that way. She cleared her throat and looked at Eudora who was looking from one to the other with a look of concern. But when she noticed Alana watching her she smiled.

"Alana dear, Sebastian will be teaching you how to fight in the upcoming battle.

You will learn how to use the skills and weapons that I have already taught you to conjure up." She paused and looked at Sebastian who still said nothing. He just sat watching Alana and when she looked back at Alana she too was watchful. "Do you have any questions my dear?"

Did she have questions? Oh boy, *did* she? For one, she knew this man. He had spied on her on more than one occasion over the last couple of weeks. She had never really gotten a good look until now and what she saw made her tremble. He was dressed in black, his hair was kept away from his face by a piece of thong and from the looks of it he could use a trim. His hair hung well past the collar of his shirt which was open at the throat revealing a smooth chest. She had never seen a real body builder, but if she had, she knew Sebastian would fit the bill. Actually he was a rather large man and his shoulders were big. Everything about him was powerful, but it was his mouth that held her still. There really wasn't anything special about it. His lips were full and looked really soft even with the hard look on his face. Even though he was tall, dark and dangerous he was also beautiful. Probably the most beautiful man she had ever seen. With his dark eyes and dark hair, if he ever decided that being a warrior wasn't worth it anymore he could always be a top model in her world. If only he could get rid of that serious look. But hey even in her world women liked the bad boys. With a shrug of her shoulders and a smile on her face she told him so. Then she lost that friendly look and narrowed her eyes and looked first at Eudora than at Sebastian who still had a puzzled look on his face. She almost laughed at that. She was sure she wouldn't get to see that look much.

"What I don't understand is why he has been following me for the last couple of weeks." she said pointing accusingly at Sebastian but looking at Eudora.

"That is easy my dear. Sebastian has been watching over you to make sure you stayed safe until your training could start. I'm sorry dear that we couldn't tell you at the time," she smiled and looked again from Sebastian to Alana. "Anything else dear?" Alana thought about it for a minute and looked at Eudora again.

"Will you be there for my training with him?" pointing again at Sebastian. Eudora didn't know what to say. She had hoped something would happen when they finally met. *This* just wasn't *it.* Looking once more at both of them she almost sighed. Neither one of them would even speak to the other. What was she going to do?

"Sorry dear. This week you will spend with Sebastian. He will show you the art of combat and finer arts of war." Then she looked at Sebastian. He nodded and stood up.

"It is time to go" he said and fell silent again. Alana didn't want to be alone with him. There was something about him that made her edgy. Looking almost hopeless she stared at Eudora willing her to understand how she felt.

"If for any reason you need me just call my name. I will be there." Eudora stood up, grabbed Alana by the shoulders and guided her to her feet. With a quick hug and kiss on the cheek she was gone and Alana was left with her second teacher. He held out his hand.

"Come," was all he said to her. Stiffening her spine she placed her hand in his and before she could even take a breath she was in another place. This time they were outdoors with lush green grass surrounding them for miles. In the distance she could make out the border of the forest which encircled them. In their open space, the sky was bright blue and the clouds floated by. In the distance a bird called to another. Closing her eyes Alana breathed in the fresh, sweet air. With her eyes still closed Sebastian whispered close to her ear.

"Things are not always how you see them." His voice was soft but held an edge to it. Alana popped her eyes open looked left to right and turned around in a complete circle. She was alone. Looking back around Alana didn't know how or where Sebastian had gone - she just knew she was alone. Taking a deep breath Alana decided to sit down and wait. She knew she should feel something but right now she didn't know what that was. She was calm and her mind was clear. Alana noticed the sky was turning dark. She didn't know what was going on, but she did know that if she didn't get a fire going she wouldn't be able to see and that wouldn't be good.

Sebastian watched from afar as Alana looked her situation over. He was actually surprised at how well she was handling everything. He didn't detect any fear, only calm. As he watched Alana struggled at first, but then a smile lit up her whole face. She stayed focused on her task. Let's see how well she handles everything else. In the blink of an eye, where Sebastian once stood there was now a black wolf with eyes equally black and he was watching his prey.

Alana was very proud of everything she had achieved. Not only did she build her fire she had conjured up a chair of all things. Basically all she did was want it and then she allowed herself to have it. This was actually not that bad. It was easy to say those simple rhymes and to remember them. With a smile still in place Alana sat down in her chair. The sky was darker. It would be very dark soon - good thing she was able to get those fires going. Eudora would be so proud and her mother wouldn't be able to believe it. And her friends? They would all just freak out. Alana almost laughed but suddenly a feeling of fear come over her. She started to shiver and the hair on the back of her neck stood straight up. Getting up slowly she turned around and coming toward her was the biggest ugliest beast she had ever seen. Its teeth were bared and his fangs stood out. Alana almost screamed. Her mind did scream. She shook her head to concentrate. She needed to stay calm and alert and she needed to remember everything she had learned from Eudora. Closing her eyes and taking a deep breath Alana prepared herself for battle. When she opened them again she was ready. Sebastian saw the change in her right away. Alana let the fear go and now she was preparing to do battle with him. He bared his teeth even more and gave a growl and started to move forward very slowly. He wanted to see what she would do. Alana was scared to death, but she couldn't let that show. She had to push that aside. She needed a protection spell and she needed it fast. That thing was getting closer. Bracing herself, Alana put her hands out in front of her and in her mind she spoke.

"Protect me in this blessed place, keep the beast at bay, guide me with wisdom to fight, and rid this evil from my sight." Alana kept chanting this over and over but as she did the beast advanced closer. She never moved. She knew that to show weakness would be her downfall. She had to rely on the faith that her spell would work. The beast was so close she could hear its breathing, but still she stared at it and kept her chant going. When the beast growled and lunged forward she never lost focus and right before her eyes he bounced away as if someone had picked him up and thrown him.

Alana could hardly believe it. She had conjured up a spell and it had worked. Looking straight ahead she saw every move the beast made. She knew she had surprised it. She could tell by the way it walked to and fro, almost as if he was watching her. She had to think of something else she might need before he came for her again.

17

Sebastian watched her closely; she had surprised him with what she knew. Eudora had indeed taught her well. This will not be as easy as he first thought, but it would be easy enough. He didn't want to end it too soon. He was curious to see what else she had. He looked toward the sky and the wind picked up its speed. Now let the fun began he mused as he approached her.

Alana watched as the wind picked up and the beast moved forward. She had to think of something and quickly. If only she had something to protect her besides the spell she had already used. Looking left then right she stopped. She wondered what else she could call for. She looked once more at the beast. It was still some distance away. She closed her eyes. What would a warrior want she thought? A sword and its shield.

Opening her eyes she worried that she would only be able to hold one or the other. Which one to choose? She made her decision. The shield would be the best. At least it would be some form of protection. The sword she probably couldn't swing anyway. With her decision made she concentrated on a shield. One that would protect her from this beast. She closed her eyes and imagined holding it. Sliding her hands through the straps it wasn't as heavy as Alana had thought it would be. Testing the weight of it she knew she could hold it with both hands actually she could feel it with both hands. She popped her eyes open and there it was in her hands. Sleek and light, it covered a good portion of her body. It was made of a shiny material. Silver with a gold heart in the middle. It was perfect.

As if it was made just for her, she held it against her shoulder with all her weight shifted to that side. She was ready. The beast was almost on her now and the wind had picked up. Alana's hair was flying all round her face, but still she didn't move. She was waiting.

Sebastian was amazed at how fast she had learned. He held back to watch. She was still calm. He could sense that she was concentrating on something. Her eyes were closed. When she held her hands out, where they once was empty was now a shield. She opened her eyes. She was ready and Sebastian knew it by the way she stood with her shield in front of her. He looked closer at the shield. It was no ordinary shield. He had never seen one before but he had heard the rumors. Only the purest of heart could conjure up that shield. His was the same in material but instead of a golden heart, his had a black dragon to mark him as a Drakon. The prophecy was true!

Alana was trembling and she was growing tired the wind was blowing so hard it was hard to hold her shield in front of her. Thank God her fires were made of Magic or they would all be out by now. The sky turned bright as lightning spread across it. Alana shivered. The first drops of rain started and before she knew it the rain was coming down hard. The wind was whipping her hair in her face brutally, making it impossible to see. She focused her eyes and looked straight ahead. The beast was breaching its way through her magic circle. It was slow going, but he was almost through. She couldn't just stand there, she had to do something! Just then the lightning flashed and there was a big boom in the distance. Everything happened so fast. The beast had broken through and now he was leaping through the air. Alana only had time to lift her shield before he leaped onto her and knocked her to the ground. She could feel his heavy breathing as he held her pinned to the ground. Closing her eyes she waited She heard a familiar voice, "Well done little warrior." Opening her eyes she noticed the same blue sky that was there when she first arrived. Where was the rain and the wind? The darkness was gone too; it was bright and cheerful again! Blinking her eyes, she looked again. Everything was still the same. She cautiously looked out from behind her shield and there stood Sebastian. The beast was nowhere to be seen.

Sebastian reached out his hand and helped her to her feet. Alana was so confused. Did she just dream all that? Looking down, her clothes were even dry and so was her hair. She noticed how Sebastian watched her. He was always watching her.

"Did I fall asleep?" Sebastian just shook his head. "That was one of many lessons you will learn." He turned on his heels and walked away. Alana stared after him. What was that supposed to mean? She hadn't understood it when it was happening and she was even more confused now. She was still holding the shield. How in the world did she conjure that? Where did it come from? Waving a hand in front of the shield, it disappeared.

She took off after Sebastian jogging to catch up to him. She was breathing heavily when she finally reached him. "What did you mean when you said I had many lessons to learn and what was all that about anyway?" she panted with a toss of her hand to indicate were they had just been. When he kept on walking and didn't say anything Alana got mad. She had to clench her teeth together to keep from growling at him. With hands down at her sides, fingernails dug into her palms and Alana lost her temper for the first time in her life.

"I don't know who the hell *you* think you are, but I am asking you a question, the least you can do is stop and answer it."

He didn't say a word and kept walking. Alana did then growl and in a loud voice, almost a scream, she said "STOP!" and threw her hands toward him as if she could make him stop. Right before her eyes Sebastian fell back on his butt, as if someone had put a wall up in front of him. Shrugging her shoulders she walked to where he sat. Maybe she could make him stop after all. When she reached Sebastian he was already on his feet with his hand stretched out in front of him. They were silent as both stared each other down. She thought she heard a sigh from Sebastian but it was so soft it could have been the wind.

"That was the first lesson you had to learn. Things are not always as they seem. Your mind can sometimes see something that isn't real. You have to know the difference." He fell silent watching her digest everything he had said. When she started to speak Sebastian held out his hand. "Come," was the only word he spoke. Alana looked down at his hand. It was large. Her hand would get lost in his. She looked back up at him and opened her mouth to speak, but when she saw the shake of his head she sighed and put her much smaller hand into his. Sooner or later they would have to talk and she had a lot of questions to ask.

Sebastian could hear her thoughts. She didn't know how to block someone out of her mind yet. He knew she was confused and had a lot of questions to ask, but right now he didn't have all the answers that she wanted. He needed to talk to Eudora. He also needed to watch her closer; his backside could attest to that, she was learning so quickly. She just didn't know what to do with all of her powers yet, but he would show her. He would teach her everything he could. She would have all the knowledge she needed, but it would be up to her if she used it. Now it was time for another lesson. This one would involve words.

Alana took Sebastian's hand and waited for several seconds nothing happened.

When she cracked her left eye open she looked at Sebastian. With a nod of his head they were in another field but this one was different. She could hear people off in the distance.

There was some kind of building over to the left, the door wide open. There were other items that she had never seen before. 'That must be the armory,' she thought. She was standing in the middle of a big circle and Sebastian was right in front of her. The silence was unnerving.

"Sebastian what is this place? Are you going to explain things to me? You have to remember I just find out about all this and I still don't know what is going on." She crossed her arms over her chest and looked directly at him.

"This is a sacred spot. No magic can enter here. You will learn how to fight without using magic." Sebastian stepped back.

"I don't understand I thought you said I will have to fight my magic against their magic. Why would I need to learn to fight without it?" She looked around again.

"This will be your next lesson. Sometimes your magic can not be used and when that happens you need to know how to defend yourself without it. Not only do *we* have sacred circles, so do the ones who look for you. If they can get you into one of their circles and you don't know how to fight, then there is no reason to teach you anymore." He stepped back in the circle. "Now I want you to show me what you can do."

Alana looked at Sebastian like he had sprouted two heads. "You mean I have to fight you? Why can't I fight someone who is more my size?" Alana wasn't expecting to have to fight. She didn't know much about it. She had been a good kid growing up. She didn't have a mean bone in her body, well not many anyway, or at least not until Sebastian showed up. What in the world was she supposed to do now? Looking around she looked for…she didn't know what, but at least she didn't have to look at him. He moved and Alana looked straight at him. He shook his head and motioned her forward. Alana sighed. What else could she do? So she moved forward and stood right in front of him. When he didn't speak or move she got angry and placed her hands on her hips.

"Well?" When he raised his eyebrow at her she almost laughed. He looked like he wanted to strangle her. "You are the teacher after all and you know I have never had to fight with anyone in my life so I'm sorry this is just a little new to me, so you have to tell me when you want me to do something or stand in some way." She sighed again and dropped her arms.

Sebastian admired her honesty. Not many people would admit they didn't' know how to do something, but here she is, still surprising him with her sharp tongue telling him just that. Maybe she wasn't so hopeless. If she was smart enough to admit to a weakness, then she would understand his discipline. She had to be ready and that didn't leave much time to teach her. He had to push her so she would know how to stay focused and have the control to harness all of her powers; he knew he had to push her and make her find her calmness where her powers were strongest. She would hate him in the end. That didn't set well with him for some reason. He didn't want her to hate him. Never before had it bothered him, but now turning away from her he forced all his thoughts away. For the good of all mankind he knew what he must do.

Alana watched as Sebastian looked at her then turned around. 'What in the world was wrong with that man?' thought Alana. One minute he was looking down to her with an amused expression the next he looked mad and this time she didn't know what in the world she had done to make him mad. She would never understand men. Yes they were fascinating creatures - one of God's finest actually - but still confusing. So Alana waited for Sebastian, the all mighty, to remember that she was there.

Sebastian took a calm breath and closed his eyes. When he turned back around his face was empty. He started toward her. Alana watched Sebastian. Not a muscle moved in his face as if he was made of stone. He started toward her. All Alana could do was take a deep breath and square her shoulders. She knew something was coming if she was to judge by that look on his face. If that was his battle face, no wonder the enemy called him the Dark Dragon; Alana knew she was in trouble.

When he pushed her, she fell to the ground and it actually hurt. He helped her up and showed her how to block a punch and then how to defend herself if she was ever on the ground. By the time he called a stop to the training as he called it, the sun was setting and she was covered in sweat and her body was screaming for a shower - a very hot one. It felt like every part of her was bruised. Suddenly she felt like she was floating and her insides felt like they had been left behind. When she opened her eyes back up she was back in her kitchen and before she had time to find her voice Sebastian spoke. "Be ready at six A.M." Then he was gone. Alana almost screamed, but she was too tired to make the effort. Maybe in the morning she would give him an earful. 'Six A.M.' - like she didn't know what he meant. She sighed and headed for the stairs. A nice hot shower was in order. After that, something to eat. And maybe work on her book.

18

Alana felt better when she got out of the shower. Maybe after a bite to eat she would be back to normal. On her way down the stairs she heard the front door open. Her mom was home. Usually she would call out to see if Alana was home, but the strain in their relationship had been hard on both of them. With a sigh she continued down the stairs and met her mom in the hall. When her mom turned to her Alana saw the sadness in her mother's eyes and the hesitation in her stance. But her mother smiled. "I didn't know you would be home so early. Have you eaten?"

Alana just shook her head no. Her mother forced a knowing smile and headed for the kitchen. "If you will give me a few minutes I will whip us both something up." Alana just watched her mother as she hurried to the kitchen. She knew this was hard on her mother. It was hard on her too, but no matter what, her mom had always been there for her and if she really thought about it her mom had only been trying to protect her and let her have a normal childhood. So with a deep breath Alana straightened her shoulders and headed to the kitchen to finally have that talk with her mom. "Hey Mom do you think you can sit down for a moment. I would like to talk to you." Alana noticed her mom's back stiffen before she turned and sat at the table. Alana took a good look at her mother. Her hair which she usually wore down was pulled back in a ponytail. There were shadows under her eyes and they looked a little puffy and red. She felt like a heel or maybe less than that. She had been so busy and focused on what she had to do she hadn't taken her mom's feelings into consideration. What had her mom been going through? If her appearance was any clue it had been rough. Alana gently took her mom's hand. She could see the surprise in her eyes and that made her feel even worse. They had always been close - more like best friends.

"Mom I don't want to fight with you. I realize now why you did it. I just wish you had given me some clue. I was just… I don't know… shocked when I found out - and angry - and I blamed you. I'm sorry Mom." Alana watched the emotions play across her mom's face. Tears welled up in her eyes.

"Honey if I could change it I would. I was somewhat shocked too." she dabbed at her eyes and sniffed. Alana was a little confused.

She thought her mom had known what was going on.
"Wait a minute. Are you telling me you didn't know about this?"
Alana watched as her mom wiped her eyes again.
"I knew what you would grow up to be, but no, I didn't know about you being a descendent of those people. Your father never told me that part. But yes I knew you were a witch." Alana took all of this in. So not only was *she* not told, but her mom wasn't told either. All of this coming up now had really been a shock to her mom too. Well except for those stories her father use to tell her. Those were actually true. He knew and he had been telling her so she would remember, and remember she did every word.

19

Sebastian paced. He had summoned Eudora and now he waited for her to appear. Damn he was tired. But he gave as well as he got. He chuckled and held his hand to his jaw - she had one hell of a right hook. He chuckled again.

"What's so amusing" Sebastian wasn't surprised when he heard Eudora's voice. She was known for her ability to sneak up on just about anyone, magic or human.

Eudora watched as Sebastian turned to face her. His usual visage was in place - the one he never let anyone past.

"I'm guessing her training went well?" She didn't give him a chance to answer. "I told you that you would work well together." Eudora watched him closely to see any sign or to feel anything from him, but as always he gave nothing away. "Well say something!" She crossed her arms in front of her waiting. If the topic of conversation wasn't so important Sebastian might have laughed at the way Eudora was looking at him. The arms crossed was a nice touch too. She almost looked like she was scolding him - as if he was a child - and that was very amusing. He decided to make her wait a little longer. When her foot started tapping on the floor he figured he had annoyed her enough.

"Her skill with magic is stronger than I first thought and even stronger than she knows. With a simple command she had me flat on my ass." Before he could finish he heard her laughter so he raised his eyebrows and crossed *his* arms. Wiping her eyes Eudora became serious again with one final chuckle.

"Go on. I will refrain from laughing again." She smiled and he could see the twinkle still in her eyes and with another sigh he rubbed the back of his neck.

"As I was saying, her magic is pure and very strong without her having to put much force behind it, but until she believes in herself none of this will matter. She has to know and be confident. There can be no second guessing or hesitation. She needs to find the key and so far she hasn't. But I think we will all be surprised when she finally does. I am training her in all forms of battle. Her human fighting skills will need more work, but I'm confident she will greatly improve. But be warned - until she believes, there will be no hope!"

Sebastian turned and stared off into space to give Eudora enough time to digest everything he had just told her. It didn't matter how much or how little that he or Eudora believed in her, or her mother and friends, it had to be Alana who believed in *herself*. It had to be *her* that unlocked the door.

Eudora had watched Sebastian during his speech. He had spoken so calmly and controlled with no emotion. She was a little worried about that. She thought for sure that Sebastian would see the special qualities in Alana. Yes she *was* very gifted - Eudora had always sensed this. And she knew that Alana's powers were already strong and growing each day. Could it be as simple as Alana believing in herself? Could Sebastian be right? Going to him, Eudora laid her hand on his arm. She noticed how stiff he became.

"Is this true? Do you really think it could be that simple?"

"I watched, in my changed form, as she pulled a shield from thin air and not just any shield. It was made from the same material as mine. The same magic, but instead of a dragon there was a golden heart."

Sebastian heard her gasp and felt the slight tremble in her hand on his arm. He turned and looked at her.

"You know what this means don't you?" He watched her eyes become crisp and clear as she nodded sagely.

"It means that the prophecy is true." She watched as something flickered in Sebastian's eyes but it was gone before she could identify it.

"I will have her ready. I will train her hard for the war to come. She will know everything there is to know about battle." then he was gone.

Eudora wondered at what cost to him, what sacrifice he would have to make. She knew the prophecy and she knew it well. She also knew of another that was made long ago only for her eyes to see in the water of her fountain. Just like the first prophecy, this one would come to pass also. She had seen the dragon in the past when the prophecy was made and she saw the dragon now in her present, and she had seen that the future was in the form, not of a dragon, but of a woman.

After her mom's confession Alana just sat there and watched as her mom got up from the table and started preparing dinner.

"How about grilled chicken on a bed of greens?"

"Sure that sounds great." She stood and went to the refrigerator and got everything ready for the salad while her mom started the chicken. Alana really couldn't blame her mom. She probably would have done the same thing in her position and her mother had provided a good life. She had always known she was different but overall she had been given the freedom to do whatever she had liked. Now it was her duty to do what she *has* to do, but saying it and doing it are two different things. She didn't know if she was ready and that's what scared her the most.

Over dinner Lily watched her daughter closely. She knew Alana was hurting and very confused. Who wouldn't be, put in a situation like she was in, having to protect two worlds that couldn't be more different? Oh Lord, what was going to happen to her baby? No one knew what they were up against - they just knew it would be happening soon. Alana's birthday was getting closer and instead of getting ready for a beautiful party, they were preparing for a war, or at least Alana was. She knew there was strength in her daughter. She had seen it through the years but was there enough to help her through this?

"Honey you know even though I hurt you and you feel betrayed please know this; I did what I thought was right at the time. Maybe then it was but I should have told you sooner. You don't know how sorry I am." Lily took a breath and looked at her daughter straight on. "I know you're scared honey. So am I, but I believe in you. I know if you put your mind to anything and you believe that what you're doing is right then you can do anything. I know you Alana. You are stubborn, intelligent and strong and those are just a few of the qualities I love about you. There are many more but above all, you never give up. I have never seen you give up anything without a fight. Now - what do you want more than anything?"

Alana heard the words as a picture of Sebastian formed in her head. She closed her mind and thought about the here and now, how to outlast whatever she was up against. Smiling she took her mom's hand. "I want freedom for all."

She kissed her mom's cheek and took the dishes to the kitchen. Her mom followed as she watched Alana clean off her plate and silverware and put it all in the dishwasher.

"Mom I'm sorry too. I understand why you didn't tell me. Can you forgive me?" She saw the tears in her eyes she was struggling to hold back. She hid them by busying herself with the dishwasher until she turned and embraced her daughter.

"I know you can do it and there is nothing to forgive. Now, it's late. I think we should both go to bed." After a quick kiss on her daughter's cheek she left Alana standing in the kitchen staring at the stairs. Maybe her mom had been tired. It had been a trying couple of days and they both had to get up in the morning. The thought of that made her groan as she made sure everything was locked and headed off to bed too. Six in the morning would come soon enough and she wanted to be at her best. She had learned a few things today and had watched every move that Sebastian made. She was confident enough to think maybe she could at least get a few hits in. She knew she could never beat him, but maybe just rough him up a little. This made her smile as she opened the door to her room and saw Eudora sitting calmly on her bed.

"Well I was wondering if you would ever come to bed or if I would have to come find you." Eudora smiled and Alana could do nothing else but smile too. There was just something about Eudora that made you want to tell her your most intimate desires - or maybe she just already knew.

"My mom and I were talking and we worked everything out." Alana rolled her shoulders. They were still sore.

"That is so lovely dear. I am glad you two are speaking again. Your aura is brighter today. So tell me how your training today was. Did Sebastian teach you much?"

Eudora knew the answer of course she just wanted to see if Alana might show any emotions toward Sebastian. She watched closely as all the emotions Alana felt played across her face. She rolled her shoulders again and Eudora saw her wince. "I know I have a lot to learn it's just he is so… I don't know, almost cruel." She sighed again and twisted her waist back and forth.

'Interesting' thought Eudora. She had never known Sebastian to ever be cruel to a woman. He was always patient. She wondered what or who had riled him but she saw the smile on Alana's face and wondered.

Alana giggled. "You should have seen his face when I yelled for him to stop and it looked like something pushed him back because, in the next second he was on the ground sitting on his ass. I'm telling you it took every ounce of strength I had not to laugh. You should have seen it!" She bent at the waist and laughed her head off. Eudora was intrigued. She heard Alana wince again as she straightened up and went to sit on the bed. "Eudora, he makes me so mad. He never just talks to me. He will tell me what to do, sure, but he never *sees* me. I am just a tool to him. Something to gain him another victory and I don't like that. He pushes so hard. I realize I don't know very much and yes I am a lousy fighter - hey I have never *been* in a fight before - but does he take that into consideration? No! He makes me work harder - but I'm not really complaining. I do understand that there isn't much time. I just wish... I don't know... just forget I said anything alright?" Alana was looking down at her hands so she didn't see Eudora's amused look.

Eudora was wondering why Sebastian was being such a beast. She could tell he had worked her hard. She could see the weariness in her face and the droop in her eyes. She was almost asleep sitting up.

"Not to worry dear. All is forgotten. Now, how about you lie down and I will tuck you in? There we go." Eudora had Alana tucked into bed and fast asleep in the blink of an eye.

As she looked at Alana she saw how small she really was. Nobody knew what she had yet to face. Could she really do it? Eudora believed in her. She might be small, but there was a lot of strength and determination too. Yes, she would be just fine and maybe she would find her soul mate in the process. When Sebastian appeared she had to mask her features to hide her thoughts because if he read them he wouldn't like it very much.

Sebastian knew she was up to something. He didn't know what it was yet, but he would find out - he always did. "I will take the watch tonight. I don't think it's safe to leave her alone." Eudora smiled that knowing smile and bowed her head and disappeared. Sebastian almost sighed with relief. He knew they would speak but not tonight. He ran his hand across his face and looked down at Alana. She was beautiful in every way and sometimes when he looked at her all he could think about was touching her - everywhere. But then he would concentrate on the task at hand and let the thought slip away for another time. He had a job to do and he would surely do that job without getting too attached or losing sight of what was more important. He looked at her again. Everything rested on her shoulders and there wasn't a damn thing he could do about it. She had surprised him today. She was learning fast. He just hoped he could teach her everything he knew before her birthday and maybe not come out looking like an arrogant bastard, but he knew in his heart she would hate him by the time this was all over. He had to push her to make her see that there was evil in the world and that soon she would become the target of those evil forces. Tomorrow would be just as hard as today, if not harder. He couldn't slacken off. Her life and everyone else's depended on him to teach her certain skills. Morning would be upon them soon so Sebastian settled down on the floor and waited for the sun to come up.

Eudora slid her hand through the water. Sebastian was having trouble with his actions and he should - pushing her so hard, but she had also glimpsed tenderness in his eyes as he had looked down at Alana. 'Poor Sebastian' thought Eudora with a wicked grin.

"What has amused you in your fountain Eudora?" asked Sebastian's father the king. Eudora turned and bowed to the king.

"How are you this evening Your Majesty?" Eudora kept her head down to show respect to her ruler even though they had known each other all their lives.

"What is this Eudora? Please rise." Eudora straightened and smiled again. "We have known each other for far too long to stand on ceremony."

With this Eudora laughed. "I know Artemis, but I couldn't help myself." The king joined in the laughter.

"Now can you tell me how all is going with my son and his charge?"

Eudora knew she had to speak carefully and word everything right or he would send someone to investigate and Eudora wasn't ready for that yet.

"So far everything is running smoothly. Alana is a first rate pupil. With more knowledge and practice she could even exceed a master's magic." With this said Artemis raised a brow.

"You really think she's that good after only a week?" This made Eudora smile. Wait until Artemis met her. He would see it too.

"I think she is better than good. She even got one up on Sebastian, but of course he won't tell *you* that." She could tell this surprised Artemis, because nobody had ever bested Sebastian.

He chuckled. "Tell me more of this girl. Do you believe she can win?"

She knew Artemis was watching her closely. "Yes I believe she can, but it's not up to me. *She* has to believe it. Sebastian thinks that is the key." She never looked away as she gave her opinion to the king.

Artemis walked to her fountain. "Interesting. Do you think she believes it? And what does Sebastian think?" Eudora followed him over to her fountain and looked into the crystal clear depth.

"I think she can do anything she puts her mind to. She is strong and intelligent and has more determination than I have ever seen in anyone else." She hoped that wouldn't put a bee in his bonnet but it was the truth. Alana wanted this more than anything she had ever wanted and Eudora had felt that from her.

"Well let us have a look at our salvation." He nodded to Eudora who ran her hands through the water and a picture started coming into focus. Before their eyes was an image she never thought she would see. Sebastian was sitting on the edge of the bed looking down at Alana with such longing and need that anybody, even the King, could see it. Sebastian gently brushed a stray hair away from Alana's face and with a sigh he got up from the bed and sat on the floor by the door. Eudora could barely look away, but when she did she looked straight at the king. He was looking at his son with new eyes. The king cleared his throat and nodded back to Eudora and as she brushed the water, the picture faded from sight.

20

Artemis was surprised to see the look on his son's face. Sebastian had always been more reserved - some would even say aloof. He finally looked at the girl to see what it was that had caught Sebastian's eye. She was sleeping on her back with one hand above her head and the other lying across her waist. She was beautiful but Sebastian had seen beautiful women before. Some of them may have been even more beautiful than the girl lying here. He wondered what it was about this particular girl that had touched something inside his son. He thought he would never see compassion in his son's eyes but it was there, plane to see along with other feelings. He wondered if perhaps his son was developing feelings for this girl. It was time to meet her and judge for himself. There had to be something to make his son turn from a warrior to a 'flesh and bone' man in the blink of an eye. Sebastian thought he was alone and so was unguarded in his feelings. This made Artemis laugh. At one time he had been just like his son. Nothing had been more important to him than his kingdom, until he met Sebastian's mother and no matter how much he fought his feelings, in the end he was defeated. And that was one war he didn't mind losing.

"I think it's time for me to meet this girl. After all, she will be the savior of not only her world but ours too." He turned and walked away. Eudora groaned silently. She didn't want them to meet yet. She wanted to give Sebastian and Alana a chance to *find* each other. She knew that if they took the time to really look at each other they would see they were fated for each other, but now if Artemis meets her she would know that Sebastian was not just a warrior, but a prince. That would ruin everything! She knew Alana well enough to know that she would close up and only see him as the prince of her father's kingdom and any feelings she might have would be put aside and she would focus only on the battle to come. That was not something that Eudora could let happen. She had to talk to the king. She had to tell him about the prophecy or all would be ruined.

21

Alana groaned when she reached to turn off the alarm clock. It was a little after five in the morning and she was not feeling like a trouper. Every muscle in her body hurt. She lay there for a moment longer before rolling out of bed. Bones moaned and her muscles groaned. She would have to do some stretches or she would never be able to make it downstairs. After that, a nice long hot shower was in order and by the time she did make it downstairs she was fifteen minutes early but with a smile on her face.

"Good morning!" she said not to anybody in particular. Her mom and Eudora were sitting at the table, both with a cup in their hands. Both looked up when Alana came in the room and both noticed her big smile and wondered.

"Good morning Honey. Would you like something to eat before you have to leave?" Alana thought she might need to eat something to keep her strength up.

"How about some fruit? I don't have much time before he'll arrive so I will need to eat quickly." When she sat down at the table a bowl of fruit appeared right in front of her. This still surprised her but she was getting used to it.

"Very good dear. You're improving. What has got you so chipper this morning? I thought you might be a little sore today." Eudora smiled again and took a sip of her tea. 'Yes,' she thought, 'this girl can do anything she puts her mind to'. She knew it the minute the fruit appeared. Eudora knew it wasn't her who had produced the fruit so it must have been Alana. Only a master could pull things out of thin air and it took years to become a master. 'Yes this is getting interesting. I think Sebastian has finally met his match.' Eudora looked from Alana to her mother's shocked look.

"Are you alright Lily?"

Lily barely heard her. She was looking at her daughter with amazement. She looked at Eudora. "You didn't just make that bowl appear. If *you* didn't then Alana must have done it. How?" Alana started to speak but Eudora held up her hand. "No, Lily. I didn't make the bowl appear. It *was* Alana and I am very proud of her! Not many can master pulling things out of thin air but already Alana has mastered it. She is learning so fast!"

Before Alana could answer, a tingle rose up her spine. Without turning to look she knew Sebastian was standing there.

Sebastian had watched unseen since Alana entered the room. Again she had on jeans and a t-shirt and her beautiful hair was pulled pack in a ponytail. He could feel the energy from her and see the fire that burned in her eyes. When she smiled everything changed. The energy was still the same, but there was a softness throughout her aura. He watched as Alana talked to Eudora and her mother. He figured she would be just dragging her butt out of bed and he would have to wait for her, but here she was. She was forever surprising him. He decided to watch a little longer. He liked watching her when she was in a happy mood. He hated knowing that once he appeared her happiness would dissolve. But the training was something that had to be done.

Alana's mother gasped. Sebastian had been so deep in thought that he hadn't seen what had just happened. He instinctively looked at Alana and saw the self-satisfied look on her face. What on earth could he have missed? He heard Lily asking about the bowl of fruit but he didn't understand why that would surprise anyone. Eudora was known for conjuring up things from than air. She loved to surprise people, but this time she looked more surprised than anyone! When he heard Eudora explain he just couldn't believe it. How did Alana, who had just discovered a little over a week ago that she was a witch, conjure a bowl of fruit out of thin air? Only a Master could do that and it took decades to become a Master. Of course there had been few exceptions - some are born to it. Sebastian had been born to it since he was of royal blood. Could she have been born with this ability? That would certainly explain her incredible pace at picking up the craft. Sebastian became determined to find out. With that, he materialized and watched as she became aware of him standing right behind her. Her back stiffened and she sat straighter in her chair. When Alana turned to look at him he held out his hand.

"It's time to go." Alana took his hand and as before, they were right back in front of the armory.

He released her hand as soon as they appeared. He did not want to touch her for longer than he had to. He stepped back and crossed his arms.

"Today we will see how good you are at casting spells for

defense."

Alana was ready. She didn't really know how to go about it but she had read a few things, so with her shoulders slung back and her back as straight as a board she mockingly asked, "Well, how about a demonstration since I don't really know what you are talking about."

For a long minute he just stared at her, which made her nervous so she raised her chin even higher and looked him straight in the eye, crossed her own arms and arched her brow. Sebastian couldn't help but smile - probably for the first time in a long while. Damn she was sexy when she was mad! Sebastian could tell she was angry even though she barely moved. Now, what to give her? Without a flicker on his face to give away his intent he decided to project a small solar ball at her. It was harmless. Even if it hit her it would do no damage.

Alana hated how he just looked at her like she was stupid or something weird. It made her less confident in her ability. Was that a smile she was seeing? No it couldn't be. Looking closer she could see that his lips were slightly turned up at the corners even though his teeth weren't showing. 'I guess that qualifies as a small smile. Not too bad. It makes him look less cruel,' she mused. Suddenly, that smile curved even wider showing off his perfect white teeth. 'It figures. He would have to have a beautiful smile that made him more real. Damn I'm in trouble now!' A light radiated from his hand so quickly she didn't have time to move before it hit her right in the chest. It really didn't hurt, but it caught her off guard and she leaned backwards and fell on her butt with her hands to her sides.

"Shit that hurt," but as she started picking herself up off the ground she heard a rumbling sound. See looked up at Sebastian to see the amusement shining in his eyes while he was trying hard not to laugh. His attempts were failing. She felt like crying. With her chin held high and her hands at her side she glared at him.

"Don't you dare laugh at me!" It almost came out in a growl she was so mad at him. All that he did in response was to raise his eyebrow and cross his arms. Once again he wore a serious look but she could still see the amusement lurking in his eyes and that hurt even more. She took all her energy and focused it all on him - all the hurt and all the anger - and let it go. God he liked to rile her up, but he could tell she was more hurt than anything else. He could see the tears swimming in her beautiful stormy eyes and those eyes were focused on him. So intense they looked, almost silver. She flung her arms out and without any warning she hit him square in the chest with a solar ball of her own. She didn't just knock him off his feet, she knocked him clear across the floor where he came to a sudden jarring halt against the wall. Trying to catch his breath, Alana panicked when she heard him wheezing. Sebastian rolled over onto all fours and breathed in and out until the pain gradually receded. How the hell had she knocked him that far across the room? She wasn't just mad she was pissed and angry. A lethal combination!

"Oh my God! What have I done?" She actually felt some satisfaction when she saw the disbelief in his eyes. Alana could still here him wheezing. She didn't know what to do.

"I'm so sorry Sebastian, can you stand? Are you hurt?"

When she reached down to help him he growled at her. She blinked and stepped back. She couldn't believe he had actually growled at her. Well this wasn't her fault. She crossed her arms in defiance as they came face to face. He was awfully close. She almost stepped back. She could see the fire in his eyes and the flare of his nostrils as he tried to regain control of his temper. Even though the situation was serious she still saw the funny side and it must have shown on her face. His brow arched up and his eyes stared right into her. Instead of giving an inch she glared back.

"I said I was sorry. You know this wouldn't have happened if you didn't make me so mad. And you want to know something?" By this time *she* needed a breath so she took a big one and released it, "I have always been a nice person and I don't get mad easy. But there is just something about you that makes me so mad. I don't like myself when I am like that!" She sighed and slumped her shoulders.

"Listen," she continued "we both have a job to do. Let's just do it. I will try to control my anger around you, but you have to be more understanding. All this - you know - I'm just learning and I can tell you now, sometimes it gets overwhelming. But you show me and I will try and learn everything I can. I know you don't like me and that's ok. I don't know if I really like you or not either. I say we call a truce for both our kingdom's sake." She turned her back on him.

Sebastian stood there and listened to everything she had to say. She was right, they had to try and get along. He wasn't even mad. He was more surprised than anything. He could probably use her in battles. She already had a lot of power. He had felt it. Actually he could still feel it. This was one witch you didn't want to make mad. He looked at her slumped shoulders and felt like the monster she thought him to be. Actually in her little speech she was wrong about one thing. He did like her - more than he even cared to admit. She had guts he gave her that. And she did get the best of him - for that she deserves his respect. He frowned again. What did she mean she didn't even know if she liked him?

"I accept this truce. Come, we have much to learn before the sun sets."

She watched him walk away, shrugged her shoulders and with a secret smile tucked away she followed. She wanted to laugh again. She had gotten one up on him and this time she actually thought she hurt him. When she was alone later maybe she would have a good laugh but for now she had work to do and she knew he would get her back eventually. She didn't mind. The look on his face and the way his big body flew through the air was worth it. She couldn't wait to see Eudora and tell her what she had done. She would probably think it was worth a laugh too.

22

Artemis had summoned Eudora and he sat at his desk thinking while he waited. He wanted to meet with this girl. The more he thought about his son, he wanted to know everything he could about her. He picked up his drink and looked into the fire that crackled close by.

"Artemis you wished to see me?"

"Sit down Eudora,' he said indicating a chair across from his desk. "Would you care for something to drink?" Eudora declined with a shake of her head. "I would like to meet this girl. Perhaps you could arrange this for me?" He would never have thought in a million years Eudora would have a problem with that, but by the look on her face and the way she remained silent told him otherwise.

"Eudora is there some reason why you don't want me to meet her? Maybe I should summon Sebastian to me and get my report from him." She could tell by the look on his face that she had made him angry.

"That will not be necessary Artemis but at this time I think it would set her back to meet you, such a powerful man."

Artemis frowned at that. "Why would it bother her to meet me when she already knows my son?" Eudora squirmed in her seat and took an extra minute before she looked at him. She had to show him a calm face so he wouldn't summon Sebastian or worse tell him to bring Alana too.

"Well you see Artemis, she doesn't know Sebastian is your son. Only that he is a warrior. She doesn't know he's a prince. I think for now it is better this way. She is comfortable with him. If she learned he was of royal blood that might intimidate her and slow the process down."

"Interesting. I wonder what other reason you have for me not seeing her. Do you care to enlighten me or do you want me to try and guess?" She knew she had aggravated him even more so she threw caution to the wind.

"If you will be patient with me Artemis I will tell you my reasons for doing what I am doing. Can you trust me?" Eudora held her breath. She had never had to ask the king for his trust before. By the way he was studying her she knew this was important to him.

He shook his head somewhat apologetically. Eudora stood and sighed. She was hoping this wasn't necessary but maybe he *did* need to know.

"Then follow me and I will show you why." She placed her hand palm side up. When Artemis raised his eyebrow she looked at her hand and precariously he placed his hand in hers and within the blink of an eye they were in her private place where only people she invited could come. He knew that whatever she was about to tell him would change things somehow. Her fountain appeared in the center of the room.

"Remember the old crone who lived here years ago? Her name was Magimus. Nobody ever knew where she had come from, but they knew her words were truths. Well, I don't know how she did it and still to this day I am baffled, but she sent me a message in my fountain before she died. It pertained to the prophecy." With this she stopped to take a breath and let everything sink in. She knew it was a lot to take in. It was still hard for her. She watched Artemis look from her fountain back to Eudora.

"Some said she was a Gypsy witch - one of the most powerful. I do know she had the sight."

"What was it that she had to add to the prophecy?" Artemis crossed his arms, so much alike were father and son, but to tell it would not be as good as to show it.

"Just look in the waters and you will see what I saw that day many years ago." She waved her hand lightly over the surface of the water. As it rippled a picture appeared. It was a mighty black dragon.

"The prophecy has finally come to pass. A beautiful little girl has been born but be warned. All is not what it seems. In order to defeat the evil and return balance to both worlds, the dragon has to protect his heart or *all* will fall." As those words were spoken a scene formed in front of them. The dragon was searching the sky. His head drops and he flies to the ground and there on the forest floor sits a little girl. As he comes forward she lifts her hand and in it sits a golden heart that lights up the night sky. The girl smiles and extends her hand even further toward the dragon. When the dragon finally stops right in front of her, her smile grows even bigger. Here in the forest the huge black dragon leans his claws out and she drops the heart into them and fades away. When the dragon looks down at the heart it also fades into his own hands. Then the picture also fades and the water turns crystal clear again. For a minute there was nothing but silence than Artemis clears his throat and looks up at Eudora.

"I don't understand. What does this have to do with my son? I understand that the girl is Alana…" his voice fades as he looks back at the water perhaps hoping for something else. Eudora knew that if Artemis studied it long enough he would figure it out. It had taken her until just recently to figure out what it all meant. Artemis looked back at her. She could see the questions in his eyes.

"Artemis you're right. That is Alana. But think how many Black Dragons have you met? I for one have only met one and you know who I'm talking about. The Dark Dragon which is your son Sebastian." Artemis stumbled a little as the truth hit hard.

"So they are connected to this? He is training her. What else can it mean?" She knew he wasn't asking her a question but she answered anyway.

"Did you not see what that little girl gave to that dragon? It was a golden heart known as the Symbol of Love among the purest of heart. Given freely, don't you see?" Eudora could tell that he didn't follow so she continued. "It means that Alana has given her heart to the dragon and the dragon now has to protect it, which means that he has to protect *her*. Don't you know the tale about the dragon? He has to always protect his treasure, which in this case is Alana." She saw realization sweep over him. "I hope now you know why we must wait. I don't really know how she feels about him yet, but if we tell her now she will feel betrayed by him and I think if that happens, she would never trust him. And we know that without trust there will never be love. But if she fell in love with him first, I think she would be strong enough to forgive him anything. She knows from the tales her father told her that when she gave her heart it would be forever. No matter how angry he might make her, she would always love him. I think when the time comes your son the Dark Dragon will play a big role in bringing peace and balance back to both our worlds." She crossed her hands in front of her and waited to see what he would say.

"For now we will leave it. Eventually I will have to speak to her, but for now we will do it your way." He shimmered out of sight. Eudora felt light headed. She needed a good stiff drink and one appeared on her table and she smiled and reached for it.

23

When Alana opened her eyes she was back in her kitchen, alone.
Sebastian had dropped her off and with a nod he was gone. She
hated when he did that and of course, he knew she would be ready
in the morning, which forced a groan. Five-thirty would come too
early. She looked around - her mom must be working late. The
house was so quiet it was almost eerie. With a shrug she headed to
her room to take a much needed, very hot shower. Every bone,
muscle, and joint she did not know about hurt, but at least she did
have the satisfaction of seeing Sebastian fall flat on his butt. She
almost giggled, but she thought if she laughed now she would
never be able to make it to the shower. Besides, her body hurt too
much.

24

"Todd you must do something. Go and see her. Take her out. You will not get in her good graces sitting around drinking all the time!"

Todd wanted to laugh. He had tried for a couple of days. He had phoned. Either nobody was home or her mother answered and would say she was out. Where could she be? He knew she hadn't been with any of her friends - he had asked. This made him mad. He knew she was ignoring him and that put him in a sour mood. How dare that stupid bitch ignore him?

She was lucky. In his opinion there were many other women who wanted him, but oh no, he had to settle on her. Well maybe for the time being anyway. It didn't mean he had to give up his playthings. He just had to make sure she didn't find out. He looked at his mother's face. He could tell she was aggravated with him. So what? He was pretty well pissed off too. Maybe if they had told him all this a long time ago he would have this all taken care of. "Mother what more do you want me to do? I have been to every place she goes to and she hasn't been there and I have called several times at her house and she wasn't there. So tell me what more do you want me to do?" Todd got up and went for another drink.

"I think you have had enough do you not?" growled his father entering the room. He looked from his son's angry face to his wife's cold icy stare. He had heard his son's loud angry voice in the hall and had come to see what was going on.

"Hello father. And the answer to your question: No I have not had nearly enough!" He splashed more whiskey into his glass. Looking defiantly at his parents he took a healthy slug. His father's fury simmered in his face, not used to this treatment from *anyone*. Nobody said 'no' to his father. His mother sat there with that look she used on anyone who displeased her and right now he was the object of that stare. Todd frowned back at her. He wasn't the one who screwed up - they were, by not telling him what was going on. He sighed and sat back down. He knew he had to hear whatever his mother had to say so he looked begrudgingly in her direction and almost snarled.

"Go ahead. Continue whatever it was you were about to say. I will be happy to take any advice you might have." He didn't care how frosty and crisp his voice sounded, he wanted both of his parents to know how unpleasant this whole experiment was to him.

With a nod from Todd's father, his mother sighed. "We know how unsettling this has been for you, but you also need to know she will reach her maturity in five days and once that happens she will be unstoppable." She stopped to take a breath and watched as her son took another sip and then snorted. That made his mother grimace. "Don't underestimate her, she will be very powerful!"

That did make Todd laugh. "Don't worry Mother, I know Alana. She doesn't have a cruel bone in her body. She doesn't have the stomach for it." He chuckled again and finished his drink. When he sat the glass on the table he sat back more comfortably in the chair, but when he looked at both his parents they both wore the same face and to him it looked like doom.

"Relax I don't know why you two are so worried. I'll take a shower and get cleaned up and go over there yet again if that will make you both feel better." Again he watched as his mother looked to his father.

"I don't think you understand what your mother has been trying to say Todd. No matter if she has the stomach for it or not, she will fight. She knows what is at stake." That had Todd's temper back up. They acted as if *he* didn't know what was at stake and that bothered him. It was like they had more faith in her than they did in him. That he would not stand for so with fire and rage burning in his eyes he spoke.

"What is wrong with the both of you? You act as if I can't defend myself. I have been at this a lot longer than she has and I know how to play the game. I can assure you I will come out the victor!" He started for the door but his father stopped him with his next words.

"Todd you have not listened to anything we have said. It doesn't matter how much you know or, as you say, play the game. You will not win. She will crush you! Listen to my words and listen carefully. When she gains all her powers you will not be able to defeat her, nor I, or anyone else for that matter. She *will* be unstoppable!" He watched his son stiffen his back, straighten his shoulders and walk out. His son now knew the whole truth and he was sure that he would now clean up, take a shower and pay a visit to that girl. All he needed to do was charm her. How hard could that be?

His wife also stood. "I do hope he heeds our warning and doesn't let his arrogance be his downfall." She too left the room and he was alone.

A drink was in order. He knew his son of course was cocky and arrogant. He got that particular trait from his side of the family - all the males were that way. They all had a shrewdness to them, but his son possessed a shallow side too. Maybe they could pull this off if his son could keep his mind on the issue at hand instead of cheap women and booze. He had heard all about what his son got up to. It was his job to know. It was a good thing he didn't possess a heart or this would be difficult. Then he smiled. He knew his son. In the end he would not let him or anyone else down. He might show a smooth exterior, but deep down he knew his son was a monster capable of anything he put his mind to.

25

After a quick shower Alana headed downstairs. Her mom was still at the shop. This was a busy week for her with lots of weddings looming. She and her staff were putting in a lot of hours to get everything done. She decided she would make a sandwich and then call Eudora. Her day had gone a little better after her little speech. Sebastian had at least explained somewhat after that and she was getting the hang of things. She wasn't as tired or sore tonight. Perhaps by the end of the week she wouldn't be sore at all. With that thought a chill ran down her spine. By that time she would need to know what she was doing. Her time would be almost up. After tonight she only had four days left. Alana swallowed hard and decided maybe she would eat later. She really wasn't that hungry right now. She needed to talk to someone. She didn't want to be alone so in the quiet of the kitchen she called Eudora. She didn't have to wait long. Eudora was right in front of her smiling and that made Alana smile too. There was just something about Eudora that made all her worries go away.

"Hello dear. How was your day?" Eudora walked to the table and produced two cups of coffee and motioned for Alana to sit down. When she did a nice steaming bowl of soup appeared along with some bread. "Sit my dear. I know you have to be hungry after the day you had. Has Sebastian kept you busy?"

Alana looked at the soup and decided she did need to eat after all. She took up the spoon and had a taste - clam chowder.

"Thank you for the soup. It's one of my favorites." She took another spoonful and a sip of coffee before continuing. "Actually I think we got a lot accomplished today." Then she burst out laughing. Eudora smiled and looked at where Sebastian was standing. She could tell that whatever story Alana was going to tell Sebastian wouldn't like it. When she caught his eye he nodded then disappeared. She didn't want him to hear when they spoke of him. That wouldn't be fair and Eudora knew this would be for the best in the long run. Once Alana found out that Sebastian had been with her without her knowledge at least she could take some comfort in knowing that whenever it was private he wasn't there. She looked back at Alana and there were tears streaming down her face and her eyes sparkled with mischief. This intrigued Eudora.

The story must be very good indeed.

"I'm sorry for laughing like that but you should have seen his face when I knocked him on his butt!" she chuckled again and tried to catch her breath. Very interesting indeed. That's twice she has got one over on Sebastian. Once she might understand but twice? How delicious.

"I do hope you plan on telling me everything so I will be able to join in."

Alana still had mischief sparkling in her eyes. "Oh Eudora if you had been there you would have laughed so hard. He was showing me how to throw a solar ball and I guess he didn't know his own strength. When he hit me with it, I was startled and I fell on my butt." She took another breath and continued with the soup.

Eudora sat straighter in her chair now. This she didn't understand. "Dear I thought you said *you* knocked *him* on *his* butt."

Alana took another bite. "Sorry. I am hungrier than I thought. First Sebastian knocked me down. I guess if I had to say, the ball wasn't that strong but since I was caught off guard I did fall back. When I stood up I could tell he was about to laugh. You know it wouldn't have happened anyway if he hadn't smiled at me before he threw that stupid ball..." she shook her head and slurped more soup.

Again Eudora smiled. She had never known Sebastian to really smile at anyone. Maybe it was only a curve of his lips - she had seen that many times.

"So anyway, I got so mad. I mean Eudora, I had never been that mad before. So I focused all my anger on him and when I threw *my* solar ball it hit him in the chest and knocked him completely off his feet. I'm telling you he flew about two feet through the air!" She picked up her spoon again.

Eudora couldn't believe what she was hearing. She had to have a talk with Sebastian and find out what all this meant. She had a mental picture of him hurtling through the air and she had to laugh. Poor Sebastian. She was sure his ego must have just a small dent in it. When Alana looked up at Eudora's face she started laughing again too. But then the doorbell rang and both stopped in mid-laugh.

"I wonder who that could be. Maybe it's one of my friends." She got up from the table with Eudora right behind her.

Eudora could see Sebastian off to the side watching and she felt just a little safer when she looked toward the door. She noticed Alana's shoulders stiffen and her relaxed demeanor became guarded. Eudora felt something was wrong about this visitor. She could feel Alana's uneasiness. She looked to check that Sebastian was still there then walked up behind Alana.

"Who is it dear?" then Eudora finally came face to face with Todd, the man who wanted to marry Alana. Alana didn't want to marry him, she at least knew that much was true.

Alana turned from Todd and looked at Eudora. "This is Todd". She turned back to Todd and with a crisp tone she asked "What are you doing here Todd?" She could tell he was not happy with how she spoke to him but he wasn't looking at her. He was looking at Eudora. He looked back at her and she could tell he was masking his feelings.

"I thought we could go for a walk and talk. We *are* still friends." He leaned in and grabbed her hand but Alana stepped back out of his reach.

"I'm sorry Todd but I can't. Eudora and I are making dinner for my mom. She will be home soon. Maybe another time," but before she could close the door Todd walked further into the room.

"I understand. Perhaps we can go for that walk tomorrow? I haven't seen much of you lately. I've tried calling but it seems you're never at home. I was hoping we could still be friends Alana." He looked at Eudora. "I think I am at a disadvantage here. Who are you?' but before Eudora could speak Alana stepped forward.

"This is my Aunt. She will be staying with us for a few weeks." Todd looked from Eudora to Alana. Tonight he would not get her out of the house - he could see that. But he had to control his anger and do what he was best at - charm. He smiled and looked back at Eudora. "It is a pleasure to meet you Eudora." He looked back at Alana. "I see you ladies are busy so I will bid you goodnight. I will however come by another time and maybe then you and I can go for a walk or maybe see a movie?"

Alana just nodded and walked beyond Todd to the door. Eudora looked at Sebastian and sent him a message to follow Todd. When Sebastian disappeared she knew he would be outside waiting for Todd to leave. Alana closed the door and locked it and Eudora put her arm around her shoulder.

"I think there is still half a bowl of soup on the table calling your name and if you're nice to me maybe I will show you my secret on how to make it hot again." She chuckled and pulled Alana into the kitchen to show her a few secrets that she might use one day.

26

Sebastian waited right outside the door far enough away but close enough to see and hear everything. When Alana closed the door on him Sebastian had to smile. It gave him great satisfaction that she had turned Todd away. As Todd started down the steps he was mumbling under his breath and Sebastian was certain that he heard the word 'bitch'. He frowned when suddenly Todd stopped in his tracks and looked around sharply. Sebastian thought perhaps he had shown himself but no, he was still invisible. This was one time Sebastian appreciated the fact that he had the rare power of invisibility but there was something still not right about Todd. He was heading in the direction of his car so Sebastian decided it was time he sprouted wings - literally - if he wanted to keep up with Todd. As the car roared to life and backed out of the driveway Sebastian was in the air and following.

27

After showing Alana how to warm up her soup, Eudora headed back into the living room and looked out the window just in time to see Sebastian transform. He kept his human body but now where his shoulders met in the back were two enormous wings that spread out in a graceful display. Of course they were as black as the clothes he wore but nonetheless beautiful. Eudora sighed. Not many had the ability to transform and it was a sight to behold. Alana came up behind her just as Sebastian took flight and Todd left the driveway. "Has he left yet?" Eudora could tell something was bothering Alana. "Yes, he just pulled out of the driveway." She fell silent and waited for Alana to speak. "Eudora I have been meaning to ask you something and since I only have four days left… do you think I can do it?" Eudora watched Alana closely. She knew she was worried and with good reason, but Eudora would not lie to her about this. "Yes I believe in you. I think you know that. I have always believed in you. Even when you were a little girl I knew you would have the strength to face your fears and the courage to keep going on. But I don't think that is really what you want to know. I think you really want to know what Sebastian thinks." The look on Alana's face told her she was right. "Maybe you should ask him." She fell silent again. Eudora wanted to tell her what she wanted to know, but *she* didn't even know *that*. But she would before the night was up. She would know exactly what Sebastian thought.

"You know Eudora, I think you're right. Now if you will excuse me, I think I am ready for bed. Would you tell my mom when she gets home I said I would talk with her tomorrow?"

Eudora smiled at Alana and walked over and gave her a quick hug. "Of course dear. Perhaps it is best that you go on up to bed. You will have a long day tomorrow."

Eudora waited until she heard Alana open her bedroom door then concentrated on calling Sebastian. She told him whenever he was done they needed to talk. That done, she sat down in the nice comfy chair by the door and waited for Sebastian to get back and Lily to get home too.

28

Sebastian looked down to see Todd's car turn into the long driveway of his parents' home. He needed to find out what he could about Todd and his family. There was definitely something not right. There seemed an almost dangerous quality to him - he had felt that - and he also had felt the rage and anger toward Alana. A rage so intense it was almost unnatural. He could understand the anger perhaps if he really wanted her, but Sebastian was starting to doubt that, but the rage was different. He had acted like a monstrous child who couldn't get his own way and that just didn't sit well with Sebastian. But he would find out what exactly Todd wanted with Alana, because he did know he wanted her, but for what purpose? Closing his eyes he thought for a minute. When he opened them he watched Todd going into his parents' home. There was a story here. He just had to figure out what that story was about and why it involved Alana.

Starting back to Alana's home, he felt Eudora's presence calling to him so instead of a pleasant flight through the evening air he transformed back into his human form and shimmered back to Alana's house where he found Eudora sitting in a chair waiting patiently for him.

"Thank you for coming so quickly Sebastian. I do hope I didn't interrupt you in the middle of anything."

Sebastian sat down. "I was finished. I followed Todd home but something just doesn't feel right with him. Have you felt that or is it just me?"

Eudora watched Sebastian closely. "Since this was actually my first time in meeting him I tried to have an open mind but you are right. Something didn't feel right with him. I was hoping it was just me, but since you also felt it, I think we need to do some checking."

Sebastian sat there and nodded. "I felt it the first time I saw him. Do you know what his parents' names are?"

Eudora shook her head. "I will ask Lily when she gets here. I'm sure she knows a lot about them and when I find out what I need to I will call you. Alana will be safe while we check. I have already put a spell on the house. When neither of us is here she will be protected and I will be alerted if someone tries to get in."

With that said, Sebastian stood. "I will wait for you to call." He disappeared. Soon they would find out everything they could about Todd and his family. Still lost in thought she almost missed the sound of a car door closing. She went to greet Lily at the door.

Lily gave her a tired smile. "Where is Alana?" Eudora took her purse and keys and put them on the table by the door.

"She was tired and so went to bed but she said she would talk with you tomorrow." Eudora could see even though she was tired she was also worried about her daughter.

"Let's go in the kitchen and I shall fix you something to eat and you and I can chat."

Lily looked at Eudora gratefully and headed off to the kitchen with Eudora hot on her heels. "You sit down Lily and I will take care of everything."

As soon as Lily sat, Eudora waved her hand in front of her and the same soup that Alana had for dinner appeared in front of Lily with a teapot and two cups. Eudora could see that Lily hadn't quite gotten used to all the magic that she had witnessed lately.

"Now you go ahead and eat. It's good, or at least Alana thought so when she had some earlier."

Lily gave up trying to understand what she could not and dug into the soup. By the time she came up for air, the bowl was empty and Eudora was still sitting there very quietly sipping her own tea. "Would you like some more?"

When Lily shook her head the table was cleared instantly except for the tea pot and cups.

"Was Alana's day alright? I know yesterday she was very sore and tired. I hate that she has to learn all of this and I will tell you another thing too. I wish her birthday didn't have to come this year." She picked up her own tea and took a sip.

Eudora chose her words wisely. She knew Lily would ask lots of questions if she just came out and quizzed her about Todd and his family, so she went another route. "From what I know, her day was actually better than yesterday. She said she wasn't as sore but after dinner Todd showed up and I think that meeting upset her. I might be wrong about that but she did go to bed right after he left."

Again Lily sighed. "I had hoped after she told him she was not interested he would just leave her alone but I don't think he liked her refusing him. He has called several times for her while she has been with Sebastian and I don't think he liked it that she wasn't at home or that she hadn't called him back. He was very rude when he asked me if I had given her any of his messages. I'm just glad she didn't marry him." Eudora watched a shiver run down her back as she took another sip of tea.

Eudora cleared her throat and asked innocently, "Is there any reason you don't like him?"

When Lily shrugged her shoulders Eudora decided to just ask, "What do you know of his family?"

Lily put her tea cup down and closed her hands around it. "I really don't know much about them at all. They have ordered flowers from me on several occasions. They're from old money and you know how some people with too much money are - they seem more fake than real. His mother, Helen, I have only meet once and that was an experience. And his Father, I have never met or talked too. I think Alana said his name was Raymond. I never really liked Todd too much. He likes things his way and that's not for Alana. She is too independent for his liking."

She picked her cup up and took another sip. This was interesting to Eudora. She wondered why Lily didn't like them, because Lily was the type who liked everyone.

"Why did you find his mother an experience?"

Lily again sat her cup down. "I don't know if you know the type, but she was too sweet and too nice with an air of...I don't know...maybe she thought she was better than me because she had more money. It wasn't just one thing about her, it was the whole picture. Do you know what I mean?" Eudora nodded. "I'm just glad that they won't be Alana's in-laws. I don't think they would treat her with respect. Actually I don't think they would have treated her good at all."

Eudora could tell Lily was tired so she decided on one more question. "Do you by any chance know their last name?"

Eudora could see the puzzled look that crossed Lily's face before she answered.

"Their names are Helen and Raymond Sinclair. Why would you want to know that?"

Eudora placed her hand over Lily's. "I want to do some checking on them. Perhaps I can find out something and if I do I will let you know. But for now I think you should go upstairs and get some sleep." She gave Lily a reassuring smile.

"I think you're right. I had a busy day today and tomorrow will be just as busy."

As soon as Eudora heard her footsteps on the stairs she summoned Sebastian. He was there in an instant.

"I think it's time we found out a little more about the Sinclair's. What do you think?"

When Sebastian nodded, Eudora placed her hand out and Sebastian took it. She took them both to her special place.

"Now let's see what we can find out about the Sinclair bunch."

On command, the fountain appeared in front of them and when she closed her eyes she spoke softly. "Show us what we need to know about the Sinclair's." Running her fingers through the water, she opened her eyes. Both Eudora and Sebastian looked into the water but nothing happened. When Sebastian looked up with a question in his eyes Eudora frowned too.

"Let me speak it differently." Eudora closed her eyes again and spoke. "Show us what we need to know about Helen Sinclair and Raymond Sinclair and their son Todd Sinclair." Again nothing. Eudora didn't know what was wrong. This had never happened to her before. She tried to ask in different ways and just like before, the waters were calm and clear.

"What do you think this means Eudora?" asked Sebastian still looking in the water for any signs.

"Honestly Sebastian, I do not know, but I think I know someone who might." She disappeared and was back in just a minute with Brigham. He was the oldest and the wisest of their realm.

Sebastian knew that his father had asked advice of him throughout the years.

When Brigham saw Sebastian he bowed and spoke in a deep voice. "You're Highness." Sebastian only nodded his head.

"Now what can I do for the both of you?" He looked at Eudora's worried face.

"I don't know what is wrong, Brigham. I have been searching in my waters for Todd and his parents' history so we can better understand them and know what we are up against here, but every time I spoke, nothing happened. I did ask several different ways and not even a ripple appeared. This has never happened to me before. What could be happening?"

Brigham looking into her fountain. "Ask your waters to look for someone else Eudora."

This puzzled her but she complied. "Show me Alana." She ran her fingers through the water and right before their eyes Alana appeared. She was in bed asleep."

Sebastian leaned in closer to get a better look "I don't understand. Why would it show Alana but not Todd and his parents?" he looked up.

Brigham was standing there stroking his beard. "Why indeed?" He asked Eudora to look for other people and every time she did they appeared.

"What do you think Brigham?" Both she and Sebastian stood there waiting for Brigham to answer.

"It seems to me these people are hiding something or that is not their real names. Tell me Eudora, why are these people so important?"

"Todd is the one who proposed to Alana. They had been dating a couple of months but she broke it off with him and now he won't leave it alone. Sebastian and I both felt like something was not right with him. We just can't put our finger on it. But now maybe it's because they are not telling the truth about their identities." For a minute a chill ran down Eudora's spine.

"I don't like this at all. Why would they have to hide their identity and what are they hiding it from?" Sebastian asked.

Brigham looked at them both. "I will try and find out everything I can but you two should stay close to Alana. I have my suspicions but until I find out, I want you both to keep a close eye on Alana." When they both nodded agreement Brigham disappeared. "I wonder what his suspicions are?" said Eudora.

"I don't know, but whatever it is I'm sure it's not good. We need to make sure Alana celebrates her twenty-first birthday and that she stays away from that whole family."

Eudora nodded and Sebastian disappeared.

29

Alana actually woke with a smile on her face and her body was no longer sore. She was getting used to all the training that Sebastian was making her do. One thing she did know for sure - she was hungry this morning. She got out of bed and headed downstairs to have something to eat. At the bottom of the stairs she heard voices from the kitchen and smiled. Good. Her mom was still home. So with a spring in her step and a smile on her face she went to investigate. When she walked in her mom and Eudora were both sitting at the table.

"Good morning you two." She took a seat at the table and got a cup to pour some coffee.

"My, you're in a chipper mood today honey."

Alana laughed. "I actually got out of bed without groaning or feeling sore, so to me, I guess that makes me chipper - and hungry!" She waved her hand in front of her and a big plate of eggs, bacon and toast appeared. Her mom just shook her head.

"I guess one of these days I will get used to all of this."

Eudora had not said anything yet. She had been watching Alana closely and for the first time she felt at peace about her and again her aura glowed bright. Alana was gaining confidence every day and her powers were getting stronger too. Eudora could feel it and was pleased.

"I'm glad to see that you're feeling more like yourself dear."

Alana smiled at Eudora. "You know Eudora I think you're right. I do feel more like my old self." She took another sip of her coffee. Eudora was glad to see it but she needed to speak to Sebastian before they started their day.

"I'm sorry you two, but there are a few things I need to do. I will see you both later." Alana looked up, smiled and said good-bye and Lily did likewise and on that cue Eudora disappeared. Immediately back in her own realm, she summoned Sebastian who appeared immediately. "Is there something wrong Eudora?"

By his stance, with his arms crossed on his chest, she figured that he preferred to be somewhere else.

"I know you have to get to Alana soon so I will get right to the point. You have been working with Alana now for a few days. How well do you think she is doing?" Eudora watched and waited

for Sebastian to speak, she could see the guarded look on his face.
He sighed. "It doesn't matter what I think Eudora, as well you
know. It all depends on what Alana thinks but if you're asking me
if *I* think she can do it, my answer would be 'yes'." Sebastian
could tell he had surprised her so he chuckled. "I can tell by the
look on your face that answer surprised you."

"You would be right Sebastian. I would have never thought you
would tell me this, but whether you know this or not I think it does
matter to Alana. You might not believe this, but I think she
respects you."

This made Sebastian snort. "I know she told you what happened
yesterday."

"Yes she did tell me and you must admit Sebastian not many
people, if any, has caught you off guard."

Sebastian shuffled his feet. "She didn't catch me off guard. There
was nothing I could do, it happened so quickly. She is more
powerful than you know. I am still feeling the sting from that solar
ball and my backside felt it this morning."

She could tell it took a lot for Sebastian to admit this and that made
her more curious. "Let me ask you something without you biting
my head off. If you two went into battle against each other who do
you think would win?"

Sebastian growled at her. She almost laughed at the look on his
face because nobody, especially a mere girl, had ever beaten
Sebastian. But maybe this time Sebastian would lose more than
just the battle and that was what Eudora was counting on.

"This is nonsense. I have to get back to Alana before she thinks
I'm not coming." He started to shimmer. "Wait! Sebastian I
have just one more thing to say. I plan on taking the time while
you are with Alana to do some investigating of Todd and his
parents and I will talk to Brigham again." Sebastian nodded his
head and disappeared. This time Eudora did chuckle. "I think my
dear Sebastian you have finally met your match." She laughed out
loud. She needed to go over the ancient books. Maybe there, she
might find something. Then she too disappeared.

30

Alana had just finished breakfast and was talking to her mom when
Sebastian showed up. He was late which was unusual. When she
arched her eyebrow at him he just grunted and held out his hand.
She sighed and said good-bye to her mom and took his hand and
they were back in their usual spot.
"Tell me Sebastian, when I will learn how to disappear like
 you and Eudora?" Sebastian just looked at her. He knew if he tried
showing her she would probably already know how to do it. It
seemed that anything and everything he showed her she picked up
quickly.
"When you're ready you'll be taught." He headed off toward the
field. "Today I have decided I will teach you how to call on your
magic. Alana only sighed and followed him.

31

Eudora was deep in her books when Brigham appeared, but he was not by himself. Artemis was with him and for some reason she didn't like the look of this. She put a smile on her face and stood to bow to her King. When she straightened up she waited for one of them to speak.

"We have been discussing everything that happened yesterday and Brigham and I both have our suspicions about who this family might be. Do you have any clues Eudora?"

Artemis waited for Eudora to speak. "I can't explain it myself. The only thing that I have come up with is this family is hiding from someone and has changed their name to protect them. What do you and Brigham think?"

Brigham stroked his beard as he always did when he was in deep thought then he looked to Artemis before speaking.

"We think if these were normal people, even if they changed their names you should still have got a reading from them. Our magic is strong and it would have been able to get through that simple ruse. But since that is not the case, there is something else working here." Brigham waited until this sunk in. He knew just when Eudora understood. He could see the horror in her eyes and on her face.

"This can't be! Please don't tell me these people have magic of their own, because if they do…" Eudora couldn't finish her sentence she was too shocked. She would have never guessed this. If this was all true then Alana was in more danger than she thought. If these people were hiding their identity from them then it only meant one thing and to think about that was terrifying.

"Sebastian and I both felt as if something was not right when we saw Todd, but I would have never thought this. I couldn't even feel his magic. Nor did I see it." She fell silent. Oh my God they had to do something they had to warn Sebastian.

"We need to let the others know and we also need to tell Sebastian everything we have found out and we also need to find out just exactly who these people are."

Artemis waved his hand. "First we will tell the others then we will let Sebastian know. Right now he and Alana are safe. Are they not training in Sebastian's domain?"

When Eudora nodded her head Artemis sighed. "Brigham I think you need to call the others. Tell them all to meet in my study. It is private there and no one will be able to hear or see anything. It is well protected."

When Brigham nodded he disappeared to fetch the others.

"Eudora I have done it your way, but now I think is the time for me to meet Alana."

Eudora swallowed and nodded her head. They both shimmered to Artemis' study. Most of the others were already there.

Artemis addressed them. "We think the dark ones have found the girl and we also think that they have known who she is for quite a while. They are protecting their identity with their magic and for now we can't break through."

All was quiet until Zephyr spoke. "What would you like us to do you're Majesty? Everyone in the room waited. Zephyr was one of the wise. Even though she was young in appearance she was probably one of the oldest of them. She had special powers and she knew of the stories and some of the dark ones. She had been around in those times.

Eudora asked, "Would you know them if you saw them Zephyr?" Zephyr looked toward her King as if for approval to answer. He nodded and she stepped forward. "I have seen many but I cannot recognize them if they are disguised."

Eudora nodded and produced her fountain. She motioned Zephyr to approach. Eudora ran her hand through the water and called for the only picture she had of Todd to come forward. First her fountain was empty but then his image floated to the surface. Most everyone around looked at the image. Zephyr was already studying the picture.

"Do you mind if I try something Eudora? It will not harm your waters but it will show us the truth. No matter how powerful they are, this potion will always ring true."

Eudora nodded and Zephyr placed her hands out in front of her and in them was a small bottle. Eudora didn't know what was in the bottle but she didn't question Zephyr. She knew she was wise and that her powers lay in the truth of everyone's soul. She heard Zephyr whisper in a language that was old - one only Eudora knew about because her own teacher wanted her to know everything of the old ways. Zephyr poured the potion into the water. First it bubbled then there was mist everywhere and when it cleared everyone in the room moved closer.

Todd's face vanished and one word took its place '*D'Ary*'. Eudora heard several gasps before the picture vanished and her water was clear once more. In their old language 'D'Ary' meant 'Dark'. Brigham stepped forward and motioned for Eudora who nodded and with a wave of her hand her fountain disappeared.

"I know of the D'Ary." With one word a book appeared in Brigham's hand. Eudora had seen this book before. It was the records book of all the people who had left their realm. When he sat the book down on Artemis' desk he moved his fingers over it and it opened to a page. "Huh. Here it is. Gideon and Bronwyn D'Ary. They had two children - Keir and Raynor. Keir died in a battle years ago but his brother Raynor still lives."

Eudora's head was spinning at this point. She couldn't believe these people were out there and they hadn't even known it.

"There magic is protecting them or we would have sensed them. They must have some kind of shield that is protecting them from us. What do you think we should do now?'

Eudora hadn't asked anybody in particular but the King spoke. "We need to find out everything we can about the D'Ary family. Brigham I want you to find everything you can about them." Brigham nodded in response. "The rest of you figure out who else is involved with them." Everyone else in the room bowed in obedience and the King addressed everyone in the room. "All of you know how important this is. Please do not fail me. You may all go about your duty except for Brigham, Eudora and you Zephyr. I would like you to stay too. We may need you."

The Queen laid her hand on her husband's arm and spoke "I think it is time we told our son and this girl who these people are."

Artemis placed his hand above hers and with a heavy sigh nodded in agreement. Eudora knew the time had come for Alana to meet the King and Queen and she hoped enough time had passed for Alana to understand. They hadn't really lied to her, they had just omitted the truth and so with a heavy heart she also nodded her head.

32

Sebastian could see she was getting tired. They had been at it a while so he decided to give her a break to catch her breath and maybe get a drink of water. When he called a halt she looked at him questioningly.

"Come we will sit and have a drink." Sebastian walked off the field and strolled over to the shed and right before her eyes two tree stumps appeared along with two bottles of water. She was thankful but she wasn't going to let him know that, so she just followed, picked up the bottle, unscrewed the cap and took a big drink. 'Huh,' she thought, 'that was refreshing.' She took another swig. When she opened her eyes she noticed Sebastian watching her. That unnerved her. He was always watching her. "What?" she said. When he just shook his head and opened his own drink she shrugged her shoulders and sat on the stump he had provided for her. She watched him take a drink and swallow. His Adam's apple worked up and down. He ran his hand over his forehead. They had worked hard so far and Alana was learning a lot. She thought back to the night before, when she had asked Eudora if she believed she could do it. She had known what Eudora would say - she just wanted to hear it, and not just from Eudora. She wanted to know if Sebastian thought she could too. She just didn't know how to ask him and she wasn't sure what he would say. So instead of asking, she took another sip. She thought she heard him sigh.

"You have something on your mind."

How did he do that? "Don't tell me you can also read my mind?" She almost said it jokingly, but when she saw the look of guilt on his face she had to ask.

"Sebastian? You can't really read my mind can you?" She was hoping his answer would be 'no' but that wasn't looking likely. She stood up.

"Oh my God, please don't tell me you actually can!" She put her hands on her hips and waited. When he didn't answer she growled and tapped her foot. This amused Sebastian greatly - his little warrior was so brave.

"I should have known. Well if you can, I hope you're getting everything I'm thinking about you right now!" She stormed off a little way. Of course she should have known this. They *were* magical. There were probably others things he could do that she didn't know about. She felt him touch her shoulder and that made her stiffen. He *never* touched her.

"Alana it is not like that at all. Yes I can read thoughts and view things that go through someone's mind, but I don't take advantage of it." He dropped his hand away. She watched him run his fingers through his hair.

"Then what way is it? Have you, as you say, looked into *my* head?" This thought embarrassed her. There were some thoughts she didn't want him to know about. He looked her straight in the face.

"Twice," was all he said, then she turned beet red. She could feel the heat in her cheeks.

"Twice? And when was that?" She was sure that her question would make him uncomfortable, but instead of showing it, he looked calmly at her.

"The first time was when I saw you at the café. You were troubled and I tried to help you relax."

Alana thought back to that morning and remembered how she had felt and then she clearly remembered how, when she had looked at him, it seemed like all the bad feelings went away. OK. Maybe she would forgive him for that one.

"And the second time was when?" She could tell he didn't want to answer by the way he wouldn't look at her and the way he rubbed the back of his neck. "Let's sit down and I will tell you."

He sat on one of the stumps that he had conjured. She stood there for a moment but eventually followed his lead. He was silent for a minute thinking about how to explain.

"Remember the first night you met Eudora?" He stopped long enough to look at her. When she nodded her head he continued. "I was there when she told you who you were and I was there when you had memories of your father. I saw everything you were recalling. Memories of you playing in your father's study and him telling you the story of the Princess and you telling him you liked that story 'bestest' of all." He went silent and watched her face. He saw that she didn't like what he was saying and he really didn't blame her, but he would show her how to block other people from entering her mind so she would not be vulnerable to anyone.

"Wait a minute! How could you know what was said that night and what was in my mind when you weren't even there?"

Now this was the tricky part. He had to tell her that he could be invisible when most others of their kind couldn't. He knew she would be mad. Hell she was going to be more than mad and this was the telling he didn't want to do.

"I was there Alana. You just couldn't see me." He waited for it to sink in. When it did, her eyes got big and round and she jumped up off the stump and glared at him.

"Let me get this straight. You mean you were there and you were invisible?" When he just nodded she started to pace back and forth. "So how many times have you been invisible and watched me?" She stopped pacing and crossed her hands over her chest. The gesture was not lost on him.

"It's not like that at all. I was sent to protect you. I had to watch over you." He got up and glared right back at her. They were both silent for a long time until tears formed in Alana's eyes. This was something that Sebastian didn't expect. He didn't know how to deal with a crying woman. He had never had to. Alana turned her back on him and he could tell she was trying to control the flow of tears. When she spoke it was no more than a whisper.

"I can't believe you spied on me like that." He watched her wipe her hand across her face and Sebastian wanted to take her in his arms but he didn't dare, so he placed his hand on her shoulder and waited for her to turn around.

"I know this probably won't help, but I was never there when you were with Eudora. She was there at the time to protect you. The only time I was there was at night or whenever you were out in the beginning. I know you probably think I've invaded your space, but it was only for your own good." He could tell that made her angry. He could see the fire that leapt into her eyes.

"I'm so tired of everyone telling me this or that is for my own good."

She walked back over to her stump and sat down. He didn't know what to say after that so he just stood there for a while and waited for her temper to cool. Alana couldn't believe he had done that to her. She didn't know if she could trust him after this. She looked up at him. Maybe after a while she might understand better, but right now she felt laid open for everyone to see. She sighed. Sebastian took the chance and walked back over and sat down.

"Alana I can teach you how to block people from getting inside your head and I can also teach you to get inside someone else's head. Would you care to learn?" He waited for her to come to terms with what he was saying. She slid a glance toward him. "You can really teach me to do the same thing?" When he nodded she spoke again. "Can you also teach me to be invisible?"

Now this was different. Only a few knew how to do this but when he looked at her he could see the hope in her eyes and he couldn't tell her no.

"I can try, but I will warn you not everyone can do that." She thought about it for a minute and again she nodded her head. Sebastian sighed with relief. "OK. No time like the present. Now you must clear your mind and close your eyes." She did just that and he watched her for a minute. "Now try and open your mind to me. Try and get inside my head." He could tell she was concentrating so he opened his mind and sent her a message. "Open your eyes." When he looked she had her eyes still closed so he tried again, but this time he closed his eyes too and unblocked his mind. He heard her gasp and he opened his eyes. She had her eyes open and she was looking right at him with amazement on her face. "Did you just talk to me?"

He shook his head no. He could see the disappointment on her face. "But I did tell you to open your eyes with my thoughts." First she showed disbelief, then she giggled and a huge smile transformed her face.

"I did it? Wow! I can't believe I really did it." Her reaction almost made Sebastian smile. He liked to see her happy.

"Now I will try and teach you to block someone from entering your mind. First you have to clear all thoughts from your mind." When she just looked at him he told her to close her eyes. "Now can you feel me tapping into your mind?" He watched her closely he could tell when she felt him in her mind. A look crossed her face than he told her to close her mind off to him, to push him out. "Open your eyes Alana." When she did Sebastian spoke again. "Now I will try and read your thoughts. Remember block me from your mind. Are you ready?" She nodded and closed her eyes. Sebastian tried to tap into her mind. He concentrated very hard but she had closed her mind off to him. He couldn't believe it. She was faster than most. Most took a long time to learn to do that. "Very good Alana, I couldn't break through."

Again she smiled as soon as she opened her eyes. "Wow! That was so cool, I could actually… I don't know…feel your presence I guess you would say." That did make Sebastian smile or at least the corner of his mouth turned up. It was hard not to laugh at the look on her face.

"OK now you have to teach me how to become invisible." She stood up and he followed her lead.

"You did well, but that doesn't mean you have perfected it, but with a lot of practice you will be able to do it in your sleep."

"Ok now c'mon. Show me how to become invisible." Sebastian hated to disappoint her.

"You have to remember if this doesn't work, then it means you just can't do it. But that's alright too. Not many can transform. Are you ready?"

Looking determined Alana nodded that she was indeed ready. She looked like she was expecting to be handed the secrets of the universe.

"Ok Alana. You need to listen closely. This is not as easy as the mind reading. You have to open your mind once again but this time let everything float away. You need to concentrate on being invisible. You have to tell yourself that no one else can see you. You have to believe it. You have to believe in yourself and your ability. Now connect with your mind and make everyone around you not see you. Can you do that?" When she just nodded Sebastian did too. "OK now try."

He watched her concentrate. She bit down on her lower lip and Sebastian almost groaned. She opened her eyes and looked at him. "Is it working?"

Sebastian was still so focused on her lips he didn't understand at first what she was asking. Then he shook his head and tried to soothe her feelings. He knew what she was trying was probably impossible. This was not something you could learn. Only the ones born to it could do it.

"Alana? Some things even you can't do. I only know of a handful of people who have this gift." When Alana looked so disappointed Sebastian took pity on her. "Let's try again. Now follow the same steps and try again." Again he watched her concentrate with all her might and again nothing happened. He actually was hoping something would. He ran his hands over his face.

"I don't think this is something you can do Alana." He could see she was disappointed.

"Maybe I can't do *any* of this. Have you thought about that Sebastian? Maybe I won't be ready or maybe I haven't learnt enough. After all, my birthday is only a couple of days away." Her shoulders sagged. Sebastian knew she needed reassurance.

"Are you asking me if I think you can do this Alana?" he watched her closely. He could see the look on her face and it was one of surprise. "Are you still trying to read my mind Sebastian?" Sebastian shook his head. He thought he saw relief pass over her face. Was she actually worried about what he thought?

"Alana look at me." Reluctantly she looked at him.

"Always the little warrior I see. I think you are strong enough to do whatever you want to and I think you have the courage to try and when the battle is upon us you will do the right thing. But you have to know this. Regardless about what I think you have to ask yourself the most important question; do *you* believe you can?" He watched as she soaked up everything he had said and he could tell she was surprised by his answer. It had shown on her face and at the same time she was pleased.

"Thank you for the vote of confidence. I might need that later and I need to thank you for teaching me the other things too. Even though I couldn't go invisible." At that point she laughed. "I guess it's not like I could just command myself to be unseen and it just happen." She laughed again and right before his eyes she was gone. Sebastian stumbled backwards slightly and he knew his mouth was open and that he probably had a stupid look on his face but he couldn't believe it. She had gone! Invisible!

"What! Tell me Sebastian. Why you are looking at me like that?" He pointed at her and she looked down. "Oh my God it worked! It really worked!" She looked back at Sebastian and laughed. It was the first time she'd ever seen him with the 'deer in the headlight' look with his mouth gaping open. She wished she had a camera right now. Eudora would not believe this.

"Alright Sebastian, you can close your mouth now. I know you're a man with few words but this is priceless!" She laughed again. Sebastian knew he looked stupid just standing there watching her, but he couldn't believe what he was seeing so he was entitled to gawk at her for a minute. Eventually he closed his eyes and shook his head to clear it and opened his eyes again. There she was, or rather there she *wasn't* and he could hear her talking and laughing and of course the joke was on him because he didn't ever think she would be able to pull it off. There were too many secrets about her and she was learning faster than most. He heard her laugh again and speak.

"Houston we have a problem." He could hear the smile in her voice and he just bet she was laughing at him on the inside. So what the hell - he smiled anyway.

"And just what problem is that? And enlighten me on who Houston is." Again she burst out laughing.

"You mean to tell me you have never heard that phrase?" He shook his head and Alana laughed even harder. "Well since you told me how to go invisible, now can you tell me how to be visible again?" Sebastian just shook his head - he was still in shock.

"Just open your mind, and let yourself be seen again." He waited and soon she reappeared. That smile was still there and it lit up her whole face and made her eyes sparkle. He was about to tell her how impressed he was when he heard Eudora's call. She didn't sound like herself. Alana had been watching him and she felt so alive. She still couldn't believe she had done that. She watched Sebastian open his mouth as if to say something then he snapped his head up like he was listening to something.

"What is it Sebastian?" she watched a puzzled look pass over his face. "Eudora is calling us. She needs to see us right away." Alana nodded and walked over to Sebastian.

"Is there something wrong?" She could tell Sebastian was distracted. "I don't know, but I hope you're ready to travel. We are needed in my realm.' When he held out his hand she took it, whatever it was it must be important for her to call them both to his realm. Finally she was going to get to see where Sebastian Lived.

33

Traveling this time for Alana felt different. It didn't just happen in the blink of an eye. She felt light headed, like she was floating through time and her breath came quicker so she squeezed her eyes tighter closed and concentrated on taking each breath. Finally she felt her feet hit a sold surface and dared to open her eyes. She gasped. They were in a hall or foyer with candles everywhere to light their way. She didn't have much time to look around as Sebastian grasped her hand and led her down a long corridor. It was amazing! The candles were just floating above them suspended in the air. She had to almost run to keep up with him. She wanted to stop and look at everything. On the wall hung several pictures. One actually looked like Sebastian but when she tried to study it he whisked her past it as if in an urgent hurry. Why would Sebastian's picture be in this place? She must be mistaken. "Sebastian look, do you think you can slow down? Where's the fire anyway?" Sebastian turned long enough to raise an eyebrow then he kept going but he did slow down just a little. Alana just stared at his back as they hurried along. Their hands were locked; this was the first time they had actually touched for more than a fleeting second and she kind of liked it even though it did weird things to her insides. Suddenly they stopped in front of a large door. When he didn't knock at once Alana looked up and she bit down on her lip; she had to remember he could read her thoughts if she didn't block him out. When she looked back up at him she stuck her chin out.

"Well are you going to knock or what?" She raised her eyebrow in question. She could see the amusement in his eyes and decided to ignore him. She raised her own hand and knocked. "What? I didn't think it would open by itself!"

'Enter' boomed from beyond the door.

Alana straightened her shoulders and waited for Sebastian to open the door. She thought she heard a small chuckle from him but she wasn't sure, then the door opened as if on its own and Alana had no more time to think about it as they entered the room.

Eudora watched as Sebastian and Alana approached. Alana was in front with Sebastian on her heels but she hadn't noticed them yet. She was too busy looking around the room. She could see that

Alana liked what she saw by the soft smile on her face. Alana turned and noticed Eudora and her smile grew bigger. Sebastian stood right beside her but he wasn't paying any attention to her. He was watching his father.

"We came as soon as we got your message" said Sebastian sparing Eudora a look before returning his gaze to his father.

Artemis had been silently watching Alana. Yes, he could see that she was someone special. Her aura was very bright. He noticed that whenever Sebastian spoke it appeared to glow even brighter. 'Interesting' thought Artemis as he watched as Alana noticed someone else was in the room. She looked him straight in the face and gave him one of her charming smiles. He understood why his son found her so fascinating.

Eudora held out her hand and escorted Alana further into the room. "Alana I would like to introduce you to our King." Artemis watched the surprise register on her face.

"Very nice to meet you." She rasped. Her throat had gone dry with sudden nervousness. "I'm sorry. I hope I did that right. You are the first king I have ever met. Or *any* royalty for that matter and I don't really know what I'm supposed to say now - maybe I should just shut my mouth."

Artemis smiled. Yes indeed. She was spirited, innocent and honest. He looked at his son and saw that he seemed a little uncomfortable and that made Artemis smile even more. He would have a lot of explaining to do, but Artemis was sure all would be well in the end.

Alana looked from the King to Sebastian than back at Eudora. Everyone was silent. She hoped she hadn't offended anyone but for some reason Eudora and Sebastian appeared to be uncomfortable. Neither one would look at her. She swallowed and looked back at the King. "I feel like I should apologize again. I don't know if maybe I said something wrong or..." she didn't have time to finish her statement as a beautiful woman came through the door and headed straight for Sebastian with a lovely smile on her face.

She gathered Sebastian up in her arms for a hug. Alana's mouth dropped open and just as quickly snapped shut. She didn't know who this woman was but right away she didn't like how friendly she was with Sebastian and she didn't like how Sebastian was looking at her. All the hard planes of his face softened and a gentle smile touched his lips as he kissed her cheek.

Alana didn't know that the King was watching her so close – as was Eudora. She narrowed her eyes and crossed her hands in front of her chest until she finally looked away. She couldn't watch this scene. She had never thought to ask if Sebastian had a wife or a girlfriend and this bothered her more than she wanted to admit. She felt like crying but instead she turned back to the scene in front of her, squared her shoulders and gave herself a pep talk. 'OK Alana you can handle this.' She took a deep breath and waited.

Artemis realized that when his Lady wife entered the room, Alana didn't know who she was. He could tell this bothered her even though she was trying hard to hold it together and not let it show. He could see why Eudora had such faith in her but it was time to introduce his wife to Alana before sparks started to fly.

"Sebastian, let your mother go so I can introduce her to Alana." He had been watching Alana the whole time and he could see this news surprised her. He watched her stiff shoulders relax and a smile replaced the frown she was sporting.

"Oh I am so sorry I didn't know there was anyone else here. You will have to forgive me Alana, it has been some time since I have seen my son."

Alana just smiled and nodded her head then the King came from around the desk and placed his arm around his wife's waist.

"Alana, I would like you to meet my wife, Queen Aurora." Alana started to bow then she looked from the King and Queen to Sebastian. He stared at her boldly. She looked at Eudora who smiled encouragingly, but she didn't look too comfortable right now. She could tell the Queen was a little curious because she looked from Sebastian to Eudora. Alana's shoulders stiffened again and she crossed her arms in front of her. Artemis wanted to laugh. She looked like one of his son's warriors - very fierce. He could tell she was clenching her teeth together.

"It's very nice to meet you, Your Majesty."

She turned her furious look on Eudora. "Excuse me! But didn't you say he was a warrior?" Alana almost growled this at Eudora through her teeth.

Eudora wrung her hands together, "Yes dear I did, but please let me explain."

Alana didn't want to hear any more of this. Her ears were ringing and her head was starting to pound She couldn't remember a time in her life when she had ever been this mad. When she held up her hand Eudora closed her mouth.

"I can't believe you didn't tell me! I trusted you!" Then she turned on Sebastian.

"And you! Why didn't you tell me you were a Prince! For God's sake!" She crossed her arms again and closed her mouth before she said anything she would regret. She could feel the tears in the back of her eyes and she willed them to stay there. She felt like a fool as it was. The room was silent. She looked at everyone. The King looked amused, his wife looked worried, Eudora looked sorry but Sebastian didn't show anything at all. If she didn't know better she would have thought he was a statue.

"What? Cat got your tongue Sebastian? Nothing to say to me now?"

His only reaction was his raised eyebrow. She growled again low in her throat. Damn it! She was going to cry. She knew she was. Sebastian started toward her but she didn't want him anywhere near her.

"STOP! Don't come any closer. I don't want you near me! Your *Highness!*" she nearly spat the words out as she held her hand up but still Sebastian kept coming. Then the first tear rolled down her cheek. She felt humiliated and the pounding in her head worsened. She didn't want him to come near her. She knew if he did she would break down and it was all his fault. This made her mad again and in a loud voice she yelled "STOP!"

She flung her arms out and with all the anger and rage she felt at being deceived, she hit him right in the chest with a solar ball and Sebastian's feet came out from under him and he slid halfway across the floor to the door. She heard a gasp, then heard the queen say something. Alana didn't know what it was, she was so focused on Sebastian. She could tell by the look on his face he was beyond mad. His face was red and his nostrils were flared and there was a dangerous look about him.

Artemis wouldn't have believed it if he hadn't seen it with his own eyes. She was more powerful than even he suspected. When his wife tried to intervene he held her firmly. "You must not interfere

in this my love. This is between Sebastian and Alana," and so far
Artemis liked what he was seeing. This was the best entertainment
he'd had in a while.

Sebastian knew she was angry. Hell he wasn't far from the mark
himself but when he looked at her he could see the hurt on her face
and he wished he could have told her earlier who he really was but
actually he never even thought of it. He had a job to do and he was
doing it.

"Alana calm down. I know you're upset but getting mad won't
solve anything. You might get hurt or hurt somebody else and we
are all here to work together". He approached her again ready for
anything she might throw at him, but instead her shoulders
slumped and it seemed like the fight went out of her. She looked
around embarrassed - a hint of red colored her neck and face.

Alana felt awful. She let her temper - a temper she didn't even
know she had - get the better of her and now she had shocked
everyone and she felt like a heel. The only one who didn't have a
shocked look on his face was the King. He looked rather amused if
she had to guess, so with her chin raised high and her shoulders
slung back she straightened up.

"I'm really sorry for that display Your Highness. There was no
excuse for the way I acted. I do hope you will forgive me." She
bowed to the King and Queen. She never looked at Sebastian or
Eudora, not sure if she could forgive them right now. She was still
angry with them. When she raised her head the King nodded and
the Queen smiled at her.

"Alana there is nothing to forgive. Sebastian and Eudora should
have told you from the beginning. If anything, they should be the
ones to apologize." The Queen looked at Eudora and Sebastian;
both were smart enough not to say anything.

Artemis cleared his throat trying to hold back a chuckle at the look
on Sebastian's and Eudora's faces. "Now that we have this settled,
if everyone will take a seat we will get down to the reason you
were both called here."

The King waved his hand and a table with five chairs appeared in
the middle of the room. When the three visitors were seated the
King and his wife took their seats. Alana was seated between
Eudora and Sebastian which didn't suit her at all but there was no
hope for that right now.

"Eudora called you both here to discuss the D'Ary family." When both Sebastian and Alana stared at him with blank looks he clarified. "You probably don't know that name but in your world Alana, they are known as the Sinclair's." Artemis crossed his hands and waited for that name to register.

"Are you talking about Todd Sinclair and his parents?" asked Alana incredulously. When the King nodded he noticed the way Alana was looking at him. Of course she would be confused at the how and why the King of another world would know the Sinclair's but after he was done today everything would be clear to everyone. "Are you telling me these people are from your world?" Again the King nodded.

Sebastian sat a little straighter in his chair and he had a murderous look in his eye. "Father are you saying that these people are the ones we have been looking for? And if so why haven't I or Eudora felt their presence?"

Eudora who had been silent finally spoke. "They have cast a spell to hide their appearance from all of us." Alana listened to everything that was being said around her and she couldn't believe it. Todd a witch? He was so…she didn't know, but a witch? That couldn't be true - could it? A shiver went down her spine. She had always felt something when she had been around that family. Now she knew what it was. She wasn't crazy after all. She just needed some clarification.

"Excuse me, I don't mean to interrupt any of you, but are Todd and his family are the evil ones trying to gain my powers? Is that what you are saying?" She still couldn't believe it.

Eudora magically produced a rolled parchment. As she unrolled it she explained how she and Sebastian felt wary around Todd and how they had tried to investigate it. She explained how they couldn't see them in her fountain and that was impossible unless they were magically concealing their true identities. She showed Alana their names on the parchment and how after their son Keir died they had disappeared only to show up in Alana's world. How they got there no one knew. Only a few could walk between worlds but they had discovered a way. Alana just shook her head. She couldn't believe all this. Her head started pounding again so she placed her hands on each side of her head. All this time and she didn't know. What if she had actually married him? Again another shiver went down her spine. No - she would have never done that. Suddenly she thought of her mother.

"Wait! We have to get back. My mother is alone. What if they try to harm her?" She stood up needing to get away and make sure her mother was safe. Eudora held out her hand and touched Alana's arm.

"They will not harm your mother Alana. They are not even aware that we have discovered their true identities." She patted Alana's arm and urged her to sit back down. As Alana sat down not quite convinced of her mother's safety there was a knock on the door. Everyone looked toward it.

"Enter" boomed the king in the same tone that he had used for Alana's arrival. The door opened and a woman entered wearing a flowing robe. She also wore a mischievous smile. She bowed to the King and Queen and looked at Alana and Sebastian.

"You're Highness, I am glad to see you are well."

When Sebastian nodded to her she turned to Alana.

"So you are the one we have all been waiting for all these years?" Alana watched the woman in front of her. She had no idea who she was, but she seemed to know who Alana was and there was something about the way she looked at Alana that made her uncomfortable.

"Alana, I would like to introduce you to Zephyr. She is the one who discovered who Todd was and why his family is hiding.'

Alana again studied the woman. She had a look about her, like she could see into Alana's soul and for some reason she didn't like that. Of course Eudora sometimes looked at her like that, but this woman hid many secrets herself.

"It is very nice to meet you Alana. When you are finished here come see me and you and I will have a nice talk." All Alana could do was nod her head. "Now I think it is time to show them what we have discovered."

When everyone stood up the table and chairs disappeared and in its place stood Eudora's fountain. They saw pictures of Todd and his brother Keir. Todd was not really his name - it was Raynor - his parents' names were Bronwyn and Gideon. They were the D'Ary family who fled after their son had died in the war and were now part of the dark side. 'If the truth be known they probably always had been,' thought Alana. She was just glad she didn't do something stupid like marry into that family. She knew the tale her Father had told her. She would give her heart to the one *she* loved - no one else could make that choice for her.

Alana looked out of the corner of her eye to see what Sebastian was doing. He was watching the fountain at everything that was being shown to them so he didn't know she was watching him. Already when she thought about it she found she really couldn't blame him or Eudora. They didn't lie to her, but they didn't tell her the whole truth. In a way she understood why. Eudora knew her well enough to know that she would have been on the defensive and self-conscious around him knowing him to be a prince. She wouldn't have been up to par, but thinking he was just a warrior made it easier to handle. 'Oh my god! Sebastian a real live prince.' She didn't know if she could get over it now. 'Pull yourself together,' she thought. She needed to be at her best so she returned her attention back to the conversation that was taking place.

"I think we need to figure out what they will try next," said the King. Alana actually liked the King and Queen. She felt understanding from the Queen but the King was more guarded. Even though he showed a calm exterior she could tell there was power underneath.

"If I were them I would try and get Alana by herself where she was not protected by any of us," said Sebastian who then looked at her. "What do you think they would do? You do know them better." Sebastian was actually asking for *her* advice. She had to think about that.

"Sebastian is right, even though I hate to admit it." This made him grunt and the King chuckled.

"So tell me Alana, what you would do in a situation if they were to somehow get to you?" She wasn't expecting that question but before she could say anything Sebastian growled low in his throat. "That will never happen. I will not allow it - ever!"

Alana wasn't expecting that response either. He took the role of protector very seriously. All went silent in the room and all looked from her to Sebastian. He stood there in his warrior stance challenging anyone to disagree.

"Very commendable Sebastian, but sometimes things don't always go the way you want them to son." Artemis had been watching his son's face and he knew he would give up everything to protect

Alana, even his life. He might think he was just doing his duty but it was much more than that. Sebastian just hadn't realized it yet. He took after him - very stubborn.

"Thank you for coming to my rescue Sebastian but you and Eudora have taught me well." She looked at the King. "To answer your question, I would try and find their weakness and use that to my advantage and if that didn't work I guess I could always distract them and just walk out unnoticed."

Eudora looked at her and then at the King. He was watching Alana closely. "Tell me Alana, how would you do that?"

Alan knew he was just appeasing her. She could tell by the look on his face and everyone else's that they didn't believe she could do anything. That made her mad but she saw the confidence in Eudora's eyes. At least one person believed in her. But when she looked at Sebastian, to her amazement he too looked like he believed in her. He nodded to her. On that cue from Sebastian she bowed then disappeared. She was watching everyone closely.

Eudora was shocked but proud, the King and Queen stood with their mouths half open, Zephyr put her hands together and clapped and Sebastian stood there and observed the reactions of the others. Even though he didn't show it, she knew he was proud of her too.

"Bravo! Bravo!" said Zephyr who was still clapping.

Alana suspected that Zephyr was not all that surprised. Like she already knew of her newly found skills. Suddenly everyone in the room, except Sebastian, was clapping. Tears were shining in Eudora's eyes, the Kings were sparkling with amusement and the Queen still looked a little surprised.

Alana was laughing when she reappeared. "God, if you guys could have seen your faces. It was priceless!" she said wiping the tears from her eyes. "So Your Majesty how was that for a first?" She was still smiling when she bowed again to the King.

"Very well done. I have to admit I wasn't expecting that. You *have* learned a lot in such a short time," and he bowed right back at her. Alana felt wonderful. She felt alive for the first time in a long time. Zephyr placed her arm through Alana's. "I think it's time for us to have that cup of tea and talk." she looked over to the King at his nod Zephyr bowed and lead Alana out of the room.

34

Alana couldn't guess why Zephyr wanted to talk to her privately.
They had left the King's study and were walking down the long
corridor. She was glad but also curious as to why this woman
would want to talk to her. She decided not to question it.
There were portraits along both walls. Some were very old,
probably ancestors and somewhere more recent. In the older ones
the men looked terrifying. She wouldn't have wanted to go up
against any of them. In almost all the pictures she recognized a
dragon symbol. Some larger and some very small, but it was there.
Eventually she came to the one she was looking for. It was the one
of Sebastian that she had glimpsed on the way in. She stopped to
study it. He looked strong and brave, standing in a meadow of
some sort with his sword strapped to his back, only the handle
showing, but she found the shield in his hands very curious. It was
silver just like her own and almost identical in shape to hers, but
that is where the similarities ended. Alana was on her tiptoes
looking at the symbol in the middle of his shield. It was of a
dragon, but for some reason this dragon looked familiar, like she
had seen it somewhere before. Getting even closer she studied the
dragon; its wings were spread wide in a flying position, its neck
was arched back and its eyes were dark, almost piercing into hers.
The detail of the portrait was mesmerizing. Now she understood
where he got the name 'Dark Dragon.' Because everything about
this dragon was dark. Black against a silver background. She
shivered slightly, but couldn't look away. Straining, she tried to get
closer forgetting everything else around her. She couldn't shake
the feeling that she had seen the dragon somewhere. She knew it
was silly. Swallowing hard she started to turn and as she did a
glimpse of gold appeared but was gone just as quickly. She gasped
and focused again on the portrait, shaking her head fast. She turned
to Zephyr and smiled. It had to be just her imagination playing
tricks on her but she could've sworn that right where the dragon's
heart would be was a golden heart. But just for a fleeting moment.
Zephyr watched Alana closely. She sensed that Alana had felt
something when she looked at Sebastian's portrait so she also
studied it. The portrait was one of the latest ones that had been
done of Sebastian which had been several years ago. Nothing

looked out of place. She wondered what Alana had seen. So she watched Alana's face. She had noticed curiosity at first but now she could see a hint of recognition then surprise.

"Alana is everything all right? You looked a little strange for a minute."

Zephyr waited while Alana looked back at the portrait again. This time she kept her feelings well hidden. Satisfied, she looped her arm through Zephyr's.

"It was nothing. Just a touch of *déjà vu.*"

Zephyr noticed the shiver that ran through Alana and decided not to press her. "Quite a magnificent beast do you not agree?" she said indicating the portrait.

"If you like that sort of thing I guess. Anyway what is with all the dragons?" Zephyr just laughed and ushered Alana further down the hall. She *was* going to take her to the gardens - one of her favorite places - but maybe the library would be a better place for Alana to ask her questions and maybe answer a few.

"We shall talk in the library. I have always loved the smell of old books." Alana noticed the way Zephyr had avoided her question but she would get some answers before the day was over. There were things she needed to know about. Sneaking a glance in Zephyr's direction she knew this was the woman who would answer some of her questions. She was certain that before the day was over she would know a lot more about Sebastian and her destiny.

35

Sebastian had watched as Zephyr took Alana out of the room. He was grateful for it and cursed because Zephyr was blunt in speaking. She would probably tell Alana things she didn't need to know, at least not right now, but he needed to talk to his father and Eudora alone. He knew there had been something about Todd he didn't like. Now he knew what that was. Todd wanted to hurt Alana and that was something he would not allow him to do, so turning his attention back to his father and Eudora he asked, "So father, what do you think we should do about the D'Ary family?" Artemis knew that Sebastian didn't like the idea of Alana going off with Zephyr, but some things couldn't be helped. "For now, I think we should wait and watch and make sure Alana is always protected. They will make a move soon and that is when we will be ready." Sebastian snorted, "You're forgetting father that Alana's birthday is only a few days away. I don't think we should underestimate them. They will try something and soon."

He looked over at Eudora. "I think we should make sure the house is well protected, maybe by a stronger spell. If I was in their position I would try and grab her before her birthday. Before all her powers transferred to her." Eudora and the king both nodded. "I don't think she should leave the house for any reason. This way we both can protect her. I know she will be spitting mad, but she must realize it will be for her own good."

Artemis laughed, "I think my son, *you* just don't want her to put you on your backside. I must admit it was an entertaining event." When Sebastian glared at his father Eudora laughed too.

"Artemis you must know this is not the first time Alana has bested him. Hasn't it happened two other times Sebastian dear?" Sebastian growled in response and Eudora chuckled again. The King and Queen who had been silent until now both laughed.

"Sebastian honey, please do tell. I do love a good story, especially when it involves my son getting tossed around by a girl."

Sebastian looked at his mother. She had an amused twinkle in her eyes. Sebastian rubbed the back of his neck and again glared at Eudora for opening her mouth but she stared back at him with an innocent smile. He sighed. What the hell he thought. All they had to do was ask Alana and he was sure she would fill them in.

36

Zephyr and Alana had just sat down when they heard the roar of someone laughing and Alana jumped. "I think Sebastian and his father are catching up."

It sounded like they were having a good time. Alana wondered what they were talking about when another peel of laughter came from down the hall, but this time it was feminine. When Zephyr clapped her hands in front of her Alana focused back on where she was.

"Now I think it is time for some tea." Zephyr spoke some soft words that Alana had never heard before, but when she heard a sound outside the library door she turned to see a servant bringing in a tray with a steaming pot of tea and something else that smelled delicious. The servant placed the tray down and Zephyr waved her away dismissively.

"Shall I pour? Would you like some cake too? Our cook is one of the best. Cream? Sugar?"

When they were both settled with their tea and cake she decided to answer one of her earlier questions. She knew how this worked - give and take. She smiled again at Alana.

"Now that we have some tea and cake it's time to answer your earlier question. You asked me about all the dragons, right? Sebastian's last name Drakon is very old. It goes back centuries and means dragon, so that is why you will always see the symbol of a dragon. It's more or less their coat of arms."

Alana took all of it in. What she didn't understand was why that dragon on Sebastian's shield looked so familiar. She knew she wasn't crazy. She had definitely seen that dragon before. She just didn't know where yet.

Zephyr waited for Alana to take in all of what she had told her. She knew that she had recognized Sebastian's dragon. Zephyr found that interesting. After taking a sip of her tea she set the cup down and looked again at Alana.

"Now will you answer a question for me?" She already knew the answer but she was testing Alana's truthfulness.

"Of course. What would you like to know?"

'So trusting,' thought Zephyr before she spoke. "I noticed the way you looked at the picture of Sebastian in the foyer and for a minute it looked like you might have recognized something in it. Back then you said to me it was a touch of *déjà vu.* I was wondering what you mean by that?" She watched as Alana swallowed hard before picking up her drink.

"I don't really know what it was. It was just like I had seen…I don't know if it was the portrait I'd seen before or if it was the dragon. It's all really crazy to me, but for some reason, that dragon on Sebastian's shield looked so familiar that it made me pause for a second." She paused while taking a sip of her drink. "I know it sounds weird to you because it sounds the same to me."

Zephyr was happy that she didn't lie. It would have been harder to talk if she had to pull every piece of information out of her. "Maybe you have seen it before, perhaps in your dreams. You do dream do you not Alana?"

Alana looked closely at Zephyr. "I don't know, maybe, but why would I dream about Sebastian's shield. It's not like dragons really exist," she snorted and took another bite of cake. Zephyr wanted to laugh but decided better of it.

Alana wondered why she was asking her so many questions. She wanted to learn more from Zephyr but it seemed like she was giving more answers than she was getting.

"Now do you mind if I ask you a couple of questions".

Zephyr appeared more guarded but she smiled in answer. "Of course. What would you like to know?"

Alana thought about it for a minute. "How long have Sebastian's family been in power?"

"That one is simple; there has always been a Drakon to sit on the throne and when it is time for the King to step down his son Sebastian will rule. Of course centuries ago there were no rulers and everyone lived in peace but that ended some time ago."

Alana knew she was leaving a lot out but maybe later she would finally get the whole truth.

"Do you know what happened two hundred years ago when Lucian and Drake became enemies?"

Zephyr paused before answering. "Alana, not many really know what happened. You have to remember it has been over two hundred years. If you really want to know, why don't you cast a spell and ask your ancestors?"

Alana took a deep breath. "Do you really mean I could just step back in time and find out?"

"No I don't mean that, but you could ask when you are dreaming and since they are your ancestors they will come to you in your dreams. You just have to know what potion to conjure and what spell to say before you take the potion. I'm sure Eudora would have explained all of this to you."

Alana concentrated, trying to remember. "I don't remember a spell to do anything like this. What would I have to do?"

Zephyr picked up her cup and waited to answer Alana. She wanted to get a better read from her before she sent her down this path. She needed to know that she would be ready to take it.

"The spell has to come from you, but you will need a few herbs to mix together. It will be like tea but it will not taste as good. Are you sure you want to find out?"

When Alana nodded eagerly she was convinced that she was strong enough to find out the truth.

"You will need to write a spell that will send you to the past in your dreams. You will have to think about the person you want to see, but let me warn you sometimes the passing can be difficult. You must drink the tea and say the spell over and over again. You will become sleepy. Your body will remain where you lie but your mind and spirit will be in the past." Alana listened intently. "Now to get back, you will have to write another spell that will bring you back to the present time. Do you think you can do that?"

Alana nodded again. "But I don't know if I can get the herbs I will need. It's not like we have them growing in my world." "Not to worry I will have them for you before you leave."

Alana was so grateful to Zephyr. She had never dreamt that she could actually go back in time. She wondered why Eudora had never told her about this. "Can I ask you another question? Is it safe for me to go to the past?" She thought maybe that was why Eudora had never told her.

"Of course. I would not send you in harm's way. Your destiny has already been chosen for you and I would not interfere with that. This would just be a history lesson on your family tree."

Alana accepted this. She felt that Zephyr would not let anything bad happen to her. The King and everyone else thought highly of her and she had been with them for many years. She trusted her.

"Now how about you tell me a little about Sebastian?
Zephyr laughed. "Where should I start? Sebastian even as a boy was very serious about his duties, but don't let that fool you Alana. Underneath that hard exterior he has a gentle soul." Alana laughed at that idea. "You think I am joking but I do know Sebastian well. He doesn't show that side to anyone but trust me, it is there. He is the most loyal of men and the most trustworthy."

Alana had to take her word for it for she had never seen that side of Sebastian, but even Eudora speaks highly of him so he can't be all that bad. She just wished maybe he could show her a little of what everyone else speaks about. Until then she would keep her opinions to herself. "Now I think it's time for me to take you back to the others, but before you leave I will give you a potion that will help you reach the past and maybe that will help you with your future." Alana hoped she was right. She needed to understand the past to maybe help her fight in the future.

37

Sebastian was wondering what was taking Zephyr and Alana so long. They had been gone a while now but when he heard the door open and saw Zephyr enter he took a breath. Alana entered wearing one of her mysterious smiles. This had Sebastian frowning. He wondered what they had talked about.

Zephyr bowed. "I have brought Alana back to you. We had a nice chat and a cup of tea."

The King summoned Alana forward. "That is nice. I hope you and my son can stay for dinner. We have a marvelous cook. I'm sure once she found out that Sebastian was here she started preparing some of his favorites. She always did spoil him."

Alana smiled toward the King. Looking at Sebastian, she noticed he had a slight frown on his face. She wondered what he was thinking, but of course he had his walls up and she couldn't sense anything from him.

"I think that would be wonderful, if your son has no problem with that?" She looked directly at Sebastian with a challenge on her face.

He grunted. She snickered and bowed at the King and Queen. "I will take that as a *yes*." She arched her brow and waited.

"I have no objections." Again Alana smiled sweetly.

"Good then that is settled." The King had watched the play between his son and Alana. He turned to Eudora; "Of course you will stay too Eudora?"

When she bowed her head he laughed. "Splendid!" When he stood up his wife was right beside him.

"Perhaps Sebastian, you could show Alana our beautiful gardens." When Sebastian just shrugged his shoulders Alana spoke up. "That will not be necessary your Majesty. I'm sure Sebastian has people he would like to see. Maybe Eudora could show them to me."

"Very well. Until dinner then." The King and his lady wife left the room leaving Sebastian, Eudora and Alana alone. Eudora looked from Sebastian to Alana then stood.

"Come with me dear. The gardens here are breathtaking. I have not seen any to top them."

When she reached the door Alana looked back at Sebastian. He didn't even look their way, so she followed Eudora out a side door that would take them to the garden.

"I hope your time with Zephyr was productive." Alana walked with Eudora and smiled. "I like her. She seems to know a lot about the kingdom." Eudora was hoping Alana would say more, but she fell silent and kept walking. "Alana dear, I hope you will allow me to explain why I kept the fact that Sebastian was a prince from you. The blame should fall with me. You see Sebastian likes to be known simply as Sebastian, so in truth he didn't lie to you. It was me. I wanted you both to be on the same level. I know now that it was wrong, I should have told you."

Eudora waited for Alana to say something but she kept walking. Eudora sighed while she kept pace with her. She knew Alana was still angry and she didn't blame her. If she was put in the same situation she would probably feel betrayed too. Perhaps as time passed she would forgive her, but for now Eudora didn't know when that would be.

Alana had listened to everything Eudora said to her. She knew she felt bad. She could hear it in her voice. She just needed to put herself in Eudora's position. Would she have said anything? She really didn't know. Maybe she would have, but then maybe not. If what Eudora said was true, would she have looked at Sebastian differently? Probably. She knew she wouldn't have tested him knowing he would soon be King of his world. 'Wow!' thought Alana as the realization sunk in. Sebastian was in line for the throne. Maybe it was for the best. She didn't know. In the beginning she would have probably handled the situation totally differently. She *would* have felt inferior to him, so in all honesty she would have always felt like she didn't measure up, so to speak. When she glanced sideways at Eudora she could tell she was very concerned so Alana stopped walking and faced her. She could see the question on Eudora's face so she took her hand and squeezed it and smiled.

"Eudora I have had some time to think about why you did it, and I do understand. You probably helped me out. I think if I had known that he was royalty I would have been so self-conscious I probably wouldn't have learned anything. I would have been too worried that I was doing something wrong."

"I wanted you to feel sure of yourself and to be able to learn everything you needed to. Perhaps I handled it wrong, but I did have your best interest at heart."

Alana chuckled. "I know you did. That is why I can't hold it against you. Now let us continue. I can't wait to see these gardens!"

Eudora sighed in relief and continued on to the gardens. She was glad Alana was able to think it all through clearly. Anyone else may not have understood, but Alana was different. She was smart enough to know it was not done intentionally. Now she only needed to find out if Alana was still mad at Sebastian. It really wasn't his fault. He *did* prefer to only be known by his first name. Once they reached the gardens Eudora would find out if she was still mad at Sebastian or not. But for now it was nice to know that *they* were still on speaking terms. Eudora looked around. She always loved this place. It was so serene and peaceful, and she did have a surprise for Alana at the far end of the gardens. There was a place that she knew Alana would be excited to see since she did look at it every night in her globe.

38

Sebastian watched through the window as Eudora and Alana walked down the path to the gardens. They stopped once and he watched as Alana smiled to Eudora and took her hand. He was happy to see that she was not mad at Eudora anymore. Eudora might not always think about her actions, but the intention behind them was from the heart.

"I wonder what you find so interesting to stare at for so long?" Sebastian was so intent on his own thoughts he never heard her enter the room. "What do you want now Zephyr? I thought you had left." He turned to look at her. She was smiling. That unnerved him because she was always smiling that knowing smile.

She bowed toward him. "She is lovely, yes?"

Sebastian just shrugged making Zephyr laugh. "Come now Sebastian. You're not that immune. Even though you would like people to think you are. Let me ask you something Sebastian. Do you dream?"

Sebastian just stared at her. He didn't know what she was trying to get at and he didn't know if he really wanted to know.

"It's a simple question Sebastian, do you dream?" She waited. She knew she was making him angry. She could tell by the flare of his nostrils and the narrowing of his eyes, but still she waited silently and watched him. She knew that he didn't know what to think of her. They had never really spoken much.

"I don't know why it should be of any importance to you if I dream or not and I don't think it is any of your business."

She knew he was getting angrier by the battle stance he had taken and the way he crossed his arms in front of his chest.

"Since you will not tell me, perhaps I should tell *you* what *I* have seen." She watched him raise an eyebrow but other than that he never moved.

"I have seen a mighty dragon and this mighty dragon has lots of secrets." She stopped to see what this information would do to him. He never moved but she had seen the slight stiffening of his shoulders. Again she smiled and continued. "This mighty dragon protects a precious treasure and in the end he will play a major role in what will come. He just doesn't know that yet. But soon he will." She bowed again and started to leave. "Wait! How do you know all of this?" She looked over her shoulder at him and for the first time since Sebastian had known her, her face was serious.

"Remember Sebastian I have the gift of sight passed down to me from my own mother. What I see shall come to pass." Again she bowed and disappeared. Sebastian didn't know what to think from their meeting. He didn't want to admit it to her, but he had been dreaming a lot lately and they had been more vivid over the last couple of days. He knew he was the dragon but that is all he understood of the dream. There was a little girl he didn't know who had smiled up at him so trustingly and she had presented him with a gift right before she vanished. That gift was a golden heart. He wondered if it had anything to do with what was happening now, or could it have something to do with Alana? Again he looked toward the window. They were too far away for him to see but he knew they were out there. He needed to get some answers and he knew the only person who could help was Eudora. He had to look into her fountain and soon. Sighing, he decided a trip around the gardens might clear his head and he hoped to see Eudora. He knew he could trust her, but he just hated to bare his soul to anyone.

39

The garden was spectacular. More than Alana expected. There were trees and flowers she had never even seen before. Maybe they were just known here, but it didn't matter to her. Everything was so beautiful and the smells were amazing. If she could bottle this up she would call it *Heaven.* Her little getaway at home was nothing like this. She had thought *that* was heaven, but after seeing this place there was no comparison. She didn't know how long they had been gone but it seemed like quite a while.

"This is so beautiful. I'm glad you showed me this but do you think we should be getting back?"

They had been walking quietly, neither bothering with words. The view was too beautiful to spoil with words. "We will leave soon. I have one more place that I want to show you." Eudora turned on the path and Alana followed. All she could see was a big wall of ivy in front of them. She followed until they came up to the ivy. Alana lifted a brow at Eudora who only chuckled.

"I have saved the best for last. Come. Close your eyes and take my hand." Alana put her hand in Eudora's and closed her eyes. She thought she heard the creak of metal. She wanted to peek but avoided the temptation. This must be important to Eudora if she wanted her to close her eyes. She actually looked like a kid about to enter a candy store. Her face was bright and rosy and there was a twinkle in her eyes. She had never seen Eudora look so excited before. There was that creaking sound again. She wondered what Eudora was doing.

"You can open your eyes now Alana." Alana didn't know what to expect when she opened her eyes but it wasn't the sight that greeted her.

"Oh my!" she said as her eyes grew wider. She could feel tears in her eyes and didn't understand why. This place was exactly the same as the one in her globe that Eudora had given to her. She stepped forward and looked all around her. Everything was the same. The trees swayed back and forth as a light breeze blew, the flowers twirled and danced as they floated to the ground where the grass was lush and the deepest of green. Small petals landed here and there making the light pink and white stand out against the green. Butterflies flew slowly around and the birds were singing a soft song. Off to the right she heard the bubble of the stream as it emptied out into the pool at the bottom of the waterfall. Walking closer she could see that the water was crystal clear. It was more beautiful than even Alana could imagine. It looked like something out of a fairytale or maybe something where fairies - if they were real - would live. She turned in a full circle with her arms stretched out wide then she closed her eyes and listened to the sounds. She was wrong before. *This* was heaven. What she had seen so far was close, but in this place she felt like anything was possible. All her emotions came to the surface at once. One tear rolled down her face then another one. She couldn't seem to stop them. Then she started to laugh. Eudora didn't know what to think as she watched Alana. She seemed so happy her whole body was glowing. At first it was a slight color now it was so bright Eudora had to squint to look at her, almost like she was looking at the sun. She was all golden with tears streaming down her face. She was laughing and crying at the same time. Eudora could feel all of Alana's emotions as she spun around in a circle. Even the birds and butterflies seemed to be watching her. Alana took a deep breath and let it out and she opened her eyes and looked right at Eudora. She had the smile still in place, but her eyes where bright almost silver in color. There were no more tears. She wiped what remained on her cheeks with both her hands. She stepped over to Eudora, laughed softly again and gave her a huge hug. Eudora was not one to be overcome with emotions, but right then she wanted to weep. But she held it together and hugged her back. She sniffed once then twice and pulled away. Alana had to laugh again. She knew she had gotten to Eudora and she also knew not many people could do that. This made her even happier.

"Thank you for showing me this place and for giving me that globe. I would have never known a place like this existed if you hadn't shown me." When she looked at Eudora her face was more serious now. "I also want to thank you for showing me how it *would* look in your fountain. At the time I thought it was cruel, now I know better. I vow to you today Eudora that I will do everything in my power to preserve this beauty. I promise you- nothing will ever take this beauty away! I will make sure of it" She didn't care how powerful the others were. She would win.

40

Sebastian had come to look for Eudora and Alana when he saw the
gate opened to Tranquility. He knew Eudora had taken her there.
He decided to go in unnoticed. When he entered, Alana was
spinning around in a circle with a smile on her face and her eyes
closed. Then she started laughing. The blossoms were falling all
around her and some had even landed in her hair, but when he
looked closer he saw that tears were also streaming down her face.
When he tapped into her feelings he was less alarmed. She was
happy. This didn't make any sense to him. She was smiling and
laughing and crying. He shook his head. Women! He didn't think
he would ever understand them. He saw how bright her aura was
and becoming brighter. A golden glow almost as bright as the sun
surrounded her. This surprised him. Even his father's aura was not
this bright. He tucked that information away to ask Eudora later.
She stopped suddenly, wiped her face and looked at Eudora. She
had a determined look about her. He listened as she spoke to
Eudora. There was confidence in her voice. Something he had not
heard before. This again surprised him. 'Had she finally found the
key?' thought Sebastian. He watched the surprise cross Eudora's
face too. He watched as Eudora led Alana out. He waited before he
too left. He looked around again. Could this place have helped
Alana find herself - to find her own strength and courage? To help
her believe? He didn't know, but he would find out soon. He
needed to talk to Eudora now more than ever. Before he
disappeared he surveyed the area again and shook his head. Then
he disappeared.
Sebastian appeared back in his father's study. He summoned both
his mother and father to him. When they arrived they looked
worried. "Is there something wrong my son?" asked his mother.
The king just watched him closely.
"No mother. I would like you to give Alana a tour of the house
while I talk to Eudora. Do you think you can do this for me?" His
mother, somewhat relieved agreed to help even though she was
puzzled by his request.
"You will find Eudora and Alana on the path coming from the
gardens."
His mother nodded and she disappeared in search of Alana.

"Why are you in such a hurry to talk to Eudora? Has something happened?" asked his father. Sebastian rubbed the back of his neck.

"Nothing has happened or at least I don't know. I know Alana is a special case but have you ever known of anyone's aura being so bright it almost blinds you?" Sebastian watched his father as he thought it over. "Everyone's aura is different. Some glow brighter than others. Why do you ask?" Artemis watched him intently.

"I know what I am about to say may surprise you but Alana and Eudora went to Tranquility and I watched unnoticed. I saw Alana's aura glow so bright it was almost like I was looking at the sun. No disrespect father but it was even brighter than your own."

This did surprise Artemis but he didn't let it show. "You have to remember where they were. That place has its own powers. Maybe her aura was enhanced just by being there. Artemis would have to check into this to find out everything he could.

"Maybe you're right," said Sebastian as he took a deep breath. "Father, will you excuse me? I need to talk with Eudora."

His father briefly nodded and left. Sebastian summoned Eudora. He prowled the study as he waited for her. He knew his father wasn't telling him everything but before he could think more on it, Eudora arrived. He could see the question in her eyes.

"We need to talk. I think your library would be a good place." Eudora just nodded and held her hand out and in an instant they were in her library.

"What is the matter Sebastian? You are not acting like yourself." Sebastian walked back and forth in front of her fireplace.

"I was there in Tranquility when you and Alana were there." He knew she was not happy about this. "I also saw her aura glow brighter than I have ever seen anyone's. I know that you saw it too."

Eudora stood in front of him. "I saw it and yes, I was a little surprised by it." She watched Sebastian closely. Something wasn't right with him. He seemed edgy and that was not like him at all. He was usually in control. "What is bothering you Sebastian? You don't look like your usual self." She heard him grunt before he rubbed the back of his neck.

"I wanted to talk to you before I saw Alana. I spoke with Zephyr and she asked me a lot of questions that I didn't have the answers to."

Eudora held her hands together in front of her and Sebastian knew that she only did that when she was nervous or unsettled. "What sort of questions did she ask you?"

Sebastian could tell Eudora knew something. "She asked about my dreams. Do you know why she would ask me this?" He watched the puzzled look come over her face.

"I don't *know* why she would ask you this. Did she explain it to you?" He could tell she wasn't hiding anything from him about Zephyr, but he knew she was hiding *something*.

"She talked about a mighty dragon. Something about secrets and protecting his treasure. Does that make any sense to you?" "How did she say she knew this exactly?"

Again he watched as Eudora wrung her hands. "She said she knew from her gift of sight. She also said the dragon would play a major role in what will come. That it *shall* come to pass, whatever that means." He heard Eudora's slight intake of breath. He narrowed his eyes and looked again at her. "You know something about this don't you?"

"What I know is not important. Are you having dreams Sebastian?"

Again Sebastian paced back and forth in front of Eudora. Whatever it was, it was bothering Sebastian. She had never seen him like this. He was always so sure and cocky. They were two of the things she had always liked about him. Now he paced around like a caged animal trying to find a way to escape.

Sebastian knew he was going to have to tell Eudora if he wanted to find answers. He just didn't like it. Finally with the decision made he turned back to Eudora and stopped pacing.

"I have had several dreams if you must know. At first I was a dragon searching through the sky. This dream came for several nights. Then I would land and wait. That dream lasted again for several nights. Then in my dreams, when I land there is a little girl with a big smile on her face like she knows who I am, even in my dragon form. I would wake when I saw her. Now though, when I dream, she holds out her hand and in it lies a golden heart. When she hands it to me she always vanishes. This dream keeps going on and on. I don't know what to think anymore. I don't know what it all means but for some reason Zephyr thinks this has something to do with the here and now. What do you think?" He had been so intent on telling his story that he never looked at Eudora once until he had finished. Her face was like stone, her eyes were huge and her face was pale.

Right from the beginning of the story, Eudora knew it had something to do with the prophecy. She was surprised that Sebastian was having dreams. That part shocked her. She didn't understand any of this and obviously Sebastian didn't either. The time had come to tell him the second part of the prophecy. There was a reason he was getting these images. It was *his* destiny after all.

"What is it? You know something Eudora. I think I have a right to know since it involves me, don't you think?" Eudora winced at his raised voice.

"I didn't mean to yell at you, I just want to know what all of this means and how Zephyr knew about it." He sighed and looked back at Eudora. By now her features where more controlled.

"Do you remember long ago the old woman who lived in the cottage at the edge of the woods? Her name was Magimus?" He shook his head. "You probably don't remember her. You were very young at the time. She dressed like a gypsy. Some said her powers were very great." She watched again for any sign of recognition from Sebastian but he had a faraway look on his face. "I remember when I was younger I had gotten too close to the woods and I saw a woman who was dancing. She had on a skirt made of different fabrics and her shirt was a bright blue. Her hair, almost white, hung half way down her back. She was humming and laughing as she twirled around. I didn't think she had seen me but then she laughed and asked what a prince was doing so close to the forest. She warned me not to go in there, that there were things in the woods that could do me harm." Sebastian paused. "I remember being curious. She had a gentle face. It started to rain so I turned to leave and get back home but she waved me forward. Told me she would make me a nice cup of cocoa. I didn't see any harm in that so I went inside. She stirred the fires and made me probably one of the best cups of cocoa I have ever had." Eudora watched as Sebastian took a deep breath and rubbed the back of his neck. "As we sat at her small table she had asked me if I wanted to know a secret. I remember leaning forward and nodding my head eagerly. She laughed - almost a cackle - and she told me that one day the prophecy would come true and I would play an important role in it. At the time I thought it was because I was the prince and would be king one day. She told me not to tell anyone about our little talk. It was a secret between the two of us." Sebastian was surprised that Eudora didn't butt in the whole time he was telling his story. She was not one known for patience. "That is the same woman you are talking about right?"

Eudora nodded her head as she waved her hand for her fountain. "I think you should see the second half of the prophecy." She knew Sebastian was going to ask more questions. "I will answer all of your questions once you have seen what Magimus sent to me through the magic of my fountain. I don't know how she did it, but like I said, she had many powers. One was for seeing the future." At her command the second part of the prophecy that she had showed the king played out in the water. Eudora watched Sebastian closely. He was surprised to see his dreams come to life in her waters. When the vision finally cleared all was quiet. Sebastian turned from the fountain and walked a few paces.

"When did you receive this message?" She heard the calmness in his voice, but she was not stupid. She knew he was anything but calm.

"I received this right before she passed. That was years ago. I didn't understand what it meant back then so I left it alone until recently."

Sebastian started to pace again. "I don't fully understand what this could mean. What? Am I supposed to save some child?" he growled and ran his fingers through his hair. Like his father he wasn't looking at the whole picture. It had taken her a while to figure it out too.

"Do you still not know who that little girl is?" she asked softly and watched the bewilderment fill his face. She motioned him forward and placed her fingers in the water. As she ran them through the surface, pictures started to form and one after another they appeared and floated away. Sebastian watched as the little girl from his dreams appeared and then vanished just like in his dreams.

He pointed at the waters and looked back at Eudora. "That is the little girl from my dreams." Sebastian's forehead creased while he concentrated on the pictures. "Tell me who it is!" he almost shouted the words.

"Keep looking. Soon you will recognize who it is."

Sebastian didn't like having to wait but soon he would figure it out as the pictures started looking more and more like her.

"Oh My God! It can't be! Why did I not recognize this sooner?" She knew he wasn't really talking to her so she ran her fingers through the water again and the last picture vanished. She waited for him to work this all out in his head. For once he didn't have her blocked and she could actually feel all of his emotions. This was something new to her. She had never been able to catch Sebastian with his wall down. She concentrated on him while he tried to decipher everything he had heard and seen. She was surprised by what she could sense from him. He was trying hard to be the big bad wolf; he hated how he made Alana feel, he had remorse for making her hate him, because deep down inside of him where he never let anyone in *she* was there. Eudora felt his wall slide into place and shut her out but she had seen all she needed to. "I still don't understand what all of this means. We all know that Alana is the only one who can defeat the dark ones. Is it because I am helping her to accomplish all of this?" Eudora knew he was only talking out loud so she stood there quietly. She heard the low growl that came from his throat as he wiped his hands across his face than he looked at her. "Do you think I have a part to play in all of this?"

She knew what he was asking. She smiled at him reassuringly. "Honestly Sebastian, I don't know. I guess we will all find out in the end. I think there is a reason for everything that happens in life, even in our world." Eudora spoke softly. "One thing I do know - we had better get back. Everyone will be wondering where we have been. Dinner should be ready soon. Don't worry Sebastian. We will figure this all out." She opened her hand and placed it on top of his and before he could say anything else they were in the library where his mother and father were waiting with Alana. Sebastian was determined that he would find out what all of this meant one way or another. He looked back at Eudora and she knew that their conversation was not over.

41

Something was bothering Sebastian. Artemis could see that he was very distracted and noticed that he was looking at Alana differently. Even Eudora wasn't her cheerful self. He had to wonder just what those two had to talk about. Of course after his son and Alana left he would talk with Eudora and find out what exactly was going on, but for now they had a dinner to enjoy. Alana knew something wasn't right between Sebastian and Eudora. For one thing, neither spoke much. She watched as the queen looked from them to her husband with concern.

"Sebastian, have you been able to see many of your friends since we arrived?" She realized that he wasn't really listening when he shook his head.

The king laughingly announced in his booming voice; "I have taken the liberty of inviting a few of them to dinner. You will meet them there, Alana."

She looked from father to son. "I think that's wonderful. I can't wait to meet them."

As she spoke, three men came rushing into the room straight to Sebastian. She gasped and watched with fear rising in her chest. Sebastian was so deep in thought he didn't notice that one of them had his sword in hand and was aiming for his head. She watched as Sebastian turned his head right as the man in front of him swung his sword. She knew it was going to be too late for Sebastian to defend himself so she did the first thing that came to mind. Instinctively she thrust her hands out in front of her and shouted; "FREEZE!" All three men stopped in their tracks like they were rooted to the floor. She heard one say 'what the hell?' as another shouted words she didn't understand. She was sure she didn't even *want* to know what they meant, but the third one just stood there looking at her shocked. The king also stood and bent at the waist laughing so hard that his face was turning red. The queen also was laughing but somewhat more regally. She always tried to maintain some level of royal decorum. Alana looked from them to Sebastian. He was already on his feet looking puzzled as if he didn't know how they had gotten into the room. The only one who had enough sense to say anything was Eudora.

"Alana dear would you mind releasing Sebastian's friends and the king's guards?" Alana looked around the room. She felt like such an idiot. With a wave of her hand she released them.

"I am so sorry. I didn't know who you were. I just saw the sword and reacted." All three men looked at her warily. The king stopped laughing and looked at Alana.

"No need to apologize. You were just reacting naturally to these three brutes bursting through the door looking frightful. At least they didn't use their battle cry. That would have raised your hackles right enough." He chuckled again and looked at his best warriors.

"Do apologize to Alana for scaring her half to death. *We* might be used to your antics but Alana isn't." All three bowed to their king and queen, smiled at Sebastian and nodded to Eudora then they focused back on Alana. She tried a smile, hoping they would stop looking at her like she had just told them they would be going to bed without any dinner. They all surprised her as they bowed to her and gave her a lopsided grin.

"Please forgive us lady. We didn't know there was company in residence." Sebastian snorted "You're all lucky she didn't send you flying across the room, since that is one of her specialties."

Alana held her head high. "You should know since I have done it to you more than once." She crossed her arms in defiance.

The king slapped his hand on his leg. "She got you on that one my boy!" He laughed again. All three men wore the same expression of disbelief. She didn't care. As soon as she said it Sebastian had lost his cockiness. Served him right.

"I guess since my son is not going to give the introduction I will have to." The king got up and moved to the first man. She had noticed he was the tallest of the three and the biggest. They sure didn't make them like this at home.

"This one here is my second in command. His name is Kohn." Again Kohn bowed to Alana but still looked at her a little uneasily. The next man was just a couple of inches shorter.

"This is one of my lieutenants. His name is Rowan." He not only bowed but smiled. Alana smiled back.

"And last but not least is Warwick. He handles the training of the new lads and the horses." Warwick was just as beautiful as Sebastian and when he bowed and smiled with a wink she knew he

was probably the biggest flirt of the bunch. She smiled back.
All three men were handsome in their own way. Kohn was dark
like Sebastian except his eyes were a light blue but still just as
pretty as the rest, even with the long scar that ran the whole length
of his left cheek. It gave him character. The scar was faded and if
you didn't look too closely you could miss it. Rowan on the other
hand was all golden. His hair was almost the same shade as hers.
His eyes were amber with little flakes of gold. Warwick too was
dark with the same rich coloring. The only difference she could see
was his eyes. They were a deep green where Sebastian's were
almost black. They all had bodies that most men would dream of
having and most women too but in different ways. She almost
laughed at her own joke. If her friends could only see these three
they would flip! Trish would go for Kohn, Katie would go for
Rowan and Jess would definitely go for Warwick because they
both were nothing but big flirts.

Everyone sat down and conversation flowed. Every now and then
one of the three would look at Alana curiously they probably
wondered who she was and what she was doing there. She didn't
blame them after what she had done to them. When they heard a
loud boom Alana jumped, startled. Everyone stood. She did too.
She realized it must have been the dinner bell but it had sounded
more like a giant gong. As they all headed to the dining room
Zephyr met them in the foyer.

"Sorry I'm late. I was busy with some potions and lost track of
time." She looked at Alana with a knowing wink. Alana
understood perfectly.

"Come! You're just in time," said the king as the doors to the
dining room were opened.

"Alana, since you are the guest you will sit at my right and
Sebastian you can take the end so you can catch up with your
friends."

The table was smaller than she expected for a royal meal. The king
and queen sat side by side at the head of the table, she sat to the
right of the king and Eudora sat next to her. Zephyr was right
across from her. Kohn faced Eudora and Rowan and Warwick sat
across from each other with Sebastian sitting at the far end. As
everyone took their seats and got settled the king clapped his hands
and dinner commenced. There was plenty of conversation that

flowed easily and the food was delicious. She remembered another time at another dinner party where she couldn't remember what she had eaten let alone if it was good. 'Now this,' she thought as she looked around 'is what a dinner party is supposed to be like.' She wished her mother could have been there. She would have enjoyed it. As a matter of fact her three friends would have enjoyed it too - at least the company.

Before too long, dinner was over and it was time for them to return to their own world. She actually hated to leave. They were in the foyer as the king patted Sebastian on the back and his mother gave him a hug and a kiss. All his friends pushed and shoved him in good fun. He grunted and growled at them. Zephyr stepped forward and gave her a hug and took both her hands. She slipped a pouch into Alana's hand. Alana thanked her and gave her a hug back. The queen was just as nice, giving Alana a brief hug and a kiss on the cheek. The king smiled toward her and bowed. Alana smiled and bowed back again. He chuckled. She liked Sebastian's parents. His father seemed like he was always jolly and his mother was very kind. All three of his friends bowed toward her but didn't get any closer. They were still wary of her. It made her laugh to see three huge men treat her that way. Then Eudora nodded and in a flash she was gone. Sebastian stepped toward Alana and took her hand and just as before, she closed her eyes and felt like she was floating in the clouds and just as quickly she was back in her bedroom.

She looked at Sebastian. He never took her to her bedroom. He always dropped her off in the kitchen or living room. He just grunted and told her that her friends were downstairs and he didn't want to scare the daylights out of them by showing up right in front of them. He vanished. Not a 'good-bye see you tomorrow.' Nothing. She shook her head.

Before she went downstairs she put the herbs from Zephyr in a safe place. She could hear her friends in the kitchen with her mother and from the sounds of it, they were having a good time. She looked at the clock and was surprised that it wasn't much later than when she had left. It seemed like she had been gone all day but it had only been a couple of hours. She loved how this time travel worked. She could go to Sebastian's world and stay for hours and back in her own it would just seem like minutes. She planted a genuine smile on her face and entered the kitchen.

42

As Alana stood in the doorway she watched all her friends laughing at something her mother was saying. She watched them enjoying themselves for a while before stepping into the room. "I see how you guys are when I'm not around. You don't even miss me at all huh?" She leaned over Katie and took a chip and munched on it. Trish was the first to react.

"We decided to wait and entertain your mom until you got home. Where have you been anyway?"

How could she tell them she just had dinner in a castle that really doesn't exist, at least not in their world? And that there had been three very gorgeous guys to entertain her. She looked for some help from her mother who gave her a sheepish look and shrugged her shoulders. She wouldn't be getting any help from Mom.

As she tried to come up with a good explanation Eudora breezed in with a couple of shopping bags.

"Alana dear, you forgot these in the car." Alana smiled and took the bags. God bless Eudora to come to her rescue. It wasn't like she could tell her friends 'Oh by the way I'm sorry I have been so busy training as a witch and trying to save not only our world, but a world you don't even know about, from evil beings that are trying to destroy everything around them. And it just so happens to be Todd and his whole family that are the evil ones.' She knew they would laugh her off or think she was making a sick joke, when all the while every word would be true. She didn't know if they could handle it or if they would even understand and she hated not telling them anything. They knew her too well. They would know she was lying so she smiled at Eudora and grabbed the bags and placed them by the door. Eudora had come up with a perfect ploy - her friends knew she loved to shop. "Sorry girls, I didn't know you were coming over. Eudora and I went shopping." The three friends looked at her with a secret smile. "Could there be something in those bags for...let me think...someone's birthday coming up in just two days?" teased Jess who was never one to keep a secret or be modest about anything. She was the one after all who had told her about her surprise birthday party last year. Alana made a face and rolled her eyes. "No! Everyone knows I can't refuse a shopping day, so when Eudora asked me I said yes."

She shrugged her shoulders and sat down next to Katie. "So what brings all of you over without letting me know you were coming? If I had known I could have gone shopping another time." She watched as all three of her friends looked at each other. She could see that something was up.

This time it was Trish who spoke up. "We just thought we would take you out tomorrow night. Just us girls before your birthday." She noticed Jess and Katie nodding and smiling at her eagerly. Now what was she supposed to say? She couldn't just say no without a reason. Of course they would come over for her birthday but they had a tradition of usually getting together to celebrate birthdays on the actual day. She looked to Eudora and her mother hoping for some help. She hated having to lie.

Katie frowned. "Don't tell us you already have plans? You know we all usually get together on b-days. It's a tradition."

Alana knew that, so she smiled, hoping it didn't look forced and lied through her teeth. "Of course! You know I wouldn't miss it for the world." She looked again at Eudora with a helpless look on her face. She knew tomorrow night her friends would be disappointed but at least maybe they would still be here and safe and maybe one day they would forgive her. As she sat and listened to their plans her brain was thinking of other things, like maybe forgetting her birthday altogether this year, but she knew that wasn't possible so she had to suck it up and keep her composure until after all of this was over. She had to stay strong for everyone.

Eudora watched as the girls twittered amongst themselves about going out the following night. They were all in good spirits except for Alana. She could see the conflict on her face. She knew she would have to deceive her friends and not keep her word and that hurt her. Eudora could see this as they talked more and laughed about Alana getting old. Before long Alana's friends were getting up to leave telling her that they would see her tomorrow night and that she should get plenty of sleep because they were not going to bring her home until after the clock struck midnight. Alana flinched but the others didn't notice. They were too busy gathering their things to notice.

As soon as her friends left, Sebastian appeared. "I forbid you from going out with them tomorrow night. You will stay close so we can keep an eye on you."

Eudora just shook her head. Women were the same anywhere and they didn't like being told what they could and could not do. She already knew that Alana wasn't really going to go. She had seen it in her face. The way she downcast her eyes to hide the hurt that was there because she knew before the night was over she was going to disappoint her best friends and she couldn't even tell them why? Sebastian should know her better but he was looking at her with accusation instead of compassion, knowing she was going to do something very difficult for her. She didn't know how to explain to her friends. She watched as Alana narrowed her eyes at Sebastian and raised her chin. They both were too stubborn for their own good. And if they weren't careful it would be their downfall.

Alana knew she couldn't go, but she sure didn't need Sebastian telling her what to do. How arrogant of him to think he could tell her what she could and couldn't do. She was her own person and that was something he needed to learn and fast so she took several calming deep breaths before she spoke.

"I know my duty Sebastian. You don't have to tell me. I'm not a child." She was so hurt and angry she didn't know what else to say. Sebastian knew she was upset even though she was blocking her thoughts from him. He could still feel her pain and he knew it ran deep.

"Good I'm glad we understand each other. This is only for your own good," and just like that he was gone.

She wanted to stomp her feet and order him back but instead she actually growled low in her throat. How dare he question her honor? So far she had done everything she was supposed to do without question - even when she didn't understand.

Eudora knew the emotions that were going through her mind right now. She needed to talk to Sebastian. He didn't have to attack her like that. She knew what she had to do and she would do it. "Dear, why don't you go on up and take a hot bath? You deserve it."

Alana just shook her head and said "good night."

Eudora waited until she heard the bedroom door close and sighed and rubbed her forehead.

"Tell me something Eudora. Why does he treat her so badly? What has my daughter ever done to him? Anyone looking at the poor girl could tell this was hard for her."

"I have no idea, but I can assure you I will be finding out." She nodded and disappeared, leaving Lily in the kitchen by herself. She decided a nice glass of wine would be good after everything that had happened. Everyone had to pretend nothing was wrong and it was the hardest for Alana. She heard the water running and wanted to take everything off her daughter's shoulders. If *she* could take on the task she would and gladly. Reaching for a glass, she got a bottle of wine out of the cabinet. She didn't drink much, but every now and then it was helpful. She poured a glass and looked toward the ceiling. She heard the water turn off and knew Alana was probably sinking into a steaming tub. Perhaps at least for a little while she could leave her thoughts and troubles at the door, but knowing her daughter the way that she did, it wouldn't be easy. There was something going on with her and Sebastian. She had never seen anyone upset her the way that he did and she had never seen anyone *look* at her the way he did.

43

Eudora summoned Sebastian to her. In a blink he was there and by his stance, he was ready to do battle. Her lips twitched. If that was how he wanted to play, so be it.

"Do you think you could have been a little more understanding? She knew she couldn't go with her friends and she hated deceiving them." She was searching for some indication of feeling from Sebastian but again, no emotions were visible.

"Sometimes I don't understand you at all. She deserves an apology from you. I told her to take a nice hot bath but when she is through you need to apologize. You hurt her tonight." She had been watching him closely so she saw his jaw tighten at those words. So the tough warrior wasn't so tough after all.

Sebastian was well aware that he had made a mistake. When he had confronted Alana he watched the light leave her eyes and he hated that he was the cause. "I will talk with her but be warned; I stand by what I said."

Eudora didn't expect much so this was something. "Fine, but you need to let her know you don't think she's a failure. You might not believe this Sebastian, but I think your opinion matters to her. You can grumble and grunt all you want but she knows how everyone else feels. She is unsure about *you*!" "We will talk when she has finished."

Eudora gave a slight nod. That was probably the best she could hope for. Sebastian disappeared and the smile she had been trying hard to conceal came forward. Yes they would talk and if she knew Alana he would be getting an earful. She needed to get back to Artemis. He had wanted to talk to her when she got everything settled and she already knew what the conversation was going to be about. She still couldn't believe Sebastian dreaming of the prophecy - at least the second half. Their destiny was tied together. Soon they would both realize it but until then they would butt heads at every turn. She couldn't wait for the sparks to fly. With one final smile to herself she disappeared in search of the king.

44

Alana was glad Eudora had suggested a hot bath. She felt almost normal. At least if she didn't think about what had just occurred she did. She would get back at Sebastian. She was just getting out of the tub when her phone rang. She quickly wrapped a towel around her slim figure and peeked outside the bathroom door to make sure he wasn't waiting for her. The coast was clear. She grabbed the phone.

"Hello?" she said as she headed back into the bathroom. She didn't want him to show up with her sitting on the bed with her hair dripping wet and a towel wrapped around her.

"Did I catch you at a bad time?" She smiled and wondered why Katie was calling her so late.

"No I was just getting out of the tub, why what's up?" she listened but Katie didn't say anything. The hairs at the back of her neck stood at attention and goose bumps spread across her back. "Katie, are you all right?" Again there was silence. She knew she was still there, she could hear her breathing.

"Sorry Alana, I was looking at the sign above me. I know it's late but my car won't start. I have tried both Trish and Jess and I get no answer. Do you think you can come and get me?"

Alana took a deep breath. She had done this before for Jess. It was no big deal. One of her friends needed her and by the sound of Katie's voice she needed her right now. She sounded scared and a little unsure.

"Of course I'll come and get you. Just tell me where you are." Alana looked for a pen and piece of paper, but all she found was a tube of lipstick and some eyeliner. Suddenly she slapped her forehead. She could do better than that and in a blink she was holding some paper and a pen. "Ok I have something to write with, now tell me." When Katie gave her directions she wondered why Katie was on the other side of town but instead of asking, she told her to hang in there and she would be there soon. She hung up the phone. Now how to get out of the house without anyone finding out or questioning her? Any other time and she wouldn't but Katie was in trouble and she couldn't leave her friend alone in the dark no matter who was out there looking for her. Think Alana. She snapped her fingers and called for her spell book. There had to be

something in there to help. She almost dropped her book when she heard a knock on her door. "Alana, are you in there?"
She rolled her eyes. Duh! Where else would she be?
"I'll be out in a minute" she yelled back. Great! Now she would have to deal with Sebastian. She could use the invisible spell but then he would wonder what was taking her so long and probably break down the door and then he would only come after her. No she had to take him out of commission but how? She had to think and she needed to think fast. Katie needed her. If only he would give up talking to her tonight and just go to bed but she knew he wouldn't do that. He was like a dog looking for a bone. Perhaps she could help him fall asleep. She remembered Eudora talking about sleeping spells but if she tried it, would it work on him? She shrugged her shoulders it couldn't hurt to try and before he knew it she would be back without him even knowing she had been gone and then for once she would have one up on the almighty Sebastian. She couldn't wait to see his face when she told him. She had to block her mind or he would know what was going on. She had a lot of things to do. First she had to get dressed and unfortunately her clothes where in the bedroom, so she closed her eyes and concentrated on her favorite jeans, underwear, bra and a sweatshirt. When she opened her eyes she almost clapped her hands. Her clothes were right in front of her so she quickly got dressed. Now as she looked in the mirror she looked at her wet hair. Could she make it dry? She tilted her head and closed her eyes again and when she opened them her hair was dry. After brushing it she pulled it back in a ponytail. Now to make him think she was ready for bed. She rolled her pants up just a little and reached for her robe. When she had it in place and tied the belt she looked in the mirror. Yep, she looked as close to ready for bed as she could get. Now she had to come up with a spell and hope it worked. She sat on the toilet and picked up her spell book. Looking down at the blank page, she tapped the pen against her lip. What to say? She closed her eyes and wished the words forward. Cracking an eye, she looked down at the paper and it was still empty. She had to clear her mind and think of something short and sweet. She had to smile at that considering who she was talking about. She finally scribbled sown some well-chosen words. Could it really work? Was it that simple? Eudora had taught her that some

spells were simple and some took a long time. Maybe this would work after all and if it didn't she would just have to try something else. Taking a few deep breaths she waved her hand in front of her book and it disappeared. If this worked she would throw it up in his face every chance she got.

She made her face as blank as possible and opened the door. Sebastian was standing close by and he was watching her. She had to block all her thoughts. She concentrated.

Sebastian knew she would still be mad at him but he didn't think she would give him the silent treatment. He thought she would come out all fire and brimstone but there was nothing. He couldn't feel anything from her, he frowned. "I think you and I should talk about earlier."

Sebastian waited for her to acknowledge that he was even in the room. He watched her take a deep breath wondering already what she was up too. She wasn't acting anything like herself. Maybe he had hurt her more than even Eudora thought. She knew Sebastian was watching her closely. She had to take a deep breath to calm her trembling body than she had spoken. "Listen to these words, I speak, close your eyes and fall asleep."

Sebastian couldn't hear what she was saying, she was talking so low. He leaned in close to catch whatever she was saying. All he heard was 'fall asleep' before she faded from his vision.

She watched astonishment come over his face before his eyes rolled back in his head and he fell to the floor. She couldn't believe she had done that. She wanted to rejoice but she didn't know how much time she had before he woke so she grabbed a piece of paper and scribbled down a note telling him what she had to do. She picked up her shoes and left her bedroom. At the bottom of the stairs she listened. She heard soft music coming from the kitchen so she knew her mom was in there, probably waiting for her to come back down from her bath. She grabbed her purse and keys and tiptoed to the door. The door creaked slightly but the music was obviously loud enough to muffle the sound. She slipped out and sat down to put her shoes on. When she stood up she wanted to yell or laugh. She wanted to do something! She couldn't believe she had actually got away with it. She was smiling when she turned toward her car at the side of the house. It was dark. She had forgotten to turn on the light but the streetlight was just enough to see by. When she reached the car she was still so full of herself. She didn't hear the footsteps behind her until it was too late. Something was blown into her face and she immediately slumped forward.

"My my. That was easier than I thought it would be. But he said you would do anything for your friends - such loyalty." In a blink they both disappeared.

45

Eudora found Artemis waiting for her in his study. When she appeared he was standing by the fireplace. "I have been waiting a while for you Eudora. What has taken so long?"

Eudora snorted. Just like him to get right to the point. Just like his son, he had few words. "Sorry Artemis. When we got back, some of Alana's friends were there so I couldn't just leave. After they left I had to break up your son and Alana…" she heard him chuckle and continued. "I think maybe you should have a talk with him. He has gone too far." She folded her hands in front of her and waited.

Artemis raised an eyebrow. "What has my son done to warrant this behavior from you?"

She snorted again. "He didn't do anything to me but to Alana. He questioned her judgment and her integrity. He hurt her very badly. He acts like she doesn't know what is at stake and I really don't think *he* knows what's at stake for *her*." She decided she would let him chew on that for a minute before she spoke again. She watched as he stepped forward. When he took his seat he motioned for her to do likewise. "Why do you think he did this to her?"

Eudora just shook her head. "Honestly I don't know why. He has been very hard on her. I'm beginning to think he wants her to hate him. He never shows anything, but when I mentioned that he hurt her I thought I saw *some* remorse. I had a talk with him but I don't think it matters. I told him she feels like a failure in his eyes and that he should apologize and let her know that she is doing well."

Artemis was surprised and disappointed by his son's behavior. He was never cruel but from how Eudora described the situation it sounded like he had been. Perhaps she was right and he needed to have words with him.

"Did he apologize? Did he even talk with her?"

Eudora stood up. "When I left him he said he would talk with her but I doubt he will apologize. He said he stands by what he said. I don't know Artemis, maybe he will." She was pacing by this time.

"Can you tell me why my son was so pre-occupied earlier?"

Artemis watched her stop in her tracks and look at him. It must be serious if the look on her face was any indication.

"Remember when I told you about the second half of the

prophecy?" The king nodded.

"Well he talked with Zephyr and she told him some things he didn't understand so he came to me." Again the king was silent so she continued. "She told him things that she had seen. Apparently he has been dreaming about the second part of the prophecy. I mean down to every detail so I had no choice but to show him." Eudora sat down again.

Artemis didn't understand it any more than she did, but after he talked with his son maybe he would know more. "I think you were right Eudora. Their destinies lie together. They just have to come to terms with it all, but for now we need to wait and see if Sebastian talks to her. From what I have seen, he at least respects her. I do believe that much."

Eudora thought about that. Maybe he was right. "For now we will leave it be. I think I should get back. You never know, I might need to be a referee." Artemis threw back his head and laughed. "I don't think that will be needed. From what I saw from Alana she can handle Sebastian." He chuckled again. "You know, he's a lot like me. Stubborn to the bone and just as hard headed. Tell him I would like to speak with him tomorrow."

Eudora chuckled too. "I think you might be right. I will tell him to come see you tomorrow, after they are done training."

With a nod she was gone.

Artemis knew how Sebastian thought. Just like his father - he remembered a time long ago, when a pretty young thing stepped within sight of him. He chuckled again. If Alana was anything like his wife she would definitely give him back whatever he was giving her and from what he had seen so far they would be seeing a great show of fireworks. Again he chuckled and decided it was time to seek his own bed and let his wife know what was going on.

46

Alana woke with a start. She couldn't move and she felt woozy when she opened her eyes. Everything was still dark and something was covering her mouth. She didn't know where she was but she did know one thing - she was in trouble. Her hands were tied behind her back and her feet must have been tied too because she couldn't move them. She didn't know how long she had been out. It could have been hours or days. All she could remember was someone blowing something in her face and hearing a woman's voice but nothing else. What was she going to do now? She thought she was helping a friend when she cast that spell. Boy was that a mistake? Now she was stuck and she didn't even know where she was or if anyone was looking for her. Sebastian had been right. He would probably love to hear those words coming from her but for now she had to think about what to do. She tried the restraints with no luck. Whoever had tied them knew what they were doing.

If only she had listened to Sebastian. From now on if she ever got out of this, she would listen to every word he had to say. She had been stupid. Wherever she was, she was alone. Not a sound came from the room. All she could hear was her own breathing and the frantic beat of her heart. Crying was not an option right now - she had to figure a way out. She tried once more to move but the ropes only grew tighter forcing her to wince in pain. She tried to concentrate to remove them but so far that wasn't working either. Why, if she had all this magic, was nothing working? She felt trapped and was starting to panic. She took several controlled breaths to calm herself.

Eudora had always told her that if she wanted something she just had to ask and let herself have it. She hated to admit it but right now what she wanted was Sebastian to come find her. She wished now that she had never doubted him or thought him foolish for always telling her it was for her own good. She had gotten so sick of him telling her that but now she realized that it was true. If only he could hear her. She would tell him how sorry she was for everything. She tried to find a more comfortable position.

Alana thought back to Eudora's lessons. She could hear her laughing as she told her, 'darling there is nothing you can't do if your heart is set on it. You will always have your heart's desire if you believe you can.'

Squaring her shoulders and sitting up the best she could she took a deep breath. Her heart's desire? Was that what Sebastian was? Her thoughts took her back to the first time she saw him in the café. Even then there was something about him. Of course he was rough around the edges and he made her mad sometimes, even furious, but when she looked into his eyes she knew that was where she wanted to be. Taking another deep breathe she was actually starting to feel calmer. She cleared her mind of everything except Sebastian's face and in her mind she spoke to him.

'Sebastian if you can hear me I am so sorry. You were right and I was wrong. Please, please wake up…I…I need you Sebastian. Wake up. Can you hear me? God I hope you can hear me…I know you're probably mad and I don't blame you but please speak to me.' She waited and there was nothing. Sighing she settled back down in despair. She had to reach him.

47

Eudora appeared in the kitchen first. She heard the music. It was playing softly. Not something she would listen too. She liked songs, not just instrumentals. She looked into the living room and found Lily sitting in a chair with a blanket over her lap and a glass of wine in her hand. On the table she noticed that half of the bottle was gone. Lily smiled up at her. "There you are. I was wondering where you got to. Would you care for a glass of wine?"
Eudora smiled down at Lily, "No thank you, and I do believe you have had enough too."
Lily shook her head and finished what was left in her glass. "Nonsense. I have only had a couple of glasses. I was waiting on Alana to come down but she hasn't yet." She shrugged her shoulders and sat the glass down. Eudora shook her head again as she picked up the wine bottle and the glass and took them to the kitchen. When she returned she had a steaming cup of coffee in her hand.
"I think you should drink this dear. Did you say Alana never came downstairs after her bath?" She handed Lily the cup and waited for her to take a sip. "No she hasn't. I thought for sure she would come down before she went to bed."
'Maybe not if she and Sebastian had a fight,' thought Eudora. Perhaps she should check on her. "Finish your coffee dear and I will check on Alana."
Lily nodded and took another sip as Eudora went upstairs.
Alana's bedroom door was half opened so she pushed it the rest of the way. She expected to find Alana in bed and Sebastian lurking about but when she stepped into the room she found a different picture indeed. Alana was nowhere to be found and Sebastian was lying slumped on the floor. A chill went down her back. Something was very wrong. She rushed over to Sebastian and shook him.
"Sebastian!" No response. She grabbed him by the shoulders and shook him again harder this time and in a louder voice; "Sebastian wake up!" This time she heard a groan. Now she knew something was definitely wrong. He was always alert. She wondered what had happened while she was gone. She shook him some more. He was coming around now so she stopped and waited for him to get

his bearings. He sat up and grabbed his head.

"What the hell happened?" Eudora looked at him closely. "I don't know. Don't you know? Where is Alana?" Eudora checked Alana's bathroom. Nothing. Back in the bedroom she spied a piece of paper lying on Alana's bed. She read it quickly to herself and looked again at Sebastian. By this time he was on his feet, if not so steady.

"I don't know where she is. The last thing I remember, she came out of the bathroom. I thought I heard her say something but that is a little fuzzy. Then everything faded and you woke me up." Again he grabbed his head. She knew he still wasn't alert or he would be tearing the house apart to find Alana. Poor Sebastian. She had cast a spell and put him to sleep. The note said that her friend needed her and she went to help.

"She is gone Sebastian. Do you know how long you have been out?" He looked at her clock on the night stand.

"What do you mean, she isn't here. Where the hell is she?" This time he yelled and made Eudora wince. She handed him the note.

"Why that little witch, wait until I get my hands on her." By this time Sebastian was pacing the floor trying to regain his senses. Lily came into the room looking worried. "I heard shouting. Is everything all right?"

Eudora went to Lily. She didn't want her to panic so she smiled. "Dear, do you by any chance have Alana's friend Katie's number?" "Yes it's on speed dial. Why?"

Eudora guided Lily over to the bed and grabbed the phone. "Do you think you can call her and find out if Alana is over there or if she has seen her?" Lily looked from Eudora to Sebastian. Sebastian looked furious.

"Could someone please explain to me what is going on?"

Eudora handed her the note to read. "Oh my God, I can't believe she would do something like this. I mean I know her friends mean the world to her but...how long ago did this happen? I never saw her leave the house." She looked to Sebastian. He rubbed his hand down his face.

"Maybe a couple of hours. I don't remember much considering she cast a spell on me."

Lily grabbed the phone and without a word hit Katie's number from speed dial and waited. After several rings Katie answered and she didn't sound like she had been awake.

"Katie? This is Alana's mom. By any chance have you seen Alana tonight?" Eudora could tell by the look on Lily's face the answer was no. "Did you have any car trouble tonight?" Again she didn't like the look on Lily's face which had turned as white as a sheet.

"No, No. Nothing is wrong. I just thought she might be with you. If you happen to see her please tell her to call home. Sorry to have woken you. Bye."

She hung up. "She hasn't seen Alana and she said she didn't have car trouble, that she went straight home after she left here." There was silence for a few seconds. Eudora was wringing her hands. Lily sat staring at the phone and Sebastian was pacing again.

In a small voice Lily asked, "Oh my God! They have her don't they? What if something has happened to her?" Lily covered her mouth as a sound escaped. Sebastian stopped pacing and looked at the two women. "Don't say that!" he boomed. "We will find her." Eudora put her arm around Lily. "I think we should all go downstairs and figure this out." She helped Lily from the room with Sebastian following.

Once they were in the living room and Eudora had Lily seated Sebastian called in a loud voice. "Kohn, Rowan, Warwick! Come to me!" Lily jumped at the heat in his voice. The three men appeared in her living room. Her eyes grew big as saucers. All three bowed to Sebastian. "You're Highness."

Eudora helped Lily to sit down and patted her hand.

"What can we do for you Sebastian?" asked Kohn.

"Alana has been kidnapped. We know how they did it. We just don't know where she is. I want you and Warwick to scout around and find out everything you can. Rowan I want you to stay here and guard the house." All three nodded then Kohn and Warwick disappeared.

Rowan walked over to Sebastian. "I will check outside and see if anything is amiss." He was out the door before Sebastian even nodded.

Lily looked again at Eudora. "Who were those men and what did they mean by Your Highness?"

Eudora looked Lily straight in the face. "Sebastian is not only a warrior dear, he is also the crown prince. His father is the king."

For several seconds Lily was silent. "Does Alana know this?"

Eudora nodded. "Yes she does, but she wasn't too happy when she found out."

Lily looked at Sebastian again. "When did Alana find out?"

Eudora looked up at Sebastian when she answered. "She found out today when she had dinner with the King and Queen."

Lily made a sound in her throat. "I bet that didn't go over well."

Sebastian snorted. "No it didn't."

Just then, Rowan entered the house with Alana's keys and purse. Lily gasped and Sebastian looked toward the door.

"Where did you find those?" Rowan walked forward and laid them on the table. "The bag was on the ground but the keys were in the door of that thing outside."

Lily again looked puzzled. "Don't tell me he doesn't know what a car is?" Eudora patted her hand again. "Yes dear he knows what it is. It's just that we don't use them in our world so he hasn't ever seen one before. Not many of us leave our world. Only a chosen few can travel from one world to another."

Lily looked around the room. "Then how did he and the other two get here?"

Eudora started to answer but Sebastian beat her to it. "They came because I called for them."

Still Lily looked confused so Eudora explained "They cannot travel without an invitation and tonight when Sebastian called them he basically gave them passage." Lily nodded but Eudora knew it was a lot to take in.

Sebastian and Rowan had their heads together talking in a soft whisper. When they were done Rowan again went to the door and slipped out. "Rowan will stay and watch the house. No one will be able to enter."

Eudora got up and held her hand out for Lily's. "I think we should give Sebastian some time to see if he can connect with Alana." They went into the Kitchen.

"I don't understand. Do you really think that he can find her?"

Eudora sat down next to Lily and magically produced a pot of tea. She poured them both a cup and handed one to Lily. She smiled. "If she can be found he will find her." Eudora took a sip of her tea and hoped and prayed that he could.

48

Sebastian was alone in the living room. He sat in the middle of the room, crossed his legs and cleared his mind. He focused on Alana. He was worried but he pushed all of his feelings aside and concentrated but felt nothing from her. He took several deep cleansing breathes and closed his eyes. Again he concentrated on her face. He cleared his mind and a chill ran down his spine. He felt fear grab hold of him. He had connected with her. She was scared and felt alone. He could hear her babbling to him but couldn't understand all of the words - she was saying them so fast. But he caught the words 'sorry' and that she was wrong. He felt the panic in her as she spoke to him. He was relieved that she was still alive, now to try and get her to shut up so he could communicate with her. He spoke to her in his mind. 'We will discuss what you did when you get home but right now I need you to tell me where you are.'
He waited to see if she received his message.

49

Alana had been babbling for so long with no answer that she was surprised to hear Sebastian's voice came to her so clearly.

'Thank God you finally woke up. I didn't think you ever would. I'm sorry Sebastian. I don't know if you heard me or not but you were right, I was wrong but in my defense I was trying to help a friend!' Even though she was still alone she felt better knowing that Sebastian finally knew she was missing.

"We can talk about that later. Are you alright? Do you know what happened? We found your purse on the ground by your car." He felt the fear vanish and calmness settle over her.

"I don't really know what happened. I left the house. I thought I heard someone behind me but when I turned to look something was blown into my face. I know I heard a woman's voice. I must have passed out and next thing I know, I wake up here and I don't even know where here is. My hands and legs are tied and there is something over my head and something in my mouth. I can tell you right now, it doesn't taste all that nice."

Sebastian couldn't believe it. Even in her dire situation she was still complaining.

"Be thankful you're still alive. Do you think you could remove whatever is on your head?" He sure hoped so. He was hoping to look through her eyes to see where she was.

"I will try." She went quiet and the waiting was killing him but he remained patient. He wondered why they hadn't done anything to her yet. Maybe they had hired a bounty hunter to find her and they hadn't handed her over yet. If that was the case they needed to hurry before the real perpetrators turned up for her.

"Alana have you got it off yet?"

"Hold your horses. Geez, it's not as easy as you think. There I got it." He could feel her relief at getting it off. "Can you tell me what you see?" Sebastian opened his mind further.

"It looks like some kind of warehouse." Sebastian could see what Alan was looking at.

"Are there any windows you can look out of?" He watched as she scanned the room.

"There is one to my left and another smaller one on my right." He looked at both of them. One only showed the night sky, but the one to the right showed another building.

"Try and focus more on the one to your right. I can't see much."
He watched her focus closer on the window on the right.

"Wow. I forgot that you could see through my eyes. There is a
building with something on it. Wait! I know that building."

He could feel the excitement in her. "Good tell me. Show me
where the building is. How you would get to it from your house?"
He watched as she recalled in her mind how to get to it from her
house. By the time she was through he knew exactly where she
was.

"Now hang on Alana. I will be there as soon as I can." He broke
the connection and opened his eyes. She was downtown in the
industrial part and if her directions were good he would be there in
no time. In a booming voice he called for Eudora. Both women
came into the room. "I have located her. I need to go."

Lily and Eudora looked relieved as he left the house. Outside he
told Rowan to keep the women safe inside the house and then he
spread his wings and was soaring through the sky before Rowan
had closed the front door. He wanted to get in and out before
anyone showed up to claim her.

Rowan walked inside and looked at both women. "Sebastian
wanted me to wait inside for him to get back." He stood next to the
front door.

Eudora sighed. 'Well,' she thought, 'at least he takes his
responsibilities seriously.'

Lily was so relieved she was fidgeting. Eudora couldn't help but
feel the happiness in her friend. "Didn't I tell you that Sebastian
would find her?"

When Lily nodded with tears rolling silently down her cheeks
Eudora grabbed her hand and squeezed it.

50

Katie had gotten hold of Trish but not Jess. She left a message on her machine. She was probably still out with someone. On her way now to pick up Trish, she knew something was wrong with Alana. Her mom hadn't sounded like herself and she didn't know why she would ask about her car. When she pulled up to the curb Trish was there waiting for her. Trish got into the car.

"Do you think that they have found her yet?"

Katie looked worriedly back at Trish then pulled out into traffic.

"I don't know, but by the sound of her mom's voice something is definitely wrong. She asked me about my car. I don't know what that was about, but we are about to find out." Katie was glad they didn't live far from Alana. After Alana's mom had called she couldn't get back to sleep thinking something was wrong with Alana. She had been so secretive lately. She knew something was going on in her life. As she pulled up to Alana's house all the lights were on. Were they still looking?

When the girls knocked on the door Rowan immediately drew his sword.

Eudora calmly held up her hand. "Put that away Rowan, the house is protected. Whoever is at the door is not evil or we would know that by now. Besides, they wouldn't have knocked." She went to the door and looked out. "It's Katie and Trish," she announced to Lily.

Lily rose. "They are probably worried about Alana and came to make sure she is all right." Eudora nodded her agreement than spoke to Rowan.

"I think it's best if you wait outside or in another room. You are a bit difficult to explain." He bowed and disappeared as Lily opened the door.

Both girls came in and looked around. It was Trish who spoke first. "Have you found Alana yet? Is she all right? We were so worried we decided to come on over. We couldn't get a hold of Jess. You know how she is, she's probably still out but I left a message."

Eudora smiled at both girls. "She's all right. Sebastian has gone to get her."

Both girls looked at each other and then back at Lily.

"Who's Sebastian? She's never mentioned him."

Lily placed her hands in her lap and looked at Eudora. She should have known Alana's friends would turn up. They all loved each other very much and they were very loyal. She didn't know what to say. Eudora stepped in.

"She met Sebastian last week at the café." Both girls looked puzzled. "Do you mean the guy who was at the club?" asked Katie. Again Eudora smiled. "Yes that's him."

"Wow I didn't even know she had talked with him," said Trish. Their conversation was interrupted by a commotion outside and someone screeching in a high pitched voice.

"Buster if you know what is good for you, you will move out of my way." Both Katie and Trish rolled their eyes.

"That would be Jess. She must have just got the message and come straight over," said Katie heading for the door. Eudora was right behind her. When Katie opened the door there was a man stopping Jess from getting to the door. When he turned around Katie lost all train of thought. There standing before her looked like a medieval warrior come to life. He was gorgeous!

"That's all right Rowan. This is Jess, another one of Alana's friends."

Jess huffed and walked past him. "Sorry I wasn't home when you called, as soon as I got your message I rushed over here." Katie just nodded as Eudora told Rowan he may as well come in also. She stepped back and watched as he came in, shut the door and stood with arms folded next to it. Katie returned to the couch. She couldn't believe she had just stood there gawking.

"Could someone please explain what the Neanderthal is doing here and why he is dressed like Genghis Khan?" In her usual style Jess flicked her head toward Rowan as she sat down next to Trish.

Sebastian was almost there. He could see the building that Alana had earlier identified to the right so he knew he was close.

"Alana, hold on. I'm almost there but I need for you to think of something happy." He knew she wouldn't understand, but he needed the glow of her aura to know just where she was. He waited but she showed no sign.

"Think of the day you were with Eudora at Tranquility."

He felt her puzzlement. "I don't know how me thinking of something happy will help you find me and anyway, I don't know what you're talking about." 'Be patient,' thought Sebastian.

"You remember the gardens that Eudora took you to right? Well the last place she took you to is known as the garden of Tranquility. It's the same one in your globe." He felt the puzzlement slip away as a calmness took over her. He could feel a sudden burst of positive energy.

"I loved that place. I didn't know it was called Tranquility but the name fits."

"Good. Think of that place and how happy and peaceful it made you feel," he said as he scanned the area for any sign of a bright glow. Sure enough, emanating from a building that was dark he saw a pale golden glow. It was coming from Alana. Landing at the door and discovering it securely locked Sebastian calmly used his strength and magic. It creaked on its hinges. He stepped into the warehouse giving his eyes time to adjust to the darkness. There was no sign of Alana. He called to her and he heard a muffled sound coming from the left where a door was closed. He headed in that direction and found the door blocked by magic, but whoever put the spell on it wasn't very strong. He broke through in seconds. As soon as he entered the room he saw her aura glowing in the corner. He surveyed the area and could detect no other magic so he rushed forward. When he got close he hit an invisible wall and he fell flat on his ass. He grunted. It seemed like every time he was close to her he was on his backside. He searched for the source of the invisible barrier and found crystals placed at four different points. He kicked one away and the force field was broken. He knelt down to Alana and removed the fabric that was stuffed in her mouth. She coughed and took several deep breaths and in a scratchy voice she spoke feebly.

"I know you're mad and probably want to give me a lecture, but do you think we can wait until I am home and can clean up a bit?" This time she looked at him. His face was very close to hers. She thought she saw something there that she had never seen before, but she wasn't sure if it was just a trick of the light or her imagination. For a second she thought she had seen compassion. Sebastian grunted and turned her around to release the ropes that were holding her when she winced. He stopped. "I don't have time to look these over right now. Do you think you will be alright until we get home?"

Alana sighed. *Home!* She couldn't wait. She nodded her head and looked away. She didn't want Sebastian to see how scared she had been or the tears she was trying not to let loose. She had messed up badly and she knew it. When he lifted her up she tried not to make a sound but her legs and hands where sore and the ropes were biting into her flesh. She could feel something sticky running down her arm. She knew by the coppery smell that it was blood. She bit her lip as he stood up with her in his arms. She could feel his gentleness as he carried her out of the building.

"Alana, close your eyes and rest. We will be at your house before you know it."

She *was* tired so she closed her eyes. She felt very light and then she felt the wind on her face and her hair was blowing about. This didn't feel like any of the other times when he had transported them somewhere so she took a chance and opened her eyes. What she saw she didn't believe. They were flying! She turned her head away from his broad chest and her eyes grew wide. Yep, they were flying!

"How is this possible? How are we flying?' She tried to get a better look at his face so she arched her head to look closer. "Oh, My God! You have wings! What are you?" He grunted again. "I will explain everything to you when we get you to safety."

She hated when he did that. She didn't want to wait until they were safe - she wanted to know now.

"We're safe enough considering we're flying. Does everyone that's magic have the ability to fly? Or are you more than just a witch?"

"Not too many have the ability. It's not something you learn. You have to be born with it. And I can change shape. That is known as a shape shifter. I *am* of royal blood."

Alana thought all of this through. If he could shift into a bird what else could he do?

"I'm not a bird. I can only shape shift into two different creatures." Shoot! Alana forgot to block him out of her mind.

"What do you mean by creatures? What can you transform into?" She knew whatever he said she wasn't going to like it.

"I can change into a wolf." Alana thought back to her first lesson with him.

"You mean to tell me *you* were that big black beast that scared the daylights out of me?"

She heard him chuckle. "Yes my little warrior and I have to say you did a very good job."

Alana swallowed. That was the first time he had ever complimented anything she had ever done. And he had called her 'his little warrior.' She was momentarily distracted by the new feelings surging through her. But she wanted to know what else he could become but she was scared of the answer.

"What else can you transform into if it's not a bird?" She knew by the way he growled she had insulted him.

"Think about what Eudora told you about my battle name. Maybe you can figure it out." He went silent and looked back up to scan where they were. Alana's mind went blank. She couldn't remember squat but as she thought back to her conversation with Eudora and thought back to when she walked with Zephyr she remembered about the dragons in the pictures. Particularly the one that was big and black with eyes just as dark. At the time she thought that it was unusual. Most had red eyes, or the ones in the books she had seen did. She looked back up at him. No, that couldn't be. But Eudora did say that his enemies would sometimes flee just by the sound of his battle cry or even his name being whispered about.

"Oh My God! You can't mean to tell me you're really a dragon?" When he remained silent Alana looked back up at his wings. They were not really feathers. They looked more like scales and they were as black as the picture she had seen in his foyer. Could that picture have been of him in his dragon form? She had actually felt as if she knew it in some way - there was some recognition there.

This was just too much to handle. She remembered Zephyr explaining the meaning of his last name. Drakon stood for dragon. She just thought it was a family crest or something.

She knew by his silence that he wasn't going to talk anymore, but before the night was over she was going to find out everything she could about him either from him or from Eudora. For now she was just glad to be going home so she made herself as comfortable as possible and enjoyed the ride. She smiled as she closed her eyes. 'My little warrior.'

Sebastian knew that she would have lots more questions. He looked down and noticed that she had relaxed and her eyes were closed. He concentrated on Kohn and Warrick and sent them a message to meet him back at the house. He told them he had found Alana and they needed to form some kind of plan to find out just who had taken Alana. They were certain it had been the D'Ary family but they had to find out if they had a bounty hunter working for them. Alana said she had heard a woman's voice before she passed out and he knew that Todd's mother wouldn't have done this herself. So who had they hired to kidnap Alana?

52

"I'm getting worried. Are you sure Sebastian knows where she is?" asked Trish.

"Wait a minute. Who's Sebastian?" said Katie looking more perplexed. "Remember that guy from the other night?" She could see Jess was still confused.

"You know? The one who was watching Alana. He was dressed all in black and very cute. She had seen him at the café too."

Trish saw recognition light up her friend's face. "Oh yeah! I remember him. But I don't think she even talked to him. Remember? We left soon after." Jess looked from Katie to Trish who just shrugged her shoulders.

"So what's up with him?" Again Jess pointed her finger at Rowan. Trish answered. "We don't know. We just got here ourselves Jess but I'm sure Eudora can explain it to us." They all looked at Eudora expectantly.

'Now what to say?' thought Eudora. As she was about to explain, Kohn and Warwick entered the room and not by the traditional method. There was chaos and screams from the three girls. Trish stood up and shouted "What the Hell!" as Katie gasped and Jess fainted dead away. Lily went to Jess somewhat bemused. She was getting used to this. Katie and Trish both looked the newcomers over. They were both dressed in the same odd clothes as Rowan. It was Katie who in a calm voice spoke to Eudora. "I think it is time for an explanation don't you?"

Eudora tried her best not to look flustered but was failing miserably. Jess was starting to come to and all three men were standing there looking at the women strangely. This was all Eudora needed. She knew she couldn't lie her way out of this so she threw caution to the wind and told all the woman to sit down and she would explain.

"First of all, Kohn, Warwick and Rowan step forward please." They did so quite calmly trying to look in place.

"Trish, Katie and Jess these are Sebastian's men."

She watched as all three men bowed to the women. Jess of course smiled at all of them and batted her eyelashes. Trish rolled her eyes. Katie was quiet as she looked all of them over.

"What do you mean, Sebastian's men?" asked Katie.

Alana had told Eudora all about her friends and she knew that Katie was the smartest of the three and probably the one who would understand the best.

"Where Sebastian lives, he is the crown prince and these men are his warriors or as you would say his guards." She indicated toward them still watching Katie for her reaction. She heard Trish snort. Eudora knew she was the realist of the group so she squared her shoulders and waited for whatever Trish was going to say. It didn't take long.

"Ok, I can understand the guard's story and even the story about Sebastian being a prince and everything but what I want to know is where does he live? And how in the hell did these guys just appear out of thin air? Do you have an explanation for that?"

Eudora could tell Trish wasn't buying any of this, even though everything she had said so far was the truth so she decided the *whole* truth would be easier.

"Sebastian lives in the otherworld. A place that is not on any maps and not a place that anyone born of your world knows about. It's magical and Sebastian is here to protect Alana from the dark ones, who are also from our world but live in yours. They want to kidnap her before her birthday when she will gain all of her own powers. You see dear we are all magical beings from a different world." She smiled. The room was silent. Then Trish started laughing. She was bent at the waist with tears streaming down her face trying to catch her breath.

"That…is…so…funny!" She wiped her eyes and looked at her two friends. "Come on guys you can't tell me you believe any of this. We have known Alana all her life. Don't you think if she was a witch she would have told us? We are her best friends after all." She snickered again and looked back at Eudora.

"I assure you dear, everything I have said is true. Alana didn't know any of this until a few weeks ago." She saw Trish was having trouble with this. For once she had a look of uncertainty on her face. She glanced again at the men standing by the door. After several seconds she looked at Lily.

"Please tell me this isn't true. I know *you* wouldn't lie to any of us." She didn't need Lily to say anything. She saw truth on her face.

"Oh my God! I can't believe any of this. Don't tell me you're a witch too?"

Lily shook her head. "No I'm not a witch. Her father was. At the time that we met I didn't know it but he told me before we married."

Jess still hadn't said anything. She was still watching the men. Katie was calm as usual. She always took things at face value and even though Trish was shocked she was starting to understand.

"What I don't understand and maybe someone can explain it to me is why would the 'dark ones' be after Alana?" Trish sighed and then ran her fingers through her hair.

Eudora answered her. "It was a long time ago but it involves Alana's ancestors. There was a curse made and despite that curse, Alana is the first girl to have been born since that time, giving her tremendous power. So the dark ones know if they can gain her power for themselves they will hold both worlds in their hands. We can't let that happen." She waited for this to sink in. Katie was the first to respond. "You mean Alana has to stop them?"

Eudora smiled. "Yes, but she won't attain all of her powers and skills until her birthday. She is already showing great signs of her gift. She already has more power than most witches that have had theirs for centuries and even some of the masters. They need to gain her heart to obtain her powers but now they know that is impossible. So now they have to try another way or destroy her."

"Do you mean Alana has to go up against these people? Do you by any chance know who these people are?" Eudora had to commend Katie. She caught on fast.

"We have just learned who they are and yes Alana will have to face them in a battle by herself. We have given her all the knowledge that we can but in the end it will be all up to her."

Trish's eyes grew huge. "You can't mean to say Alana has to fight these people. She doesn't have a mean bone in her body much less the skills to fight." Everyone heard the snort from the other side of the room. Trish narrowed her eyes "Let me guess. You have something to add?"

Kohn stepped forward. "I don't think we have anything to worry about with her. She has more power than most and she unarmed all three of us. She has even put Sebastian in his place." All three men laughed. Trish looked again at Eudora who saw the question in her eyes.

"Alana did disarm them and she has put Sebastian on the floor several times. Don't worry her skills at fighting and magic are above the norm." This time even Eudora chuckled. "She even sent Sebastian flying through the air to land on his backside."

Trish had a look of disbelief on her face.

"I assure you, Alana is more than ready to face whatever the D'Ary family can dish out to her."

Trish glanced at Katie and then back to Eudora. "D'Ary family? Are they the dark ones? I have never heard that name before."

"Of course you haven't. That was their name in our world, but in your world you do know them very well. Sinclair."

"You can't be serious!" shouted Trish but Katie spoke in a calmer voice.

"Do you mean Todd and his family?" When Eudora nodded she heard some unladylike words leave Trish's mouth that had even the men raising their eyebrows.

"You wait until I see that worm." Trish had to stop and take a breath. She had gotten all worked up. Eudora was shaking her head.

"You can't confront him - any of you. He has a lot of power and he could kill you with just a thought if he wanted to. Their magic is the same as ours. They just use theirs for evil."

Katie shivered and Trish's face looked a little pale. Eudora started to say something else when right there in front of her, Sebastian and Alana appeared and again chaos broke out. Everyone jumped up and ran to see if Alana was Ok. Sebastian shouted for calm and to give them some room as he carefully laid Alana on the floor.

"I don't know why, but I have tried several times to get these ropes off her hands and they won't move. What should we do?" Eudora came forward to examine the ropes. Just as she thought, they were made of a powerful magic that not even Alana could break. She thought back to something she had learned years ago from a wise wizard and looked to Lily.

"Lily dear, will you go get some scissors?" Lily ran toward the kitchen and came back with them in her hand. "Now I need you to cut the rope around her feet and hands. I…" before she could finish Sebastian was interrupting her.

"What are you doing? I have tried everything. If I couldn't get them off her what makes you think Lily can?"

Eudora knew Sebastian didn't like to feel helpless but this time not even his magic could help. She nodded to Lily and told her to cut the rope. Lily, with shaky hands cut through the ropes on Alan's feet and then the ones on her hands. Alana cried out but before anyone else could get to her Sebastian was there rubbing the circulation back into her legs and looking at her hands. There were tears streaming down Alana's cheeks but when she looked up she noticed that all of her friends were there.

Eudora was standing near her. "They were worried dear and came over to see if you were all right. I had no choice but to tell them considering that Kohn and Warwick appeared right in front of them."

Sebastian was still amazed that Lily, a simple human had broken her bounds. "How did she do that?"

Eudora chuckled. "They placed a spell that our magic couldn't break the bounds. They didn't count on us having a human to help and because of that she was able to cut them off. You see she is neutral and has no powers. They didn't count on that and didn't bother sealing the ties against shall we say 'non-magic'?"

Alana was finally getting some feeling back into her legs and hands. She would be sore and raw in the morning.

Eudora assessed the injuries to Alana's ankles and wrists. "I will be back shortly dear. I have some herbs we can use to take away most of the soreness and maybe they won't be so raw in the morning."

Alana nodded. She was still a little surprised to see all of her friends there. Sebastian watched Alana closely. He could feel her pain. Her wrists were bleeding where the ropes had cut the skin. "Lily, do you think you could get me some wet towels so we can see how much damage was done? A couple of dry ones too?" Lily nodded and started for the kitchen. One of Alana's friends went with her. He thought it was the shy one. What was her name – Katie?

"You two. I think Alana said your names were Trish and Jess?" Both girls nodded but didn't say a word. "Can you go upstairs and get a hot bath started for Alana?" Both girls jumped up and went off, happy to be able to help. When he heard them overhead in Alana's room he questioned his men.

"Did you two find out anything? Alana thinks it was a woman who kidnapped her."

Kohn stepped forward. "We checked everywhere. Nothing. Do you want us to go out and look some more?" Sebastian thought about it. If they hadn't found out anything by now they probably wouldn't have any more success. "No. I think you should stay here. We might need you later." All three bowed. "Alana?" Sebastian didn't know what to say to her. She had been very brave, even though she had done something stupid, he understood her reason. He admired her loyalty.

"Please Sebastian, if you're going to yell at me do you think you could wait until tomorrow? I'm not really up for a lecture right now. I know what I did was a mistake and it was wrong. You don't have to worry. It won't happen again."

He didn't like the way she sounded - so defeated.

"Alana, look at me." When she did he wanted to shake her. Did she think him that much of a monster that he would kick her when she was down? "I'm not going to lecture you. I think you have done enough of that for both of us." He could see the surprise in her face. "You do?"

"Yes I do. I was just going to tell you what a good job you did in staying calm and clear headed enough to lead me to you. That was very brave my little warrior."

He heard one of his men snort but when he looked at them they shut up and went to the other side of the room.

"I think tomorrow we should have that talk after you get a good night's sleep." She nodded.

"Do you think you can get up now, or should I carry you over to the couch?" He heard her wince as she tried to get up.

"I might need a little help. My legs are still a little shaky."

Sebastian held his hands out. When she tried to stand again he was there to help her to her feet. The process was slow but he knew she needed to do this as much on her own as she could. When she reached the couch Lily and Katie came back into the room. Lily had a bowl in her hand and some towels thrown over her shoulder. Katie had a glass in her hand.

"We thought she might need something to make her feel a little better and maybe make her relax."

She handed the glass to Alana who sniffed it and looked up, "This smells like whiskey."

Her mom laughed. "Yes it is, and I want you to drink it all but not at once. Take a few sips now."

Alana obeyed and when it hit her throat she coughed. "This stuff is awful. How can people drink this?"

Katie laughed this time. "You might be right Alana but it will make you feel better. Once Sebastian starts to clean your hands you will wish you had a good stiff drink." With that, Alana downed half of it. It wasn't so bad that time so she sat the glass down and gave him her hand. "I think I'm ready."

Sebastian took the bowl of water and sat it on the table and took one of the towels that Lily handed him. He dipped it in the water and as gentle as he could he wiped away the blood to see the raw skin below. If he could get his hands on Todd right now he would be a dead man.

Alana was trying to stay brave as he finished one hand and went to work on the other. She was biting down hard on her bottom lip. Sebastian saw this and hated having to hurt her, but in order to cleanse the wounds he had to do this.

He heard the other two come down the stairs. They sat down out of the way. When he was about through Eudora reappeared with some bottles in her hand.

"I think I have everything we will need. Good Sebastian, you have cleaned the wounds nicely." She sat the bottles down and examined Alana's wounds. She 'tsked' in sympathy.

"I had her friends run her a bath. I think once that is done you can put whatever you brought on her wounds and bandage them up." Eudora nodded and looked at the other girls in the room. "I think for tonight that you should all stay, just to make sure nothing else happens."

Trish stood up. "What do you mean? Do you think that scum would come after us?"

Eudora knew Trish was trying to be brave, she saw her fear in her aura. In fact all three were scared and not just for themselves but for Alana too.

"I don't know what he would try but he used Katie once. Next time he might actually kidnap one of you to get to Alana."

Sebastian added "I think she is right. It would be better if we could make sure you are safe tomorrow. I will send my men to watch over each one of you."

Jess stood up quickly. "I want the big one in the middle!" Then she smiled at Warwick who winked back at her. Katie rolled her eyes and Trish jabbed her with her elbow.

"What?" she said innocently as she rubbed her side. Everyone except for Sebastian laughed.

The whiskey was working judging from Alana's lopsided smile.

"Do you think you could make it upstairs by yourself?"

She tilted her head to one side. "I think so. My legs aren't hurting as bad now." To prove it she stood up. She wasn't exactly straight on her feet but that had more to do with what she had drunk than anything else.

"Good. Now I think it's time for your bath." When she headed in the direction of the stairs he looked at Eudora. She knew what he was asking so she took her bottles and followed Alana. When the girls started to follow too, Sebastian held up his hand.

"Let Eudora help her. She will know what to do. We need to talk." The girls sat back down. He saw Lily looking at the stairs with concern.

"Lily maybe you could go up and make sure Eudora finds everything Alana will need." She looked relieved to be able to help her daughter.

"I think I will. If anyone wants anything down here, the girls know where everything is."

53

All was quiet in the living room. The men watched the girls and the girls watched the men.

'This is ridiculous,' thought Katie. Nobody wanted to be the first to speak so she felt she might as well. Usually it was Trish who had the big mouth but for once even she was looking wary. "Sebastian you wanted to talk to us?"

"I wanted all of you to stay so we could discuss Todd. If any of you run into him do not let it be known that you know about his true identity. If he were to find out it would be dangerous." Sebastian looked at everyone to make sure they all understood the gravity of his words. He could see that the girls were scared but he had to caution them. They had to accept how dangerous Todd could be. Hell, even Sebastian didn't know how dangerous that was but he did know that when you back someone into a corner they will usually strike.

"I don't understand. Are you telling me that little weasel could actually hurt us?" said Trish. She was still confused but she didn't see how someone like Todd could hurt anyone. He was too preppy. Not manly like the ones in the room now and God were *they* gorgeous. All were too handsome for their own good, especially Warwick. Now that was one hot specimen. There was something about him that made her insides want to stand up and take notice.

"Don't underestimate him - any of you! He might not look the part but he is evil through and through." said Sebastian.

"I always said he was too perfect. Now I know why." said Jessica. Sebastian just shook his head. Yeah she might be beautiful but she lacked substance. Beauty only lasted for so long thought Sebastian. Again he looked toward the ceiling as he heard movement. Alana on the other hand - she had beauty *and* substance. And one hell of a killer smile, if and when she ever honored you with one that is and because of his role as her mentor, he didn't receive one very often. But when he did, it did strange things to his insides. That he didn't much like. When he woke up earlier and found she was gone something inside of him took over. All he knew was he had to find her and soon. That was a feeling he didn't want to feel again. Collecting his thoughts he addressed everyone again. "Just remember what I said and don't go looking for him."

"What should we do if he contacts us? I don't know about the others but I don't think I can just smile and carry on a conversation with him," added Trish. She folded her arms in front of her as if to show some measure of strength.

Sebastian came over and stood before her. He watched her eyes go wide as she took a big gulp of air.

"You need to act just like you always have toward him. If not, it could mean your life! Do you understand?" He waited for her to nod nervously before he looked at the others. Jess still had a dazed look but also nodded her head. Katie on the other hand stared right back at Sebastian with a level of intelligence that was almost scary. She nodded but never took her eyes off his gaze. Satisfied that they understood the danger Sebastian turned to his men. He gave them a knowing nod and all of them disappeared. He heard a small gasp from the girls - a distinctly disappointed gasp from at least one of them. They would eventually get used to all of this magic to-ing and fro-ing. He turned back to the girls and looked them over again. Everyone might say that Katie was the shy one but he knew better. He saw in her aura more inner strength than any of them so he directed his next words to her.

"I think maybe it's time for everyone to get some sleep. I know all of you know your way around so I will let you find a bed." He turned to go upstairs when Katie spoke.

"Wait, where are you going? There are only three bedrooms upstairs. I know who are sleeping in two of them and the three of us are going to sleep in the guest room. So you will have to take the couch. And where are your friends going to sleep?"

Leave it to Katie to find the logic in everything thought Sebastian. "I know how many rooms are in this house and my men won't be sleeping. They will be watching the house and I won't need the couch I will be watching Alana." He expected her to object but instead she surprised him with a smile. "Oh." She said knowingly. With that he was on his way upstairs. He wanted to get to Alana and see how she was doing. He knew she was in good hands with Eudora and her mother but he wanted to see for his own peace of mind. He heard footsteps behind him and over his shoulder he saw all three girls following him. He started to say something but Trish beat him to it.

"We want to make sure Alana is all right before we turn in too."

Sebastian studied all three women. He knew if it came down to it they would fight tooth and nail for Alana. That was good to know. She had such good friends so he nodded and continued up the stairs. When they approached the door Sebastian knocked and waited. Lily opened the door and smiled at everyone. "Come in." Eudora looked up. She could tell by all the anguished faces they were wanting to know how Alana was doing.

"She is resting right now but I think she will be fine in the morning. The herbs I brought seem to have done the trick. Of course she will be a little stiff in the morning but the pain should be gone by then."

All three girls looked down at Alana then they backed up and said good-night and headed for the guest room. Sebastian, she noticed, still stood where he was, looking toward the bed but keeping a respectful distance. Lily stayed long enough to kiss her daughter's forehead then she too left for her own bedroom, content that her daughter was in safe hands.

Sebastian was still standing there just staring at her forlornly. "She knows what I can do, Eudora, or at least what I can transform into." Eudora knew the time would eventually come for her to know.

"What did she have to say about that?" She watched closely for any sign from Sebastian. She knew he was very worried.

"She didn't say much. I was trying to get her here safely. I told her we would talk tomorrow." She sensed he was leaving something out.

"Did you tell her everything?" She watched as he ran his fingers through his hair and down his face. "I will tell her everything tomorrow." 'So he didn't tell her about the second part of the prophecy,' she thought. "Sebastian, please take what I am about to say as womanly advice." She waited for him to nod before she continued.

"Make sure you tell her everything. She is giving you a chance to be honest. Don't disappoint her by leaving anything out. " She heard him sigh as he finally walked over to the bed and looked down at Alana.

"I will tell her everything by tomorrow night. There will be no more secrets." Eudora was satisfied with that. She gathered her things up.

"I will leave you know and report back to the others and let them know what is going on." She didn't wait to see if he was listening. She disappeared as quietly as she always did. Sebastian stood there looking down at Alana. By tomorrow night she would know all of his secrets. He didn't want to explain *any* of them to her but it was necessary. He just hoped he didn't give too much of himself away in the telling. Damn he was tired. More tired than if he had fought a mighty battle. He looked around for a chair and found one in the corner. It wasn't very comfortable but he really didn't need it for comfort. He was going to sit there next to her bed all night to make sure nothing happened to her. His men were outside and they were his best, which set his mind at ease somewhat. But they didn't have long before her twenty-first birthday.

He looked down at her again and thought back to when he first saw her. She had certainly come a long way in that short time. At first he hadn't thought that she could do any of the things she would need to do but so far she had surprised him with all the knowledge she had absorbed. He remembered when Eudora had asked him if she could defeat the dark ones and at the time he wasn't really sure. Now he knew better. She could do anything she set her mind to and probably even do them better than most. Of course she hadn't received all of her powers yet but from what he had observed they would do nothing but enhance the powers she already had. So did he believe in her? Yes he most certainly did. He knew in the end that *she* would be the one standing.

54

Eudora had notified Artemis that she was coming. She hadn't told him why but she was sure he already knew the reason so she wasn't surprised to see not only the king but Brigham and Zephyr waiting for her when she entered his study. She bowed and as she came forward she realized that he already knew what had taken place.

"What has happened Eudora? What do you have to report?" She could hear the worry in his voice so she put him at ease right away.

"Everything is fine Artemis. Sebastian has handled the situation." She saw some of the anxiety dissipate from his stance.

"We know some of what happened. Perhaps you could enlighten all of us?" Eudora explained the situation to her king and added that now that the crisis was over, they needed to be extra diligent for the sake of everyone's safety and also to discover who had kidnapped Alana. Someone had been commissioned by Todd. They would find out.

"Kohn and Warwick combed the area but found nothing or no one to speak of what happened. They are at the house now protecting everyone." The king looked puzzled. He obviously didn't know about Alana's friends finding out everything.

"I think there is more to this than even we know. Perhaps you could start from the beginning and explain everything?"

Eudora knew this was not going to be easy. They had survived for centuries in complete secrecy. Now more humans knew about them than ever before but she did have faith in Alana and her friends that their secret would be safe so she took a deep breath and started. Everyone was quiet as she told the story. A few times she noticed Brigham stroking his beard but he didn't interrupt. The king sat in his chair with a look of amazement at times but Zephyr looked knowingly at Eudora as if she already knew the full story. When she was done she sat patiently and waited.

Brigham was the first to break the silence. "These friends of Alana's you spoke of. Do you think they will remain quiet about everything they have seen so far?"

Eudora was ready for that question. "I have the utmost faith in Alana's friends. They will not say anything to anyone. They love Alana like sisters and their loyalty is unquestionable. We have nothing to fear in that quarter."

Brigham nodded his head slightly and Eudora gave a sigh of relief. He had accepted what Eudora said as truth. She continued; "I think everyone should be on watch. There are only two days until Alana reaches her maturity and gains all of her powers. Until then she will be vulnerable to attack. It was wise of Sebastian to have the men stay. They will be of help if he needs them."

After much discussion it was agreed that Zephyr and Brigham were to investigate if Todd had hired a bounty hunter, and if so who. Artemis would keep everyone informed and Eudora was to return to Alana's house to reinforce all of the spells of protection. The battle was almost upon them and they all knew what they had to do to keep Alana safe.

55

Alana was in a deep sleep, dreaming of dancing and laughing in her garden. She loved that magical refuge. It was her special place now. She would remember it always even if she never saw it again. It was ingrained in her memories. Sebastian had called it Tranquility. A perfect name for it. When you were there, all your troubles seemed to float away. In her dream she turned and looked all around her and she gently swayed. The trees seemed to sway with her and the blossoms twirled almost in slow motion in their descent from the trees. The birds were singing a gentle song. All was peaceful. But suddenly the birds stopped singing and the sun disappeared leaving a chill in the air. She stopped her dancing and looked around. Something was very wrong. The trees were still and the blossoms stopped their movement. All was quiet and still. Too still. The place was still beautiful but without life and warmth. A chill went down her spine. She heard a faint whisper of someone laughing in the distance but it wasn't a friendly laugh. She covered her ears to escape the noise but it only grew louder and crueler. 'Who are you?' she whispered. The laughing stopped and all that remained was the silence. She searched around again and still she saw nothing. A breeze touched the side of her face almost in a caress but it chilled her to the bone.

The whispered words became louder and clearer and made her blood run cold. 'Soon I will have you. You cannot run or hide from me. Soon you will be mine and you shall die.' The eerie laughter pitched and faded in the breeze and all was quiet again.

56

Sebastian must have fallen asleep because he woke up to Alana's voice. *'Who are you?'* he heard her whisper.

He didn't know if she was having a bad dream or not. She was so still in bed but he could hear the fear in her voice. He decided against waking her. She shivered in her sleep as sweat beaded on her forehead. He tried to get inside her head but something was blocking him. He knew it wasn't Alana. She was too deep in sleep to be able to block him out so someone else was doing it. He decided it *was* time to wake her. He leaned forward to shake her when she suddenly sat upright in the bed. She was breathing hard and her face was pale. Whatever had happened, it wasn't good. He focused on her face but she was still hanging onto the dream. Her pupils were dilated and her heart was racing. As he touched her arm she pulled away and looked at him. He could tell she wasn't seeing *him*. "Alana it's me, Sebastian. You are safe."

He didn't mean to sound so gruff but it was needed to bring her back to reality and away from whatever she had seen in her Dream. It worked. Her eyes focused on him and her body relaxed. She threw her arms around his neck and started to cry. He didn't know what to do. He usually avoided crying women, always feeling helpless. She held on to him like she never wanted to let him go. The only thing Sebastian could do was try and comfort her. Whatever had happened in her dream had scared her to death - he could tell by the grip she had on him. He placed his arms gently around her and held her close as he whispered encouraging words. He didn't know what he was saying - he just wanted her to stop. She was crying so hard that her whole body was quivering. He just sat there and let her cry. Maybe this was what she needed. He rubbed her back and held her tight. It seemed like hours before the sobs grew quiet and her breathing became normal. He felt her relax against him and thought she had fallen asleep again. He liked having her in his arms. It felt right. This was the closest they had ever been and his body was having a hard time with it. He started to move and heard her small voice.

"Please. Just another minute." Her voice sounded raw and small to him so he did the only thing he could. He gathered her even closer and ran his hand up and down her back trying to comfort her. He didn't know if it was working or not but something was working on *him*. Looking down at her he noticed her head was lying on his shoulder with the back of her head to him. He was glad she wasn't looking at him right now. He was sure that if she saw his face right now it would scare her or confuse her - he didn't know which. All he knew was that his shirt was soaking wet from her tears and she was moving her head closer to the side of his neck and he could feel her breath caress him.

Alana had been so scared at the time she didn't really know what was happening until she heard Sebastian's voice. She knew then that everything would be all right.

Sebastian was there with her. She was so relieved she had thrown her arms around him and let all of the emotions of the last couple of weeks come to the surface. She was scared to death. She didn't know if she had it in her to accomplish what she was expected to do. She had so many people relying on her and she also had people out there that wanted her dead. Now that was a scary feeling. She knew the voice in her dream. She had heard it so much over the last couple of months and still it unnerved her. It was a good thing she trusted her instincts. She heard Sebastian talking to her. She didn't know what he was saying but it sounded comforting so she relaxed and let everything else go. After a time when her tears had stopped she realized this was probably the closest she would ever get to Sebastian so she wanted to enjoy it while she could. He had actually made her feel better and she felt safe when she was with him. She felt other feelings too, but she wouldn't let him or anyone else know that. Right now she couldn't believe she had cried all over his shoulder. He had tried to move but she stopped him. She wanted to just sit there and feel his strong arms around her. She knew it didn't mean anything to him. He was just trying to comfort her and she did appreciate that, but she wanted him to feel more for her than just an obligation or even a duty. She slid her head closer to his neck and inhaled. He never wore cologne but his scent was intoxicating to her senses. He smelled of earth, pine, the sun and all male. She didn't really know what that meant but when she was close enough to get a good whiff he always smelled the same - all male.

If she could bottle his scent she would call it 'Longing' because every time she was close to him she yearned for everything about him. Wasn't it ironic? He was the one man she wanted but couldn't have. That thought almost brought back the tears. She took another deep breath to try and get rid of the lump that had formed in her throat. She had been so busy with her own thoughts that it took her a minute to come back to reality and when she did, she sighed again. Sebastian was holding her but not how he had been before. Now he was keeping her more at a distance. She could feel it in his body language so she took one more deep breath, masked her feelings and looked up into his face.

Sebastian was trying everything he knew not to react to the way Alana was blowing on the side of his neck. It was so soft and light - almost a lover's caress. He knew she was only breathing but it was still doing funny things to his insides. Her breath warm and soft against his skin. He had to get back to the reason he was holding her. He closed his eyes and concentrated on the battle to come. When he opened his eyes he was ready until he heard her take a deep breath and look up at him.

Sebastian knew when he looked into her eyes that he was in trouble. What he saw there, he was sure, was mirrored in his own eyes. Even with her eyes all red and swollen, her nose runny and her face blotchy from crying she was still the most desirable woman he had ever met. He leaned back before he did something stupid. He thought he saw disappointment in her eyes but it was quickly masked. Could she have felt something too? Shaking away all thought of desire he focused back on Alana.

"Do you think you could tell me now what you dreamed about?" Sebastian tried not to show any of the feelings that were boiling inside of him.

For just a minute Alana thought Sebastian was going to kiss her but instead he pulled away from her. Maybe she had been imagining it because she wanted it so badly.

So she broke the contact and sat up, put her legs under her butt and told him about her dream. As she talked he listened. She got to the part where Todd invaded her dream and how he had taunted her with his laughter and how he told her she would be his before long. How when she was his he would kill her. She shivered at the last and placed her arms around her middle.

"I thought Eudora put a spell on the house so anything bad or evil couldn't Enter?"

Sebastian couldn't believe that Todd had actually gotten into her mind and tormented her like that. He knew his tactic. He was trying to scare her so she would be less confident once she had to come face to face with him. Todd thought he knew her but he obviously didn't if he was foolish enough to think that this would keep her from her purpose. If anything it would make her stronger. "Eudora put a spell that no one could physically enter but Todd didn't physically enter. He used his mind against you. Remember our first lesson when I told you things weren't always what they seemed?" He watched her nod "Well he entered your mind while you slept and entered into your space and he was able to manipulate everything in it. You didn't see it coming so you didn't have a chance to block him out." Again he watched her. She shivered slightly. "I didn't know it was possible for him to enter my dreams or my head for that matter." She looked up at him. "Can you do the same?" At his nod she thanked God she hadn't had any dreams about him that he could see. She would be mortified if he knew how much he affected her or if she was honest with herself how much she did care about him.

Sebastian didn't know what she was thinking. She had learned well to block someone out when she wanted to and right now whatever she was thinking she didn't want him to know. Today had been a long day and they only had a few hours left before daylight. He knew she needed to sleep. "I will talk to Eudora in the morning and make sure she reworks her spell to make sure he can't enter your dreams again, but for now I think you should try and get some sleep. Daylight will be here before you know it." She nodded her head and lay back down and closed her eyes and listened as Sebastian went back to the chair he had left. It was several minute before she could actually relax enough to try and go to sleep. She was curious about him. He told her they would talk tomorrow about what had happened that night. She couldn't believe he could actually change not only into a wolf but also a dragon! She had already seen his wings and if the picture she had seen in his foyer was any indication she had already seen him in his full dragon form, but a picture was different to real life. She wondered how big he was in his dragon form. She didn't know much about them but what she did know they were huge. She was still thinking about him as she drifted off to sleep.

57

Todd opened his eyes and looked around the room. It had taken more out of him to enter her mind than he thought it would. He took a minute to focus. He didn't want anyone else to know how drained he was. If that stupid bitch Star had done her job right he wouldn't have had to enter her Alan's mind. She would be right there in front of him but Star had underestimated Alana and so had he. Alana's abilities were far better than he had expected. She was learning very fast indeed and had escaped just minutes before he reached her. He had been so mad. He knew now that he shouldn't have taken it out on Star. Well maybe not so much. Yes, she deserved to have been punished for not watching Alana closer and letting her escape but he had been a bit extreme. Maybe after all this is over he would summon her back. Next time she would be a little more co-operative. In future when he asked her to do something for him she would be better. She would have a lot of time to think about it considering she was stuck in between. She was not in this world or any other. He had sent her floating around in total blackness between realms. Of course he would have to end this soon. Too long in the abyss between here and there tended to send one insane. That would be a waste of a good shape shifter. "Well were you able to access her mind and find out anything?" Now that was the part no one would like. He hadn't been able to find much out as she had been dreaming. Dreaming of some stupid place with lots of trees and flowers. She had been so happy until he showed up and scared her half to death. Maybe her powers aren't so strong after all. He knew she had been scared, he could feel her fear. Perhaps it had been one of the others helping her to escape. Oh well. He would have her in the end.
"No mother I didn't find out much. She was dreaming so there wasn't much to see." He knew she didn't like his answer by the way she curled her lip up. "Could you at least feel her powers?" He had felt very little from her except her fear. "I didn't feel a big wave of power if that is what you are asking. Honestly I didn't feel much power at all." And he hadn't or at least he told himself that he hadn't. He had been more intent on scaring her than anything and she *had* been scared. That almost made him want to laugh, to

know he was so close to having her.

"Now what do you think we should do? You know the house is protected by strong magic that even we can't break. How do you suggest getting to her?" Todd looked around while waiting for a response. Most of the people there were dressed in robes of black with hoods that covered most of their faces. He knew a few of the men present but most were unknown to him. When one of the hooded men stepped forward he carried a wooden stick that looked as old as he was. He was a stranger so Todd looked in question toward his father who nodded to the man.

"This is Ciaran. He is one of the elders. He has devised a spell, not to get into the house but to disarm and enchant. We will go after the mother. The girl will have no other choice but to attempt to rescue her if she wants her mother to stay safe and alive. She owns that flower shop so we know she will be there. When she closes it up tomorrow we will be there waiting."

Todd thought it was a good plan. He tried to get a better look at the man under the robe but all he saw was the gleam in his eyes as he handed his father a parchment of paper. His hand was boney and very pale. No wonder he was an elder. He probably needed that stick to help him stand up. Just as the thought formed in his mind he was lying on the floor. He jumped quickly to his feet.

"What the hell was that for!" he yelled at the old man who stood before him laughing.

The old man went quiet and pointed his finger at Todd "You should know better than to mock your elders." He then stepped back among the others. Todd couldn't believe it. The old man had heard his thoughts. He heard his mother snort and he looked toward her.

"Todd this is not a game. You must be ready for anything!" Todd wanted to snap an answer at his mother but he knew better. He would be ready damn it. He *was* ready! No weak female was going to defeat *him*. She didn't even have her powers yet and he knew Alana. She didn't even have it in her to do battle with him or anyone else for that matter. Look how easy it was for Star to get her. Of course she had escaped but she had people working with her. On her own she would be no match for him. He would make sure of it. He stood up and stared at both of his parents.

"Tell me what I am to do and I will make sure to deliver her mother by tomorrow night."

His father gave a slight nod and called him forward. His mother moved so he could get a better look at the paper that his father held. "You need to study this. It will take all three of us to say it." Todd leaned forward and looked at the paper. He read it over in his head. '*The Power of Magic times three will strengthen our power to enchant thee to come with us peacefully.*' It was a simple enough spell. He figured it would be harder than that. He was about to ask his father about it when the old man stepped out again. "Don't be fooled by how simple the words may appear. They are very powerful when said by three together. If anyone is protecting her they won't have a chance to resist. The words not only enchant her to follow but also to disarm any that protect her." He slipped back amongst the others and with a dismissive wave from his father they all disappeared.

"Do you understand Todd? This is something that we all have to do together and every word has to be repeated as they are on this paper."

Todd understood damn it. He was tired of everyone treating him like a child. He knew what he had to do.

"I wasn't questioning the words father, just how simple it seemed. I know my role and my duty." He had to control his temper he knew. His mother looked down on him and his father wasn't much better but he would show them. He would show them all that he was not one to mess with. By tomorrow evening he would have Alana's mom and hopefully within hours after that he would have Alana and her powers. That made him smile as he watched his father roll the paper back up and both his parents leave the room. He decided to have a drink before he made his plans for Alana. He would be doing things his way, not the way of his parents or the elders. This was his chance to become what he was always meant to be - the most powerful man in the world.

His phone rang just as he was about to take a drink. He picked it up on the second ring. "What?" he growled into it. He listened for a few minutes and then hung up. Apparently Alana's stuck up friends still hadn't come home. He wondered where they could be. He had his own people watching them to see if maybe he could use them for his own means. Of course no one thought about her stupid friends, but he had. And not a one of them had made it home yet.

Jessica was the hot one. He actually wouldn't mind taking a crack at her. Even though she was hot she was also stupid as shit. Trish was the smart ass of the group and the one he hated the most. She had always looked at him like he wasn't good enough for Alana. That made him laugh to himself. He wouldn't mind sending her to the gates of hell but only if he could watch. He actually laughed out loud that time. Now Katie, he didn't really remember much about her. She always had her head down and never looked him in the face. He knew he could have fun with her too but only if he could find out where they were and why they hadn't made it home yet. They were his backup plan. He already knew Alana would do anything for them but next time he had to make sure he had one of them for plan B. He had no doubt that Alana would come if she knew one of her friends were in danger. He never really understood why they were friends in the first place. They were all so different. He shrugged his shoulders, decided one more drink wouldn't hurt and so poured another one. He sat down in one of the chairs and loosened his tie. He wished now he hadn't been so harsh with Star. He could sure use her tonight but there would be plenty of time for that once he took care of Alana and all her goody-goody friends. He would destroy every last one of them.

58

Alana woke up gradually but it wasn't as quiet in the house at it usually was. She could hear voices downstairs. At first she didn't know where she was until she looked around. Her head was still foggy from sleep. When she sat up straight in bed she groaned. Her body was still sore from the previous night's adventure. The clock on her nightstand read seven-thirty. She couldn't believe she had slept an hour longer than normal. She eased out of bed and did a few stretches to loosen up her body. She expected that Sebastian would have come upstairs and dragged her out of bed for being late. She shrugged her shoulders somewhat disappointed and decided to get dressed. In the bathroom, when she looked in the mirror she groaned. Her eyes were all puffy and bloodshot and her head didn't feel much better. She wished that she had a spell to make her look fresh and revived. She made a mental note to add one to her book as she splashed cold water on her face and brushed her teeth. She felt a little better. Now to do something with her eyes. She looked in a drawer and found some eye drops. As she applied them she thought back to the night before and groaned. She had cried on Sebastian's shoulder and now the thought embarrassed her. He must think her weak. How was she going to face him today? If she could stay in her room and hide she probably would. Looking back at the mirror, her face and eyes did look better. Good thing, because she was really not one to hide. Taking a deep breath she left the sanctuary of her bathroom.
The voices were louder now. Everyone was already up and in the kitchen. Stealing herself she went downstairs to face everyone.

Sebastian looked back up at the clock. It was almost eight o'clock. He wondered if Alana was up yet. He had given her more time to sleep today knowing she needed it after the night she had just experienced, but soon he would have to wake her. They needed to get a move on. Today was their last day to work out any kinks in her training. He knew she would be sore but nothing could help that. They still needed to work. Eudora had been watching how impatient Sebastian was, looking at the clock every few minutes. She was aware that he had given Alana some extra time to sleep this morning. He was softening toward Alana she could see. Sebastian hadn't told her everything that happened last night but she knew Todd had invaded her dreams. She had taken care of that this morning. He would not be able to do it again. This time her spell was stronger. By what Sebastian said, she had been very frightened last night and it had taken her a while to get to sleep. 'Poor girl,' thought Eudora, 'she has so much on her shoulders it is a wonder she hasn't gone mad.' But she had faith in Alana's strength. She might look small and fragile but there was real strength within her.

She quietly approached Sebastian and discreetly asked, "Would you like me to go and see if she is up yet?"

Sebastian looked at the clock again. "If she isn't down here by eight then we will check on her."

Eudora started to say more but everyone in the room went quiet. She looked toward the door and saw Alana standing there with her usual smile in place, but Eudora knew she was a little weary.

"Dear, we have all been waiting for you. I hope you slept well? Do your hands or legs hurt?" Alana turned and gave Eudora an appreciative smile.

"I'm fine Eudora, thank you for asking, but I could use a cup of coffee!" she laughed and everyone in the room started talking at once. She walked over to the table and took her seat without looking at Sebastian. She was too embarrassed.

Her mom placed a cup of coffee in front of her and as she took a sip she looked around the room. Everyone was there except for Jessica. When she looked at her friends with a questioningly look Katie rolled her eyes.

"Jessica is still in bed. You know her, she doesn't believe in getting up before nine unless she has to. Her beauty sleep she calls it."

Everyone in the room laughed then Trish piped in. "Like she really needs it, but you know her. She swears by it."

"Honey would you like something to eat? I think you should eat a little something." Alana knew her mom was worried. Alana was too, but instead of showing it she put another smile on her face and for the first time looked at Sebastian. He was watching her. "I'm sorry I overslept. Do I have time for something quick?" When he nodded Alana looked back at her Mom. "What did you make?"

"Eggs and bacon dear."

Alana made a face. She didn't think she could stomach that today so with a wave of her hand a big bowl of fruit appeared in front of her.

She heard the clank of a fork and looked up. Trish was staring at her with mouth agape. Her friends had never seen her use magic. She looked at Katie to see what her reaction was. She looked like nothing unusual had happened. But Trish was still looking from her to the bowl of fruit.

"Damn that was freaking amazing. Can you do anything else? Can you like, ask for something and it just appear?" She was waving her hands like Alana had done. Alana laughed at the amazed look on Trish's face. It wasn't often to see Trish look so animated with her hands waving about but before she got a chance to answer Katie spoke up.

"I for one think it's incredible." She gave Alana an encouraging smile.

"Come on you two. I am still the same person I was before. It's just now I can do more things – special things." She shrugged her shoulders as if it was the most natural thing in the world and picked up her fork and pierced a piece of pineapple. As she watched both of her friends she had a twinkle in her eye.

"Look Alana, you just caught me off guard. You know we're behind you one hundred percent. We've been through a lot together - this one takes the cake I might add - but no matter what, we will always be there for you."

Alana shook her head in amazement. She was afraid if she spoke right now she would cry. Katie even gave her a nod and a wink with a big smile on her face.

"You know I just got to thinking, maybe it's a good thing to have a witch as a friend. No more flat tires. No more bad hair days and the most important thing? You could turn any of those idiot men out there into a frog!" All the women at the table, including Eudora burst out laughing but the men didn't see what was so funny.

"You do have a good point Trish. I will have to keep that in mind." Alana took a final bite and stood up. "But for now you guys are on your own. I have work to do."

Both girls nodded. They knew Alana and Sebastian needed to get to training. They also knew how important that was.

Sebastian had been watching Alana. She looked a little tired but other than that she looked like she always did. It was good to know she had such loyal friends. He could tell by Trish's speech that they would stand by her no matter what and he promised himself that he would make sure all her friends stayed safe. Stepping forward he looked at everyone at the table.

"I want each of you to pair up. You are not to leave this house unless one of my men is with you. Do you understand?" He waited for everyone to reply before continuing. "My men will be your shadows until this is over. If you don't have anything to do it would be easier if you stay in the house. It is protected by Eudora's spell and no one can enter. Lily, I don't think it would be wise to go into your shop today. Make arrangements with one of your staff. You have to remember these people are desperate. They will try everything in their power to get Alana to come to them and you are an obvious target to help them achieve that."

Lily was not happy with this but she nodded her head anyway.

He was satisfied that everyone would do what he asked. He looked to his men. "If for any reason you need me just call. I will hear." All three stood and bowed.

He stepped closer to Alana and held out his hand. When she placed hers inside his they vanished.

"Wow! That is so cool. I don't think I will ever get used to seeing people just disappear like that." Trish stood and took her dishes to the sink.

Eudora watched as everyone followed her lead. She too would do everything she could to make sure these girls and Lily stayed safe. After everyone cleaned up, the girls headed into the living room leaving her and Lily alone in the kitchen. She waved her hand and all the dishes were stacked neat and sparkling.

"Sebastian's right you know. If they wanted to get to Alana they would go through you and I know you don't want Alana to worry about your safety." She knew she had her with that speech when Lily sighed.

"I will do as you both ask, Eudora. I don't like it but for my daughter's safety I would do anything. I need to call Becky and make sure she can go in and work without me today." Eudora watched Lily go to the phone and speak with Becky. When she hung up she looked back at Eudora.

"Becky said she would open the shop. She thinks I am getting everything ready for Alana's birthday." She covered her face with her hands as a sob escaped. "I haven't even had a chance to think about her birthday. This was to be the most important one for her and she can't even enjoy it." This time Lily didn't try to hide the tears or the anguish in her voice.

Eudora stepped forward and gave Lily a reassuring hug. "Lily we are going to throw her the biggest and best twenty-first party that we can. Perhaps not all the people you planned to invite will be here but at least her family and best friends will be." Eudora was actually warming to the ideal.

"Girls!" she shouted "Could you come in here for a minute. Will one of you go and wake Jessica up. We need to discuss Alana's birthday party."

Katie volunteered to wake Jessica as the other three got out pens and paper and Lily made more coffee. They would make sure even if no one else could come that Alana had a birthday she would always remember. Of course since she would also receive all her powers it would be memorable anyway.

Eudora reminded herself to make sure the King and Queen were invited.

60

Hot and sweating, Alana needed a break so she held up her hand. "Do you think we could take a break? I need some water." She was concerned that Sebastian would think her weak but right now her throat was dry and raw and the headache she had managed to push away earlier was coming back.

Sebastian had been expecting her to call a rest break and was surprised that she had endured so long before doing so. He was impressed with her more and more each training session. She actually was doing better than he had anticipated. She had certainly come a long way in the last week.

They walked over to the stumps where Alana sat down and held out her hand. A bottle of water appeared. She was definitely getting better, she felt. She no longer had to concentrate as much. It was mostly second nature now. Sebastian joined her and produced his own bottle of water.

They were silent as they rested and drank their water. Sebastian wondered what was going on in her head. He should never have shown her how to block him.

Alana was trying to figure out a way to bring up the previous night and talk about what happened, both at the warehouse and later on. She just didn't know how to mention it without being blunt. That was not one of her strong suits - more Trish's style. She snuck a peek at Sebastian from under her lashes. She had tried a couple of times to read his thoughts but he always kept up a wall too thick to penetrate. Well, she was hoping *he* would bring it up but since that didn't seem likely she resigned herself to raising the subject herself. The only way to do that was to just blurt it out.

"I was hoping we could talk about what happened last night when you found me." She sat there and waited.

"I have been waiting for you to ask. I figured it would be sooner. What would you like to know?" She could kick him for making her be the one to ask. He spoke so calmly. Before she was through with him she was determined to make him squirm.

"I must admit, I've been wanting to ask all day but I thought you would tell me when you were ready but you didn't. Now I'm curious why." He just sat there "What I want to know is everything?" She thought she saw his jaw clench.

Sebastian stood and walked a few steps away with his back to her, searching for the right words. Alana sat there and waited patiently. Eudora had told him that he should tell her about his dreams but he never thought it was the right time or place. Instinct had always told him to wait.

"I am a Drakon and was born of royal blood so I can do more than most. Some of my ancestors also had the ability to transform but not all and only men could accomplish this. My father is one who doesn't have this ability. I can transform into two different creatures as I said last night. I can take to the ground and to the air." He turned when he said the last. "I think the best way to describe it is to show you both transformations. You must not be afraid. Even in these forms I am still me and in full control. I have the same thoughts, the same reasoning and the same desires and passions."

Alana's heart skipped at the last part. She nodded and prepared herself with some excitement at the anticipation of seeing him change into a beast. Even so, she let out a tiny scream as he transformed into the wolf. He looked so terrifying but she remembered what he said and just held her breath as he approached her. 'Relax Alana I won't bite you.' Her eyes widened. "You can still talk to me when you're in that form?" She watched amazed as he nodded his head up and down. She couldn't believe it. She had to close her eyes just for a second to accept that even though there was a wolf in front of her it was still Sebastian.

'I know it's a lot to take in right now,' he said.

She opened her eyes and narrowed them at the wolf. "All right buster, you need to stay out of my head unless I let you in. Is that understood?"

Sebastian walked forward and sat down in front of her. She was more amazed when he picked up his paw and extended it out to her. 'Agreed,' he said in her mind. She didn't really want to touch him but she took his paw into her hand and was pleasantly surprised at how soft his fur felt. She was tempted to rub his head before she caught herself and pulled her hand back.

"Ok, I think you have made your point with wolfie here." She watched as he changed back to human form. It was pretty incredible to be witness to something of this magnitude. Sebastian was standing again in front of her. "Wolfie?" he questioned.

She laughed, "Well it was either that or scream." Sebastian was pleased by how well she was handling all of this but the hardest was yet to come.

"When I change this time try not to scream. I know it will be hard but remember it is still me and that I control everything. You will see." Alana heard the seriousness in his voice and she knew from the picture what he would look like so she prepared herself for it. She took a deep breath calmed her already fragile nerves.

"Ok I'm as ready as I'll ever be." Sebastian stepped back even further. He watched Alana's face as he transformed. Her eyes widened and her face paled some but she stood firm and craned her neck and arched her back to look up at him. Alana thought she had been ready this time until now. She had to bend half way back to look up at him. For a minute she thought she was going to pass out but she took another deep breath and tried to calm down.

"Holy Shit!" she shouted. "I mean I knew you were going to be big but this…Oh my God!" She took a few steps back and still the dragon stood there like a statue. He was actually starting to scare her. "Sebastian, say something! You're starting to freak me out." The dragon leaned further down to try and get closer to her; she forced herself to stay put.

'For a minute you left me speechless with your choice of words.' She thought she heard a chuckle but did a dragon even know how to laugh? Again she looked up at him.

"Very funny, I was just a little surprised that's all." When he leaned further down she put her hands up.

"All right. All right. I was more shocked than anything. I thought I was going to pass out until I reminded myself it was just you." She studied him closely. He was totally black. Even his eyes were as black as the night. His feet or claws, whatever they called them, were almost as big as she was. He had scales that covered every part of the underside of his belly, all tiny in form. Even his head was covered but on the upper side the scales were different. They were bigger and thicker and there were spikes that rose up along his back. His wings were large. She had seen them the night before when he was human but they seemed bigger. Today they fanned out into a point and grew smaller as they came back to the point where they started at his back. His tail was long and ramrod straight. It looked dangerous. He even had smaller looking wings that fanned out on both sides of his head where small horns protruded from his skull. There were even spikes sticking out from his chin. She hadn't seen his teeth yet but she was sure they would be huge. Could he breathe fire? She thought she had heard they could do that somewhere. She knew when she got home she was going to do some research on them and find out everything she could.

'Have you had a good look yet?' She looked up sharply. She had been so busy looking him over she never thought about how he might feel.

"I'm sorry if I was staring. You are the first dragon I have ever seen and there is a lot of you to look at. By the way, can you breathe fire?" Again she thought she heard a chuckle in her head.

'Yes I can breathe fire and go ahead and look. I *am* the only dragon you will ever see.' She raised her eyebrow at that.

"Do you mean you are the only one of your kind?" When he nodded she almost laughed. She was actually talking to a dragon, even if it was really only Sebastian.

'Would you like to go for a ride?' He caught her off guard and her mouth dropped open.

"You can't be serious. You mean like you are?" Again she heard a chuckle and this time she knew she wasn't imagining it.

"Yes, I mean like I am." Alana looked at him cautiously. She didn't want to hurt his feelings. She just didn't think she was ready to go for a ride on the back of a dragon.

"I don't know Sebastian, maybe another time. I'm not so sure about all those spikes." As she spoke the spikes disappeared.

"How'd you do that? 'I can call for them at will. They are for battle.'

"I would be afraid of falling off. Maybe another time," and just like that he transformed into his human form. Alana was grateful he didn't push her about the ride.

She was not only afraid of falling off but she didn't think she could just climb on top of a dragon and say giddy up.

"One of these days I'll take you for a ride over my kingdom. We have lots of magical places.

Alana smiled. "I bet your friends and Eudora think it's amazing to watch you transform and to know they actually know a real fire breathing dragon," she snickered.

Sebastian had a serious look on his face. "I have never shown anyone else the transformation. Of course some have seen me afterwards in the sky or on the battlefield but I have never let anyone get as close as you."

Alana was astonished and moved by the gesture he had made. She thought for sure everyone, at least those closest to him, would have seen him change. She wondered if he had ever held anyone so closely before.

"I'm honored that you showed me. I just assumed because of that picture in the foyer that everyone had seen you up close."

Sebastian shook his head. "That was done by a battlefield artist who got a close look at me when I was in battle some time ago. He did a remarkable job considering he only saw me for a brief time. Some of my enemies in battle may have gotten a longer look and they probably wished they hadn't. But nobody has ever seen me transform."

She noticed he seemed a little uncomfortable telling her all this but she really did feel honored. For whatever reason he had decided to show her, she was grateful. Now she had to show a little vulnerability.

"I also wanted to thank you for last night. I know you probably won't believe this but that was the first time something like that has ever happened. Usually I suck it up, but I don't know if it was the effects from earlier or the fact that my life had been threatened. Anyway I just wanted to thank you." She really tried hard to look him in the face but she just couldn't. She felt like a coward and hung her head, when she was trying to give an apology for needing help. She was more than a coward - she was embarrassed - that at her lowest point he was there to witness it. She noticed also that he had gone quiet.

He had a stern look on his face. "Alana never apologize for being human. I accept your thanks and I know you well enough to know that wasn't like you. Can you not give me a little credit? I'm not the monster you think I am." She could tell she had made him mad but she didn't know where he got the idea that she thought him a monster. She put her hands on her hips.

"Listen you. Just because I wouldn't take a ride on your back doesn't mean I think you're a monster. If you want to know the truth I was a little scared. There, now you know." She crossed her arms.

Sebastian looked at her puzzled "I wasn't even talking about that Alana. I knew you were scared that's why I didn't push you."

"I don't get it then. I have never looked at you as being a monster. Maybe a little arrogant and cocky but never a monster. You've been hard on me and I didn't like it very much. But now I know why you did it. If I win…" there was a catch in her voice. Darn it. She wanted to sound confident so she started over. "You pushed me so I would work harder. I get that now. Of course at the time I thought you were being mean and sometimes cruel. I know you don't like me much but I do respect everything you have done. I am who I am today because of the way you pushed me to do my best." That was more open than she wanted to be but once she got started she couldn't help it. She wanted to make sure he understood that she had never thought him a monster.

Sebastian hadn't expected that little speech. She was mad. He could tell by the glow that burned around her body in her aura. She had been so compassionate about how she felt about him. She actually said she respected him and understood why he had pushed her so hard. By this time her face was turning red and she had started to shout but she was wrong about one thing. He did like her and he respected her more than any other woman so while she stood there with her arms crossed breathing hard he did the one thing he had wanted to do since the first time he had seen her in Eudora's fountain. He pulled her close. The fire left her eyes and a look of surprise came over her face. He whispered close to her lips. "You talk too much." Then he kissed her.

61

Eudora had all the girls in the kitchen making plans for Alana's birthday. Jessica wasn't happy about being woken up but she got right into it when shopping was mentioned. They decided a theme party would be ideal and Eudora actually liked what was suggested. It was fitting since Alana would be attaining all of her powers on her birthday that they dress up as magical creatures. The theme would be called 'One Magical Evening.'

Katie was in charge of costumes, except for Alana's. Eudora had something special in mind for her. Jessica would organize the decorations. They didn't want it to look too much like Halloween, more like a magical place. Jessica had the perfect idea. Lily of course took care of the flowers while Trish was in charge of the cake with Eudora's help of course. It was too short notice to order one so they were going to come up with one of their own and even though Sebastian wasn't there yet, they were putting him in charge of keeping Alana away from the house so they could get everything ready for the surprise.

Sebastian's warriors would be there. They would come as themselves. Eudora was going to talk to the King and Queen and make sure they showed up in all their finery - Sebastian too. He wouldn't like it but she figured for Alana he would play along. For security, Kohn would shadow Trish and Rowan was going to follow Katie but Jessica had insisted that Warwick go with her. With all their plans in gear Eudora called the men into the room. They would need different clothes as they were still in their battle gear. For this she asked Jessica for her help - she was the most fashion oriented after all. She did study it more than any of her friends. When the men were properly dressed she gave each one instructions about who guards who. She could tell by their smiles that she had made the right choices. Could there be romance in the air between these three couples? She shrugged her shoulders. Anything was possible. Look at Lily and Edmund. The first in centuries to marry outside of their kingdom and look what happened there. They broke the curse and had a beautiful daughter. Speaking of which, she went back into the kitchen. Lily was on the phone. She heard flowers being mentioned so she must be talking with her friend Becky.

Eudora wanted to go to see the King but she didn't want to leave Lily alone just in case Lily got into her mind to go to her shop and make sure the place was running right. She also had to go to her library. The outfit she had in mind for Alana was there and by the time she got through with her, Alana would look just like a Princess. And perhaps a prince that she knew would actually act on his feelings. She was convinced that Sebastian had feelings for Alana. She had watched him enough over the week and when she had been kidnapped he was like a mad man. He growled at everyone who got close to her when he finally brought her home. She was also certain that Alana had feelings for him. She had watched her too. They both watched each other without the other one knowing. She thought it was amusing. They were probably wondering what the other one thought. She was going to try and talk with Alana some time tonight. Maybe she could find out something from her since Sebastian wasn't going to give anything up. Lily said good-bye and hung up the phone.

"Lily did you get all the flowers arranged? Will your friend Becky do them?" Lily sat down next to Eudora.

"I told her what we would need. I will have to go and pick them up tomorrow though. The shop is only open until noon and they are too busy with other deliveries to bring them here. Besides, she would wonder why I didn't pick them up myself and probably ask questions. As it is she thinks I am busy getting everything ready." Eudora didn't like the idea of Lily going to the shop but she didn't voice it. Tomorrow she would think of some other way even if she had to go and get them herself. She studied Lily. This must have been killing her. Even though tomorrow was her daughter's birthday it was also going to be a difficult day. She waved her hand and a pot of tea appeared with two cups. "I think we need to relax for a while. The girls have everything under control."

She watched as Lily poured tea for both of them.

"Have you already picked out Alana's birthday present?" She asked, trying to keep Lily's mind off everything else.

"I have had her birthday present since she was born. Edmund gave it to me. He said we were to pass it on to Alana when she turned twenty-one. I do wish Edmund were here to see that. He would be so proud of his little girl."

Eudora had been relaxing in her chair but the mention of Edmund made her sit up straight. She tried to sound as calm as possible when she asked if Lily had already wrapped it. When Lily shook her head and took another sip of tea, Eudora's curiosity got the better of her. "Would you mind if I see it?"

If Lily wondered why, she never asked. She excused herself from the table and went to fetch it. Eudora wondered what Edmund would have given Lily that was so important he told her to wait until she was twenty-one. Perhaps it was just a human tradition. Lily soon returned with the gift.

"I had almost forgotten about it until the other day when I was looking for something in my chest and found it. There was a note from Edmund reminding me not to forget," she laughed as she put the small box on the table. "May I see it?"

Lily passed it to her. On touching her palm she felt that whatever was in the box was important. She could feel the magic emanating from the box. Such power! Eudora smiled back at Lily. She didn't want her to give away her thoughts. The box was a small cube with gold etching all around the edges and down the seam in the middle where a gold symbol rested. The symbol she did not recognize. It was formed in a circle but when she looked closer it looked like a small golden heart in the middle. She had to take another breath. She felt even stronger now about the importance of its contents. She reached for the latch and heard a click as the box came open in the middle. Both sides separated to reveal the precious contents. Nestled on a bed of blue velvet lay a golden heart on a chain. It was a locket. She didn't attempt to open it - that was for Alana to do. But she had seen this heart before in her fountain waters. This was the same heart that the little girl had given her dragon. She had been right. Alana was Sebastian's heart even though he didn't want to admit it now. He would though and soon. She closed the lids and latched the box and with a smile she handed it back to Lily. "It's beautiful."

Lily looked down at the box. "Yes it is. I know it meant a lot to Edmund. He said it had been in his family for a very long time." She got back up and went to put the necklace back. Eudora wondered could it be that it was passed down through generations to be given to the firstborn daughter. If what she suspected was true then that necklace had originally belonged to none other than Rianna.

62

Sebastian had wanted to do this for a long time. From her reaction when his lips touched hers he knew that he had taken her by surprise. Her body went rigid. After a few nips of her bottom lip she sighed into his mouth and relaxed slightly. He slid his hand further up her back cradling her neck in his hand. Pulling her even closer she parted her lips so he took full advantage and laid siege to her mouth. He couldn't seem to get enough. He heard a groan in his foggy brain. He thought that it had come from Alana then realized the sound had come from him.

He felt a light touch as her hands traveled up the front of his shirt and came to rest right over his heart. He knew he should stop but for the life of him he couldn't seem to pull away. The heat radiating from their bodies set him on fire. They fit together more than perfectly – more as one entity. If his life ended tomorrow he would die a happy man.

Alana couldn't believe what was happening. One minute she had been hurt and furious with him and then she was in his arms and everything about it felt right. She had never experienced anything like she was feeling now. She slid her hands up his chest and could feel his heartbeat beneath her palms. His heart was beating as fast as hers, she knew. She felt alive for the first time in her life.

Sebastian held her so close she hardly had space to breathe. She had opened up to him completely, holding nothing back. When she slid one of her hands along his neck and let it rest on the side of his face she felt him pull away right before he broke the kiss and held her at arm's length.

Sebastian had never lost his head but right now he had just forgotten about everything. He held her away from him and looked into her flushed face. Her eyes were luminous and bright with a touch of desire blossoming in her face. Her aura was as golden and as bright as the sun as it circled her body. He hated doing it but he had to release her. He spoke in a gruff voice. "That should never have happened."

Sebastian saw the desire dissolve, replaced by a question in her eyes. He couldn't look at her with her lush lips swollen and her breath coming quickly, like she had just run a marathon. She was confused by his behavior. He turned his back on her to block her out

of his head. Even if it felt right, neither one of them needed a distraction right now. He had a job to do as her teacher and she had a job to do as his student. There was no room for emotions. He felt a light touch on his back and tried not to react. "Why did you kiss me Sebastian?"

He could hear how hurt she was. He took a calming breath and cleared his mind. He hated to hurt her but right now she didn't need to be focusing on *him*. Sebastian turned to look at her. She still had a slight plumpness to her lips but her eyes had cleared and her face was as blank as his. Her aura had faded.

"I think for the time being we should forget about it and continue what we started." The slight droop in her shoulders told him that he had hurt her again. "It's time to get back to work."

When she tilted her head to the side Sebastian thought that she was gearing up for an argument but instead she surprised him yet again. She squared her shoulders, nodded and walked back over to their training field. He ran his hand along the back of his neck and followed her, a little disappointed that she hadn't put up a fight.

'*That's what you wanted,*' said a voice in the back of his mind. He knew it was for the best. They needed to finish what they started and then maybe...he didn't know. Maybe they could talk more.

63

Eudora was still in the kitchen when she heard voices in the living room. She got up and went to see which one of the girls had returned. When she entered she almost laughed. Trish and Jessica were directing their guards where to put all the boxes and packages. They were being good sports, even with all the muffled words and grumbling. She couldn't believe they had gotten so much done in such a short time.

"Did you by any chance leave anything in the stores?" She did laugh then as both men answered 'No!' in loud voices.

Trish blew the hair from her eyes. "I have to tell you Eudora, when Jess has her mind set and it has to do with fashion or decorating she can get things done. It seemed like everyone in the stores knew her and wanted to help."

They heard Jess laugh as she directed Kohn to put the boxes he was holding down. "Of course they all know me. I make shopping a priority and I spend just as much time in stores as I do at home." Both Trish and Eudora rolled their eyes as the front door opened again and Katie and Rowan came in. Both had their hands full.

"Dang, Jess. Did you buy out all of the stores or what?" The girls all laughed and the men all groaned.

Just then Lily came into the room. "My goodness. It's a good thing I cleaned space in my sewing room. Looks like we'll need *all* of it."

Two hours later they had everything stacked neatly in the sewing room and they were all ready for a cold drink.

Eudora was glad when Lily offered to make some iced tea. It looked like they would need it. When everyone filed out to the kitchen Lily Eudora put a charm on the door to allow anybody access except Alana.

Lily and Eudora made their way to the kitchen. The girls were fixing glasses with ice for the tea and getting together a snack of chips and salsa. The guys were already seated at the table so Lily and Eudora took their seats as the girls brought drinks and snacks to the table. After everyone was seated Jess looked at Katie.

"I hope you were able to find some really cool costumes for all of us. Well except the guys since they will be wearing their own clothes."

"I think everyone will be happy with what I got them. Jess, you will be a gorgeous wood nymph and Trish, I decided since you are the boldest of the bunch you will be a Goddess. I will be a fairy with beautiful wings. And Lily I thought you would look good as an Angel." Both of Katie's friends were happy with her choices for them. Lily liked the idea of being an Angel.

"Eudora I figured since you are who you are, that you had something in your own wardrobe to wear?"

Eudora smiled at Katie. "Dear, you are right. I have plenty of things to choose from. Now I have decided to invite Sebastian's parents." She saw that no one had expected that. Even the guards looked surprised. "After all, it's not every day that a prophecy comes true, but tomorrow, a prophecy we have waited centuries for will finally come to pass."

Everyone at the table looked at each other excitedly but it was Jessica who actually clapped her hands together and with a radiant smile looked at Eudora.

"You mean to tell us that a real King And Queen will be here tomorrow night? Oh my God! I can't believe we're actually going to meet royalty!" Jess clapped her hands again and looked off into space.

Jessica was already planning what she was going to do and say to them. Trish rolled her eyes and looked at Jessica. Kohn stood and also looked at Jessica but his look was one of distain.

"You have already met royalty. Sebastian is the crown prince of our world." Eudora had to commend Kohn on his loyalty to Sebastian. Jessica's eyes grew huge at the look on the men's faces. They were all looking at her with the same look of disapproval, even Warwick who had seemed to have taken a fancy to her.

"Oh my God! You're right. I really never looked at it that way. Wow! That means he'll be King one day!" Katie almost choked on her tea.

"You have to forgive Jess. She really doesn't keep up with things like that. She hadn't really meant any disrespect to Sebastian." Kohn sat back down with a grunt.

"Way to go Jess," said Trish. Jess looked around the table, her bottom lip starting to quiver and tears sprang up in her eyes.

"I'm sorry. Katie's right I didn't mean...I mean to say..." she sniffed and started over. "When we met Sebastian, we didn't know he was royalty…well not until after Eudora told us. By that time I just saw him as Sebastian - Alana's warrior friend…Oh, I'm messing this all up." She closed her mouth and decided she had said enough when Eudora shot the men a rather critical look. They all looked a little uncomfortable and Katie and Trish where staring daggers at them for upsetting their friend.

Kohn cleared his throat. "We accept your apology Jessica."

Jess looked up with watery eyes and smiled. Warwick who was sitting close to her reached over and gave her a napkin to wipe her eyes.

"Now that all the drama is over, maybe we should think about dinner. Alana and Sebastian will be here soon," said Trish as she got up and headed for the kitchen followed closely by the other two girls. Eudora looked at all three men. "I think you three should patrol the area just to make sure everything is as it should be while we get dinner started." All three stood and as fast as they could without appearing over anxious took up their patrols outside. She smiled to herself as she too went into the kitchen to see what was on the menu for tonight.

64

On the other side of town there were three others sitting down for dinner, but this dinner was more somber. Todd looked at his mother and father and wondered if they even liked each other. He knew that they didn't love each other. He had known that for years. Hell, you could wonder if they even liked *themselves*. The only noise was the clink of silverware as the meal was eaten in silence. His mother always wore a sour face and his father never showed anything. No wonder their family was the way they were. But he remembered a different time before his brother had been killed. Now *he* had been the exception in the family. He had been nothing like the rest of them. His father had pushed him to do his duty even though his brother didn't understand what the war was about and look what happened. There he was - dead now. Todd had looked up to his brother at one time but after his death his heart was only full of hate for everyone and the damn war. He had been about nine then. His brother was probably the only person he had ever loved. Now sixteen years later he had turned into something that his brother wouldn't approve of. There was nothing he could do about it now. He actually liked his life. The power and money felt good and soon he would have more power than anyone could comprehend and that made all of this - he looked around again with a smirk on his face - bearable. "What has got you looking that way Todd?" He let his memories fade and looked at his mother. "I was just thinking about tomorrow." He knew not to mention Keir's name. No one had spoken it since they buried him.
"I'm glad to see you're finally taking your duty to this family seriously." Todd growled at his mother under his breath. He hated her and he hated his father even more. They were both the reason Keir was dead. Do his duty to the family? What a joke. More like making sure his mother and father lived comfortably all of their lives but he promised as soon as he gained what he needed from that bitch Alana, he would take care of his parents. Maybe he would send them on a holiday far away. Maybe he would give Star some company. He had to smile at that as he looked at his mother. "Yes mother. I plan on taking my duty to this family very seriously from now on."
His mother snapped her head up and glared at him. She had

detected some sarcasm. His father smiled and told him it was good and after they took care of Alana, everything that they had worked so hard for would be theirs along with all the power that came with it. Todd had to agree with him but there was only one little flaw. It would be all his, not theirs, and when everything was over he would make sure they both knew it.

65

Since the girls and Lily had dinner under control Eudora decided to go and see Artemis. When Kohn appeared at her summons she gave him instructions to watch the girls while she visited the King. When he nodded obediently Eudora disappeared and reappeared in the king's foyer and walked to his study. She knocked and waited until he boomed out his usual invitation, "Enter!"

He was sitting in a chair by the fire with his wife in the other across from him. They both greeted her with genuine smiles.

"Eudora, what brings you here?" asked Aurora.

Eudora bowed to them and approached. "Eudora, what have I told you about bowing? We have known you too long for that," the King laughed.

"I'm sorry Artemis. It's just a token of respect." He dismissed that with a snort and raised an eyebrow as if to ask the reason for her unannounced visit.

"I have come to invite the two of you to a special event."

Again the King raised an eyebrow. "What special event would this be?"

Eudora smiled. "We are having a birthday party for Alana. I thought you both would like to be there. We are calling it *A Magical Evening* since it *will* be to some effect. Not only will it be her birthday but also the day when she attains her full powers. It will be a time to remember. Will you both honor us by coming?"

Before Artemis could speak, Aurora clapped her hands together, "Oh how I do love parties." Eudora watched the glow spread across Aurora's cheeks. Artemis saw it too. "I guess you have your answer," chuckled Artemis.

"How should we dress, Eudora? I know things are different in that world." She could tell Aurora was already thinking about what she had in her closet.

"That is the beauty of this party. We want you to be yourselves. We want you to dress in all your royal finery." Aurora clapped her hands again and laughed softly. "I can't wait. What will Sebastian wear?"

Eudora smiled again. "I will send him to retrieve his royal robes and crown later. When we are ready for you we will send for you." She suspected Sebastian wouldn't be too happy to leave the house and travel home but Eudora couldn't take the crown. Protocol only allowed it to be handled by the rightful owner or his appointed servant. "Now I have to get back. Sebastian and Alana should be back by now and I have one more stop to make to get Alana's costume. I told her girlfriends and mother that I would provide her gown. I have the perfect one in mind."

Aurora looked at her with a puzzled look. "What will she be then?" Even the King leaned forward in anticipation.

"I want that to be a surprise to everyone but I think you will like it." Artemis and Aurora both nodded as Eudora said her good-byes and departed.

She reappeared in her library and immediately opened the trunk in the corner releasing the aroma of jasmine throughout the room. It had been a while since she had been in this particular trunk. What she was looking for was wrapped in tissue. Pulling the gown out, she inspected it closely. It was as perfect as the day she had first placed it in the trunk. That preservation spell had worked beautifully. She sifted through the trunk for the rest of the items she would need. When she had recovered them all she conjured up a big white box and put everything inside. She repeated the preservation spell to make sure everything remained well protected. The gown was centuries old after all. She smiled. Alana would make the perfect Enchantress. She had been born to the role. Eudora looked around one last time. She would call for her own robes tomorrow but for now she needed to get back. Dinner was probably over by now and the ribs she conjured up to feed everyone before she left would not stay around long and she was in the mood for some good old barbeque.

Alana and Sebastian arrived to the smell of barbequing ribs and Alana's mouth started to water immediately. All her friends were in the kitchen along with her mom and they were chatting and laughing. Katie suddenly noticed their presence. "You're both back!"

The others all turned to look. She felt like she was on display. "Hi honey, Sebastian. Alana, why don't you go on upstairs and take a shower. Once you're done, dinner should be ready. We're having ribs." She laughed at the look on Sebastian's face.

"Don't worry. You'll love them. I'll be back in a few minutes." She turned and left him alone with everyone staring at him.

"Where are my men?"

It was Trish who answered. "They are outside somewhere protecting the house." Sebastian nodded and left.

"God he's such a hunk! Alana is so lucky." Jess had a dreamy look on her face as she watched him leave. "Hello! Earth to Jessica." Trish waved her hand in front of Jessica's face.

"What? You mean to tell me none of you think he's a hunk?" She folded her arms in front of her. Katie giggled. "What happened to Warwick?"

Jessica shrugged her shoulders. "What about him? He's cute too but there's just something sexy about that one." She looked to the door again.

"Yeah. We know what that something is. He's a prince!" everyone laughed, even Lily. "Come on girls give her a break."

Jessica stuck her tongue out at both her friends and laughed too. "Well that definitely gives him brownie points. And if you must know, I wasn't thinking of myself on this one I was thinking about Alana."

They all stopped what they were doing and looked at her.

"What? Come on you can't tell me you haven't noticed the way those two look at each other?" Jessica realized that none of them had. "Watch them tonight at dinner. You'll see. I'm not saying another word." She went back to chopping the tomatoes for the salad. Everyone else went back to work too but it wasn't Trish's nature to be quiet. "Do you really think Alana has a thing for him?" Jess nodded. Trish looked at Katie and Lily.

"Have you two noticed any of this?" Both shook their heads.

"I mean, I'm not saying he's not a hottie with a great bod. Hell, all of them are hunks with the capital H but I will reserve judgment until tonight." She looked again at Jessica who gave her a saucy look and went right back to chopping the tomatoes.

"Who is a hottie and who are we not judging?" All four women jumped and turned with a guilty look.

"Oh, it's only you Eudora. You scared the daylight out of me." Katie touched her chest and took a deep breath.

Eudora raised her brow in that questioning way. Trish walked to the doorway and looked around it. Seeing the coast was clear she nodded to Katie who couldn't wait to include Eudora in the girlie chat.

"Well, Jessica seems to think that Sebastian and Alana have a thing for each other. She says she has seen them giving each other the look. We were arguing with her because none of us have seen it." Trish urged her on with an impatient nod. "What do you think Eudora? We're going to watch them tonight at dinner."

All eyes were on Eudora. Even Lily, who was trying not to appear interested waited for Eudora's reply.

"Jessica, I have to say you are very observant. I agree with you. I too believe that there is 'a thing' between them," she said trying to sound as modern as the girls.

Jessica smiled at everyone in triumph as Katie and Trish both looked dumbfounded. Lily stopped pretending that she wasn't interested and looked right at Eudora hopefully.

"See, I told you. So if any of you would have been looking you would have seen for yourselves. Now I think we should get dinner on the table." Jessica grabbed the salad and brought it to the table just as Alana came into the room.

"I feel so much better after my shower. Do you guys need any help?" Everyone talked at once. She was a little puzzled until Jessica came up to her.

"We can handle it. Why don't you go tell all those hunks out there that dinner is ready." Alana laughed at Jessica and headed for the door. Looking back twice, she shook her head not knowing what had been going on. Whatever it was they sure didn't want her to know. It might have something to do with her birthday. She wouldn't put it past them to have a party anyway. She smiled at that. She did have the best friends a person could have. If she could just get over this afternoon as easily as Sebastian had. He hadn't mentioned it again for the rest of the day. He had actually worked her even harder than he ever had before. Her arms were sore from holding one of those godforsaken swords that felt like they weighed a hundred pounds. She desperately wanted to know what had happened but she was too much of a coward to ask. She was afraid of the answer he might give. Well she wasn't going to dwell on it. She had more important things to think about right now. She needed to be ready and focused. She had a niggling feeling that something was going to happen tomorrow. She knew she was being foolish with the house protected and all the magic that was in the house, but still she couldn't shake the feeling something important was about to happen. Tonight she needed to do the spell Zephyr had shown her if she wanted answers. She had a feeling that tomorrow would be too late. She shivered as she went to the door. Rowan was at his post so she told him it was time for dinner. He nodded and within seconds all three men were coming through the front door. She called for Sebastian in her mind. She waited a second and called him again. She started to worry when he didn't appear and was about to try again when suddenly he was there. "Dinner is ready," was all she said as she left him standing in the living room as she headed for the kitchen.

The food smelled good and she was so hungry. As she took her place at the table she saw the guards looking at the ribs a little warily. Katie laughed at them and urged them all to try them. "Trust me. Once you try them you will become addicted." She looked right at Warwick as she said it. Katie looked at Alana and rolled her eyes. Alana laughed and looked down the table at Sebastian. He too was looking at the ribs heedfully but when Rowan took one and took a bite he looked at the others with a barbeque smile.

"They are very good." After that all the men dug in and were smiling with barbeque all over their faces. The girls all laughed and settled into their own meal.

Alana enjoyed watching the pleasure come over Sebastian's face as he ate the ribs. It was the first time she had ever seen him show any kind of emotion. When he looked up, their eyes met and again he put that wall up to keep everyone out. Alana sighed and looked away. For just a split second she got to see pure pleasure on Sebastian's face and it took her breath away. Again she peeked through her lashes but he never returned her glance so she went back to eating her dinner. She didn't know she had an audience as she had watched Sebastian but three people had watched with dawning clarity. Jessica on the other hand had a smug smile for everyone.

66

Alana excused herself to go to bed right after dinner explaining that she was so tired. She had overheard Eudora tell Sebastian that his parents wanted to see him and him saying he would go right after dinner. This was the perfect opportunity for her to try the spell that Zephyr had helped her with. She went into her room and closed the door and turned the lock. She was well aware that Eudora or Sebastian could get in but no one else could. Eudora was busy with everyone else and Sebastian had gone to see his parents so she had time. No sooner had she started for her dresser when there was a knock at her door. She groaned and closed her eyes. "Honey it's me. Can I come in?" She couldn't keep her mother out so she unlocked the door. Her mom was standing there smiling. "I have something for you. I know it's not your birthday for a couple of hours but I wanted you to have this tonight. Your father wanted you to have this for your twenty-first birthday."
Alana didn't know what to say. Her father; it had been so long ago since she had seen him. She could barely remember his face. She opened the door wider for her mom to come in. She could do the spell later.
"I know you're tired. I promise I won't stay long. Here. Open it." With shaky hands, Alana took the package. It was a blue velvet box lined with gold and a clasp in the middle with a symbol on it. She took a deep breath and closed her eyes until she felt ready. She took the clasp between her fingers and pulled it open. Nestled in the middle of the blue velvet was a golden heart on a chain. Picking it up, she felt a lot of energy and warmth move through her body. She looked at her mom.
"When did he give this to you?" She had tears in her eyes. Lily took the chain and turned Alana slightly to allow her to fasten around her slender neck.
"The day you were born. He gave this to me and was very adamant on that day that he wanted you to have it when you turned twenty-one." She slipped the necklace around Alana's neck. Alana reached down and looked at the necklace again. It was beautiful. She would wear it always. She hugged her mom.
"Thank you. I needed this tonight." Lily kissed her forehead and got up.

"I won't keep you any longer. I know you have had a hard day," she smiled at Alana and left her to rest. Alana couldn't believe this. Something from her father. She sniffed, wiped her eyes and went and locked the door again. More than ever she needed to try this spell. She went to her dresser and removed the pouch that Zephyr had given her. She decided the bathroom was the best place. At least if Eudora or Sebastian turned up they wouldn't come into the bathroom. That room would be private and peaceful. She had collected everything she needed during the week. Gathering it up, she locked herself in the bathroom.

'OK,' she thought, 'you can do this.' She closed her eyes and took several deep breaths to calm her nerves and to focus. That done, she opened her eyes and went to work. She placed all the items in the middle of the floor and sat down Indian style. Zephyr said she would have to steep the herbs in boiling water. She bit down on her lip. She had plenty of water but how to boil it? 'Of course!' she thought as she slapped her forehead. '*I* can do it. I am a witch after all.' Quickly she conjured up a pot and filled it with water. She placed the candles around her in a star. Zephyr told her they would help with the spell and repel evil spirits while attracting benevolent ones. She remembered the order Zephyr told her to place them in. The white symbolized truth and strength. That one was to go to her left behind her elbow. The blue which represents psychic and spiritual awareness was to be second place at the point in front of her. The third one was pink, for love and friendship and overcoming evil went behind her right elbow. The fourth candle was yellow representing confidence. It went in between the white and blue and the fifth one was orange for courage between the blue and pink. The last one was the gold one. It represents intuition and protection and went directly behind her. She was to sit in the middle of the candles. Zephyr said it was a witch's symbol of protection and of positive power and energy. She hoped it worked. She went back to the pot and pointed at the water and watched it boil, still amazed at her new found abilities. She produced a cup and placed the herbs into it and added the boiling water carefully. While letting it steep for a few minutes and allowing it to cool. Alana called for her spell book and refreshed her memory. Satisfied, she waved her hand again and the book vanished. She pointed at the candles in the order she had placed them and watched as a flame appeared from every wick. Now she took the cup, sat in the center of her symbol and waited the prescribed two minutes. She had placed a clock on her bathtub so she wouldn't forget about the time. She was still a little shocked from her mother's visit. She touched the necklace again feeling certain that it meant something. The energy she could feel from it was powerful. When she was finished with her spell she would go downstairs and talk to Eudora. She was sure she would know something about it but for now she had to keep her focus on what she was doing. Looking at the clock, it was time. Zephyr said she had to drink every drop in one go and then say the spell. She did as advised and when the potion was all gone Alana closed her eyes and spoke.

'*Turn the hour back in time…Give me the past so that I might know… What happened all those years ago…Show me now what I wish to see…Show me now and blessed be.*'

As Alana opened her eyes a bright light came out of nowhere and almost blinded her. She closed her eyes to protect them but after a few seconds she slowly opened them again. She blinked several times and looked around. She was in someone else's bedroom. It didn't look like any bedroom she had ever seen. The walls were made of some kind of stone. There was one small window right in front of her with wooden shutters over it. There was a bed, if you could call that a bed, to the left. It was made of a dark wood. Very rustic looking and surrounded by curtains. It looked like something made a long time ago. At the foot of the bed was a matching trunk. Alana was starting to think she may have made another big mistake when she swung around and saw a huge fireplace that took up most of the wall. There was a fire burning, casting all kinds of shadows around the room. Alana didn't see a lamp but there *were* candles. Some hung on the wall, others were placed throughout the room on stands. There was a door she was sure went out into a hallway and another that probably went to a closet. These doors were huge and also rustic with black rings. She assumed the rings were used to pull open the door.

'Oh great,' thought Alana. She had traveled back in time but to where she didn't have a clue. She walked further into the room intending to look out the window when she heard a clank come from somewhere and the door over at the side opened. She started to turn around but before she could, she had been picked up and thrown against the wall.

She didn't really hit it hard but she was still a little dizzy from the shock of it all. She tried to move and panicked. All she was able to do was move her head. She turned her eyes in the direction of the door and lost all train of thought. A woman stood with her hand out and was looking at Alana with a frosty stare.

The woman was beautiful, even with the fire in her eyes. Her hair was very long and it brushed the floor as she walked forward. It was the same color as Alana's. Her skin was so fair she looked like a porcelain doll. Her eyes looked silver. Maybe it was just the light. She appeared to be very small in build. Maybe five foot four, if that. She was wearing a blue velvet dress different from any Alana had ever seen. It was a one-piece that fit to perfection, cut expertly to emphasize the curve of her neck. The sleeves went down to her wrist and belled out into a point. Some kind of belt circled her waist and then hung low to the ground. The dress was full length and so reached the floor. It was stunning. Her hair was braided with ribbons running through it and she had a headpiece that circled around her head and sparkled in the candle light. Alana could tell that they were real gems of the highest quality. The piece curved around and dipped down on her forehead forming a V shape. The stones were small with one larger central stone shaped like a teardrop. The woman was now standing just a few feet from Alana. She was still looking at Alana like she was some kind of criminal.

"Who are you? And what are you doing in my bedchamber?" 'That figures,' thought Alana, 'her voice is soft as velvet.'

"Speak!" She didn't really shout but it was loud enough to wonder if this woman was friend or foe.

"I'm sorry my name is Alana Vaughn. To be honest I don't know what I'm doing here." More quietly she muttered, 'stupid spell.'

The woman came closer. "Are you a witch then?"

Alana almost groaned. She shouldn't have said anything. Witches were burned in some parts of her history. Why not here? She looked back at the woman. "I guess you could say that. I'm learning."

The woman tilted her head in curiosity. "What are you wearing?"

Alana tried to lean forward. She didn't see anything wrong with what she was wearing - a pair of jeans and a t-shirt.

"These are jeans and a t-shirt," she said as she watched the woman inspect her clothing fascinated by what she saw. "Why do you dress like a man?"

Alana couldn't help it - she laughed. "Where I come from women dress like this all the time."

The strange woman stepped back just a little and narrowed her eyes. "Pray tell, where is it you come from?"

Alana looked at the woman. 'Man they talked strange in whatever time this is.' She thought carefully before answering. "I am from Georgia. You know, the peach state?" She could tell the woman had no idea where Georgia was much less probably what a peach was. "I do not understand this Georgia and who is peach?"

Alana knew this was going to be a long night.

"Do you think you could let me down now? I mean you know harm."

The woman smiled and it lit up her whole face. Alana had to admit, she was beautiful and from what she could see, flawless. And she had a twinkle in her eye that Alana didn't quite understand.

"Of course you will not harm me. This chamber is protected. No one with evil intention can enter." Alana narrowed her eyes.

"Why didn't you say that in the first place?" The woman laughed it was almost musical. She waved her hand and Alana fell to the ground sideways. As she landed softly on the floor her necklace fell out from her t-shirt. She heard the woman gasp and looked up at her. Her face was pale. The woman pointed her finger at the necklace. "Where did you get that medallion?"

Alana looked down at her necklace. "It's not a medallion. It's a necklace and my father gave it to me. Why?"

The woman came forward to look at the necklace more closely. Her color was starting to return. "And who is your father? What is his surname?"

'Again with the strange words,' thought Alana standing up. The woman still hadn't taken her eyes off the necklace.

"His name was Edmund Von Drayton. Now let me ask you a question - who are you?"

The woman bowed as she stared at Alana. "My name is Rianna. Some call me Rianna the Enchantress."

Alana's eyes grew huge and she felt dizzy as if she was about to pass out. "No you can't be her!"

The woman laughed again. "I can assure you that is my name given to me by my mother. Her name was Alana. You know it means 'beautiful' don't you?"

Alana nodded. She needed to sit down. Without being invited, she walked over to the fireplace and sat in one of the chairs. She couldn't believe she was actually sitting in the same room as her great, great…she didn't even know how they were related. She looked back up at Rianna who had a sincere look on her face. She didn't want to say too much because she didn't know what time she had come back to. "Are you married Rianna?"

Rianna looked puzzled. "Yes I'm married. Why do you ask such a question?" Alana felt she still had to tread lightly. "I was just curious." Rianna laughed and gave her a knowing smile. "Are you wanting to know about the curse?" Alana sat up straighter in her chair.

"What *do* you know about the curse?"

Rianna sat next to Alana. "We know Drake was angry with my Lucian and some say he cursed us." She moved her shoulders slightly. "You mean you don't believe it?"

Rianna laughed again. "Drake was bitter toward Lucian and me. He never understood. It was not up to him or Lucian. It was *my* choice and I chose Lucian."

Alana knew all this. What Rianna didn't know was the things that happened in between when the curse was made.

"Well I don't know if this will affect the future or not, God I hope not, but Drake did cast a spell and for a long time there *were* no daughters born." Rianna stood and paced the room.

"This can't be. How much time passed before the curse was broken and a daughter was born?"

Alana shifted uncomfortably in her seat. She didn't want to look at Rianna. "Please. I need to know if my legacy continued."

Alana finally looked at Rianna uncertain about how much to tell her but she felt she had to tell her everything. She took a deep breath. 'Dorothy, you're not in Kansas anymore,' she thought.

67

Alana told Rianna everything she knew about the curse and no daughter ever being born until her. Rianna sat through the whole story without interrupting.

"So now you know the whole story and that I am the first daughter to be born in two hundred years." Rianna just sat there looking into the fire.

"Rianna, maybe I shouldn't have told you. I cast my spell to find out some answers. I will be turning twenty-one in just a few hours and there are dark forces who mean to destroy me and take my powers."

Riana whipped her head around. There was fire and determination in her eyes. Alana would hate to be on the wrong side of her.

"I will make sure that doesn't happen." She got up and went to a trunk and opened it. She pulled out a thin piece of sheer material and held it out to Alana.

"I don't understand. What is it?"

Rianna draped the fabric over her arm and smiled at Alana. "This was given to me by the Faerie Queen for a service I did for her kingdom. It may look fragile but I assure you, it can hold up against even a stubborn sword or dagger. It was made with faerie magic. I give it to you."

Alana shook her head. "No you may need it. I can't take this from you."

Rianna countered with a slight laugh. "You are not taking it from me. I will cast a protection spell on it so only you or I can call for it."

Alana looked at Rianna in amazement. "You mean I can just call for it like I do for my spell book?

Rianna drew the fabric from her arm and reverently placed it back in the trunk. "Exactly. All you have to say is 'I call on the fairy magic bestowed to me.' You won't even have to put it on. It will know what to do."

Alana looked at her with disbelief. Rianna closed the trunk and once again turned to Alana.

"There is something else I would like to show you." She waved her hand and a sword and shield appeared. Alana's eyes grew wide again.

"Where did you get that? I have seen both of them. I even pulled the shield out of my mind the other day when I was battling Sebastian in training."

Rianna held another knowing smile. "By giving you these things now, they are available to call on wherever you are and more importantly *when*ever you are. Even though you called on the shield what to you was a few days ago, it came to you because I gift them to you now. I know that is difficult for you to comprehend but this too will become natural to you as you progress in our art.

Alana touched her fingers to her forehead this was all so confusing. "You mean to tell me that because I came from the future and met you, in my future I can call on these things because of this night."

Rianna smiled and nodded. "You are grasping it nicely. It has to be. You would not have been able to do it any other way. Even though you are a descendent of mine, I would have had to make everything available to you with a spell. Just like your spell book, my magical possessions are the same. They only answer to me."

Alana was starting to understand but decided to go with it rather than struggle in her mind. She had an intuition that she could trust Rianna and felt very comfortable with that thought. She *was* her great, great something grandmother after all.

Rianna grabbed Alana's hands and looked her straight in the face. Her hands were warm to the touch and she could feel the energy and power radiating from her. Alana fell silent as Rianna spoke. "All that I have and all that I own from now until the day I die will belong to you - always." Alana felt energy and warmth flowing through her body and for the first time she could feel her own power and energy. She smiled at Rianna with tears in her eyes.

"Thank you for everything. I know I haven't done anything yet but I know in the end everything you have given me will be invaluable for the battle to come. And I feel so much better prepared for having them."

Rianna must have read something in Alana's face.

"My dear Alana. You were named I'm sure, after my mother. You are my descendent. I have faith in your abilities to conquer all. You just have to believe in yourself enough and have the confidence to erase all doubt." Alana cast her eyes down.

"What is it Alana? Is something wrong?" Alana couldn't help it.

She felt like she could tell Rianna all of her secrets and desires. She told her all about Sebastian and how he is her teacher and Eudora, how she had helped her with the first part of her training. She told her how much faith Eudora had in her but she didn't know how Sebastian felt about anything. Rianna listened as Alana poured her heart out. When she was through she wiped her eyes.

"I can't believe I just told you all of this. I haven't told anyone." Rianna touched her check. "We are kindred spirits who understand one another. You need to give him some time. I know his family. They are a stubborn lot."

Alana looked up. She had forgotten that Sebastian would also have ancestors in this time. Rianna leaned forward and touched the golden heart with a gentle caress.

"You know, my mother gave that to me when I was a little girl. It's a symbol of true love." Alana was surprised.

"This necklace is yours?" Rianna touched it again and held it in her hands.

"Yes at one time it was mine. Now it is yours. You know it opens?" asked Rianna as she turned it over in her hands and looked in the back. She looked puzzled.

"No I didn't know that. How do you open it? I don't see a clip or anything."

She looked down and watched Rianna touch the smooth surface on the back. "That is strange. There was a small indent in the back for you to put your finger on. All you had to say was 'open' and it would open."

Rianna dropped the necklace and went to her dressing table. When she came back she had the same exact heart in her hands.

"How can this be? I am wearing the same necklace that is in your hand!"

Rianna turned her necklace over and said the word 'open' and it opened to show a small hiding place.

"Magic is unique in its own way. There has to be a reason why yours won't open."

Alana looked closer at the necklace. "It just *looks* like a locket." Rianna looked at her. "I don't understand this word 'locket.' What does it mean?" Alana laughed. "Where I am from they make necklaces with lockets that open at the side with a small clasp or a little button to push to release the lock. That way the locket opens to put things in - sometimes secret things.

Rianna's eyes widened. "And what secrets do they hide inside?"
Rianna closed her necklace and looked up at Alana waiting
for her to answer. "They don't all hold secrets. Most of the time
they hold photos or mothers put locks of their children's hair so
they will always have them near their heart."

Rianna looked shocked. "Why would they punish their children
like that? And what is this word 'photo? What does that mean?"
Alana almost sighed there was a lot Rianna didn't know and she
probably shouldn't be telling.

"The hair is for luck and to bring them closer and a photo is…a
kind of picture. Like your paintings." Alana looked around. There
was a tapestry of a castle hanging on the wall so she took Rianna
by the hand. "You see this? We call this a picture and I can make
one of you say, with a device called a camera and get it developed
and you could see yourself…" Alana could see she was confusing
poor Rianna even more. "Never mind. I do have one question for
you though. Our legend tells us that Drake told everyone that
Lucian cheated. Do you know what that was all about?"

Rianna sat down. "I'm afraid that is my fault, not Lucian's. They
both agreed they would not call on me, that their friendship was
important to both of them. When I found this out I was furious
because by this time I had already fallen in love with Lucian and I
thought if Drake was any kind of friend he would be happy for
Lucian. So I pursued him. I made sure I was to be wherever I
thought he would be. It didn't take long for Lucian to realize he
loved me just as much. Drake went into a rage. It wasn't really me
he wanted. He knew that whoever I married would gain more than
just my love. He knew my husband's powers would grow whoever
that eventually turned out to be. He believed Lucien cheated him
out of my powers - not me. He lusted after them more than he did
me. Lucian tried to talk to him but he wouldn't listen. That is when
sides were formed and Drake eventually made the curse just before
his death. He knew he couldn't have me. My powers were great
and he didn't want anyone else to have them. He had become a
wicked and bitter man yet still, Lucian mourned his death."

Alana could tell that Rianna still felt guilty about what had
happened. She sat down next to Rianna and took her hand.
"You should not feel guilty about any of this. Both men made their

choices and I'm sure Lucian doesn't regret the decision he made and would choose you again if the choice was there to make." Rianna looked into Alana's eyes. "You are right." She stood. "Now I think we need to get you back to your own time." Rianna spied the relief on Alana's face.

"I don't know what to do! Zephyr only gave me enough herbs to get here. I didn't even think about getting back!"

Rianna took Alana into her arms and gave her a warm hug.

"You have to remember that you are special. Your powers are different to others –even Zephyr's. They train and practice their magic but we *are* magic. We can do anything that our heart desires. Always remember that your magic comes from your heart."

Alana had trouble taking all of that in. She still had trouble believing she was so powerful. Of course others had told her but hearing it from Rianna, the one she actually inherited her powers from put a different light on everything.

"Now let's see if we can get you home." She called for her book and thumbed through it and after a few minutes she stood up.

"I have just the spell to send you back without all the herbs or candles." She looked up and smiled at Alana. As she waved her hand to make her book disappear she reached out to Alana and hugged her again. "I am glad to know that my legacy is going to someone who will not take advantage of it or use it for evil. You truly are the purest of heart Alana. I believe in you. Now you must find a way to believe in yourself too."

She kissed both of Alana's cheeks. "I am glad that I got to know you. Now close your eyes."

Alana was so choked up she couldn't see anything anyway so she closed her eyes and waited.

'I send you back through space and time…to the place you were when you came to me…travel safe Alana mine and bravely face your destiny…'

Rianna pointed her finger and swirled it through the air toward Alana. Light swirled around her body until nothing was left but a few tiny sparkles.

Rianna looked out the window and said a prayer to Diana the moon goddess to keep Alana safe. She smiled softly as she turned from the window. She would tuck this chapter of her life away and occasionally bring it out to remember when a descendent of hers traveled two hundred years into the past to save two worlds.

68

Alana felt like she was floating on a cloud. Her whole body felt
light and a calmness like she had never felt before had settled over
her. She tried to open her eyes to see where she was but they felt
heavy and she couldn't lift them. She hoped Rianna's spell would
work and she would get back to her room safely. If she turned up
anywhere else she would have a lot of explaining to do. One
minute she felt like she was soaring and then suddenly she felt like
she was plummeting. A scream was only avoided by the fact that
she was too scared to open her mouth. She could feel her heart
beating inside her chest. 'Am I going to die?' she wondered. Her
stomach gave that same lurch she got from riding a roller coaster
and suddenly it all stopped and she could feel something solid
beneath her hands and her bottom. Eventually she plucked up the
courage to take a peek. She cracked one eye open and peered
through her lashes. She let out a breath she had been holding when
she realized she was back in her bathroom. Opening her eyes fully,
her heart beat a little sturdier and her stomach found where it was
supposed to be. Alana got up on shaky legs and looked around.
The candles were still where she had put them but they were no
longer burning. She needed to clean up the mess and jump in the
shower so she hurriedly stashed the candles under the sink. She
was almost finished cleaning up the mess when there was a gentle
tap on the door. "Alana dear, are you all right in there?"
She took a calming breath before answering. "Yes I'm fine. I'll be
out in just a minute."
She hurried and jumped in the shower. After drying off, she
hurriedly threw on a t-shirt and some sweats. When she came out
of her bathroom Eudora was there sitting on the edge of her bed.
"Sorry I took so long." Eudora waved it away. "No problem dear."
Eudora noticed Lily had given Alana the necklace. She could see
the chain. She wondered if Alana had figured out how to open it
yet.
"I see your mother gave you the necklace from your father. Alana
touched the chain and pulled the heart out and looked down at it.
"Yes, its beautiful isn't it?" Alana held the heart out for Eudora to
look at. When she touched it again she felt the power it contained.
Turning it over she noticed that the opening she had seen the other

day was gone. She decided not to say anything right now. She would talk with Alana tomorrow before the party. Everything was arranged.

"I don't want to keep you long dear. I just wanted to see how you were doing."

Alana smiled at Eudora. "Actually Eudora, I feel more like myself than I have in a long time."

Eudora looked at her closely. There was something different about her. She couldn't put her finger on it right now but her aura seemed even brighter. She smiled and patted Alana's hand.

"Get a good night's sleep. I will see you in the morning." Eudora left her to hopefully get a perfect night's sleep and rise refreshed. Alana closed her eyes and blew out a big sigh. 'That was close!' she thought. It took everything she had to keep her mind blank so Eudora wouldn't guess that she had actually traveled back in time. She giggled to herself. She couldn't believe it! She looked back down at Rianna's necklace. Even though it was hers now she would always see it as Rianna's first. She studied the back but there was still no opening to it like Rianna's had. She started to drop it back to her chest when she noticed there was a small piece on the side that she was certain hadn't been there moments ago. As she touched the side and pressed it, the heart gave a small click as it sprung open. She almost laughed out loud. Rianna had been listening when she briefly explained lockets from Alana's time. Inside was a tiny piece of paper. She took it out and snapped the locket closed.

With care she unfolded the piece of paper. In a delicate hand it said *'Call for my book and it will explain everything to you.'*

Alana folded the piece of paper back up and replaced it in the locket. Once done she looked toward the bedroom door and concentrated. It locked. With that done, she closed her eyes and concentrated on Rianna's book and in a soft voice she spoke.

'I call for Rianna's spell book.' Magically a very large book rested in her upturned hands. It was old and heavy. On the front of the book was the same symbol that was on the box that contained her necklace.

She opened it up to the first page and wrinkled her nose at the old musty smell. On the first page it read; *'Rianna's Enchanting Secrets.'* Alana liked that. The name fit Rianna considering she was an Enchantress. She opened it up to the next page and there she saw her name. This was just so weird to know that one of her ancestors from two hundred years ago was writing to her now. It was amazing and she was glad she had gotten the chance to actually be in the presence of such a wonderful woman.

"My *Dearest Alana, How did you like how I changed the lock on our necklace? I remembered what you told me about the lockets in your time. I think that is why yours did not open when you were here. We were not looking in the right place. I had already changed it. I have left everything I have to you. Now all you have to do is call for it. I have placed protection spells on everything, so no one else can call for anything that was mine and now is yours. Remember the faerie armor I showed you while you were with me? I'm sure you do. Please promise me you will wear it on your birthday. It will fit under anything you wear - that is the beauty of the faeries' magic. I have a gift for you on your birthday. You will receive it on the day. It has been in safe keeping for you on such an important day. It has been passed down over the years. You will know it when you see it. I'm sure you're wondering how I know you are reading this the night before your birthday? Because I know you Alana mine. You are a curious woman and I know you would have found the lock by now. Tell me I'm right. I know as I write this you are smiling down as you read. Now on to the battle you talked about that will come. My shield and my sword are ready for you whenever you call for them. They are now yours to pass on to your own daughters. Your necklace has its own power of protection. While you wear it you will always be protected, it is after all the symbol of our true destiny. Your heart holds all the power in your world and in mine. I know you are struggling, wondering if you are good enough or if you have the power. Well Alana, you have all the power you could ever want at your disposal. Just remember dearest, you are magic, while everyone else around you merely practice magic. You are the future. You will face your destiny with courage and strength and a clear mind and you will defeat the evil that dares to try and take what is rightfully yours. What most don't understand is that they cannot take what is not given freely. You will prevail. I am very proud of you. Look on page twenty-one at the bottom. Your special number. There is a spell that has been passed down for generations. It has never been used. Only a true descendent of mine can say the spell and make it work. Few know of the spell since it has never been used before. When you say the spell you have to believe it with your whole heart. It is there if you need it. All the females in our family that have gone before us will always be here watching over you. Our magic is intertwined. So Alana, I wish you the best in life and in love. I hope you find that special someone as I have. I regret nothing in my life - it was complete. I will always think of you. Remember me always. Tell your daughters the story of you going back in time to meet your great-great-great-great-great grandmother. I was blessed to have met you...*

Forever,

Rianna

Alana had barely been able to read the last words from the tears that were now gliding down her face. She had wondered how they were related. Now she knew. She would keep Rianna's name alive and she would tell any daughter she might have all about how she had traveled back in time to meet a wonderful woman who was her grandmother. She wiped her tears away and looked at page twenty-one. She was confused to find it blank. She ran her hand over the page and where there hadn't been any words before, they now appeared. Alana looked closely at the spell. After she read it, she understood immediately what it meant. She closed the book and with a heavy heart she waved her hand and it disappeared. She sniffed and took a deep breath. Alana wondered what was keeping Sebastian. She looked to the door and did what Eudora had done the first night they had met. She asked it to unlock and it obeyed. Yawning, she longed for bed. Morning would come soon enough. She had to get some sleep or she wouldn't be any good to anyone in the morning. Even though they were trying hard to hide it, Alana knew something was up. Everyone had been giving each other sly and secretive smiles all through dinner. Her friends had left after dinner. Sebastian's warrior friends followed each one of them home. She wondered how their nights were going. She also wondered what Rianna had meant by a birthday present as she closed her eyes and fell asleep.

69

Sebastian had arrived back from his parents' and was greeted by Eudora. He hated the fact that she wanted him to dress up in his royals. It made him feel like a pompous ass but he didn't complain. It was the least he could do for Alana.

"What is on your mind Eudora?" Sebastian almost smiled at the innocent look she was giving him.

"I don't know what you mean." She crossed her arms and Sebastian couldn't help a chuckle.

"Come now Eudora. I know you want something so just spit it out." He watched as the innocent look lifted.

"Oh all right! I hope all went well with Alana today?"

He knew she was fishing for information he just wondered how long he should make her wait for it. "Her training is complete."

Eudora's eyes widened. "So she is ready then?"

Sebastian shrugged his shoulders. "She has been ready since the day she was born. She just had to prepare for it."

Eudora was surprised. "So do you think she *is* ready? Can she do it?" She knew they were questions he didn't want to answer but these were the easy ones she was asking.

"Eudora, you know as well as I do. She can and will do anything she puts her mind to."

She tried to read him but he still kept that wall in place. "I know that. What I'm asking is do you think she can win?" She had asked this question once before and Sebastian hesitated when he answered. She wondered what that answer would be now.

He looked her straight in the face. For the first time he was letting her see and it surprised her.

"She will win. I will not let her die, even if I have to give up my own life." She could tell by the little he was letting her in that he was speaking the truth. Now to the harder questions.

"Did you tell Alana everything?" She was disappointed as he blocked all thought out of his head again.

"I told her everything she needed to know."

Eudora crossed her arms again and raised her eyebrow. She knew what he was saying without saying it. He didn't tell her about the second part of the prophecy.

"I know you might not think she needs to know but I think you're wrong. She does need to know." She could tell she had upset him by the way he ran his hands through his hair and started pacing back and forth. "Fine, I will tell her tomorrow."

She had to be satisfied with that. "Now, we need you to keep Alana busy tomorrow until I call you. The girls and Lily have worked so hard on her birthday. I would hate for the surprise to be ruined."

Sebastian stopped pacing. "What would you like me to do with her? I already told you she has learned all there is to learn."

Eudora sighed. What a stubborn man - like father like son.

"Tell her you want to go over a few things with her. Just keep her busy until I call you. Can you do that?" Sebastian nodded. "Is that all?'

Eudora almost rolled her eyes but instead she just nodded and watched Sebastian disappear. She knew where he was going - where he went every night - to watch over Alana.

70

Sebastian stood admiring Alana while she slept soundly. She was lying on her side with one hand tucked under her pillow and the other resting under her chin. What he had told Eudora was the truth. She had been born to her magic and that he and Eudora had only prepared her to use it. He was about to turn and leave her to her privacy when he caught sight of her necklace. It was not something he had seen her wear before. He gently touched the chain as it rested against her neck and felt its power and warmth. He wondered where she had gotten it. Alana moved in her sleep revealing the locket which had been hidden beneath her. Sebastian staggered backwards. Nestled under her chin, close to her own, was a golden heart and it was glowing bright in the darkened room. He couldn't believe what he was seeing. Leaning in to get a closer look it glowed brighter. Sebastian stepped back again and the heart's glow diminished. He moved to the other side of the room and looked at the heart. The glow was extinguished. Testing his theory further, he again moved forward and found that the closer he got to Alana, the brighter the heart glowed. He now had no doubt that the heart around her neck was the same one he had seen many times in his own dreams. The one that a little girl with chubby cheeks and an angelic smile had given to him. He knew what it meant. The prophecy that had been handed down through the years, that Eudora had kept hidden until recently, was true. He and Alana were bound together. He needed to talk with Eudora and find out where she got that necklace. He disappeared and immediately stood in the kitchen. He didn't want to leave the house and Alana unprotected so he summoned Eudora to him. Alana was having a wonderful dream of her childhood when she was young when her father was still alive. She was in his study playing, watching him work. That had always been a happy time to Alana. It was one of the only memories she had of her father. *'Don't forget what I told you poppet. You are the princess!'* She laughed and skipped to the door and out of the room but instead of being in the hallway she found herself in a forest. She didn't feel scared at all but looked all around her at the beauty. An old woman appeared beside her. She smiled and asked the old lady who she was and what she was doing there. The woman placed a gentle hand on her face.

'*My name is not important child. I have been waiting for you.*'
Alana laughed. She didn't know why but she did not fear this
woman dressed in a worn blue woolen dress that had been mended
several times with patches of darker blue. Her hair was as white as
a cloud and just as messy. Her skin was all wrinkled and she
leaned heavily on a wooden stick.

'*Why have you been waiting for me?*' Alana replied. She was
fascinated by the woman. She knew she was old but her crisp blue
eyes were sharp as she looked down at Alana.

'*I have waited a long time for this day to come child. Let me tell
you a story about a beautiful princess with special powers.*' The
old woman paused to look again at Alana who still had a huge
smile on her face.

'*My daddy said I was the princess.*' The woman again laid her
hand on Alana's check.

'*Your daddy was right child. You* are *the princess.*' Alana clapped
her hands and stood there waiting for the old woman to finish the
story. She had always loved stories. Her father had always told her
the best stories.

'*In this story the princess meets a mighty Dragon and she gives
this dragon her heart to protect because this is what dragons do.*'
Alana's eyes had grown fearful.

'*Do not be afraid, child. This dragon is your destiny. He will
protect you at all cost. You must understand this.*'
Alana stood there and nodded her head.

'*Good child. Now listen to me carefully. There will be a battle. You
must call on your dragon. He will always be there to protect you.
Do you understand what I am saying to you?*' Again Alana
nodded.

'*Now I must go child. Just remember; do not be afraid.
Your dragon will come.*' Alana gave the woman a lopsided grin. '*I
will not be afraid, I promise.*'
The old woman smiled as she walked off into the forest.
Alana sat down on the ground. Even though she was in her body as
a child it was her mind as an adult that she was listening too. She
was confused. She didn't understand any of what was going on.
This was the first time she had this dream. Looking around her
again she wondered if she should get up and try to find her way out

of the forest. She understood part of what the woman said. The rest was so confusing. She didn't know what she had meant when she said to give her dragon her heart. She needed her heart to live and breathe surely. Alana heard a noise in the distance. Strangely, Alana knew she should be afraid but for some reason she was very calm. The trees above her rustled as a huge gust of wind blew the leaves. She looked up and gasped. Coming down fast was something large and black. Still she was not afraid. She watched as a huge black dragon came closer and landed right in front of her. She had to smile at the look on its face - it looked just as confused as she felt. The dragon looked at her and she felt that something about it was familiar. Her chest started to feel warm and something was glowing below her shirt. She reached inside and pulled out her necklace with the golden heart. She knew what to do. Alana pulled the chain from around her neck and watched as the golden heart glowed brighter as the dragon leaned in closer. She smiled up at the dragon and held her hand out. At first the dragon just stared at her than he extended his own arm. She smiled again as she dropped the heart into his claw.

Alana woke with a start. She looked around and her room was empty. She didn't know what that dream was about. She reached for her necklace and gave a sigh of relief. It was still there. She was more confused now than she ever had been before.

'Was that dragon Sebastian?' she thought. 'It sure looked like him. And if so, what did it mean?' Had she already given her heart away to Sebastian? She really didn't know how she felt about him right now. She knew she cared about him and what he thought, but did it go further than that? *Could* he be her one true love? Right now she didn't know and she was more tired than when she went to bed. She lay back down and closed her eyes. Maybe her dreams were over for one night.

71

Sebastian didn't have to wait long for Eudora. "What is it Sebastian? Has something happened?" She was worried.

"No nothing like that Eudora. I just had a question to ask you." Eudora blinked at him. "Well by the sound of your voice it's obviously very important." Sebastian sat down and Eudora followed him.

"I went to check on Alana and as I stood over her bed watching her sleep I noticed a chain around her neck. I had never seen it before. At first I didn't think anything of it until she moved and I saw what was at the end of that chain. When I leaned in closer to get a better look it started to glow and the closer I got the brighter it got. Can you explain this to me?"

Eudora knew Sebastian was rattled. She was intrigued to hear that when he got close the heart would glow. That, she hadn't expected. "Alana received it as a gift from her mother. It was originally from her father's side of the family passed down and was to be given to Alana on her twenty-first birthday. I think it belonged to Rianna." Sebastian's head snapped up. "What makes you think it belonged to Rianna?"

"Sebastian did you by any chance touch it?" She knew before he answered that he had.

"I only touched the chain." He got up and started pacing. She hated when he did that.

"Well I was able to hold the heart in my hands and I can assure you there is a lot of power in it."

"I too felt its power just by touching the chain. It became warm and there was more power there than I have ever sensed in an object before." He went back to pacing.

"That is why I feel it was Rianna's. She is the only one who could have wielded that much power. I think you should tell Alana the rest of the prophecy tomorrow before it is too late." She heard him sigh before he sat down again.

"I will tell her everything tomorrow Eudora. When would you like me to have her out of here?"

Eudora knew he felt conflicted. "We think it would be best if you were out of here by at least eight-thirty. The girls will be here at nine and we have a lot of work to do."

Sebastian nodded and rose to leave. Eudora laid her hand on his arm and felt his tension. "Everything will work out Sebastian. You are a good teacher. Alana has learned well from you." She released his hand as he looked up.

"You have taught her well too Eudora. We both have done what we were intended to do." With that said Sebastian disappeared. Eudora smiled. "No Sebastian. You still have more to do. If only you would open your heart."

72

Alana actually felt good as she prepared for her day and yes, she had to smile, today was her day. She was still struggling to understand the dream and considered talking to Eudora about it. She would later but right now she needed to get dressed and have something to eat and her favorite coffee. She looked at the clock; seven-thirty. She was not a morning person at all but since all this training had started her body was on auto-pilot and woke her up early. Previously she would have moaned and groaned. Now she always awoke feeling refreshed and ready to start her day. She doubted that Sebastian had anything planned for her, so she could relax and take it easy today and maybe not worry about the impending doom she was having to face. She was going to take a break from *everything*! As long as she stayed in the house everything would be fine. She dressed quickly and headed downstairs with an extra bounce in her step. Entering the kitchen, her mom and Eudora were both sitting at the table as usual.

"Good Morning. Isn't it a beautiful day?" She took her usual seat and poured some coffee. After savoring the first sip she looked up at her mom and Eudora.

"What?" she asked as she noticed the surprised looks.

Eudora recovered first. "By any chance dear, have you looked in the mirror this morning?" Puzzled, Alana went to the mirror in the hallway.

"Oh My God!" she yelled. "What is going on Eudora?"

Both her mom and Eudora smiled at her. She was standing there glowing brighter than the sun with a look of astonishment on her face.

"Happy birthday honey," her mom said as she looked from Alana to Eudora. "Yes dear, Happy Birthday."

Alana sat down somewhat dazed. "Will this go away or will I always be like this?" she asked waving her hands in front of her face. Eudora gave her a patient look.

"No dear, you will not always be like that. It is the transformation of your powers. I must admit it's brighter than I expected but it is normal I assure you."

That really didn't help thought Alana as she took another sip of her coffee. "Please tell me Eudora, I won't be like this all day will I?" Eudora shrugged her shoulders she really didn't know. "Even if you are honey, I think I can find a few pairs of sunglasses for Eudora and me to wear." Both the older women laughed and Alana had to admit that it was all rather amusing. Sunglasses would definitely be a requirement of the day. She too started to laugh and the more she laughed and smiled the brighter she became. Eudora and Lily shielded their eyes. "I'm sorry. Am I getting brighter?"

When both women nodded she waved her hand out and two sets of sunglasses appeared.

"Tough! I guess you two will just have to wear these because today is *my* day and I'm going to enjoy it!"

Eudora and Lily put on the sunglasses and together they looked at Alana and gave her a saucy smile. She had to chuckle at that.

"Honey would you like something to eat?" Alana shook her head. "Don't worry about it Mom. I have it all under control."

She stood up and theatrically waved her hands in front of her. A breakfast feast fit for a king appeared. She looked at both them both and with a saucy smile of her own sat back down ready to tuck in.

"Wow! You didn't have to try so hard. I remember the first time you conjured something up it seemed like you had to concentrate so hard."

Alana shrugged her shoulders as she picked up her plate and started filling it with eggs and ham and some crispy bacon - her favorite. She slathered jam on a piece of toast.

"It's easy now. I just have to think about it and there it is," she said and pointed with the knife that was in her hand. "Go on now. I didn't work so hard for all this to go to waste." She chuckled at her own joke and took a bite of her toast. Eudora and Lily began filling their plates.

Eudora noticed right away that things had changed with Alana. She was more certain about herself. Perhaps it was the transformation of her powers that made her feel this way. Eudora didn't have anything else to go by since this was the first time they had ever had to hide someone's powers to protect them. She would talk with Sebastian later and see what he thought. She looked at the clock. Sebastian should be arriving soon.

Sebastian showed up just as they finished breakfast and enjoying the coffee. Alana was surprised to see him. "Hello Sebastian. Would you care for some breakfast? I made it myself." She shrugged her shoulders and smiled at Sebastian. He looked to the two women who were still wearing their sunglasses. Looking back at Alana he had to shield his eyes.

"Eudora could you please explain to me what is going on?" he said but kept all his focus on Alana. Eudora and Lily both laughed. He looked away from Alana long enough to narrow his eyes at the two women.

"What is going on here?" He didn't quite yell but his voice was raised somewhat. He looked back at Alana. "And would somebody tell me why she's glowing?"

"It has something to do with her receiving her powers today - all of them." She pulled her glasses down and looked him in the eye. Sebastian knew what she was saying.

"Well if you're through Alana, I think we should go." He held out his hand. She looked at it in puzzlement.

"What do you mean, go? Where are we going?" She looked to Eudora who smiled.

"There are a few things we need to go over."

Eudora knew Alana was hoping to have the day to herself but it couldn't be helped. She would be in the way and she didn't want the surprise to be ruined.

"But it's my birthday. I thought..." she closed her mouth when she saw the look on Sebastian's face.

"Oh all right - doesn't mean I'm going to like it though." She placed her hand in his and they were gone in the blink of an eye.

Lily sighed. "That was close. I thought for a minute she was going to let her stubborn streak get the better of her."

Eudora chuckled. "I thought the same thing too. But I think she came to the decision that no matter if it is her birthday, she has a job to do. Poor Alana. Sebastian *was* actually going to give her the day off until I told him to keep her busy."

73

Todd and his family were just finishing their own breakfast. "I think we should go to the flower shop right before noon. They close at noon and the less people there the easier it will be to accomplish our task."

Todd groaned to himself. It was always 'we' when *he* would be doing most of the work. Of course they would help in snatching the mother, but after that it would be up to him and there was no 'we' in that. Before the day was over he would have all that he had ever wanted. Once they had her mother they planned to bargain her life for Alana's powers. What they didn't know was, he didn't just want her powers he wanted her to pay for rejecting him. Nobody rejected him! Especially no one like her. His friends had all thought him crazy when he had asked her out. Back then there was something about her that intrigued him and he had since learned what that was. Even though he couldn't feel her powers then, he must have sensed them on some level.

"Don't worry. I will be ready before noon."

He got up from the table and on his way out he smiled to himself. Before the day was up he would not only have Alana's power but he would have her life too.

Alana was surprised they weren't in the field when they 'landed.'
She had to admit it had taken a little longer to get here. She turned
in a circle inspecting her surroundings. They were in a clearing
close to the woods. When she looked toward the woods a shiver of
recognition ran down her spine. "Where are we?"

Sebastian had been watching her and saw the shiver as she had
looked toward the forest. "We're in a clearing close to where I live.
I thought today we would do something different."

She crossed her arms, raised her eyebrow then she narrowed her
eyes. "And just what did you have in mind?"

He bowed to her and transformed to the dragon. When he spoke
she heard it in her mind.

'I thought for your birthday, I would take you on a ride.' She stood
there with her eyes wide and looked at him.

'If you're scared I understand.' He watched as her eyes narrowed
again.

"No I'm not scared. How am I supposed to…" she waved her
hands up and down. "Where will I sit and how do I get on?"

He could see she was nervous. 'Leave that to me Alana. I want you
to just enjoy.' He lowered his body to the ground flat on his belly.

'Now all you need to do is climb up." She looked at his face and
then looked at what she would have to climb. Even flat on his belly
he was still at least seven feet or so off the ground.

'Don't worry Alana. I won't drop you.' She looked doubtful but
sighed and started the climb anyway.

"You know what Sebastian? At one time I thought you were my
protector, to slay the big bad dragon. When all along you were the
dragon!"

Sebastian chuckled. It rumbled low in his belly and vibrated all the
way up to where she was sitting. She slapped his scales. "Stop that
or you're going to make me fall off."

Sebastian had to hand it to her. She was actually doing better than
he thought she would. She had accepted him for what he was. He
had been afraid she might feel repulsed by what she saw.

'Alana. I might be the big bad dragon but I will always be your
protector.' She clucked her tongue as he felt her settle on his back.

"All right, I'm here. Now tell me what I'm supposed to hold on to while you go flying about?" He could hear that she was short of breath. "You know it's not too comfortable up here either." 'Hold out your hand.' She did so. "All right, now what?"

'You're the witch. Conjure up something!' He waited to see what she would do. He felt something around his neck. At least it wasn't a rope, or at least he hoped it wasn't. 'What did you decide on?' he asked. He was a little curious. "Hush. I'm not done yet"

He waited another minute and felt something soft land between his shoulders. He wanted to turn and see but he was afraid he would unsettle Alana and send her tumbling to the ground.

'Are you settled now?' he sounded impatient.

"Almost. Does that feel comfortable?" He really couldn't feel much but he could hear her settling down. "There I think I'm as comfortable as I ever will be."

He turned his head then. She was sitting on something that looked close to a saddle.

'What exactly have you put on me?'

She laughed and patted the side of his head.

"I know you're not a horse but that was the closest thing I could think of. With a few modifications of course." He could feel the pride of her accomplishment. 'You didn't use a rope did you? You need something strong and a rope might break.' He wanted to take her for a ride but he didn't want to drop her either.

"No smarty pants. I didn't use a rope. I thought of that too. It's a leather strap and with a little magic, it won't break. I think I am as ready as I will ever be."

He stood and looked over his shoulder. She was sitting there pretty as you please in something that looked like a saddle that had high sides. It looked made of leather. She was strapped in from the waist by the leather strap she had around his neck. He watched as she looked down. Her face paled slightly and she swallowed several times and closed her eyes.

"I'm ready." He waited. She cracked one eye open and looked at him. "Well?" she said.

'I think you should keep your eyes open so you can see what's going on.'

She opened both eyes. "Ok. Are you happy now? You better not go too fast Sebastian!" she yelled as he took off into the air.

"Ho…ly Crap!" she shouted over the wind whipping by. He took it slow at first to let her get used to being up so high.

'How are you doing Alana?" She said something but he couldn't hear with the wind sailing by. 'Speak to me with your mind. I can't hear you over the wind.' He waited.

'Oh my God! Sebastian this is amazing!' He turned to look. She was glowing again and her hair was whipping around her face but her eyes were wide open and she had an amazing smile on her face. 'This is better than any amusement park ride any day.' He looked ahead of them to watch where he was going. For several minutes they just flew across the sky, neither one speaking as they enjoyed the ride.

'Sebastian, can I ask you something?' He didn't like the sound of this. 'What is it?' 'How many other girls have you done this for?' Alana waited for him to answer. She didn't know why it was important to know, but it was.

'You are the first Alana, Happy Birthday!' It made her heart warm to know that this was something only they had shared.

'Well Sebastian, I have to admit this is probably the best birthday present ever, besides what my father gave me.'

Sebastian didn't ask what that was - he already knew. Eudora had told him and he understood. 'Thank you.' He was glad he wasn't in his human form. He would probably slip up and do something stupid like kiss her again. She had spoken so softly he was touched that this meant so much to her. 'The day isn't over yet. I have plenty more to show you.' He decided it was time to just enjoy and not talk. He flew even higher and faster. He knew he had to keep her busy but no one said he couldn't enjoy it too.

75

After waiting for almost an hour outside the flower shop Todd and his family were starting to wonder if Alana's mother was even in the shop. Todd looked at his watch. It was after twelve now. Where could she be? They watched as the last woman came out of the store. She was older than Lily but was locking the doors.

"Do you think she may not have come in today because of it being the girl's birthday?" asked his mother.

Todd answered sullenly. "Well it's safe to say that woman who just locked the doors and walked off was the last one out. So she *must* have stayed home today. I guess Alana's birthday is a fair reason for not turning up at work." Todd was steaming inside. He walked over to the shop and looked in the window. All the lights were off so no one was inside. He decided to check it out further but when he tried to enter the shop there was something blocking him. He snarled and walked back to his parents.

"She was definitely the last one. They have put some kind of spell on the shop. I couldn't enter. We need to go back to the house and find a way to break the spell they have put on her house." Both his parents nodded.

"If I know her mother they will be having a party tonight for her birthday. We just have to figure out how to get in."

He walked off without caring whether his parents followed or not. He had to get back to the house and talk to Ciaran and find out if there was any way to break their protection spell. He needed to get inside that house and he needed to do it tonight.

76

Eudora was glad that she had Kohn and Rowan pop over to the flower shop to fetch the flowers. Lily had called her friend Becky to tell her they would be coming in the back way and would pick up all of the flowers. They were back at the house within minutes with the most beautiful flowers she had ever seen. They had roses the palest of pink to the darkest of pink and there were rich purple ones that almost looked silver. Eudora had never seen that color before. They would use the pink throughout the house except for the living room. The special purple ones would go in there. Lily explained that Alana loved those ones best, how they would change from a dark purple to a light and even sometimes blue and silver. She had always said they were alive. That is why she wanted them in the living room and pink was one of Alana's favorite colors so she had found every shade of pink rose she could. Lily had Katie and Jessica help her with the flowers as Trish helped Eudora with the cake. That left the men to do any heavy work like moving tables and arranging chairs.

"So Trish, since you are the designer, what kind of cake should we make?" Eudora let Trish sketch the design and she was going to put it all together.

"Actually I already had something in mind, before you know… all this?"

Eudora understood what Trish was saying. "But I spent a lot of time last night thinking and what I have come up with, I think everyone will like. I just hope it's not too complicated for you to make."

Eudora waved that away. "If you can draw it my dear, I can make it. Now let's see what you have come up with."

Trish opened her sketch pad and handed it to Eudora. "Be honest and tell me what you think? I wanted to show it to you first to see if you could do it."

The way Trish was biting her lower lip told Eudora she was nervous but it was simple enough and to the point and anyone who knew Alana would understand the meaning. The cake was in the design of a castle on a hill with trees all around. The flags stood high above the towers. When Eudora looked closer at the flags she saw one had a dragon on it. It was perfect with simple enough lines. All this sat on a base of grassland with people scattered around. Some looked like witches and faeries and others looked like warriors. She raised her eyes and looked at Trish.

"It's beautiful dear. What made you draw the people the way you did and that flag there with a dragon?" Eudora pointed to the tallest tower where a black dragon stood boldly on a flag.

Trish shrugged her shoulders. "Doesn't every castle have a dragon somewhere in the background?"

"I think its lovely dear and I think Alana will love it also. Now let's show it to the others before I get started. I know they will like it just as much as I do."

"I hope you're right Eudora. As far as the people go? I thought it was best to put the ones who wanted her to be happy and safe." Eudora was touched. She had seen one that looked like her along with Sebastian and his warrior friends. They found the other girls and all agreed it was the perfect cake for Alana.

"You know she always said she was looking for Prince Charming not Mr. Right." Jessica was looking down at the picture as she said it. All the girls laughed.

"I remember her saying that too Jess," said Katie. "Yeah and I remember Jess, that you said, 'but it was fun with Mr. Wrong until Mr. Right came along'" said Trish. Jess laughed and gave them a saucy smile. "Well it is you know."

"I think you did a beautiful job Trish. Alana is going to love it," said Lily as she gave each girl a hug. "She is going to love everything you all have done."

Eudora nodded. "Now back to work everyone. We don't have much time and we still have a lot to do." Eudora and Trish both went back into the kitchen. Eudora was going to make her cake as magical as she could without losing any of the charm or detail. Eudora looked at the clock. They only had a few hours more before dark and she wanted to make sure everything was ready so everyone had to stay busy. They would all need about an hour to get ready and she knew Alana would need some time too. She smiled. They would do it. With everyone working together it would get done.

Sebastian decided it was time for them to take a break so he
spotted a field below and headed for the ground.

'You still doing alright back there?' Alana was still enjoying
herself. Her cheeks were red from the wind and her hair had come
loose from her ponytail. It hung down her back in disarray but with
that smile and the gleam in her eyes she never looked more
beautiful. He lay as close to the ground as he could to let her climb
down.

"Oh my God, Sebastian. That was unbelievable. I will never forget
it as long as I live." She was brushing her fingers through her
tangled hair as he got up and transformed back into his human
form.

"I'm glad you liked it. I thought I would give you
something no one else could." Alana couldn't believe it. Sebastian
actually grinned at her. Of course it wasn't a real smile but it was a
start.

"Thank you. I don't think anyone could top that," she beamed at
him again.

"I thought if you're hungry we could have something to eat."
Alana was hungry. She didn't know how long they had been gone.
"That would be great. All that flying worked up my appetite. I bet
it did yours too, especially with a passenger."

Sebastian produced a blanket with a subtle wave of his hand and
followed it up with a basket of goodies. Alana grabbed the basket
so Sebastian could lay the blanket out on the ground. She placed
the basket down and opened it to see what was inside and looked
up at him in puzzlement. "What? You don't like it?"

Alana shook her head. "No it isn't that. It's just all my favorite
food!" She pulled out an array of fruits and cheese with crackers
and some turkey meat. "How did you know what I liked?"

"Alana I've watched you eat countless times. You always favor
fruit and cheese and every now and then I would see you eat a
turkey sandwich, so I thought I couldn't go wrong with any of
those items." She smiled at him.

"Thank you. They *are* all my favorites." She picked a grape and
popped it in her mouth. She handed out food and drinks and they
sat there and ate a leisurely lunch and looked out to the horizon.

They were both comfortable enough to eat and just watch the scenery and take a few minutes to just enjoy life.

78

Todd reached his house before his parents. He called for Ciaran to meet him in his father's study. By the time Ciaran appeared his mother and father had also turned up.

His father spoke before Todd had a chance to open his mouth.

"Ciaran, we need you to find out how to break a protection spell. The girl's mother never showed up today and we need to get into their house. We know they will probably be having some kind of party so we want to have the element of surprise. Do you think you can manage that?"

Todd was furious that his father had spoken to Ciaran. He had wanted to be the one to find out first if it was possible.

"I will see what I can do,' answered Ciaran. 'I will have to study it."

Todd's father nodded and Ciaran bowed and disappeared. "If there is any way to get into that house, Ciaran will find it," said his mother.

Todd couldn't stand being in the same room with them anymore. "When he finds out anything, I will be in my room, preparing for tonight."

He turned and left, not even waiting for permission to leave. He wanted to look in his own book and see if he could come up with something. He had some spells even his mother and father knew nothing about. They were even too dark for them. He was convinced he would find a way to get to her before the night was up, even without his parents' help if need be.

They had finished their lunch and were enjoying the glorious weather. Alana admired Sebastian as he sat there gazing at the surrounds and looking really relaxed. She hadn't really seen him like that very often. She wanted to talk to him about her dream. She probably should talk to Eudora about it first though.

"Sebastian I think I had a dream about you last night." She watched as the relaxed look dissolved and he became wary.

"What do you mean - you think?" he said as he looked at her so intensely she had to look away. The light was fading from the horizon - it would be getting dark soon.

"I dreamt I was in my father's study. He was telling me the story about how I was the princess telling me again never to forget. I was a little girl. I laughed and promised him that I would always remember it. I remember skipping to the door and when I opened it, I was in some woods. They looked like the ones by your house. There was an old woman with the most intense blue eyes. She was very old. She spoke to me and told me she had been waiting for me. She went on to tell me about a mighty dragon."

Alana recognized the blank look on Sebastian's face. It was a little paler as if she had shocked him or made him mad but the blankness told her he was hiding something.

"She finally told me he would protect my heart and then she vanished. I sat down in the woods and waited. She had told me not to be afraid and that my dragon would come. Suddenly, from the sky a big black dragon swooped down right in front of me. My necklace grew warm and started to glow. I don't know how I knew, but I did, that this was *my* dragon and he was there to protect me. Even though I was a child I had the mind of an adult. I took my necklace off and handed it to him. That is when I woke up, but the funny thing is, that dragon looked like you. Do you think you can explain it to me?"

Just for a minute, while she was telling him of her dream, his wall had slipped and she got to see a glimpse inside and she could tell he knew something about it. He ran his hands through his hair and looked away. A muscle in his jaw twitched. He sighed, stood up and took several steps away. She waited patiently and after what seemed like minutes she urged him to answer.

"Please Sebastian. I need to know what that dream meant. You have always been straight with me and I respect you for that. Don't shut me out now!" She wanted to shout. She wanted to stand up and tell him to look at her but she knew if she did that he would clam up and she would never find out. Sebastian was a lot like her. They both had a stubborn streak.

Sebastian didn't know what to say. He couldn't believe she'd had a dream almost the same as his. She had been a little girl in his too. Eudora had been right. She did have a right to know. He looked off in the distance. Eudora would probably call him soon, so it was now or never.

"Her name is Magimus. She lived in a cottage close to the woods. Some said she had great powers. That she could even see into the future. The dragon you saw was me. I have been having a dream similar to yours but mine starts by finding you sitting on the ground. You were a child and you had a big smile on your face with a trusting look in your eyes. You handed me the necklace and vanished."

After he finished the story he braced himself and turned around. She was looking at him with an owlish look. She blinked several times, opened her mouth but shut it again.

"There is a second part to the prophecy. Eudora kept it hidden for years from everyone. She has just recently shown my father and me. Magimus sent her a message in her fountain. She doesn't know how she did it still to this day. Eudora didn't know what to do with this information so she had kept it to herself. It was long before you were born. She had locked it away for years and forgotten about it. She didn't even know if she should believe it or not but now we know it's true. You have the evidence around your neck." She touched the necklace and looked back at Sebastian.

"What did this woman say to Eudora?" Sebastian looked off in the distance again. Alana didn't think he was going to answer until he turned back around and looked at her again.

"She said the prophecy will come to pass and a daughter will be born, and in order to defeat the evil ones the dragon must protect his heart at all cost or all will fail."

Alana ran her hands through her hair and stood up. She had to take all of this in. How had an old woman managed all that?

"I should tell you everything. Eudora and I both felt the power

from your necklace. Eudora thinks it came from Rianna."
With the mention of Rianna's name Alana bowed her head. She knew she had to tell Sebastian about her trip back in time. She looked at him sheepishly.
"I think you need to sit down Sebastian. I have a few more things to tell you." Sebastian watched as she paced around. She wouldn't even look at him so he sat and waited. "All right Alana, I'm sitting?" She stopped pacing.
"I don't think it was right of you two to keep what you knew from me. If I hadn't told you about my dream, I doubt you would have told me anything, so I think what I'm about to say will make us even." She stopped pacing again and looked at him. When he nodded for her to continue she bit down on her bottom lip.
"You have to promise me." Sebastian knew whatever she had to say was worrying her. "I promise."
"Now remember, you can't be mad and I don't want you to say anything until I finish. You got that?" He nodded again.
"The necklace *is* Rianna's. I cast a spell to find out why the curse was made in the first place. Instead of someone coming to me or me getting a vision or something, which is what I expected, I went back in time two hundred years and met my grandmother. Well actually you have to put a handful of 'greats' in front of that. Rianna is my ancestor. We talked. She showed me things and told me what had happened. Lucian did nothing wrong. Rianna pursued him. He had promised Drake he would not go after her, but what they didn't know was it was *her* choice and she had chosen Lucian over Drake. Drake was so enraged because he thought his friend had betrayed him, when all along it was Rianna." She closed her eyes and waited for Sebastian to blow up. She knew he would, even though he had promised not to. But after several seconds and he hadn't said a word she braved a peek under her lashes.
Sebastian was still staring at her intently. She knew by the way his nostrils where flaring that he was mad.
"Remember Sebastian, you gave your word you wouldn't say anything."
He ran his hands through his hair. "I'm not mad. I actually understand why. When did you do this?" Alana bit down on her lip again and smiled at Sebastian. "Last night when you went home." She sat down in front of him.

"I don't regret what I did. It was an experience I will never forget."
For some reason tears formed in her eyes.

Sebastian wasn't mad - he was amazed. She had done all that last
night! He was actually proud of her. She had more power than any
of them realized. He could tell it had been an emotional trip for
her by the way she was trying so hard not to cry and to find out not
only was she a descendent but also that her grandmother had been
Rianna the Enchantress. She must have been about Alana's age
when they met. Of course it would be an experience. She would
remember it, who wouldn't?

Sebastian looked again at her. "I'm glad you got to have the
experience Alana. Was she helpful?"

Alana's tears were retreating. "Oh, Sebastian. I wish you could
have been there. She told me and showed me so much." Alana held
out her hands and Sebastian watched as a large book appeared.
"This was Rianna's. She gave it to me with everything else."

Sebastian was astonished. Usually when a witch passed over,
everything of theirs went too. But Rianna had made sure Alana
received everything of hers. He wondered what she meant by
'everything'.

"She gave me her shield and sword. They were the only ones of
their kind and now they belong to me, along with this."

Alana opened the book to the first page so he could read the
inscription. "She named her book *Enchanting Secrets.*"

Alana nodded. "That's not all she did." She turned to the next
page and Sebastian saw a note to Alana. "She left me a note telling
me what was hers is now mine and that nobody else can claim it
but me."

She closed the book. Sebastian had wanted to read more but Alana
waved her hand and it vanished. He started to say something when
he heard the call from Eudora.

"Eudora is calling. I think we should pack up and go."

She watched as he got rid of everything. She couldn't tell if he was
mad or not. He had said that he wasn't and he hadn't yelled so she
had to take his word for it. He held out his hand. She put her hand
in his and waited.

"Alana no matter what happens, when the battle comes, you will
be ready. You have learned well from both me and Eudora and for
the second part of the prophecy, I will protect you. Nothing is

going to happen to you. Do you understand?"

Alana smiled. "I'm glad to know, you believe in me. I had my doubts if you ever would. You might not know this Sebastian but it does matter to me what you think. Your words mean a lot to me."

Sebastian nodded and then they were off.

80

"Everyone listen up, we need to be quiet. I just summoned Sebastian so they will be here in a minute." The room went very quiet. She wanted this night to be special for Alana. It wasn't everyday a girl received the gift of great power. She knew Alana was strong enough to handle it though.

Eudora had asked Sebastian to drop Alana off in her bedroom so she wouldn't see what was going on downstairs. She listened at the top of the stairs and was amazed that a room full of people could be so quiet. She chuckled as she knocked on Alana's door.

Alana opened her eyes. She wondered why Sebastian had brought her to her room. Usually it was the kitchen. She must have shown some of the confusion on her face.

"Eudora wanted me to bring you here. She has a gift for you." Right after he said it there was a knock at the door. Eudora entered full of cheer.

"Hello my dear, Sebastian." Alana smiled and Sebastian nodded before he disappeared.

"Go ahead and get cleaned up dear, I have a surprise for you." Alana could just bet what that surprise was. She listened to see if she could hear anything from downstairs but all was quiet. She wasn't expecting that. She figured her friends would be there.

"Are my friends here yet Eudora?" Eudora smiled. "Not yet dear. But I'm sure they will be here soon. Now - how about that shower?"

Alana laughed and headed into the bathroom. Before she closed the door she heard Eudora say she would wait right there for her. Again Alana took a record shower, brushed her teeth and came out of the bathroom with a towel wrapped around her body and one around her hair.

Eudora was sitting on the bed. "I have a gift for you my dear. Actually it's not from me. It was passed on to me to hold until a daughter was born and she was supposed to have it on her twenty-first birthday."

Alana was intrigued. Could this be the present that Rianna had mentioned? She watched as Eudora pointed, twirled her finger and a box appeared on the bed. Alana looked from the box to Eudora. "Go ahead dear, open it."

She didn't have to tell her twice. She sat on the edge of the bed and slid the lid off the box. The first thing she noticed was the smell of jasmine. It reminded her of Rianna's chamber. When she pushed the tissue back she gasped. Under the tissue paper was the same dress that Rianna had been wearing the night before. So that was the present she had been talking about. When she lifted the dress out and a note slipped to the floor Eudora bent over and picked it up.

"Look dear, a note." She handed it to Alana and took the dress. Alana opened the note and read it.

'Alana mine, this gown always brought me luck. Wear it on your special night. R'

Alana almost started to cry right there, Eudora noticed.

"What is it dear?" Alana handed Eudora the note. Eudora looked at Alana. She knew who had written it, Alana could tell, so she sat down and told Eudora all about what she had done the previous night. That she knew the dress was Rianna's because she had been wearing it that same night. Alana almost laughed when she got done telling the story. It was probably the only time she had ever seen Eudora speechless.

"Eudora, you should see your face. You look like a fish out of water with your mouth opening and closing like that. I would laugh if this wasn't so serious! Please don't be mad at me. I was just trying to find out everything I could about the curse."

Eudora regained some of her composure. "I'm not mad dear, far from it. I think it's remarkable that you were able to travel back and meet her. What was she like?"

Alana couldn't contain her enthusiasm. "She was amazing and so beautiful. The stories didn't lie one bit. And she left me everything of hers Eudora, even her spell book."

Eudora's eyes grew wide. She had never heard of this happening before. She wanted to talk more about it but there was a house full of people who wanted to wish her a happy birthday.

"For now we shall leave it, but I want you to tell me everything later." Alana nodded keenly.

"Now I think it's time to get you into this dress."

As Eudora started to put the dress over Alana's head Alana stepped back. She had almost forgotten the faerie armor. "I have to put something on first!"

Eudora looked at her questioningly. Alana waved her hand and closed her eyes and felt the softness of the material as it slid down her body. She opened her eyes and looked down. It covered her body completely. Eudora gazed at the material in awe.

"This was a gift from the fairy queen to Rianna for some service she had done for them. It is faerie armor and Rianna said even though it looks delicate it's very strong." She ran her hand over it and she couldn't believe how transparent it was. It was almost invisible.

Eudora touched the edge of her sleeve. "I have heard of such a thing. Whatever she had done for the faeries it must have been big for them to have gifted her with something like this. It supposedly takes years to make something so delicate yet so strong."

Alana smiled. "Now I think I'm ready for the dress." Eudora helped her with the dress. It slid down her body and flowed to the ground – a perfect fit. It was just as beautiful as the night she had seen it on Rianna. She looked up at Eudora.

"I think I need to get this wet mess on top of my head dry. I would like to wear it in a braid like Rianna had hers and if I'm right there should be some ribbon and a crystal and gem headpiece to go along with it." They looked in the box and Alana was right but there was also a pair of silver slippers that matched the dress perfectly.

"Now that you have everything, let your fairy godmother take care of your hair," laughed Eudora.

Alana closed her eyes as Eudora dried her hair with the flick of her wrist and with a few more hand gestures she had it braided with the ribbons of blue and silver intertwined in Alana's hair. The last thing to do was put on the headpiece. Alana may have thought they were crystals but Eudora would bet that they were real sapphires in different shades of blue with a few diamonds set strategically between them. When she was through she had to admit that Alana would be the most beautiful at the ball so to speak. "Alana dear, you can open your eyes now."

When she did, she took a deep breath then turned to look in the mirror. That breath escaped in a sigh. "Oh my God, Eudora. I look so much like her. I mean I knew there were some similarities but...I actually feel like a princess, Eudora. I know it was only a story..." her voice faded as she looked in the mirror again.

Eudora came up behind her and looked at their reflection. She placed her hand on Alana's shoulder and smiled. "Alana you *look* just like a princess." She couldn't wait until Sebastian saw her. She patted Alana's shoulder. "I think your friends should be here by now. Put your shoes on and we will go downstairs."
Alana turned from the mirror and while she put her shoes on, Eudora sent Sebastian a message to let him know they were on their way downstairs. This would be a night to remember.

81

Ciaran had summoned all of them to the study. Todd had found maybe one spell that just might penetrate the barrier that had been put in place but he was curious to see what Ciaran had come up with first. By the time he got there, his mother and father were already there. Several items were set up on a table. There were different bottles and herbs and a chanting pot sat in the middle. His father nodded to Ciaran when Todd stood next to them. Ciaran came forward.

"I have found a spell. It won't break the protection spell but it will suspend it for just a second to let you in but your timing has to be perfect. You will only have a few seconds."

Todd snorted. "If you can make it old man, I will get in."

His mother turned sharply and gave him a glare. His father ignored him. "What do we have to do Ciaran?" Todd watched as the old man went to the table where everything was assembled.

"We will need blood from all three of you and we will need the blood of a shape shifter." Todd's head snapped up. His mother and father looked at each other.

"I don't know where we can find a shape shifter, do you?" his mother asked his father who stood for a minute thinking.

"I knew a few long ago but it would take a while to find them." Todd cleared his throat and everyone turned to look at him.

"What will you need the shape shifter for?" Ciaran looked impatiently at Todd. "We will need their blood to cloak you. It will only work for a few seconds though."

Todd knew what the old man was implying. The shape shifter would be sacrificed. Could he do that to Star? With an evil smile he looked at everyone. He would sacrifice his own mother if it meant he would get his revenge on Alana.

"I can bring you a shape shifter." His parents looked at him in surprise. Ciaran nodded. "Very good."

He moved to the table and commenced adding things to the pot as he chanted over it. He picked up a wrapped object and Todd watched closely as he separated the fabric. He silently removed an athame from the sleeve of his cloak. Never having been privileged to witness a high ceremony, Todd was watchful. The ceremonial dagger, he saw, had a serpent that curled around the hilt and two rubies to represent the eyes.

"First I will need the blood from the father, followed by the mother and then the son." Todd's father stepped up and rolled up his sleeve. He was silent as Ciaran chanted more words and slid his knife over flesh and let the blood drip down into the bowl. Next the mother stepped forward and did the same but Todd heard a slight wince as the knife cut into flesh. His mother was human after all. Then it was Todd's turn. He walked up, rolled his sleeve and looked from his mother to his father as Ciaran chanted again in a strange language. He never even felt the pain as his blood dripped into the pot and mingled with his parents' blood. When he was through, he picked up a towel and wrapped it around his forearm.

"Now Raynor, I will need the shape shifter." He hated that name. It reminded him too much of the past. He shook his head and concentrated. He had sent her to the in between. It didn't take him long to find her and when he did he called to her. She appeared in front of him. He knew she would be mad. Her arms were crossed and she was looking straight at him. She was so furious she never noticed the others in the room.

"How dare you send me somewhere like that?" he could see the fire spitting out of her eyes.

"Sorry love. Good thing I need you now." Before she could do anything he had her tied with magical ropes.

"What is this?" she yelled and looked around. It was then she noticed the other people in the room. Her face paled. "What do you want with me?" Todd walked over to her and with the back of his hand he gently touched her face and smiled.

"All I need from you love, is your blood." He nodded to the old man. He never looked back again as the old man went to work. He heard Star scream several times.

"Ciaran can you not shut her up?" scolded his mother. Todd didn't look at the gruesome scene but both of his parents did. After several seconds the screams had faded. Todd needed a drink but he knew if he had one, his mother and father would be furious. He looked at them both again. They weren't even watching him. He shrugged his shoulders and went to the decanter and poured a healthy drink. The hell with it he thought. He needed a drink. Before the night was up Alana would be his. He smiled as he took a sip and waited for Ciaran to finish his dark work.

Eudora went down the stairs first. She wanted to make sure that Alana was the center of attention and all eyes were on her. There was some soft music playing in the background, lights had been dimmed. Candles had been lit and placed on every available surface. The room was perfect and the smell of roses was everywhere. She was proud of everyone for the beautiful job they had done. It all looked whimsical with a touch of magic here and there. The king and queen were on their way and they were bringing Zephyr. She wanted to help celebrate Alana's coming of age. Everyone was in their place and dressed for the part. She smiled at all three girls. They looked stunning in their outfits. Lily stood by the girls and the men stood behind them. She scanned the room for Sebastian. He didn't like to dress up but too bad. This was a special occasion. He was standing near the fireplace. When he saw Eudora he nodded and moved forward. She looked back up the stairs and watched Alana descend, a vision to behold. Quickly she turned to see the reaction on Sebastian's face. She knew he hadn't expected what he was seeing and by the look on his face he didn't like it much.

Sebastian felt stupid dressed as he was. Eudora had called him and told him they were ready. He had passed the word around and they had all lined up by the stairs to watch Alana arrive. He couldn't believe what he was seeing. Of course he had seen her dressed up before but not like this. She had a soft smile on her lips and her eyes sparkled from all the candles that illuminated her. She had a soft glow all around her head. Breathtaking! He looked to see what everyone else thought. All three of his men were looking at her differently too. They had only seen her in jeans and a t-shirt with her hair pulled back in a ponytail with no make-up but what they were seeing now was more than just beauty. He didn't like the looks that passed between the three of them. Even Warwick showed more than a gentlemanly admiration. He would have to keep his eye on those three and make sure they behaved. He felt that he would have to make sure that he too behaved. It took everything he had not to rush over and take her in his arms to let everyone know she was his. He had to shake his head to clear the images of them rolling around on a set of sheets with her glorious hair cascading over his arms as she looked up at him with passion filled eyes. He closed his eyes and took several calming breaths. Alana paused at the bottom of the stairs. She looked around at everyone and when her eyes met his, her mouth formed a perfect 'O', surprised to see Sebastian dressed like that. He had even worn his crown. Alana composed her features and gave him a smile full of mischief and maybe a touch of wickedness. He couldn't help it. He smiled back.

Alana had guessed that they were secretly planning something for her birthday but hadn't imagined anything so beautiful. She felt tears well in her eyes and blinked them away. She was ecstatic. All her friends were there with her mom and Eudora. She could even see Sebastian's men. She scanned the room to find Sebastian. Sebastian stood before her, not as a warrior but as a true living and breathing prince charming. She only just avoided releasing the surprised 'o' that had formed on her lips. He was dressed like royalty. The gems in his crown winked at her in the candle light. She knew she had the look of a deer in the headlights but she didn't care. Sebastian was so beautiful standing there proud and uncomfortable at the same time. When their eyes locked she felt a warmth seep into her body. She took a deep breath and smiled at him.

Just once, for her birthday she wished he would loosen his control and have fun. He never showed anything of himself. She started to look away but right there in front of everyone, Sebastian - Drakon the mighty dragon and warrior - smiled at her. It was a true smile of pleasure that made her insides turn to liquid and her breathing to grow shallow and rapid. She had to look away. He did things to her that shouldn't be allowed and right there and then Alana, the descendent of Rianna, fell in love for the first time in her life.

Eudora had been watching both. She didn't know what was happening but by the looks and heat they were both generating it was big. She almost fell over when Sebastian actually smiled. She looked from him to Alana. She could see that her prediction had proven true. Love was in the air.

83

Alana was on cloud nine. The King and Queen were there, along with Zephyr. She felt so honored that they had come. Her family and friends had done a wonderful job. She did indeed feel like the fairy princess in all her father's stories. This was one birthday she wouldn't soon forget. They ate an enormous meal, the likes of which she had never seen. The cake was so beautiful she was speechless when they brought it out with candles glowing, adding even more candlelight to the room. Trish had designed it beautifully and Eudora had created it true to the finest detail, right down to the dragon on the flag. Alana couldn't have asked for more.

They cleared all the furniture from the living room, magically of course, so they could dance. Alana danced with the King first. She had always found him a little bit frightening but he soon had her at ease. All her friends were in awe over him and his Queen.

Sebastian stood in the background and watched it all. Alana was so beautiful that he could hardly breathe. She was dancing the first dance with his father. At first he felt jealous that his father had the pleasure of dancing with her first but when logic returned to his somewhat befuddled brain he knew that protocol must be followed. Alana had a glow about her and her smile brightened the whole room, outshining the countless candles.

"She's beautiful isn't she son?" He looked at his mother.

"Yes." He didn't elaborate. He was distracted by the way she kept looking at him.

"I have seen a difference in her tonight. She seems more confident, more sure of herself."

Sebastian was still looking at Alana "I noticed it too. She *is* more confident. Do you know, she traveled back to Rianna's time and I think that has something to do with her newfound confidence."

"When did she do this?" She glanced over at Alana with a look of respect. Sebastian was glad to see that his mother liked her.

"Last night. Her mother gave her the necklace she is wearing. It belonged to Rianna." His mother turned and looked at him.

"It must have been some conversation between the two of them. The first time I met Alana I could see her strength and courage but she lacked confidence. Now I see a very strong, self-assured woman with even more strength and courage."

Sebastian finally tore his gaze from Alana.

"Rianna didn't take anything with her when she died. She left it all to Alana." He could tell this news shocked her.

"How can that be? I have never heard of anyone being able to do that. The laws have always been there to protect the ones passing and the ones who are still left."

Sebastian looked back at Alana as he answered. "I know Mother. Rianna was quite a woman. I saw her spell book with my own eyes. She left it all to Alana." His mother shook her head.

"Incredible." She looked back at Alana with new eyes.

The dance ended and everyone clapped. The King had a jolly look on his face. "Thank you for the dance, my dear." Alana bowed to him.

"The pleasure was all mine. Thank you for coming. I'm honored." He waved it away.

"Now, where is that son of mine?" He said this in a booming voice and looked around. "Ah, there you are Sebastian. It is time for you to dance with this lovely lady." Sebastian stepped forward and took his father's place as the music started.

"I will try not to step on your toes. I don't dance much." Alana laughed and the sparkle was back in her eyes.

"Somehow I suspected that would be the case, but don't worry, I'm sure you'll do fine." They smiled at each other as everyone else in the room watched. Eudora judged that by the way they were looking at each other that no one else existed but them. Even the King and Queen noticed it. When she saw Lily was with the royal couple she decided to join them.

"They make a beautiful couple wouldn't you say?" She hadn't really asked anyone in particular. Lily continued watching the couple dancing while the King and Queen exchanged a secret smile.

"Yes I do believe you're right Eudora," said the King. All four of them watched the couple in awe as Alana's glow grew brighter. They heard one of Alana's friends gasp.

"Oh my, look, she's glowing!" All eyes were now on Alana and Sebastian.

"I think perhaps we might be planning a wedding in the near future," said the Queen. Lily nodded with certainty.

Zephyr had kept to the background enjoying the atmosphere, but she was feeling increasingly anxious. Something didn't feel right. She finally decided to alert Eudora and the King and Queen. She quietly approached the group and caught Eudora's eye.

"What is it Zephyr? Do you feel something?" The King and Queen and Lily all turned to her. It seemed that whatever she had to say, it was important.

"I just have an eerie feeling that something isn't right. We need to be on guard." Everyone nodded and Lily looked nervous, afraid for her child.

"I will go and speak to Kohn and he can alert the others." Eudora watched as Zephyr moved away on her errand.

"You don't think they would try something now do you, with so many of you in the house?"

Eudora knew by the crack in Lily's voice that she was scared for her daughter and tried to reassure her with a smile.

"Don't worry Lily everything will work out."

Eudora looked across the room at where Kohn and the others were standing. She knew Zephyr had spoken to them by their watchful looks and stance. She nodded to Kohn who bowed to her. If anything happened they would be prepared.

84

The ritual had taken longer than Todd had anticipated. They were now on the sidewalk outside Alana's home and would have to be quick if they wanted the spell to work without alerting those inside. Music drifted from the house drowned occasionally by laughter. His blood was pumping fast - soon he would have her. It was a shame they had to get rid of Star but it was for a good cause.

"Is everyone ready?" his father looked around at everyone. Ciaran had accompanied them. You never knew when another wizard would be helpful. All four nodded. Todd took a deep breath and waited.

Ciaran stepped forward and cast the potion towards the house while chanting words that the others didn't understand. When he was done he slammed the end of his staff onto the ground. A blue streak shot out of the ground and circled the house.

"NOW!" he shouted as everyone disappeared.

85

Alana was so happy now that she was in the arms of the man she loved. They were dancing in front of all her family and friends. Sebastian was about to whisper something to her when Alana's smile faded, her face grew pale and a shiver racked her body. He tightened his grip on her waist.

"What's wrong Alana?" he shouted. Everyone in the room looked at them in shock.

"Alana's eyes glazed over as she looked toward the door. "They're here," she whispered in a shaky voice.

Sebastian mentally alerted Eudora and Kohn. He looked around the room and spotted Rowan and Warwick. Likewise he commanded them to gather the girls away from the door. He was about to tell Zephyr to keep Lily safe but she had already reached her and was placing a protective arm around her. Looking back at Alana, she still had that distant look on her face. He shook her.

"Come on Alana. I need you." He heard the gruffness in his own voice and hoped it would help snap Alana out of whatever was holding her attention.

A loud boom came from the door as a blast tore the door off the hinges. Sebastian grabbed Alana and shoved her behind him.

Alana could hear the commotion but she couldn't seem to break away from her fear. She was petrified and couldn't move. She kept chanting in her head, 'it's time, it's time.' A loud noise had emanated from outside the house and then she had heard his words. He needed her.

Todd looked around and smiled. "Well, well, well. It looks like someone is having a party and didn't invite me." He didn't know who all these people were. He could see Alana's three stupid friends cowering behind three men who he guessed were their boyfriends.

"You're not welcome Todd." He swung around to look at Trisha, the smart mouth one of Alana's friends. He had never liked her. He smiled in her direction as she hid behind her boyfriend.

"Damn Trisha. I didn't think you had it in you. But if you were smart, like I know you are, you'll shut your stupid mouth." He snarled the words as he gave her another cruel grimace. "I'm here to wish Alana a happy birthday and give her my gift." He laughed as he said that. He looked around for Alana. He knew she was there - he could feel her fear.

"Come out, come out, wherever you are." Some woman he had never seen before stepped forward.

"I think you should leave. There is nothing here for you."

Todd narrowed his eyes. How dare she talk to him with that tone?

"Get out of my way woman. You have no idea who you're dealing with." He whipped his hand out and threw a fireball in her direction.

She never moved nor blinked as the fireball soared toward her. She held up her hand and a shield blocked it from touching her. She laughed, "Nice parlor trick Raynor." She threw him a challenging smirk.

He didn't know who she was but she was certainly not of this world. The woman looked beyond Todd.

"Hello Ciaran. It's been a long time." Todd looked on as Ciaran stepped forward and bowed. "Hello Zephyr. Yes it has been a long time."

Todd was confused. "You know this woman Ciaran?"

"Yes from a different time, long ago."

Todd peered at the woman. "So I guess you are a witch too?" She laughed. "Something like that."

Todd narrowed his eyes. "No matter. I came for Alana and I shall have her." Alana could hear voices. She needed to regain control of her emotions. She just couldn't let Todd and his cronies destroy her home and family. She was glad Sebastian was standing by her. She would be in Todd's control by now if it wasn't for him. He had an arm holding her protectively. She closed her eyes and concentrated on all she had learned. A voice came out of nowhere.

'Remember Alana mine, you are magic, while they only practice theirs. You must stay strong.'

She opened her eyes and took one more calming breath. Rianna was right. She could do this.

'Remember the dragon will protect your heart'

She looked down at her necklace and knew what she had to do. She bent her head and took the necklace off. She put it in Sebastian's hand. He looked into her eyes as she spoke to him in her mind.

'Sebastian. I'm giving you the most important thing in the world to

me. Remember you have to protect it.' He looked down and saw the heart in the palm of his hand. He looked back into her eyes as she touched his shoulder and smiled. She stepped out from behind him.

Sebastian knew she was ready but he didn't want to let her go. The heart in his hand felt hot, prompting him to consider the situation. She had trusted him enough to know he would protect her. He slid the heart around his neck and watched. This was Alana's fight. He would only intervene if she needed him.

"I think you were told to leave Todd. I think you should leave now." Alana spoke softly but with conviction in her voice. Todd looked at her and smiled again. Finally he had his prey within sight.

"Why Alana, I didn't even recognize you, looking the way you do." He waved his hand out in front of him as he looked her up and down. He heard a growl right beside her. He didn't know who the man was but apparently he didn't like the way Todd was looking at her. He smiled at him as if to ridicule the way he was dressed.

"Alana do you honestly think you can make me leave?" He didn't like the way she was looking at him. She seemed different.

"Don't you dare put your filthy paws on her Todd!" yelled Trish as she broke away from the man who was holding her behind him. She ran toward them, but before she could get to them Todd laughed at her audacity and pointed in her direction and slung his hand sideways.

"No!" roared Alana and all three of her friends went flying through the air. Alana flung her arms out and stopped Trish from hitting the floor. She was paying attention to Trish and never saw the fire ball that Todd threw her way. She glimpsed Sebastian running in her direction and swung her head around. She would never be able to put up a protective shield before it hit her and by the volume of the ball it was strong. She closed her eyes and braced herself for whatever would happen. One minute she was standing and next she was on the floor trying to catch her breath. Chaos broke out everywhere. Fireballs and solar balls flew from both sides.

Suddenly she saw Sebastian was lying on the ground. Around her, everything faded as she moved toward him. His face was pale and there were scorch marks on the front of his shirt. Tears sprung in her eyes.

"Sebastian get up, please, I need you." She shook him but he didn't move. His eyes remained closed. "Remember Sebastian, you're my dragon. You can't die. You have to protect my heart. Not only did I give you that necklace to protect but you also have my own heart. Please wake up Sebastian." She put her head on his chest and touched her necklace. With an anguished whisper she cried. "I love you." Tears fell on his chest. She felt a hand touch her back. She looked into Eudora's face.

"He...can't...be...gone Eudora. I won't...allow it!" She wiped the back of her hands across her eyes.

"Alana you have to get up. They need you. I'll look after Sebastian." Alana looked around to see her friends crouched down with her mother, protecting Trish who was lying still on the floor. Sebastian's mother had woven a protection shield around the group. Kohn and the other warriors weren't much good against Todd and his family. Zephyr was doing everything she could, along with the King. Alana looked down at Sebastian one last time and then stood up with determination burning in her face. She had never been so angry in all her life. Rage was boiling in her blood. She had to stop Todd even if it meant destroying him. She walked into the middle of the room, not fearing the fireballs that were flying around. She heard one of her friends gasp. "Oh my God, look at Alana."

Even though it was only a whisper, Eudora also heard and drew her attention away from Sebastian. Alana was glowing all over but not her usual glow of gold. It was more orange, as if her gold of purity was tinged with the crimson of her rage. Even her hands had sparks flying from them. She heard a groan and looked back down at Sebastian. "Alana?" he groaned again.

"Don't worry for Alana, Sebastian. I think you need to worry for those other guys."

"What?" He felt so weak he was certain that had been no ordinary fire ball. Todd was aiming to kill. He got up on his hands and knees and coughed several times. He looked at the chaos all around him. His mother was doing her best to keep Lily and Alana's friends safe. Zephyr and his father were helping his three warriors. They had been no match alone for the intruders. In the middle of the room he saw Alana standing alone. She looked like she was on fire with flames shooting from her hands.

"What the hell happened? I need to get to her." He started to stand but sat back down on his butt. Eudora placed her hand on his shoulder.

"I don't think we have anything to worry about Sebastian. She thinks you're dead you know?" He looked anxiously at Alana and could see that she had been crying.

"She thinks I'm dead?" Sebastian touched his chest. Not a mark on him but his clothes were scorched.

"I probably should be. That was a death fireball and it hit me right in the chest. I don't understand it." He shook his head to clear his mind.

Eudora reached down and touched the chain around his neck. He had forgotten about Alana giving it to him.

"I think this chain saved your life. I don't know what kind of magic is in it but it seems to contain some very powerful protection."

"I think you might be right Eudora. I can certainly feel it."

Eudora looked again at Alana. "I think her anguish for you has turned into rage." Again Sebastian tried to stand but he was still too weak.

"Sebastian you have done everything you can. It is Alana's turn to do what she was born to do."

Sebastian nodded and looked back at the scene in front of him. Alana's sights were on Todd. She held her hand out and put all of her family and friends under a shield of protection. Nothing could get in or out no matter how strong their magic. She knew hers was stronger. She thought she heard her mom scream amongst the chaos, but she wasn't certain. She had to stay focused on the people in front of her. Ciaran stepped forward and tried to knock the shield down. He chanted but to no avail.

"You are wasting your time. You will never break my spell. I *am* magic. You are nothing!"

She flung her hand and the old man slid across the floor. Todd looked from him to Alana.

"How did you know what he was saying?" Todd didn't even know what he was chanting and he knew his parents didn't either. The old man got up and came forward. All Alana did was laugh. She was so focused on Todd she never saw the solar ball come flying through the air until it hit her. It never even fazed her. She thought she heard someone yell from within the protection shield but she was too focused on what was going on in front of her.

Sebastian was able to stand up. His mother and father ran toward him with relief.

"I thought you were dead," cried his mother as she hugged him tightly. His father smiled at him and placed his hand on his shoulder.

"We're so glad you're all right son." Sebastian smiled and looked back at Alana as he spoke.

"Is everyone else all right?" By this time everyone had crowded around to watch Alana. Trish was holding her arm gingerly. She didn't think it was broken, just bruised. Zephyr approached Sebastian and touched the necklace.

"I see the dragon has protected his heart." Sebastian lowered his head but managed a smile.

"No Zephyr, I think the heart protected the dragon. I think if it wasn't for this heart, I wouldn't be here right now."

Jess was the only one who caught on to the dragon part.

"What did you mean by dragon?" Everyone turned to look at her.

"What? Why is everyone looking at me?" Sebastian pointed at Alana. "It's OK Jess, your friend there saved my life. You see, she's the princess and I'm the dragon sent to protect her and the opposite just happened. She protected me when she gave me her heart."

"No Sebastian. If it wasn't for you, Alana probably would have been toast. The way you knocked her out of the way and took the fireball in the chest, you saved her life too," said Lily as she looked out at her daughter. "Now what are *we* supposed to do?"

Eudora went to her and patted her on the shoulder. "This is Alana's destiny. She has to do this alone. She understands that. She put the shield up to protect all of us so she could do her job." Lily sniffed and nodded. They all went quiet as they watched Alana.

"I wouldn't try that again if I was you Helen. Or should I say Bronwyn?"

"So you know who we are? That doesn't mean you can fight all of us. Our magic is strong."

Alana laughed "Yes I'm sure you think so but I have a little secret for you D'Ary. I *am* magic and you merely tinker with yours."

She narrowed her eyes and growled at Alana. "How dare you? You are nothing! We have had our powers longer than you. Now, Ciaran say the spell!" yelled Helen. Ciaran stepped forward and lifted up his staff and let it fall to the floor. A flash of blue appeared and headed for Alana. It circled her. Todd's mother laughed.

"Now whose magic is stronger?" She laughed a cruel laugh. "Now finish her Todd!"

He stepped forward just as Alana threw back her head and spread her arms wide. The blue ring that was around her broke and faded. She watched as Bronwyn's eyes grew wide. Alana was tired of this game. She needed to get back to her friends and family. She needed to see about Sebastian. She felt the rage come to the surface again.

"You are all fools like Drake had been. You think you can take what is not yours, freely given. I would never give my powers to you." She braced her hands out at her side and concentrated on the spell in Rianna's book. She looked at each one of them in turn. "You!" she boomed in a loud clear voice as she pointed at Todd, "You took something away from me that I loved." She watched as he snarled his lip and smiled. She pointed at the rest of them. "And you wanted to take away everyone else I loved." She closed her eyes and with all of her heart she concentrated. When she opened her eyes again light poured out of them and wind whipped around the room. She started to float high above them with her arms spread wide. She spoke in a clear booming voice.

"*Purest of heart, give me your Light…Lend me Your strength…help me to fight…Vanquish this evil from my sight…Let there be peace for all tonight…and for life…*"

A wind picked up and swirled around the four people standing in front of her. "Do something Ciaran!" yelled Todd in a strangled voice. "This can't be happening. You are nobody. How can this be?" Their shrieks continued as the circle around them grew smaller and smaller. It finally came together and there was a loud boom as the ground shook and a bright light burst forth and sprinkled down all around like rain and then faded away. Alana floated back to the floor as the light that was surrounding her faded away. Everyone behind the protection shield cheered. She turned and with a wave of her hand the protection shield disappeared as Alana collapsed.

86

Sebastian ran to Alana as everyone else was still cheering. Nobody except Sebastian had seen Alana collapse. He reached her and fell to his knees. Gently, he lifted her head and looked at her pale face. She had been amazing. He had watched her with fascination as she fought the D'Ary family. Now her body was so cold, when just a minute ago it had been almost on fire as she vanquished all four of them at once. It had obviously been too much for her. He felt a wetness on his face and realized he was crying.

"Please Alana. You must wake up. Do you know how proud I am of you? You can't leave me now Alana. Not when I have figured out how much I love you. I have for a long time. I was just so afraid to admit it to you or even to myself. I need you. Please, you *can't* go."

Sebastian leaned down and kissed her cold lips. His big body shook as the tears rolled down his face. He looked up and for the first time in his life he prayed.

As everyone hugged and kissed, Eudora sensed all of Sebastian's emotions flooding through her mind. He was hurting.

"Oh my God!" she called. She was pale as the cheering stopped abruptly and they all saw what had turned Eudora ashen. Lily cried out and ran toward her daughter followed by the rest of her friends. Zephyr and Eudora followed behind the King and Queen. Kohn held a weeping Trish and Rowan and Warwick were comforting Katie and Jess. All three were crying. Lily held Alana's hand. Sebastian gave Eudora a pleading look.

"You have to do something Eudora. I have never asked you for anything. I am asking you now. You *have* to save her!"

Eudora hated seeing him like this and feeling all of his pain. She wrung her hands in front of her and let the tears fall. "I'm sorry Sebastian. There is nothing I can do."

He threw his head back and let out an enraged battle cry sending shivers down everyone's spine.

Alana was floating, surrounded in white. She was confused, not knowing where she was or why she was there. But it seemed so peaceful, she closed her eyes and relaxed. She thought she heard voices in a distant whisper. She caught some words.

"Need…Love…" She even felt someone's anguish. She pushed it aside and went back to the peaceful place she found so inviting.

'Alana.' She opened her eyes and looked around.

"Is someone there?" Her words echoed back to her. She mentally shrugged her shoulders and closed her eyes again.

'Alana.' Someone whispered again. This time Alana sat straight up.

"I know someone is there." She looked all around. Suddenly something floated by her. She tried to see what it was but everything was misty white. "Please show yourself."

The white cloud dispersed and a bench appeared in front of her. She sat down. *'Alana, mine.'*

Alana got up and looked around again.

"Rianna is that you?" She waited.

A light appeared so bright that she had to shield her eyes as someone touched her shoulder. When she opened her eyes Rianna was standing in front of her.

'Alana you need to go back. You are needed there with the others.
Go back? Alana didn't know what she was talking about. Everything was fuzzy to her.

"Go back where?" Rianna pointed with her hand and Alana looked down. She gasped as her memory came flooding back to her.

"Sebastian! He's alive!" She smiled and leaned in to hear what he was saying. It was difficult to hear. She managed to make out just a few words here and there. It must have been him whispering. She heard her mother and watched as she ran over and took her hand. Tears welled in her eyes to see everyone so upset. She watched as Sebastian turned to Eudora. He was asking her something.

"What is he saying? I can't hear." She leaned in closer.

'He is asking her to save you.'
Alana might not have been able to hear what was being said but she could see and feel Sebastian's anguish.

"What can I do Rianna? I don't want to see him hurting like that."

Rianna delicately touched the side of Alana's face.

'*Do you love him Alana?*' Alana looked down and watched as he threw back his head and screamed at the top of his lungs. Her tears flowed freely.

"Yes. I love him," she whispered as she watched her proud dragon weeping.

'*Then go to him. It is not your time to be here. You made me very proud today Alana mine.*'

Alana hugged her and whispered, "Thank you grandmother."

Alana watched as Rianna smiled and floated away.

88

Eudora touched Sebastian's shoulder. "I think I know what might work Sebastian." He looked up at her hopefully. "I'll do anything." Eudora knew it was true.

"You must give her your heart." Sebastian looked at her puzzled. "I don't understand what you mean, Eudora." "Do you love her Sebastian?"

He answered without hesitation. "Yes. I love her. I love her!"

Eudora touched the chain around his neck. "She gave you her heart to protect. Now you have to give her yours in return."

He still didn't understand until he looked down at the necklace she had given him. It was the same one she had given him in the dream. When he picked it up and turned it around, in the center of the golden heart was a black dragon with its wings spread out wide. He looked up at Eudora.

"How can this be?" Eudora smiled. "You are bound together now. Your hearts are intertwined by the love that you share."

She touched the chain again. Sebastian placed Alana on the floor and took off the necklace and placed it in her hand. He closed her hand around the heart and held it tightly. He leaned in close to her ear.

"I give you my heart Alana. Forever." He looked into her pale face and placed the necklace around her neck. It rested in the center of her chest. He leaned forward and kissed her lips. He felt warmth now where they had been cold.

"Her lips are warm! They were cold before." Where the chain rested, it started to glow. He looked down at the chain and back up into Alana's face. Her skin didn't seem so pale. He held his breath as he waited for a sign. He watched as her lashes fluttered and then her eyes opened. She groaned and in a soft voice barely above a whisper she spoke his name. He didn't think he was ever going to hear that voice again. The color was coming back to her face. He smiled down at her.

"Why is everyone crying?" She tried to sit up. Sebastian helped her. Everyone stopped crying and laughed but soon the tears started floating again – with joy.

Alana touched Sebastian's damp cheeks. "I thought you were dead," she whispered. "And I thought you dead also."

"No. Rianna told me to come back. I was needed." She shook her head to try to clear it. Eudora stepped forward. "Did you see Rianna my dear?" Alana looked around again.

"Would you help me stand up Sebastian? My throat is dry. I need something to drink." He nodded and helped her to her feet. Someone brought a chair and a glass of water. Absently she thanked both and sat down and drank. She looked at Eudora.

"I saw Rianna and she explained a few things and sent me back." Sebastian looked toward the heavens and whispered a quick thank you to Alana's grandmother. Everyone hugged her and told her how glad they were. Sebastian didn't even object to his warriors hugging her. He now knew she was his. They told her what had happened and what she had done. Her eyes went wide. She didn't remember much of it. All she could remember was how mad Todd had made her. They all joked with her that they didn't want to get on her bad side.

She looked up at Sebastian. "It's over then? I don't have to worry about them anymore?"

He nodded and was surprised when she flung herself in his arms. She started crying like a baby. He looked over her head at everyone. They knew what he wanted and silently they left the pair alone and headed for the kitchen.

"I'm sorry Sebastian…" she sobbed. "I don't know what came over me."

He ran his hand up and down her back. "It's OK Alana, let it all out. I was so proud of you. You were amazing. You stood up to all four of them at once and protected everyone else at the same time. I am honored that I got a chance to see you in action."

She leaned back and gave him a watery smile. That's when she noticed that the necklace was back on her own neck. She touched it and looked up at Sebastian.

"How did I get this? I gave it to you. It was made of magic you know? It had a protection spell placed on it by Rianna herself. She told me it would protect whoever was wearing it but when I saw you on the floor not moving and the front of your shirt was burnt, I saw red. After that I don't remember much."

Sebastian caressed the side of her face. "Look at the heart, Alana." She gasped. "It's got a dragon in the middle of it. How did that happen?"

Sebastian waited for her to look up at him. This time he didn't hold anything back. He let her look inside his soul. Tears formed in her eyes again as she grabbed the front of his shirt and pulled him forward. She laughed through her tears.

"For months you have spoken just a handful of words to me. Now you have so much to say. I know you were only thinking it but I knew you were just gearing up to speak them. Though they were all nice, I was only interested in three of them. I love you too Sebastian."

Her lips touched his and they were both lost. He pulled her to him and whispered those three words that interested her the most.

The End

Epilogue

It had turned out a bright and beautiful day. The castle was abuzz as they waited for news of the baby's arrival. There was much celebration for their princess, who was due to give birth at any time. As the dignitaries of the villages and faraway lands were downstairs waiting for the new arrival, the proud parents to be were upstairs in their chambers with Eudora and Lily in attendance. "Sebastian! We need you now!"

He looked at his wife nervously but was strengthened by her radiance even in her current situation. The sight of her still managed to take away his breath. He took his wife's hand. She smiled lovingly at him just as another contraction tore through her small body. Gently, he cooled her face with a wet washcloth. Like most new fathers, Sebastian wished he could take the pain away for her. Gallantly, he decided then and there he was never going to touch his wife again. She squeezed his hand.

"Don't worry Sebastian, the pain will be over soon." She smiled into his eyes. She could never have enough of just staring at him. She loved everything about him. Even the wolf wasn't so bad now. Alana reached inside his mind.

'Never say or think that again. When we hold our baby it will be all worth it and anyway, I like having you touch me.' She watched as his eyes darkened even more. He leaned forward and kissed her on the lips.

"But love, I hate seeing you going through all this pain."

Eudora chuckled and rolled her eyes. "Don't worry Alana dear. He might say he won't touch you again but in a few weeks, when you're ready, he will conveniently forget that he ever said anything."

Lily looked up at her son-in-law and watched him blush. She chuckled too as she guessed some hidden communication had been going on.

"Eudora stay out of my head. Those are private thoughts between me and my wife."

Even though his voice was stern he had a smile on his face. In fact he had worn a smile almost constantly since the battle. Eudora was happy with the change in Sebastian since meeting Alana. He wasn't so controlling and Alana had him wrapped around her pinky finger. When this little one came into the world, he or she would have him right there too. It had been a year and a half since they married and peace had found its way into both worlds.

"You know Sebastian? I don't know if I have ever told you this before, but I am glad you have made my daughter so happy. Her father would have liked you." She watched as he looked from her to his wife and she saw the love for each other shining in their eyes.

Alana panted again as another pain hit her. They were definitely closer so it wouldn't be long now. As both Eudora and Lily worked to get everything ready, Sebastian whispered to his wife while he cooled her face with the washcloth again.

Lily was glad she was able to be here for this day, even though she lived in her world and Alana lived in Sebastian's she could come and go when she wanted. She would just call and Sebastian or one of his friends would come and get her. Even Alana's friends were downstairs waiting. Of course they were all hugged up to Sebastian's friends. She wondered if anything would come of that as another contraction came and Alana couldn't help it - she screamed this time. Sebastian looked panicked.

"Can you not do something for the pain?"

Lily smiled up at him. "Relax Sebastian. It won't be long now." Eudora was the one delivering the baby - she had done this many times. Lily was just there to help and could tell Eudora was very experienced so she wasn't worried about her daughter's well-being.

Eudora took Alana's hand. "Alana dear, the next time you have a contraction I want you to push. Do you think you can do that for me?"

Alana nodded and bore down as the next contraction hit her.

'Poor girl,' thought Lily. She had been in labor now for eight hours and she knew she was tired but she never complained or yelled at Sebastian as some wives were known to do when they were in the throes of childbirth. Lily was so proud of her.

"All right Alana. You're doing really well. I need you to give me one more big push and you're going to be holding your baby in a minute."

As the next contraction hit she gritted her teeth and pushed with everything she had. In the next instance she heard a loud cry.

Alana was glowing and smiling from ear to ear, mostly with relief but also with the motherly response to her baby's first sound. Sebastian looked like he was about to pass out.

Eudora smiled at the happy couple. "Congratulations Mommy and Daddy. You have a baby girl!"

Lily smiled through the tears and sweat that were streaming down her face. She held a blanket out to Eudora who put the now quiet little girl in it and handed the bundle to Alana.

The two older women watched as Sebastian looked down at his baby girl in wonder and as Alana billed and cooed to the baby with tears of joy. Sebastian held his daughter as they cleaned Alana up and changed her gown. When they were through they heard a gentle knock. The King and Queen stuck their heads around the door. "Can we come in now?"

Eudora waved them forward. "And here are the proud grandparents of a baby girl!" Sebastian held the baby out to his mother.

"Oh she's so beautiful. Look at your new granddaughter Artemis." The baby was passed around as the two proud parents watched protectively.

"What have you decided to name her?" asked Aurora.

Alana looked toward Sebastian and he smiled down at her.

"We want to call her Rianna Marie." Everyone looked up and smiled.

"I think that is the perfect name for her," said Artemis as he wiped his eyes. They decided to let the happy couple have a few minutes alone with their new daughter. They were dying to go and spread the news anyway.

Lily handed Rianna back to her mother and kissed her daughter. After everyone left the room, Sebastian sat back down next to the bed and leaned forward and kissed his beautiful daughter and then his beautiful wife. "I love you Alana."

She smiled up at him with all the love in her eyes.

"I love you too Sebastian." While they were gazing at each other they heard the trumpets start blowing and the cheers ringing out as the happy grandparents and the godmother told everyone nearby. Word would soon spread around the kingdom. They both smiled down at their sleeping daughter as the castle people and villagers chanted in loud voice.

"All hale, Princess Rianna!"

They both laughed. "Her important day and she is sound asleep," said Alana as she too closed her eyes and thanked Rianna. If it wasn't for her book of Enchanting Secrets none of this would have been possible. She fell asleep with a smile on her face.